A Christmas Miracle for the Railway Girls

Maisie Thomas was born and brought up in Manchester, which provides the location for her Railway Girls novels. She loves writing stories with strong female characters, set in times when women needed determination and vision to make their mark. The Railway Girls series is inspired by her great-aunt Jessie, who worked as a railway clerk during the First World War.

Maisie now lives on the beautiful North Wales coast with her railway enthusiast husband, Kevin, and their two rescue cats. They often enjoy holidays chugging up and down the UK's heritage steam railways.

Also by Maisie Thomas

The Railway Girls
Secrets of the Railway Girls
The Railway Girls in Love
Christmas with the Railway Girls
Hope for the Railway Girls

A Christmas Miracle for the Railway Girls

MAISIE THOMAS

PENGUIN BOOKS

PENGUIN BOOKS

UK | USA | Canada | Ireland | Australia
India | New Zealand | South Africa

Penguin Books is part of the Penguin Random House group
of companies whose addresses can be found at
global.penguinrandomhouse.com

Penguin
Random House
UK

Published in Penguin Books 2022
001

Typeset in 10.75/13.5 pt Palatino LT Std
by Integra Software Services Pvt. Ltd, Pondicherry

Printed and bound in Great Britain by Clays Ltd, Elcograf S.p.A.

The authorised representative in the EEA is Penguin Random House
Ireland, Morrison Chambers, 32 Nassau Street, Dublin D02 YH68

A CIP catalogue record for this book is available
from the British Library

ISBN: 978–1–529–15826–7

www.greenpenguin.co.uk

CHAPTER ONE

June 1942

With their tools over their shoulders, Mabel and the other members of her gang of lengthmen walked from the station to their allocated length of the line. Finding their starting place, they dumped their knapsacks and got going. Bernice wasn't the sort to allow slacking. The first job was to hoe out the weeds from the railway tracks, then they set to in pairs, getting on with the real task of the lengthman, which was to level the railway bed on which the permanent way was laid. While one of each pair used a crowbar or a pickaxe to raise a sleeper, the other had to shovel the ballast back underneath. In due course, the same length of track would need exactly the same work to be done again because the ballast shifted every time a train travelled along the line.

It wasn't long before Bette took off the old jacket she wore for work and dropped it on top of her knapsack. 'Lots of folk hate working outdoors in the winter because of the cold. Me, I don't mind, because this job keeps us warm. It's the summer when I'm not so keen.'

'I don't care how hot it gets,' said Mabel. 'I shan't be stripping off. I'm not going to fall for that one again.'

'You were unlucky, that's all,' said Bernice.

'Unlucky with bells on,' Mabel answered.

'Ah, but you met your Harry as a result,' said Bette.

Mabel couldn't suppress a smile. 'That's true.'

She'd had a tough time two years ago, in her first summer on the permanent way. Working in a sleeveless blouse, she had ended up with badly sunburned arms, which had blistered. She hadn't thought anything of it when some of the blisters burst, but after that she'd become unwell and eventually collapsed, waking up to find herself in hospital, where she was told that soot and dirt had got into her bloodstream via the open blisters and she'd gone down with blood poisoning. It had been a truly ghastly experience, but – and it was a very big but – as Bette had pointed out, it was when she was laid up in hospital that she had caught Harry Knatchbull's eye. Harry, her very own cheeky blighter.

'How long have you two being seeing one another now?' asked Louise. 'It must be coming up for two years.'

'It's about time you made it official.' Bernice stopped working for a moment to wipe the back of her hand across her forehead. 'Look at our Joan, married a whole year as of the beginning of this month, and with a gorgeous new baby. He's a month old now, bless him.'

That made Bette laugh. 'Everything comes back to Max, doesn't it, B? I swear that if I said "Pass the salt", you'd find a reason to say what a good baby he is.'

Mabel laughed too. 'And why not? Max Hubble is the most adorable baby ever, as any of his honorary aunties will tell you.'

The four of them worked on, stopping mid-morning to take off their thick gloves and sit beside the tracks for a drink from their flasks. Later, when Bernice announced it was time for dinner, they walked to the nearest lengthmen's hut. This was constructed from railway sleepers standing up like planks of wood. Inside, more sleepers had been stacked to create makeshift benches, but there was no need to take shelter indoors today, not like they had to in winter. The real reason for coming here was to have a hot drink, freshly prepared. Bette shook the old iron kettle to ensure it contained sufficient water before she placed it on the brazier.

Once the tea was made, they sat outside, producing their barm cakes and sandwiches. There was fish paste in Mabel's barm cake and she wouldn't have been surprised if the others had paste as well. There wasn't that much choice these days. A picture sprang into her mind of Mumsy's pre-war picnics, with dainty finger sandwiches, delicious meat pies, salads, and summer fruit complete with a jug of cream. Oh, yes, and bottles of wine and home-made cordial standing in wine coolers packed with ice.

And here she was with fish paste! Mind you, one of the advantages of having a billet in number 1 Wilton Close was that Mrs Grayson was a wizard in the kitchen. She was a fellow lodger who had assumed responsibility for all the cooking and baking, while Mrs Cooper, their landlady, took care of the house alongside working as a cleaner. On top of doing the catering for the inhabitants of Wilton Close, Mrs Grayson also used the kitchen to produce jams and chutneys, which she sent to the WVS kitchen located at Darley Court, where her friend Mrs Mitchell was the housekeeper.

Today in Mabel's snap tin was a slice of walnut cake. When she took it out, she caught Louise looking at it and immediately held it out to her.

'Here, have a taste. Go on. It's delish. According to Mrs Grayson, it's eggless and fatless, but I swear you'd never know.'

Louise took a tiny bite and closed her eyes for a moment in appreciation. 'Lovely. Thanks. My mum's a good baker an' all, but she gives the boys the lion's share.'

'More fool her,' Bernice said bluntly. 'Sorry, Lou. I know I shouldn't speak against your ma, but the whole point of rationing is that we all get the same.'

Louise shrugged.

Bernice tilted her head back to drain the last drop from her mug. 'C'mon, girls. Back to work.'

Mabel replaced the lid on her snap tin and put it and her mug back into her knapsack, easing them in beside her bottle of hand lotion. You couldn't get the real thing for love nor money these days, but there were recipes in abundance in women's magazines and this one smelled faintly of roses. Also in her knapsack was that most essential of all items, toilet paper. There was a toilet, if you could call it that, built onto the side of this particular lengthmen's hut – a tiny add-on containing a bucket that was smelly and profoundly unpleasant to use. It was a toss-up which was less awful: using the bucket or nipping behind a bush.

They walked back to their section of permanent way. The sky was azure blue, almost cloudless.

'A perfect summer sky,' said Bette. 'Mind you, the war has taught us a clear sky isn't necessarily something to be appreciated.'

'Will we ever look at a sky like this again without fearing a clear night for the Luftwaffe to come calling?' asked Bernice. 'I know the raids have dwindled to practically nothing these days, but I still wonder.'

Mabel nodded. The most recent air raid over Manchester had been in May, the night Max was born, and the previous one had taken place as long ago as January, but even so, she wasn't taking anything for granted. Manchester had suffered heavy air raids throughout the second half of 1940 and it hadn't been until the autumn of 1941, less than a year ago, that the attacks had started to tail off.

'My younger brothers loved the air raids,' said Louise. 'They thought it great sport to identify the planes and collect pieces of shrapnel.'

'I hope the war will be over long before Max is old enough to do any of that,' said Bernice, and for once the others didn't tease her about bringing her precious grandson into the conversation.

As they arrived at the place where they'd left off earlier, they stood to watch a train go by on the furthest track. Two locomotives pulled a long line of goods wagons that took ages to pass by. Every time she saw a pair of locos working together, Mabel wondered whether there was more to it than simply hauling a heavy load. Was it in part because these were locos that in peacetime would have been retired before now? Many older locos were still at work because of the war.

It was the same for people. Numerous old folk had come out of retirement to step into the places of men who had been called up. And not just old folk – women too. Housewives and mothers who before the war would have spent their lives inside the home now did long hours of war work before going home to cook and clean and put the children to bed. Girls who, pre-war, would have worked only until they got married now carried on working, doing their bit for the war effort. That was what everyone did, everyone in the entire kingdom: their bit.

'You and me will work together until tea break,' Bernice said to Bette, 'and Mabel with Lou.'

In some gangs of lengthmen they always worked in the same pairs, but Bernice liked to chop and change about. Mabel liked that. She felt it strengthened them as a group. Not that you had much breath left over for chatting when you were hefting a sleeper or shovelling ballast, but swapping the pairs made you feel you all knew one another.

Bernice was the sensible, no-nonsense sort, which made her an effective boss, but she was kind-hearted too and her heart had positively turned to mush ever since the arrival of her baby grandson. Bette, with her double T, E, like Bette Davis, her copper-coloured hair that peeped out at the front of her turban and her hourglass curves, had been a barmaid before the war but had taken to working as a lengthman as if she'd been born to it. That left Louise. Though she was careful not to let it show, Mabel had always felt rather sorry for her. At the start of the war, she'd looked thin and undernourished, though like so many who had grown up in deprived circumstances, she had benefited from wartime rationing. She would always be as slim as a reed because she had that sort of build, but she didn't look underfed any longer.

But that wasn't the main reason for Mabel to feel sorry for her. Lou came from a pretty rough background. Her father, who by all accounts had been a violent man, had abandoned his family before the war, whereupon Louise's older brother Rob had stepped in and taken up where he'd left off, fists an' all. Then, early last year, Mabel and her chums had worked together to catch a thief who was helping himself to a secret store of food. The thief had turned out to be two thieves, one of whom they had caught. The other was Rob Wadden, who had escaped and disappeared for good.

Hoping that her thoughts hadn't shown in her face, Mabel cleared her mind and applied herself to lifting the next sleeper. Although her muscles were strong and her body was now honed after more than two years of hard physical labour, it was still an effort. She was proud to have a tough physical task to perform rather than, say, something clerical. Pops might be a rich factory owner, but Grandad had been a humble wheeltapper. Mabel had loved him dearly and she still missed him. Working as a lengthman made her feel they were connected.

'What are you smiling at?' Louise asked.

'I'm remembering my grandad.'

'The wheeltapper? It takes real skill to do that. You have to be able to hear the tiniest fault.'

Mabel knew Louise's praise was for wheeltappers in general, not for Grandad personally, but she felt chuffed all the same. She hid it beneath a laugh. 'Not like us, eh? Shovelling ballast.'

Louise laughed too. 'Ah, but this is precision shovelling, putting exactly the right amount under the sleeper, and you've got to keep it level.'

She stopped talking as she suited the action to the words. When she had finished, Mabel lowered the sleeper back into place, then stretched her spine.

'One more,' said Lou. 'Then we'll change over and you can shovel and pack.'

'Deal,' agreed Mabel.

They carried on until Bernice called a halt for their tea break. They walked across the tracks, lifting their feet clear with each step, and settled themselves at the side. The ground was hard and bumpy, the grass thin and coarse, but who cared so long as it was dry? Out came the flasks. The tea that had been poured in early that morning had cooled somewhat by this time, but again, who cared? It might be cooling and wartime weak, but it was tea and that was what counted.

Finishing hers, Bette lit up a cigarette and lay on her back, blowing smoke into the air. Mabel tilted her face towards the sun, closing her eyes in pleasure at the feel of the warmth on her skin.

'How's your mum getting on with her cleaning job, Lou?' Bette asked.

Mabel poured a thousand blessings on Bette's head. It was a question she would have liked to ask, but she always felt constrained from doing so. As the person who had arranged for Mrs Wadden to lend a hand when needed in Mrs Cooper's little cleaning business, Magic Mop, she didn't feel she could ask in case Louise thought she was lording it. Lou could be a bit spiky about personal matters.

'Fine, thanks.' Louise took out the remaining half of the cigarette she had started at dinner time. 'She likes the work and the money helps. Things were rather tight after Rob went.'

'Aye,' said Bernice. 'I expect they were.'

After Rob went? Mabel looked at Bette and Bernice, neither of whom batted an eyelid. Mabel had to glance away for fear of her own eyelids batting like crazy. After Rob went! Louise said it as casually as if he had gone off to join the army. The man was a wartime criminal, and a violent brother to boot. For all Mabel knew, he was a violent son too. To hear Louise now, you'd never imagine he had given her a serious beating before he disappeared. After he went, indeed!

'And with your Clifford leaving school this summer,' Bernice added, 'that'll be a bit more money coming in. He won't earn much at fourteen, but it all adds up.'

Soon it was time to return for the final stint, carrying out the work that gave them the name of lengthmen. A length was the space from one set of joints in the track to the next and each gang was required to do a certain number of lengths every day. When they had finished, they walked back to the station where they'd arrived this morning and waited for the next train to Manchester Victoria. It came chuffing along the track, white clouds puffing from its funnel. Chuffing and puffing both ceased as the train coasted alongside the platform. The brakes squealed and the train slowed, then there was a loud clunk as it halted, doors already banging open and passengers emerging.

Those waiting on the platform pressed forward. There was a feeling of urgency these days when boarding a train. So many passenger trains were full to bursting even before they started off and there was always the worry you wouldn't get aboard.

'Think slim, girls!' Bette said and the four of them squeezed on.

They had to 'think slim' all the way to Victoria, where Mabel's heart lifted as it always did as the half-spicy, half-sweet scents of steam and smoke crept into her nostrils. This was the smell of the railway and she loved it. To her, the railway meant Grandad.

Passengers surged up the platform towards the barrier. On the adjacent platform, a guard was walking the length of the train, slamming doors and checking those already closed were secure as he prepared the train for the off. Mabel and the others joined the crowd working its way past the ticket collector and onto the concourse that stretched out beneath the overarching metal and glass canopy. Opposite the platform was the long line of ticket-office windows contained within an elegant sweep of wood panelling, and over at one end were the buffet and the restaurant, the exterior walls of which were tiled in pale yellow, as was the bookstall. The restaurant boasted a glass dome on its roof, as befitted a first-class facility.

Bernice must have caught Mabel looking, because she said, 'I can't look at that dome now without shuddering. Just imagine if it had fallen in when our Joan was in there having Max. As if giving birth in an air raid wasn't bad enough.'

They went to the Ladies, each of them using the supposedly 'Out of Order' cubicle that meant they didn't have to queue up with members of the public.

Louise stood beside Mabel at the mirror above the basins. 'Are you meeting your friends in the buffet before you go home?'

Before Mabel could answer, Bette thrust her face in between theirs, her eyes twinkling in her reflection.

'Of course she isn't, you daft ha'p'orth. She'll be heading home at a run to get ready for darling Harry. Won't you, Mabel?'

Mabel laughed, too excited to feel embarrassed. 'Since you mention it . . .'

She wasn't seeing him just tonight. She was going to be with him tomorrow evening too, at a dance to which Cordelia had invited all her friends. Mabel felt tingly with happiness all the way home.

She loved living in Wilton Close. To begin with, she'd shared a bedroom with Joan and the two of them had become good friends. These days, Mabel shared with Margaret while Alison bunked down in the small bedroom at the end of the landing that in former times had been the box room.

When Mabel opened the front gate and entered the garden, Mrs Cooper and Mrs Grayson were sitting on kitchen chairs in the sunshine, shelling peas into a large cream-coloured bowl.

'Hello, Mabel dear,' said Mrs Cooper. 'Have you had a good day?'

Mabel joined them on the lawn, sitting at their feet. Before the war, she would have thought nothing of helping herself to a few juicy peas from the bowl, but no one did things like that now. Food was precious and you didn't fritter it away.

They chatted for a few minutes, then Mabel stood up.

'I'll go and get changed.'

She ran upstairs to take off her work clobber and put on a skirt and scoop-necked top before carrying her corduroy trousers and old shirt outside to give them a good whack against the wall, jumping backwards so the day's dust didn't settle all over her. She hated to feel dirty. Mind you, no matter how grimy or sweaty her own job was, it was nothing compared to Margaret's work as an engine cleaner.

Soon Alison and Margaret arrived home and it wasn't long before the girls were setting the table while Mrs Grayson and Mrs Cooper finished off in the kitchen.

When they sat down, Mrs Cooper said grace.

'Thank you for our meal and thank you for Lord Woolton and please bless the brave men of the Merchant Navy. Amen.'

'And thank you for Mrs Grayson and her magic wooden spoon,' Mabel added.

Mrs Cooper looked flustered. 'I'm not sure you should say thank you for something that doesn't really exist.'

They tucked into tomato macaroni followed by stewed apple. Afterwards, Margaret rose from her place. Her hazel eyes had sometimes looked strained earlier in the year, but now they were warm and serene.

'I'll wash up and put the kettle on,' she said. 'I imagine you two are dying to linger over a cup of tea, aren't you?' She looked at Mabel and Alison.

'Very funny,' said Mabel as she stood up, Alison following suit. She addressed Mrs Cooper. 'Excuse us dashing from the table, Mrs C, but you know how it is.'

'I think I can guess.' Mrs Cooper smiled.

'You're welcome to come out with us, if you like,' Alison told Margaret.

'Thanks, but no. I'm going to the flicks with Persephone. We're going to see *The Maltese Falcon*.'

'Ooh, I like Humphrey Bogart,' said Alison.

Margaret nudged her. 'You're not supposed to go all dreamy over another man when you're about to go out with Joel.'

Mabel and Alison went upstairs to get ready. Mabel changed into the apple-green dress she had worn last summer as one of Joan's bridesmaids. They had all worn something pretty and they'd had matching lacy boleros and also white knitted flowers attached to their hats, so that even though their dresses were all different, they still had a similar appearance.

Mabel brushed her dark brown hair, securing it away from her face with a pair of diamanté clips and letting it hang loose down her back. Then she went along the landing to Alison's room, where she found her fastening her pale yellow dress.

Alison laughed. 'Look at us. A pair of bridesmaids.'

Mabel helped Alison do her hair – and just in time too, because the doorbell rang and Mrs Grayson called up the stairs.

'Harry's here.'

Mabel darted back into her room to pick up her beaded evening bag, then ran downstairs to greet Harry with a quick kiss before standing back, feeling a little breathless as she drank in the sight of his dark eyes, generous mouth and broad forehead. He had taken off his cap, showing his slicked-back short back and sides and the slight widow's peak. He was so handsome that her heart drummed in her chest. It wasn't just that he was good-looking. It was also because he was in uniform. Mabel had a thing about men in uniform. They looked so much more attractive than fellows in civvies. The combination of Harry's looks and his RAF blue was enough to make her bones melt.

Harry escorted the girls into town, where they were to meet Joel outside the Ritz Ballroom on Whitworth Street. Joel would be coming straight from work, having got ready at the end of his hospital shift. Mabel felt like an old married woman as she smiled in pleasure at the sight of Alison's sparkling eyes and pink cheeks when Joel appeared. Compared to herself and Harry, the other two hadn't been going out long. Joel was good-looking, but he wasn't in Harry's league.

It was always a delight to be at the Ritz, with its graceful pillars and art deco features, and the balcony above where you could sit at the tables and look down onto the dancers and the famous revolving stage, if you felt so inclined. Personally, Mabel was far more interested in being on the dance floor.

They chose a table before taking to the floor for a waltz followed by a quickstep. Mabel felt weightless as she whirled round in Harry's arms. How she loved him! Early in their relationship, she had been distraught to discover that his original interest in her had stemmed from finding out about her father's money, but he had worked hard to convince her that since then he had truly fallen in love with her. From then on, their love had deepened and he meant the world to her – just as she knew she meant the world to him.

'Shall we sit this one out?' Harry suggested.

He escorted her to their table, holding the chair for her as she sat down, then he went to buy drinks. When he returned, he pulled his chair closer to hers. Oh, the temptation to snuggle against him! Plenty of other couples these days showed their feelings in public in a way that would have been unthinkable before the war, but Mabel, although she was happy to show affection, had never quite shaken off the influence of Mumsy and her etiquette book, much as she had been tempted. Nobody was better acquainted with the rules of social behaviour than Esme Bradshaw. It came from being new money and the determination not to make any blunders.

'I've got something to tell you,' said Harry.

His dark eyes were serious and alarm flickered into life inside Mabel.

'What is it?' she asked.

'Don't panic. You'll think it's good.'

'But you don't?' Mabel asked at once. 'Sorry. Tell me what it is and I won't interrupt.'

'Last year, the Air Council put a two-hundred-hour maximum on any single tour of duty. What's meant to happen now is that you do your tour of duty, then you're rotated for six months before your next tour. It's normal to spend the six months working in the OTU – that's the Operational Training Unit – training up the next batch of pilots and so forth.'

'Or bomb aimers, in your case,' said Mabel, making sure she kept her voice steady as she said the words.

'And my tour of duty is coming to an end,' said Harry.

'I understand if you feel disappointed to be grounded, but obviously it'll be a relief to me.' And how! Bomb aimer was said to be the most dangerous position.

'There's something else,' Harry went on. 'RAF Burtonwood is going to become an American airbase. I'll be leaving there.'

Mabel's breath caught in her throat. Having Harry close to Manchester had always been something to be grateful for.

'Where will you be sent?' This time, there was no keeping the tremor out of her voice.

'I don't know yet,' said Harry. 'It could be anywhere.'

CHAPTER TWO

Cordelia sat in front of her triple-mirrored dressing table, making the final adjustments to her ash-blonde hair. Before Kenneth had entered the bedroom, she had skilfully arranged her hair around a stuffed stocking to create a stylish shape. Satisfied, she reached for her earrings. For everyday wear, she loved her pearls, but for evenings out she had several sets of precious and semi-precious stones. This evening she chose pretty sapphire drop earrings and a matching sapphire on a silver chain. Kenneth would willingly have bought her gold, but she preferred silver. It looked better against her skin. She reached behind her neck to fasten the clasp.

Kenneth was standing before the long mirror set into the wardrobe door, concentrating on fastening his bow tie beneath his wing collar. Twelve years older than Cordelia, he had always been a good-looking man and now, in his middle fifties, he was distinguished and likely to remain so into old age. Evening dress sat well on him, the smart black with silk lapels adding to his gravitas.

'Another Saturday night, another fundraiser,' he remarked.

Cordelia looked at him through the reflection. 'I shall enjoy attending one I haven't had a hand in organising.'

In common with everyone else she knew, she worked tirelessly for the war effort. By day she was a lampwoman, cleaning and replacing the lights on wagons, carriages and signals. At home, she was the local collector for the Red Cross's Penny a Week Fund, as well as having her regular night-time work as a fire-watcher. When she wasn't doing all that, she often helped organise events to raise money for the armed forces.

She'd always been good at that sort of thing. Before the war, as the wife of a solicitor, it had been important to be skilled at arranging dinner parties and bridge evenings and she had sat on various charity committees, where, hiding her impatience at the patronising drivel spouting from the lips of certain ladies who had wanted the glory without any of the graft, she had deftly organised auctions, musical evenings and dinner dances. Now, in wartime, her repertoire had expanded to include beat-the-clock crosswords, jumble sales, ping-pong competitions and quizzes. She'd recently had a new idea for a potato-growing competition. Why not? Everyone seemed to be growing potatoes like mad so as not to be so reliant upon wheat, which had to be brought across the Atlantic by the Merchant Navy.

'I'll go and see if Emily is ready,' said Cordelia.

Outside Emily's room, she tapped softly on the door and went in, her heart melting with love and pride at the sight of her beautiful daughter, with her heart-shaped face and dainty chin. Her eyes were cornflower blue and her brown hair still had a natural tendency to curl, whereas all her friends had lost their baby curls years ago. Emily was wearing a dress Cordelia had lent her, a simple mint-green gown with a skirt that flared when she moved, thanks to the masses of tiny pleats.

'You look lovely,' said Cordelia.

'Thank you for lending me the dress, Mummy.'

'It's good to give it one last airing before pleats are banned by the new austerity regulations next week.'

'It's only new pleats that won't be allowed,' Emily pointed out. 'Existing pleats will still be permitted.'

Cordelia smiled. 'If that's your way of hinting that you might wear the dress again, I'm sorry, darling, but the answer's no. It's important to be seen to follow the rules. The dress must be put away until after the war.'

'But the war might go on for years yet.'

Cordelia felt a stab of sadness. She was old enough to remember the last war, the one that was supposed to end all wars. When that had started, everyone said it would be over by Christmas, and look how long it had dragged on. It had been interminable. This coming September, they would have been at war for three years. Three years! How could this have happened again so soon? How old would dearest Emily be when it ended?

Cordelia placed her hands on Emily's slender shoulders and kissed her. 'Nothing would give me greater pleasure than to see you looking beautiful in that dress time after time, but not until after the war.'

Emily gave her a cheeky smile. 'Fashion will have moved on by then.'

'Classic styles never go out of fashion,' Cordelia retorted. Goodness! She sounded like her mother-in-law. 'Come along, darling. Time to go, but first you need to show Daddy how you look. You'll knock his socks off.'

Emily giggled. 'Are you going to make him change from long socks to ankle socks when the new regs come in?'

'Certainly not, you cheeky little minx. No one can see how long a man's socks are – and you're not to tease him.'

As Cordelia had known would happen, Kenneth thrust out his chest in sheer pride at the sight of his daughter looking so beautiful and grown-up. Cordelia felt proud too – and enormously grateful. Kenneth's original plan had been that when she finished at boarding school, Emily should live out the war in the relative safety of Auntie Flora's home in Herefordshire. Emily, however, had had other ideas and had arrived home unexpectedly this time last year. It had been extremely naughty of her, of course, but . . . but Cordelia had been overwhelmed with delight to have her at home and had begged for her to be allowed to stay. She completely understood why Kenneth had wanted Emily to live with Auntie Flora, but it had been so hard for Cordelia not to have her daughter at home with her.

They both loved Emily so dearly. It was their daughter who made their marriage worthwhile.

The long windows in the hall had been boarded up for the blackout with thick material on lightweight wooden frames, but someone had pasted silver stars and RAF roundels onto the fabric. At one end was the stage, where the dance band played a dreamy waltz, and at the other end stood trestle tables holding the raffle prizes. Kenneth had purchased twenty tickets each for Emily and Cordelia. Around the dance floor were large circular tables where guests sat and chatted or where half-full glasses standing in front of empty seats showed that places were taken.

Kenneth had bought not one but two tables, paying for every seat and leaving it to Cordelia to invite their friends. That was typical of Kenneth. He had never been afraid to put his hand in his pocket. It was one of the things Cordelia appreciated about him; that and the fact that he wasn't showy about it. Some people liked their generosity to be recognised by others, but Kenneth wasn't one of them.

He wasn't alone in his generosity. Even though their seats had already been paid for, Cordelia's guests had all paid a second time. It hadn't come as a surprise to Cordelia that her friends had stumped up. Everybody did what they could to boost the war effort.

She looked around the table where she was sitting. These people were friends and acquaintances of long standing.

The wives were the ladies with whom Cordelia had enjoyed croquet tournaments and intimate little afternoon teas at the Claremont Hotel before the war. The husbands were similar to Kenneth, well-to-do, rather stuffy. Up until last Christmas, this was the only kind of table Kenneth would have countenanced sitting at.

Over on the other table sat – well, actually, sat just Dot and her husband, and Margaret. All the other places were empty because the rest of them were dancing. It was a great joy to Cordelia that she'd had Kenneth's blessing to invite her railway friends. Last summer, her pleasure at her daughter's unexpected homecoming had soon been tempered by Emily's snobby attitude towards Cordelia's railway friends, especially working-class Dot, an attitude that was in perfect harmony with Kenneth's. With her husband, her daughter and her formidable mother-in-law all ranged against her, not only at her choice of friends but also because of her insistence that these girls and women would continue to be her friends after the war came to an end, Cordelia had, after much heart-searching, regretfully concluded that her duty lay with her family and she must walk away from Dot, Persephone and the rest for ever.

But then she'd been buried alive and her rescue had been due in no small part to the very friends her family scorned. What a difference that had made. Kenneth and Emily had completely changed their tune. Adelaide, Kenneth's mother, hadn't been best pleased, but Kenneth and Emily wouldn't be swayed.

So Cordelia's friends were here tonight on a table originally paid for by Kenneth. Dot and her husband, who was an ARP warden. Mabel and her handsome beau, Harry Knatchbull, whose good looks and broad shoulders together with his RAF uniform were drawing plenty of glances his way. Alison and her boyfriend, Dr Joel Maitland.

Cordelia liked Joel. If she was honest, she preferred him to Harry Knatchbull, whom she had always suspected of being a bit too full of himself.

Joan and her signalman husband Bob were here, as were Margaret and Persephone, the two single girls of the group. Margaret appeared happier these days, which was good to see. Cordelia had always sensed a certain reserve in her. Being reserved herself, she could always recognise it in others. After Margaret's long estrangement from her father, was their being reunited the cause of Margaret's more relaxed attitude? On top of that, Margaret's brother, who had for a spell been listed as missing in action, was now known to be in a field hospital. It was pleasing to think of things looking up for Margaret.

Cordelia smiled to herself. It was good to have her special friends here – though they weren't all here, were they? And never would be again. Lizzie, Mrs Cooper's only child, had been tragically killed early in the war, and Colette had died in a bomb blast last December. Then there was Joan's sister Letitia . . .

Cordelia sat up straight. Now wasn't the time. She had a duty as a guest to make the most of this occasion. Moreover, her duty as the hostess of these two tables was to ensure that everyone enjoyed themselves.

Excusing herself, she went over to the table her railway friends were using. Joel and Alison, Mabel and Harry, and Bob and Joan were returning to their seats. Persephone was also being escorted from the floor by her current partner. When she had entered the room, the men had practically elbowed one another aside in their eagerness to ask her to dance. She was the loveliest girl present, with her honey-blonde hair and those beautiful violet eyes. Best of all, she was lovely on the inside too, a thoughtful and considerate girl who was always happy to step in and help.

Cordelia slipped into the seat next to Joan.

'You shan't mind if we leave soon, shall you?' Joan asked. 'We want to get home to Max.'

'Of course you do. I'm just pleased you were able to come.'

'I did wonder if it was right to leave a young baby for the evening,' Joan admitted. 'Gran thinks mothers shouldn't go gadding about, but Bob's mum volunteered to look after him and she all but pushed us out of the front door.'

'Good for her,' said Cordelia.

'Even so, we don't want to be late back.' Joan looked around. 'Where's Mr Masters?'

Cordelia glanced vaguely over her shoulder. 'He said he was going to bribe the band to play "It Had to Be You".'

'Is that your special song?' Joan asked.

Cordelia almost laughed in sheer surprise. 'No. We don't have one.'

How could they have one? That was what lovers had and she had never been in love with Kenneth. She had been a good wife to him, the perfect partner for a prosperous gentleman of the law who had a certain position in society to uphold. But love? That had never entered into it.

Now, though, she looked around the table. Harry was whispering in Mabel's ear, making her face light up with laughter. Joel listened to Alison, both their expressions showing their devotion. And the look that passed between Joan and Bob was so full of tenderness that Cordelia's heart ached.

These three young couples had so much love to give one another, so much happiness to share. Did they have any idea how lucky they were?

CHAPTER THREE

Mabel walked home from church arm in arm with Mrs Grayson, telling her all about last night's dance. She had a special place in her heart for Mrs Grayson. They had met when she had moved into Mrs Grayson's house as her lodger back in 1940. To start with, Mabel had found her landlady downright odd. Not only was just about everything in the house – lampshades, waste-paper baskets, cushions, plant holders, coat hangers, hot-water bottles, doorstops – dressed in knitted covers, but Mrs Grayson never set foot outside her own front door and hadn't done so for years. Not until Manchester had endured the devastation of the Christmas Blitz and Mabel had resolved to prise Mrs Grayson out of the house to seek safety in next door's Anderson shelter had Mrs Grayson finally shared the desperate heartbreak that, along with a lack of family support, had gradually resulted in her becoming agoraphobic.

Then, when others were being bombed out courtesy of Herr Hitler, Mrs Grayson had lost her house thanks to a bombshell of a different nature, when her long-estranged husband had demanded that she leave the premises so that he could move in with Floozy, his bit on the side. As distressing as that had been for poor Mrs Grayson at the time, it had, looking back, been the best thing to have happened to her in years, because that was when Mabel's railway chums had taken her under their joint wings and helped her move in with Mrs Cooper. Later, when Mrs Cooper's house copped it in an air raid, the two of them plus Joan had moved into Wilton Close, thanks to Cordelia, who was friends with the owners. Mr and Mrs Morgan had gone to North Wales for the duration to be near their son. Young Mr Morgan worked in London for the Inland Revenue, which had been transferred, lock, stock and double-entry ledgers, to Llandudno until the war was over.

These days, Mrs Grayson was able to walk to nearby places as long as she had a trusted friend to keep her company, and it was easy to see how much better she was for it. Her eyes were brighter, her skin smoother, her cheeks plumper. Mabel knew only too well from her own grief and guilt after her best friend Althea had died how inner unhappiness and turmoil could adversely affect outward appearance.

She glanced back over her shoulder. Behind them, Mrs Cooper was walking with Alison. Margaret had gone to church with her father somewhere near Alexandra Park.

They arrived at Wilton Close, a quiet cul-de-sac with two pairs of semi-detached houses on each side and another pair at the top. The front gardens, which must have been so pretty before the war, were now given over to growing vegetables. Everyone did that these days. Even people who lived in flats had window boxes of salad leaves.

They went into the front room for a cup of tea.

'Tony didn't come yesterday,' Mrs Cooper remarked, 'so I suppose he'll come today.'

Mabel laughed. 'Smile when you say that! He's good to come and help us.'

'I know, chuck,' said Mrs Cooper. 'I don't meant to be ungrateful. It's just that—'

'—with three strapping girls on the premises to dig for victory,' Mabel finished jokingly, 'there's no need for him to keep coming back every weekend.'

'It's not good for him,' said Mrs Cooper. 'Coming here, where he always used to come with Colette . . .'

'Perhaps it keeps her memory alive for him,' Alison suggested.

Mrs Cooper seemed to deflate a little. 'Yes, of course.'

'He must be desperately unhappy, poor fellow,' said Mrs Grayson.

'I understand about wanting to feel close to Colette,' said Alison, 'but it's not as though he joins in and chats when he's here. Sorry if that sounds mean.'

'He never did join in, not even when we still had Colette,' said Mrs Grayson. 'He spent all his time digging the garden and doing odd jobs.'

'He probably wanted to keep out of the way of all the gossiping women,' said Mabel. 'You know how full of visitors this place can get at the weekend.' She'd belatedly realised that the others were being serious and was sorry she'd made light of it.

'I think he must be a deeply shy person,' said Mrs Grayson. 'We owe it to him and to Colette to make sure he knows how much we appreciate his attention. Don't forget how he battled his way here at the start of the big snowstorm to advise us on preventing burst pipes.'

'He might not be the most sociable chap,' said Alison, 'but he's a good sort. I'll never forget how protective he was of Colette. He worshipped the ground she walked on. He must miss her dreadfully.'

'Poor chap,' said Mabel. She didn't say so out loud, but she promised herself she would join Tony in the garden for a while that afternoon, just to show willing.

For Colette's sake.

Mabel spent an hour in the garden with Tony. Margaret came out too. Mabel harvested the early potatoes, which

Margaret took indoors to wash. Mabel looked with pleasure at the neat row of lettuces.

'They're ready to be picked now,' said Tony. 'I'll sow another batch next week. I'll get the leeks planted out as well.'

Mabel made an effort to chat and Tony was polite, but no one could accuse him of being the life and soul of the party. Mabel found it better to get on with the work in near silence. It wasn't her preferred way, but Tony didn't seem to mind.

She glanced his way surreptitiously. He had gone thin after Colette died and the weight still hadn't come back. Poor beggar. Losing his beloved wife had clobbered him good and proper. She remembered her own anguish when Harry's plane hadn't returned from a mission on time and the horror of the hours of waiting. Harry had come home safely in the end, but Colette was gone for good.

'I'll stop now if it's all the same to you,' said Mabel.

She went inside to wash her hands and scrub her nails. Tony appeared in the scullery doorway.

'The Scouts are here to collect the salvage.'

'What is it today?' Mabel asked.

'Paper, tin cans, rags.' Tony smiled. He didn't often smile. 'You name it.'

Mabel indicated the salvage box in the corner. These days, so many items were being taken away to be reused in some way that they dropped everything in the same box and sorted it on collection day.

'I'll sort it out,' said Mabel.

Tony stepped inside. 'No need. I'll help the lads do it.'

He picked up the box, securing it under one arm, already sifting through it with his free hand as he disappeared. Mabel dried her hands and went into the front room.

'It's the longest day today, isn't it?' said Margaret.

'Do we still have a longest day with double summer time?' asked Alison. 'Or is it an even longer longest day?' She laughed. 'The land of the midnight sun.'

Mabel smothered a sigh. It certainly felt like the longest day, and not in a good way. Yesterday had been the same. What if Harry was posted to the back of beyond? She would miss him dreadfully. She hadn't said anything at home so far. Yesterday she couldn't bear to because she felt rather wobbly and didn't want to blub. Today she didn't want to cast a cloud when she, Alison and Margaret had prepared a special surprise for Joan.

Realising she had left her wristwatch on the scullery window sill, Mabel went to fetch it. In the hall, she stopped in surprise. Tony had taken his jacket from the hallstand and had one arm thrust into a sleeve. The other sleeve dangled while he used his free hand to open the front door.

'Are you going?' Mabel asked. Silly question. She could see he was. As he turned, she was concerned to see how drawn his face looked. 'Are you all right?' Another silly question.

'Sorry – I have to go. I – I've just remembered something.'

'Come and say goodbye.'

Mabel stood aside so she wasn't blocking the doorway to the front room. Tony always said goodbye before he left, but today he shook his head.

'Sorry – no. I'm in a hurry.'

And off he went. Well! What was that about? Mabel fetched her watch and returned to the front room.

'Tony's gone.'

'Has he?' said Mrs Grayson. 'He didn't say goodbye.'

'He suddenly remembered something important.'

Mrs Cooper stood and went to the bay window, as if to catch a glimpse of him. 'He's gone.' Then she smiled and said, 'But here's Joan,' and went to open the front door.

There was a clicking of paws on the floorboards beside the hall runner, then Brizo shouldered open the door and came into the room, trailing his lead. He was an appealing fellow, with floppy ears and a shaggy coat that was gingery in places and golden brown in others. Joan and Bob had adopted him at the beginning of the year, just before the country had vanished beneath several feet of snow. Brizo was a friendly dog and although he was rather bouncy, he was gentle, especially when he was with baby Max. His nature also made him suitable for his job on Victoria Station, where he wore a little collecting box attached to his back by a leather strap around his middle to collect money for charity. Now that Joan had left the railways, one of the others collected him and brought him home at the end of each day.

Brizo did the rounds, pushing his damp nose into everyone's hands, his tail wagging madly. Joan walked in and they all looked round, but she wasn't carrying the baby. Mrs Cooper followed her in and her arms were empty as well.

'Have you left Max at home?' asked Alison.

Joan laughed. 'He's sound asleep, so I've left him outside in the pram.'

'Instead of us playing pass the parcel with him, you mean,' said Mabel.

They chatted for a while, then Alison, unable to hide her smiles, said, 'We're glad you've come, Joan, because we've got something for you.'

Mrs Cooper exchanged glances with Mrs Grayson. 'Can me and Mrs Grayson take Max for a walk?'

'You don't have to leave,' Margaret said quickly.

'This is your surprise for Joan,' said Mrs Grayson. 'It'll be nice for you girls to have some time together without us breathing down your necks.'

'We'll take Brizo an' all,' said Mrs Cooper.

As the two ladies set off with the pram and the dog, Mabel watched them from the window.

'Mrs Grayson looks proud pushing the pram. It's quite a beast, isn't it?'

'I'm so lucky to have it,' said Joan. 'Prams are like gold dust these days. Most mothers-to-be have to put their names down to get one and the baby is probably a few weeks old, if not older, by the time it appears. This pram has been in Bob's family for years, being passed from baby to baby. Auntie Marie's daughter had it most recently. It's a proper coach-built one.'

Alison disappeared upstairs for a minute. When she came back, she was holding her hands behind her back.

'This is from all of us,' she said. 'It's not wrapped because there's no such thing as wrapping paper these days. All three of us helped make it and it's for you, or rather for Max, with our love.'

Mabel smiled as Alison produced a little folded garment and handed it to Joan, who carefully shook it out and held it up. It was a small pair of dungarees in two shades of green rayon velvet.

'How sweet,' Joan exclaimed. 'Don't you just adore baby clothes? They're so tiny – though I can see this is big enough for Max to grow into.'

'Do you recognise the material?' Margaret asked.

Joan frowned.

'The night Max was born,' said Alison, 'Margaret and I were scrambling all over the station canopy, extinguishing incendiaries. This is the dress I was wearing. Mabel lent it to me.'

'Let's just say it wasn't returned to me in mint condition,' said Mabel, 'but it didn't matter. All that matters is that Margaret and Alison helped keep you safe while you had Max.'

'It wasn't me,' said Alison, 'not really. Margaret was the brave one, the one with the initiative. I just followed on behind, not quite believing what I was doing.'

Margaret chimed in. 'Mabel sacrificed her dress so we could make something for Max that you might want to have as a keepsake after he's grown out of it.'

'What do you mean, "might"?' asked Joan. 'Of course I want to. I know everyone is supposed to pass on baby clothes, but I'm going to keep this for ever.' She brushed away a tear. 'This is so sweet of you – and it was so clever of you to think of it. Thank you. I love it – and I love all of you.'

She got up to hug them all, then sat down again, wiping away more tears with her hanky before she cleared her throat and laughed. Mabel, Margaret and Alison looked at one another, exchanging indulgent smiles.

Margaret stood up. 'Time for refreshments. Mrs Grayson has made some cordial.'

She and Alison went to fetch it. Joan watched them go, then she turned to Mabel.

'Are you going to tell me what's wrong?'

Mabel's skin tingled. 'Wrong?'

'Don't pretend,' said Joan. 'You weren't quite yourself at the dance last night. Do you want to talk about it? You could walk home with me later.'

Mabel made a decision. 'There's no need to keep it private. I'll tell all of you.'

When the others returned with the tray, Mabel explained about the likelihood of Harry being posted away.

'So you don't know where to?' asked Joan. 'Oh, Mabel.'

'Then there's the other way of looking at it,' said Mabel, lifting her chin. 'We're jolly lucky to have been so close all this time. Think of all the wives and sweethearts who don't get to see their chaps for months, if not years, on end.'

'That's true,' Margaret agreed, 'but it doesn't make it any less of a blow for you.'

Mabel's heart felt full as gratitude swelled inside her at her friends' understanding.

'Maybe Harry will want to get engaged,' said Alison. 'After all, you did catch the bouquet at Joan's wedding.' She caught her breath in a gasp of shock. 'I'm so sorry. I shouldn't have said that. That was the old me speaking. You don't want to be like the old me,' she added emphatically. 'I was so desperate to get engaged that I could barely think of anything else.'

'I'll be honest,' said Mabel. 'When I caught the bouquet, Harry and I looked at one another and it was a sort of promise between us.' She smiled, warmed by the memory. 'But you're right, Alison. If I'm going to get engaged, it has to be at the right moment and for all sorts of happy reasons, not because things are desperate.'

She heard herself sounding brave and sensible, which was precisely the impression she wanted to create – and it was how she felt, up to a point. But at the same time, a chilly unease rippled through her. Things had been stable for her and Harry for so long and now they were going to be shaken out of it.

What did the future hold for them?

Mabel and Louise paused for a breather out on the permanent way. It was Mabel's turn for hefting up the sleepers so that Lou could pack the ballast underneath, both of which were physically demanding jobs, especially beneath the June sun, but Mabel wouldn't swap her job with anyone. She loved what she did and took pride in helping to keep the railways running safely. Some people talked about their beloved dead relatives watching over them. Mabel wasn't sure about that, but she knew that if

Grandad was keeping an eye on her, he'd be chuffed to pieces to see his best girl working on the railways he had devoted his life to.

Louise looked as if she was about to say something, but she didn't; then she changed her mind again. 'Mabel, can I ask you a favour?'

'Of course.' Mabel hid her surprise. Louise had never sought her help before.

'It's our Clifford – you know, the oldest of my little brothers.'

'Not so little now,' said Mabel. 'He's about to leave school, isn't he?'

'Aye, he is. That's the problem. He has to get a job and so far he hasn't managed to.'

'I'm sorry to hear that.' It was the standard polite response, drummed into Mabel courtesy of Mumsy's etiquette book. As soon as she said it, Mabel wished she'd said something warmer. It wasn't like Louise to share a problem and Mabel wanted to appear interested and helpful.

'We're heading towards the back end of June now and it'll be the finish of the school year before you know it. The thing is,' said Louise, choosing her words, 'it's not easy for Clifford being related to Dad and Rob.' Her thin face coloured, but she persevered. 'Round our way, we're known as a – a rough family, but that isn't fair, because that was Dad and Rob, not the rest of us. Cliff's got a good reference off his teacher, but so far no one has offered him an interview, let alone a job, while other kids have got jobs to go to simply because the school arranged them. I thought maybe if you could help him write an application letter, it could help. His written English isn't up to much, any more than mine is or I'd help him, but I thought that you . . .' Her voice trailed off.

31

About to utter the formal 'I'd be happy to,' Mabel said instead, 'Of course I'll help. Poor kid. It can't be easy being held back because of your dad.'

'It's not a problem you've ever had,' Louise said with a touch of the old dryness.

'No, it isn't,' Mabel agreed cheerfully. 'I'm lucky.'

She left it at that. Much as she wanted to offer her willingness and reassurance, she didn't want to come across as privileged or, heaven forbid, superior. She left it to Louise to suggest arrangements. Would she receive an invitation to the Waddens' house? But no, Louise got Clifford to meet them in the Worker Bee, a café in town.

Clifford was thin, like his sister, only he was tall and gangly, his sleeves not long enough. The shorts he would exchange for long trousers the day he started work, assuming he could get a job, showed off skinny legs and he walked with the telltale crackle that said his tatty old shoes were lined with newspaper.

'He's shot up,' said Louise. 'One thing about the war: school dinners have improved.'

Before Lou could object, Mabel went to the counter and ordered tea for two, fruit cordial for Clifford and a cheese scone each. Clifford wolfed down his scone with a big grin, then rolled his eyes when his sister gave him a sharp nudge and told him not to be greedy. Mabel offered him half her scone. She wanted to give him all of it and buy another plateful, but she mustn't look like Lady Bountiful.

Louise delivered another dig in Clifford's ribs. 'Miss Bradshaw's here to help you. What do you say?'

'Thank you, Miss Bradshaw.'

'You're welcome, Clifford,' said Mabel. 'I thought we could make a few notes on the back of this old letter, then I'll give you these pieces of paper for you to write your own letters. The paper isn't brand new, but it's decent quality and there's writing on one side only.' Determined that no one should object to her largesse, she went on without stopping. 'Now then, why don't you tell me why you'd be a good person to employ?'

'Well . . .' said Clifford. 'I'd work hard.'

'Good. We can use that. What else? At school, what are you good at?'

'Not much, really. I like PT more than sitting in the classroom.'

'Team games?' asked Mabel. 'That shows you play by the rules. We can find a way of wording that.'

Clifford looked at her with open admiration. 'I'd never have thought of that, miss. I never knew PT was going to help with a job.'

Mabel smothered a smile. She had learned a lot from listening to Pops. Gradually, she drew a few useful examples from Clifford, but there was still something missing, though she couldn't put her finger on what.

'D'you think this will really help me, miss?' Clifford asked. 'I want to get a job. My mum says we need the money. I really want to help my mum. She works her fingers to the bone and goes without so she can give me and my brothers the best she can. With our Rob gone, I want to be the man of the house, but not like Rob was, not thumping everyone and making us all cringe away from him. I want to look after the family. I know nobody wants to employ a Wadden, but if somebody will just give me a chance, I'll show them what I can do.'

The air that Mabel breathed in seemed to fill her with satisfaction. This was precisely what was needed. 'I think you should put that in your letter.'

'No!' Lou exclaimed.

Mabel looked at her. 'You said yourself that it'll be hard for Clifford to find work because of being a Wadden. Let's face up to that and put it in his applications. Let him say how much he wants to look after the family and be a help to his mum. That shows his good character and without saying it in so many words, it also says he's different to his dad and Rob.'

'I don't know.' Lou squished her eyebrows together. 'I thought you were going to say things like him not being late for school.'

'What do you think, Clifford?' asked Mabel. 'It's your letter.'

Clifford bit the insides of both cheeks, which had the effect of thrusting his mouth forwards in a dramatic pout. Then he nodded. 'I want to do it, Lou. I want the bosses to know that I might be a Wadden, but I'm not *that* sort of Wadden.'

CHAPTER FOUR

June gave way to July and the Pathé newsreels were full of the battle raging in Egypt. Wherever Cordelia went, she heard people discussing it – at church, on the bus, queuing up outside the butcher's and the fishmonger's. No doubt it would be mentioned today in Wilton Close. She was on her way to do her monthly check of the property, something that Mr Morgan, the owner, had made a requirement of the arrangement whereby Mrs Cooper became the house-keeper for the duration.

It wasn't far to walk from Cordelia's house on Edge Lane to Wilton Close. Cordelia didn't enjoy doing the monthly check. She hadn't minded to start with. It had seemed nat-ural to keep an eye on the new housekeeper, but over time Mrs Cooper had become a valued friend and someone Cordelia admired and now it felt vaguely disrespectful to Mrs Cooper, who was a proud housewife, though she never seemed to mind.

Normally, Cordelia got the inspection over and done with as soon as she set foot inside the house, but this after-noon, hearing a familiar voice in the front room, she went in there to give Dot a hug.

'What's that for?' Dot asked.

'I've been thinking about you on the way here.'

Dot caught on immediately. 'You mean what's going on in Egypt.'

'Both your boys are out there,' said Cordelia. 'Personally, I find it hard enough having Emily accompany me on fire-watching duty. I'm far more worried about what might happen to her than I am about myself. It must be a thousand times worse for you thinking about Archie and Harry out there.'

'Aye, well, I shan't deny it's a worry, but there's nowt to be gained by fretting.'

Although Dot put on a brave face in public, Cordelia was in no doubt that she must do a lot of fretting in private. Cordelia's heart ached for her, but she could see that Dot didn't want to talk about it just now.

Cordelia turned to Mrs Cooper, but before she could speak, Mrs Cooper said, 'Monthly inspection, is it? Help yourself. Tony's upstairs, putting up shelves in Alison's room.'

'That's good of him,' said Cordelia. 'How is he?'

'Same as ever,' said Mrs Grayson.

Cordelia looked into the dining room and kitchen, noting that everything was clean and tidy, as always, then she went upstairs. As she turned the corner on the half landing, Tony appeared at the head of the staircase, carrying a big cloth bag over his shoulder and a dustpan and brush in his other hand. It took Cordelia a moment to realise where he had appeared from.

He took a step backwards to allow her onto the landing.

'Afternoon, Mrs Masters.'

'Good afternoon, Tony. I thought you were working in Alison's room.'

'I am – I was. I put shelves up.'

Cordelia knew it was her responsibility to pursue this. 'Alison's room is down there.' She moved her hand, indicating to her right. 'Yet I could have sworn you came from over here.'

Tony glanced left towards Mrs Cooper's and Mrs Grayson's rooms. Then he looked steadily at Cordelia. 'Yes,

I did. I opened the window in Alison's room and it was a bit stiff, so I thought I'd better check the other windows too.'

'I see.'

'It's not as though I don't know my way around the house. I've done a number of odd jobs.'

'I know you have. I'm sorry to have questioned you, Tony, but Mr Morgan holds me ultimately responsible for the house.'

'Yes, Mrs Masters.'

'Did you have Mrs Cooper's permission to enter the other rooms to check their windows?'

Tony looked at his hands. 'I never thought to ask. It only took a moment to check each one.'

'Well, please remember next time.'

'I intended no discourtesy.'

'Of course you didn't.' Cordelia smiled. 'We'll say no more about it, but please remember what I said.'

'Thank you, Mrs Masters.'

Tony disappeared down the stairs. Poor chap. It was so good of him to help out and she had torn him off a strip when he was just being thoughtful.

She looked into each room before going back down.

'Tony's done a good job of putting up those shelves. He even swept up after himself. Where is he?'

'He left,' said Mrs Grayson. 'He said goodbye as soon as he came down.'

Cordelia was dismayed. The poor fellow. She really had embarrassed him, hadn't she? Oh well, it couldn't be helped. He oughtn't to have entered the other rooms without asking, but she was sure he wouldn't do it again and she certainly wasn't going to make a mountain out of a mole-hill by mentioning it.

Soon she and Dot, Mrs Cooper and Mrs Grayson were sitting together over a cup of tea.

'What do you think of this here dried egg?' Dot asked Mrs Grayson.

'It's not as good as the real thing, obviously, but needs must. I can't say I'm keen. It changes the consistency of the baking. The end result isn't as moist.'

'The new rationing year starts at the end of this month,' said Cordelia. 'They're going to reduce the number of points per person.'

'Things are going to get harder before they get easier,' said Mrs Grayson.

'Sweets and chocolate are going on the ration,' said Dot. 'That won't be popular.'

'No, it won't,' Cordelia agreed, 'but we'll all accept it and get on with life, same as we always do.'

Dot looked at Mrs Cooper. 'You seem quiet today, love. Anything wrong?'

Mrs Cooper looked round at them. She gave her head a little shake, as if recalling herself to the present. 'I'm thinking of Mrs Redmond. She's one of the ladies I clean for.'

Cordelia's heart thumped. 'Did she receive a telegram?' It was the obvious question.

'No, nowt like that, thank goodness. Her house was burgled.'

'No,' breathed Mrs Grayson.

'When?' asked Dot.

'That's just it,' said Mrs Cooper. 'She can't be sure. There was no broken window or anything to show someone had got in. When she realised her necklace was missing, Mr Redmond said she must have mislaid it, though she was sure she hadn't. A few days later, she found an ornament had gone and that was when she knew for definite they'd been burgled.'

'The poor lady,' said Dot.

'The police got her to check the whole house,' said Mrs Cooper, 'and her emergency money had gone an' all.'

'How did the burglar get in?' asked Mrs Grayson.

'That's what makes it worse,' said Mrs Cooper. 'According to the police, there were no obvious signs of a break-in, so she must have accidentally left the back door unlocked.'

'They blamed her?' asked Cordelia.

'It couldn't possibly have been Mr Redmond's fault,' Dot said sarcastically, her voice softening as she added, 'What a miserable thing to happen.'

'She's very upset,' said Mrs Cooper. 'Now listen, we've talked about rationing and a burglary. Has anyone something cheerful to say?'

'How about Christmas?' Cordelia asked.

The others gaped at her.

'It's only July,' said Dot. 'And everyone thought I was starting early last year when I brought it up in September!'

'I know,' said Cordelia, 'but I have an idea and it'll take some planning if it's going to come off.'

'What is it?' Mrs Grayson asked.

'I'm thinking of organising a Christmas dance.'

'Oh, yes,' Dot responded immediately. 'That War Weapons Week dance you organised last summer was splendid.'

'Now we've got American forces over here,' said Cordelia, 'I think we should show them some festive hospitality.'

'A dance for the Yanks?' said Dot. 'Why not – as long as we're allowed to come too, of course,' she added with a twinkle.

'A dance for everyone,' said Cordelia, 'but with the specific aim of offering friendship to our American cousins, who'll be a long way from home.'

She glanced at Dot, whose own sons hadn't had a Christmas at home since before the war. The sadness in

Dot's hazel eyes showed she was thinking the same thing. Then her eyes cleared and she smiled.

'It sounds a grand idea and if you need help, count me in. I haven't forgotten the way everyone pitched in and helped with the Christmas Kitchens last year.'

'Thank you,' said Cordelia, pleased. 'Keep it under your hats for now, but I hope Miss Brown might be amenable to hosting the dance at Darley Court.'

'That makes it sound very swish,' said Mrs Cooper.

'I'm sure the Americans will be most impressed,' said Mrs Grayson.

'That's the general idea,' said Cordelia. 'I'm going to a fire-watchers' training session this afternoon. A number of local groups will be attending, so it's being held at Darley Court. If Miss Brown is available, I'll have a word with her.'

'If you see Mrs Mitchell, give her my best,' said Mrs Grayson.

Cordelia smiled at her. 'I will.'

In a roundabout way, Mrs Mitchell was responsible for Mrs Grayson's presence here in Wilton Close. She was Mabel's father's cousin or second cousin or something, and she was the person who had sent Mabel to live with her friend Mrs Grayson in the first place.

An idea popped into Cordelia's head. Mrs Grayson had been unable to attend the War Weapons Week dance last summer, nor had she helped at any of the Christmas Kitchen venues, but might it be possible to get her to Darley Court?

When Cordelia and Emily arrived at Darley Court, a few people, some of whom were known to them, were standing about on the drive chatting near the porte cochère, the grand drive-through porch that protruded from the front of the mansion.

'So that guests can emerge in the dry,' Cordelia explained to Emily.

'It must have been wonderful in the days when carriages came here and the footman climbed down to help the ladies descend.'

Mr Wayne, one of the fire-watcher organisers for Chorlton, approached them and ticked their names off his list. Shooting back his cuff, he looked at his wristwatch.

'On a fine day like this, we thought we'd let everyone congregate out here rather than inside.'

Soon it was time to go in.

Beside Cordelia, as everybody headed for the front door, Emily said, 'I can't wait to get in and have a look.'

Cordelia, who knew from Persephone what had been done to the interior to protect it, feared that Emily might be in for a disappointment. Darley Court had been put to bed, as it was called, for the duration and all the wood panelling had been covered in hardboard, as had the paintings. Down in the cellars, collections of various artefacts from the museum and some private collections were in storage. Even so, walking up the shallow stone steps and through the grand door into the hall was a special moment. Yes, Darley Court might not be as impressive as in peacetime, but nothing could take away the splendour of the handsome staircase that led up to a square half landing with an elegant statue of Aphrodite in an arched alcove. Stairs rose from one side of the half landing and high above was a vaulted ceiling.

The group was taken into a long room with windows along one side overlooking what before the war would no doubt have been a gracious flower garden, but which was now a market garden. Chairs had been set out in rows, facing tables at the far end, behind which some men stood talking and looking important. They took their places behind the tables and once their audience was in place, Mr Wayne stood up and called the meeting to order.

The men took turns to introduce themselves and say their piece. One warned against complacency.

'It is essential that we continue our work, even though we aren't being bombed on a nightly basis. Don't forget the tip-and-run bomber, getting rid of the last of his high explosives before heading for home. Remember also the punishment for those who fail to do their duty. An ARP warden was recently fined forty shillings for neglecting his duty.'

The next man stood up. He had a kind face and a pleasant manner. Introducing himself as Mr Sidwell, a local organiser from the Ordsall district, he talked about spreading the word regarding the role of the fire-watcher, both to entice new recruits and to increase public understanding of what they did.

'A fee of half a crown is paid to anyone who gives a talk or a lecture.'

Emily nudged Cordelia. 'Tempted?'

'I'm sure there are plenty of men who like the sound of their own voices,' Cordelia murmured.

The next speaker read from the 1942 *Home Guard's Handbook* – yes, actually stood there and read from it! It would have proved much easier to listen to had he explained the rules in his own words, but no, he went through them verbatim: the duties of the street captain, how to call off-duty members in an emergency by blowing whistles or banging dustbin lids, when to call on reinforcements from neighbouring parties, and so forth.

At last Mr Wayne stood up again. He thanked the speakers and said that after a break for tea, there would be stirrup-pump practice outside, using thunderflash fireworks. The audience perked up at the promise of that.

Leaving Emily in the queue for tea, knowing she had the social confidence to make conversation with strangers, Cordelia took the opportunity to go in search of Miss Brown. Returning to the hall, she happened to find Persephone coming downstairs wearing a tweed jacket and jodhpurs. She lived here with Miss Brown, her titled parents having decided at the outset of the war that she would be safer on the edge of Manchester than at home in Sussex, which would be in danger of having leftover bombs dropped on it when the Luftwaffe headed for home.

'That was the official reason, anyway,' Persephone had explained on one occasion. 'Personally, I think it was to stop me hightailing it to London to get a job on a news-paper.'

Now, Persephone greeted Cordelia with a smile. 'Run away from your training lectures?'

'Something like that. I'm hoping for a quick word with Miss Brown, if she's available. I don't have an appoint-ment.'

'Don't worry about that,' said Persephone. 'She was giving the gas decontamination people what for the last time I saw her.'

'I don't want to interrupt,' Cordelia began.

Persephone waved a dismissive hand. 'Trust me, if the head of gas decontamination is still here, he'll thank you for it. Miss Brown isn't someone you want to get on the wrong side of.'

Persephone took Cordelia along a couple of corridors to Miss Brown's office. A large desk stood in front of the window, its chair positioned so as to look out at the view. Around the walls were shelves with books and military helmets from years gone by and there was a metal spiral staircase in one corner. Occupying much of the floor was a table covered by a giant map of Darley Court's extensive grounds, showing how they had been laid out for wartime crop rotation.

Miss Brown might be in her seventies, but she was nothing if not hale and hearty and her eyes were sharp and clever. She wore spectacles, which she often took off and waved about to emphasise a point.

'I'll leave you to it,' said Persephone.

'To what do I owe the pleasure, Mrs Masters?'

Cordelia quickly explained her idea to hold a dance for both the locals and the American soldiers.

'I assume you have a ballroom,' she finished, realising she didn't know for certain.

'We do, though not a large one. Would you care to see it?'

'Could I possibly return another time?' asked Cordelia. 'I need to get back to my training. I really just wanted to ask if you'd agree in principle.'

'By all means,' said Miss Brown. 'And how efficient of you to start planning so far in advance. Now I mustn't keep you.'

Cordelia returned to her fellow fire-watchers, who were now assembled outside. There was an air of excitement at the prospect of heavy-duty fireworks. Cordelia fell into conversation with a couple who were probably closer to sixty than fifty. They introduced themselves as Mr and Mrs Hancock. Mr Hancock was a grocer.

'Where's your shop?' Cordelia asked.

'Levenshulme,' said Mr Hancock, 'and we have three shops. My family has been in the trade for a long time,' he added with a smile.

'Our son is here somewhere.' Mrs Hancock looked around. 'Oh, there he is. Raymond!' She gesticulated to somebody behind Cordelia.

Judging by his parents' ages, Cordelia expected Raymond to be at least in his twenties, but she turned around to find a good-looking lad of seventeen or eighteen. He had dark hair and his eyes, though not quite dark enough to be called brown, were darker than the usual hazel.

'Our change of life baby,' Mrs Hancock whispered. 'Mrs Masters, allow me to introduce Raymond. We're making the most of having him at home. He'll be eighteen at the end of the year and can't wait to be called up. You know what they're like when they're young.' She sighed. 'Raymond, this lady is Mrs Masters.'

'How do you do, Raymond?' Cordelia said. 'My daughter is here somewhere too, though I've lost her for the time being.'

'Is she the same age as Raymond?' asked Mrs Hancock.

'A little younger. Sixteen.' Catching sight of Emily, Cordelia beckoned her over. 'It might be pleasant for Emily and Raymond to pal up for the rest of the afternoon in among all us oldies. Emily, darling, come and meet Mr and Mrs Hancock.'

Cordelia placed a loving hand on Emily's arm as she performed the introductions, feeling a thrill of motherly pride at her daughter's charming manners. She caught Raymond's eye and he politely stepped forward.

'Emily, this is the Hancocks' son, Raymond.'

Cordelia looked at Raymond as she spoke. Then she looked at Emily – and felt a rush of surprise.

Emily was dazzled.

CHAPTER FIVE

Since Joan and Bob had come back to live in Chorlton, Mabel, Alison and Margaret had between them taken over Brizo duty from Dot. Joan's beloved dog had an important and valued job at Victoria Station. With his shaggy coat of gingery golden brown, his long, fuzzy ears and soulful brown eyes, Brizo was a very appealing chap. When he wore his little collecting box strapped to his back, few people could resist dropping in some coppers.

While Joan and Bob had lived in Withington, it had been Dot's job, whenever her shifts permitted, to collect Brizo each morning and deliver him back again at the end of the day. Now, though, with the Hubbles only a stone's throw from Wilton Close, and with three chums eager to help, Brizo needn't miss a day at the station. Between them, Mabel, Alison and Margaret could easily manage, no matter who was on which shift.

'But not tomorrow,' Persephone said decisively one evening when she had popped round with a knitting pattern for Mrs Grayson from Mrs Mitchell. 'Mabel and I have got the day off and Brizo deserves a day off too. He's earned it.'

Accordingly, the two of them met at Joan's in the morning, where they cooed over Max before Joan produced Brizo's lead, sending the dog bouncing around joyfully.

'Sit down, sweetie.' Persephone spoke in a mild voice that didn't sound at all commanding, but Brizo instantly plonked down on his bottom, his tail thrashing to and fro on the floor.

Joan shook her head, smiling. 'I wish I had your knack.'

'Brizo doesn't give you any trouble, does he?' Persephone asked, surprised.

'No. He's a good boy, but he doesn't hang on my every word like he does for you.'

Mabel laughed. 'That's because when you come from an ancient family like our Persephone does, controlling dogs and horses is in the bloodstream.'

Persephone took the ribbing good-naturedly. 'When I was a sprog, we had a dog as our nanny, like in *Peter Pan*. Seriously, dogs are wonderful with children. Look how Brizo adores little Max. He'd never let any harm come to him.'

Joan scratched Brizo's ears. 'I know.'

'Are you sure you won't come with us?' asked Mabel. 'We can wait while you pop Max in the pram.'

'I'd hold you up. I know Persephone wants to take Brizo for a good run. You can't do that with a pram.'

Mabel and Persephone set off, with Brizo trotting beautifully by Persephone's side.

'What have you been up to?' Mabel asked.

'At Darley Court, I've been helping the land girls harvest the shallots and do a summer pruning of the fruit trees, and at work I've been showing a new ticket collector the ropes.' Persephone laughed. 'Such a glamorous life I lead.'

'Talking of work,' said Mabel, 'I helped a lad with a job-application letter a while back and his sister tells me he's got a job to go to when he leaves school. Isn't that grand?'

They went to the long stretch of ancient water meadows that bordered the River Mersey. Here, they let Brizo off the lead so he could enjoy snuffling along the ground. Then they went along the path above the riverbank, alternately walking and running so that Brizo got plenty of exercise and fun, until they almost reached Turn Moss. Mabel had been feeling light-hearted, but the sight of the gun emplacement had a sobering effect. It didn't matter how sunny the day was or how pleasant the company, you could never get away from the war.

'Shall we drop in at Wilton Close on the way back?' Persephone suggested.

They left the meadows, walking up Limits Lane, past the line of old cottages behind their privet hedges. Stopping at the corner to put Brizo back on his lead, they headed along Edge Lane, where Cordelia lived. Mabel glanced at Cordelia's house, with its half-moon stained-glass fanlight above the red front door, and the bay window to the side of it. Mabel had lived here briefly in 1941 after Mrs Grayson had been forced out of her matrimonial home by her rat of a husband. Prior to that, Mabel had assumed Mrs Grayson was a widow, which was the automatic thought when a lady with the title Mrs lived on her own.

When they got to Wilton Close, Mabel unlocked the door while Persephone unclipped Brizo's lead, quietly asking, 'Are you going to be a good boy for me?'

'Look at the adoration in his eyes,' chuckled Mabel. 'I swear that one day he'll learn to talk just so he can say, "I'd do anything for you, Miss Persephone." It's only us,' she called.

Mrs Grayson appeared from the kitchen. 'Oh – it's you.' She twisted her wedding ring.

Persephone went to her. 'Is something wrong? You seem distracted.'

'Not me, dear. Mrs Cooper. She's in the front room. I'll be there in a minute. I'm just making a pot of tea.'

'I'll lend a hand,' Persephone offered.

Mabel took Brizo into the front room, where Mrs Cooper sat in her usual armchair, looking pale and upset. Mabel crouched beside her.

'What's happened?'

Mrs Cooper looked at her. 'It's not me. I'm perfectly all right, chuck. Don't fret about me.'

'But something's happened. I can tell.'

'It's Mrs Pearce, one of my ladies. You remember what happened to Mrs Redmond?'

The door opened. Mrs Grayson came in, followed by Persephone carrying a tray.

'You shouldn't be fetching and carrying, Miss Persephone,' said Mrs Cooper.

'Too late,' said Persephone, putting down the tray. 'Shall you be mother, Mrs Grayson? Get your nose out of the way, Brizo. This isn't for you.'

When they were all settled, with Brizo leaning against Persephone's chair, Mrs Cooper had a drink and then explained.

'Mrs Pearce has been burgled – that's one of my ladies, Miss Persephone. There was no break-in. She had no idea anything was missing until she looked for her mother-of-pearl-handled fish knives and forks. They were in a velvet-lined box, very smart – a wedding present. She turned the house upside down looking for it, even though it's hardly the sort of thing you put away in the wrong place. Then she realised other things were missing an' all.'

'Did she report it to the police?' asked Mabel.

'Yes, but there was nothing they could do. It's poor Mrs Redmond all over again.'

'Mrs Redmond?' asked Persephone.

Mrs Cooper told her about the first burglary. 'And now it's happened again. It's silly of me to be upset. It's not as though it happened to me. But when you're a cleaner and you look after a house regular like, you sort of get to feel the place belongs to you, if that doesn't sound daft.'

'Not at all,' Mabel said loyally. 'It's a sign of your devotion to your job.'

'It's a sign of what makes Magic Mop so reliable,' Persephone added.

'Bless you for saying so,' said Mrs Cooper.

'I hope they catch this scoundrel,' said Mrs Grayson.

'If it's the same person. It might not be,' Persephone pointed out.

Mrs Cooper shuddered. 'Don't say that. It's horrible to think of one person being such a rogue, let alone two.'

'Poor Mrs Pearce,' said Mabel.

'She lives on Edge Lane,' said Mrs Cooper. 'Mrs Masters recommended her to me.'

'We must have walked past her house earlier,' Persephone realised. A frown clouded her brow. 'It must make Mrs Pearce's skin crawl to know someone has been inside her house like that.'

'And has been all through, looking for valuables,' said Mabel. She imagined it happening at her own home, Kirkland House, picturing how upset Mumsy would be, and Pops would be furious. 'It's just like an invasion, isn't it?'

It was a sobering thought. Invasion didn't just mean Herr Hitler and his army. It could mean something a lot closer to home.

CHAPTER SIX

TEST MATCH
BEESON'S v HITLER

LUNCH SCORE	219
CLOSE OF PLAY	542
THIS WEEK'S INNINGS	
Mon	497
Tues	511
Wed	542
Thurs	
Fri	
Sat	
Good coils – total so far	1550
LAST WEEK'S INNINGS	3122
Increase on same point last week	114

Remember . . .

Quality First!!

As she tidied her hair, Betsy leaned forward a little to examine her reflection. Her blue eyes looked tired. Everyone's did at the end of the day, but it was not an exhausted, world-weary sort of tired. No, the girls and women working at Beeson's were tired in a satisfied kind of way, because they had worked hard and surpassed yesterday's figures.

That was what it was all about – producing more coils than they had yesterday. No, actually, that wasn't true. It wasn't just about increasing production. It was about quality as well. *Remember . . . Quality First!!* was what it said at the bottom of the scoreboard. Coils of inferior quality weren't counted.

Popping her comb into her handbag, Betsy glanced round.

'Coming?' asked Heather.

Heather was in her thirties, the mum of four children who had been evacuated to the depths of Wales. That was why she was here at Beeson's, to help win the war so her children could come home. That was why a lot of women worked here, because they were mums desperate to have their children back, or because they were the wives, sweethearts or mothers of men in the services . . . or because they were war widows.

They were all here to help bring the war to an end and the atmosphere in the small factory was determined, but that didn't mean it was grim. On the contrary, it was a cheery place to be, with plenty of chatter going on. Sometimes they spontaneously sang along together as they worked, every day turning two hundred miles of wire into coils of precisely the correct size and structural integrity.

Structural integrity. Betsy smiled to herself. That was one of the things she had learned since she'd been here. She loved her work and took a quiet pride in what she had achieved.

Heather linked arms and they joined the throng returning to the shop floor, where six days a week they sat at long workbenches beneath low-hanging lamps. In the factory where Betsy had had her first job straight out of school, working as a packer, everyone had dashed out of doors the moment they put on their coats at the end of the day, but here at Beeson's everybody crowded back inside to see the day's final score.

They called them scores because that was the way Mr Beeson presented them. He was in his late sixties, an avuncular gentleman with a kindly manner, though his clever eyes showed he was nobody's fool. Nothing got past him, least of all shoddy workmanship. He walked with an odd, lurching gait, thanks to an artificial leg that he'd got courtesy of the last war. Now he had three sons away fighting, one in each service. As soon as war had been declared, he had turned his vacuum-cleaner parts factory over to the production of coils and now, a keen supporter of cricket even though he hadn't played in many a long year, he used a cricket scoreboard to keep his workers abreast of their output.

Betsy and Heather joined the others gazing up at the board, which stood on a platform so it was easy to see.

'Look what we managed this afternoon,' said Florrie. She was a card, was Florrie. Her stated ambition had been to bag an airman and everyone had been astonished, Florrie included, when she had fallen madly in love and got engaged to a merchant seaman.

'That's a fine day's work, girls.' Ida patted the side of her turban, which was what she did when she was pleased with herself.

'Looks like we're on course to beat last week's innings,' Marjorie commented.

'But don't forget . . .' Ida began and the whole group joined in with a will.

'Quality first!'

They all laughed. It was a good way to end the day. Yet again Betsy was glad she worked for Beeson's. She'd been here since just before Christmas. She hadn't intended to stay in London; she'd meant just to pass through and carry on to somewhere else. But at the end of a long and exhausting night's travel, she had stumbled off the train at Euston Station. Feeling numb with shock and thinking fresh air might do her good, she had ignored the station buffet and gone outside in search of a café.

She had nibbled her way through a round of toast topped with carrot marmalade, aware of the noise level around her increasing as the tables filled. Suddenly two women had descended on her table, asking, 'You don't mind, do you?' as they scraped chairs back and plonked themselves down.

Betsy had learned later that these two women were Ida and Marjorie. They had joked about how they were only going to be ready for Christmas by the skin of their teeth because they were so busy at work. Betsy had been about to sympathise with their long working hours when she realised they didn't feel hard done by. Quite the reverse. They'd chosen to work overtime.

'Beeson's is a fine place,' said Marjorie. 'We love being there. We all feel we're part of a big national effort to end the war.'

Ida had laughed at that. 'That's what she said to the Duchess of Kent when she visited Beeson's. Now Marjorie says it to everybody every chance she gets.'

There was mockery in Ida's voice, but it was pretend mockery. Betsy could tell that because of the pride in Ida's eyes as she looked at her friend. That was the first time Betsy saw Ida touch the side of her turban.

Now the women started to leave the scoreboard and head for the doors. There was a bit of jostling, but not on purpose. Betsy and Heather remained linked until they got outside, then they said goodbye and headed their separate ways. The late July evening was sultry, full of the city's dust and noise. Sandbags were piled up outside every shop and office, and windows were criss-crossed with anti-blast tape.

Betsy joined the queue at the bus stop. A bus trundled into view and she raised herself on tiptoe to see the number on the front, but it wasn't hers. She liked going on the bus, but if it was packed full, she might walk. She liked walking too. In fact, she liked everything about her new life now she'd got used to it. Even though she'd been here since before the end of last year, it still felt new. New and fresh and full of possibilities. Not just possibilities either, but actual promise, and she appreciated absolutely everything. She hadn't felt this way before in her whole life, but she did now and it was a wonderful feeling.

Another thing she liked was the way she had coped. Prior to this, she would never have believed she could do it, but it had turned out that she was entirely capable. Was it big-headed to admire something in yourself? Betsy knew there was no conceit in her feeling. If anything, there was a touch of surprise.

How lucky she'd been. She liked her job; she liked her billet. The only regret she carried around with her was that she missed her old friends. It had been hard leaving them, especially in the way she had, but there had been no choice in the matter. She had new friends now and she truly liked them, but nothing would ever make up for the friends she'd had to leave behind – to abandon. That was how it had felt. Her new friends were dears, but she had to be careful not to get too close. Just in case.

Anyway, she ought to be accustomed to being at a distance from those around her. Hadn't that been the pattern of her life in recent years? But it wasn't something she had ever got used to, not really, not in the sense of accepting it. It was only when she had made new friends at the start of the war that she had truly understood how lonely she'd been before that.

The bus appeared. Passengers alighted and the waiting queue edged forwards. When it was her turn, Betsy stepped onto the wooden platform at the back, holding the pole to keep herself steady before taking another step up into the aisle between the seats, all of which were full. She would have to stand. She usually did. Even if she got a seat, she generally gave it up to an older lady.

Reaching her stop, she got off the bus and walked to the tall house where Mrs Perkins, the landlady, occupied the ground floor, letting her two upstairs floors to lodgers. Betsy lived quietly. She was on nodding terms with her fellow lodgers and some of the neighbours, but mostly she kept herself to herself. The friendly camaraderie at the factory had so far answered her need for social interaction, together with a weekly trip to the flicks with Heather and two nights a week helping at a soup kitchen, though Betsy was starting to feel she was ready to go out more.

Her room was on the first floor at the back, overlooking a walled yard with a coal bunker and the outside toilet. A pair of ancient bathtubs filled with soil acted as Mrs Perkins' vegetable patch; she was out there with her watering can.

Betsy's first job upon arriving home was to polish her shoes. She changed into her slippers and armed herself with the tools for the job, a tin of Cherry Blossom and a pair of brushes she'd bought second-hand, one for spreading the polish and the other for buffing it up to a shine. She had made a bibbed apron from a piece of gingham off the market. She wore this when cleaning her room and also when she polished her shoes.

She popped it over her head and tied it behind her back, picking up her things. Downstairs, she stepped aside to let

Mrs Perkins in through the back door to fetch more water. Betsy didn't polish her shoes in the backyard, because she had soon found when she came to live here that it was embarrassing to do that if someone came out to visit the lavatory. She did her shoes in the side passage instead, placing them on the pantry window ledge before she twisted the opener on the Cherry Blossom. It was running low and she didn't know if she'd be able to buy more. Were the nation's shoes less shiny because of Hitler?

All the windows were open because of the heat, so Betsy clearly heard the doorbell, but maybe the sound hadn't carried into the backyard to Mrs Perkins. With a shoe in one hand and a brush in the other, Betsy walked along the passage to see who was at the front door.

As she stopped at the corner and looked across, every muscle in her body squeezed tight and she couldn't breathe. It couldn't be – it couldn't . . .

The man turned and looked at her. Hazel eyes. A narrow face – narrower than it used to be. Gaunt.

The hairs lifted at the back of Betsy's neck and up and down her arms. She seemed to feel them rising one by one.

'Hello, Colette,' said Tony.

CHAPTER SEVEN

How long had she stood there? It felt like a hundred years. The world swooped around her. Her skin went clammy, but her mouth was dry, her tongue like sandpaper. Above all, what Colette felt was sheer disbelief. How could this be happening? How could Tony be here? Colette felt light-headed; something was restricting her breathing.

The front door opened and Mrs Perkins appeared. Tony turned to her. His lips moved and Mrs Perkins replied. Colette could see it happening, though she couldn't hear a single word. She was trapped inside her own little bubble. The air pressed hard against her, but instead of being warm on this hot day, it was as cold as ice. She ought to be shivering, only she couldn't, because she couldn't move at all. If she did move, she might shatter into a thousand pieces. It was only shock that held her in one piece. Shock – and fear.

Oh my goodness, fear. She pressed a hand to her stomach, dragging in shallow breaths. How had this happened? How could this have happened?

The words uttered by the other two started to penetrate Colette's bubble. At first it was like listening underwater. Then the words took on a more coherent shape, a structural integrity. Like Beeson's coils.

'You most certainly will not go upstairs to Miss Cooper's room, young man,' Mrs Perkins declared. 'This is a respectable household. I don't allow shenanigans of that sort.'

Tony drew himself up taller. Although he was answering Mrs Perkins, he looked directly at Colette when he said,

'This isn't Miss Cooper. This isn't Miss anything. This is Mrs Naylor. My wife.'

Oh my goodness, oh my goodness, the *fear*.

Colette found herself in the parlour. She hadn't set foot in here since the day Mrs Perkins had interviewed her as a prospective tenant. Why was she in here now? Why wasn't she running up the road and round the corner to the bus stop? Why wasn't she hiding behind a hedge – or in a back alley – or under a bridge on the canal?

'Shall we sit down?' said Tony.

Colette subsided into a chair. Why? Why was she sitting? She should be running for her life. But what was the point? He had found her. Oh my godfathers. She remembered Margaret saying that. Oh my godfathers.

Tony didn't sit down. Even though he had said 'we', he didn't sit. He remained on his feet. He produced a cigarette, but his hands shook and he fumbled over lighting it before sucking in a long drag. He blew out a long stream of smoke.

'Good God,' he said. 'Good God.'

His voice was soft, reasonable. He sounded mildly bewildered. He sat down and immediately got up again. Once more, he inhaled, shaking his head as he blew out smoke.

'Where's your wedding ring?' he asked.

Colette automatically hid her left hand beneath her right – why? Why 'automatically'? Shouldn't she have outgrown such responses by now? But evidently not. Tony still had the power to make her cringe with guilt. She had thought herself brave and independent. Had she been wrong?

No.

She wasn't wrong. She refused to be wrong. Leaving Manchester as she had done had taken courage. Starting a new life had taken courage. Finding a billet and a job, making friends – everything had taken courage, right down to finding out which bus to catch.

She had been brave and she mustn't crumble now. She removed her right hand and laid her left in her lap.

'I don't wear it any more,' she said. 'I haven't worn it since—'

Tony cut her off. 'Well, you can jolly well fetch it and put it back on.'

She swallowed. It was on the tip of her tongue to claim the ring was upstairs, so attuned was she to appeasing Tony. But that wouldn't work, because he would expect her to produce it. She had to tell the truth. She wanted to tell the truth.

'I sold it. I sold it and gave the money to the railway orphanage.'

Crushing his cigarette into the ashtray, Tony breathed hard. Were those tears in his eyes? Before she could be certain, he turned from her and stood in the window, placing his fingertips on the table bearing the aspidistra. His shoulders slumped. Was that a sniff? Was he weeping? Evidently so, because he pulled out his handkerchief from his trouser pocket and mopped his face before turning round again. In spite of his obvious distress, there was a grim flicker in his eyes.

'You *sold* it? You sold your wedding ring? I can't believe it.'

'It's true. I – I don't consider myself to be married now.'

Tony's eyes narrowed. 'Don't you? Well, I do and the law does. You're my wife until death us do part and don't you forget it.'

He swung round, crashing his fist onto the table, making the aspidistra jump. Colette jumped too. For a moment, she shook, then she froze.

'How?' Tony demanded. 'How could you do it? How could you leave me?'

With a massive effort, Colette did her best to pull herself together. She had found independence these past months since leaving Manchester – hadn't she? Now she must stand up for herself.

'How . . .?' The word rasped in her throat. She swallowed and had another go. 'How did you find me?'

Tony laughed, a harsh sound, surprisingly high-pitched. 'How did I find you? Is that all you have to say for yourself? Never mind that you ran away. Never mind that you pretended to be *dead*.' He leaned forward from the waist, bending almost double, thrusting his face towards her. 'Never mind that you sold your wedding ring. Never mind all that, oh no. All she cares about is how I found her.'

Tony threw himself into an armchair. He sat forwards, elbows balanced on knees. His head tilted as he looked at her.

'All right, then. I'll tell you. You can thank the new salvage regs that came in back in – March, was it? All waste paper has to be salvaged, every little scrap and no exceptions. You're not allowed to burn paper now.'

He came to an abrupt halt and fell silent. Thinking? Although he lowered his eyes, Colette glimpsed them darting this way and that, as though Tony was locked in a battle with his thoughts. Then he looked up, sitting back in the same moment – not merely sitting back but actually lounging. It was the only word for it. He put his right ankle on his left knee, his right knee sticking out sideways. It took Colette by surprise. Tony never sat like that. He always crossed one knee over the other. Tidy. Controlled. That was Tony.

'So there I was at Wilton Close,' he said, sounding positively chummy as he lit another cigarette, 'and the Scouts came round to collect the salvage, so I took it out for them. I happened to glance in the box and there was an envelope with your writing on it. No, no,' he corrected himself. 'Get it right, Tony. Let's be precise. It was part of an envelope that had been ripped into pieces, and all I could see was *Mrs J Coop* and *1 Wilton*. It was your writing – though it couldn't be your writing, could it, *Colette*?' His tone sharpened. 'It couldn't have been, because you're *dead*.'

'Tony—'

His gaze flicked her way, rendering her silent. 'Can you imagine what that was like for me?' The foot that was balanced on his knee dropped to the floor and he leaned forward. 'I thought I was seeing things. I couldn't believe my eyes – that is, I told myself I shouldn't believe them. I told myself it must be an old envelope – except what reason would you ever have had to write to Mrs Cooper? You saw her every blasted week. So I knew it couldn't be your writing, except that I knew perfectly well it was yours. D'you know what I did next? Well, do you?'

'No,' Colette whispered. Dear heaven, it was like the old days. Tony angry and her creeping about, trying to keep the peace. The pitter-patter of her heart was the same too.

'I upended the salvage box and rummaged through all the tatty scraps of waste paper. That's what I did. I knelt on the side path, picking through the rubbish like a starving urchin desperate for crumbs. The Scouts thought I'd gone mad. I found the other bits of the envelope and I fitted them together. *Mrs J Cooper, 1 Wilton Close, Chorlton-cum-Hardy, Manchester, Lancs.* Ring any bells?'

Tony inhaled so deeply that he all but sucked the remains of his cigarette down his throat. He thrust the end into the ashtray and ground it into the thick glass. He looked ready to explode and Colette quivered. Instead, he slumped, his voice going quiet.

'Even then it might have been an old envelope . . . except that the postmark said different.' Tony shook his head. 'My God,' he whispered. 'My God.' When he glanced at her, his hazel eyes were dark with pain. 'Aren't you going to ask what happened next? I searched Mrs Cooper's bedroom, that's what. That know-all Mrs Masters nearly caught me in the act, but I got away with it.' Scorn gave his lips an ugly twist. 'It took a few apologies and a bit of forelock-tugging, but her sort likes feeling they're better than the common working man.'

Colette's hands clenched as indignation made itself felt. She had always admired Cordelia and hated to hear her being disparaged like that. She ought to speak out and defend her friend, but she was in the grip of shock. Besides, when had she ever spoken out?

'I read your letters, *Betsy*,' Tony went on. 'Mrs Cooper keeps them tied up with ribbon, stupid old biddy. Mind you, I'm glad of it, because it helped me find you.'

Colette frowned. She had put her new address on the very first letter and on no letter since. When dear Mrs Cooper had written back to her that first time, she said she'd memorised the address and Colette mustn't put it at the top of any future letters. Mrs Cooper had also said she'd clipped the address off the first letter and burned it.

'My letters didn't have this address on them,' Colette said.

'No, but you mentioned a factory and although you didn't name it, you mentioned making coils. The postmark and a factory making coils: that was all it took.'

Fresh unease trickled through her. It must have shown in her face because Tony smirked.

'That's right. I made enquiries when I got here. I found Beeson's, waited outside . . . and followed you here.'

He had followed her. He had *followed* her and she'd had no idea, no telltale prickle at the back of her neck to warn her.

63

Tony shot to his feet, crossed the room in two strides and leaned over her, his hands on the arms of her chair, trapping her.

'You left me. You *left* me. On purpose. Why? How could you? I still can't believe it.'

'I . . . wasn't happy.'

Fastening her in the chair like that might be aggressive, but the clouded gaze was all confusion. 'I gave you everything. A home of our own, generous housekeeping. Before the war, you never had to go out to work.'

'You . . .' Colette closed her eyes. He was close, so close, too close. She forced her eyes open and looked into his. 'You controlled everything.'

'Of course I did. Husbands do. It's our job. A man who doesn't is feeble and doesn't deserve to be married. He's henpecked.'

'You controlled *me*.'

'Controlled you?' Tony swung away, planting himself in the middle of the room. 'I *took care* of you. I *cherished* you. Ask anybody – ask your precious railway friends. They'll all say the same. They'll say I watched over you and protected you. They'll say I was the best husband a girl could wish for.' He dragged a hand through his hair, disrupting its brilliantined smoothness. 'I know exactly what they'd say, because they all said it to me after you died. Everyone practically queued up to tell the grieving widower what a lucky girl his wife had been – your friends included.'

Grasping the arms of her chair, Colette pushed herself to her feet. Her legs felt as if they were filled with water, but she made herself stay standing.

'Tony . . .' She ought to speak loudly, firmly; she ought to shout from the rooftops, but all that emerged was a croak. 'I'm sorry I hurt you.'

He took an eager step towards her. Colette began to retreat, but the backs of her calves hit the chair. She stepped sideways instead.

'Come back to me,' said Tony. 'That's all I ask. I swear you'll never regret it. We'll let bygones be bygones.'

'I can't.' Colette shook her head. 'I've got a life here now. I – I don't want to come back.'

'Yes, you do. Whatever madness made you do what you did – you were overwrought. I said all along that that night-time work in the marshalling yard was too much for a sensitive sort like you. I've come here in good faith, Colette. Don't you care how badly you hurt me? Losing you all but destroyed me. Look at me. Look how thin I am – that's grief, that is, because I lost the love of my life.'

Tears sprang into Colette's eyes. Lord, she wasn't feeling sorry for him, was she? After the way he had controlled her every response throughout their marriage? His words, his feelings, the look in his eyes all appeared genuine, but that was how he did it, wasn't it? That was the way manipulation worked.

Colette swallowed. She tried to make herself taller. In the firmest voice she could muster, she said, 'I'm not coming back with you.'

Tony's face hardened. 'You have to.'

She shook her head. He couldn't drag her out of the house. He couldn't pick her up and carry her to Euston Station.

'Tell me this, then,' said Tony. 'You signed your letters Betsy and your landlady called you Miss Cooper. Betsy Cooper – short for Elizabeth Cooper.' He smiled unpleasantly. 'Did Mrs Cooper help you run away? Did she hand over her dead daughter's identity to you? Don't try to deny it. It's the only explanation.'

Colette lifted her chin and shrugged.

'That's fraud,' Tony said quietly. 'You've committed fraud.'

'I don't care. I'm still not coming back with you.'

'You might not care about yourself, but you care about your precious Mrs Cooper, don't you? Taking on someone else's identity is fraud in peacetime. In wartime, as well as being fraud, it's a serious crime. There'll be a hefty fine at the very least, and very likely imprisonment – and you aren't alone in having committed the crime. You wouldn't want Mrs Cooper to be reported to the police, would you?'

Colette stared at Tony in horror, then she rallied. 'You can't accuse Mrs Cooper without also accusing me. Do you really want to do that?'

Tony sighed and looked sad, but then his eyes – did his eyes twinkle? 'Ah, but you have a loving and forgiving husband to speak up for you, a husband who will do his utmost to gain the sympathy of the court; a husband who will promise to keep a firm eye on his erring wife in future now he knows what wrongdoing she has been led into. Yes, you'll be punished and I'll pay the fine – because that's all it will be, a fine. With your adoring, hard-working husband supporting you every step of the way, you'll simply be fined. Whereas Mrs Cooper, a working-class widow, will end up disgraced. Even if she escapes a prison sentence, I expect the people who own that house in Wilton Close will come rushing home to do a full inventory. So, my darling, I repeat: you wouldn't want Mrs Cooper to be reported to the police, would you?'

CHAPTER EIGHT

Oh, how it had all come flooding back! The sight of Emily all starry-eyed when she met Raymond Hancock had startled Cordelia, not just because her baby had displayed such an obvious sign of growing up, but also because of the sharp sense of recognition that had made Cordelia catch her breath in wonder. That was exactly the way it had happened to her all those years ago. She had taken one look at Kit and in that moment, everything had changed. Everything had fallen into place.

Was that how Emily felt now? Was she on the verge of falling in love? Or had she already fallen? That was how quickly it had happened for Cordelia. One look at Kit and she had fallen – dropped like a stone – as if all of her life up until that instant had merely been a prelude to that one extraordinary moment of recognising her soulmate.

She had adored him. Even now, she felt a fluttering in her belly at the memory of her long-ago love, the love that had never left her, even though Kit had been dead for years.

How clearly she recalled the anguish when her parents, especially her father, had been determined to keep them apart. Kit had volunteered as soon as war was declared and had gone marching off in high spirits. Cordelia had secretly written to him every day, his replies coming first via her old school friend and then care of a post office a couple of miles away.

Then his letters had dried up. She'd tried not to worry, but the silence dragged on.

Kit had been dead and gone for months before she found out. It wasn't until his brother came home on a brief leave near the end of the war, with Cordelia's letters to Kit in his knapsack, that she found out. In the end, pushed by her parents and too unhappy to fight, she had married Kenneth.

Kit was the great secret of Cordelia's life. Her all too brief relationship with him was the defining incident that had shaped all the years that had followed. Since losing him, she had become the perfect wife to Kenneth, but it was Emily she lived for, Emily who mattered most in the world.

Cordelia vowed to herself that she wouldn't set herself against Raymond the way her parents had ranged themselves against Kit. She wouldn't potentially destroy her daughter's chance of happiness. She wanted to be all that was loving and sympathetic. She longed to give Emily the support she herself had never had.

After that first meeting during the training session at Darley Court, there was an informal get-together one afternoon at Mr Wayne's house for the younger fire-watchers, not just in the Chorlton area, but from further afield too.

'Just lemonade and cards and pin the moustache on Hitler,' Mr Wayne explained to Cordelia, and she subsequently explained to Kenneth. 'It would be good for some of the younger fire-watchers to have a bit of fun together.'

'Fun?' Kenneth raised his eyebrows.

'Supervised fun,' said Cordelia. 'If we don't let her go' – she said 'we', but really she meant 'you' – 'she'll be the only absentee, which would be a shame.'

'Very well,' said Kenneth. 'She may go.'

Good. Cordelia didn't say it out loud, but her heart rang with it. She was careful not to display her delight. Kenneth mustn't see it and nor at this stage must Emily. Let Emily meet Raymond once again and see if she was still dazzled.

Cordelia smiled to herself. Of course Emily would be. To suggest otherwise would be like saying Cordelia might have gone off Kit before their second meeting. Impossible. Laughable.

And apparently impossible for Emily too.

When she arrived home, looking utterly adorable in a flowery skirt and ankle socks, Kenneth called her into the sitting room to ask her about her afternoon.

Emily gave the briefest possible description, then said, 'I'll go and take my shoes off,' and ran upstairs. To be alone? To dream of Raymond?

After a minute or two, Cordelia followed. She tapped on Emily's door and looked in. Emily was standing in front of her mirror.

'May I come in?' Cordelia stepped inside and shut the door. 'I thought you were putting your slippers on.'

'Oh – yes.' Emily sat on the bed to unfasten her shoes. They were her old school shoes.

'I wish you didn't still have to wear your school shoes,' said Cordelia, 'but new ones would be a wasteful use of points. Maybe we can find something suitable second-hand on the market.'

'Yes, please, Mummy,' said Emily.

How things had changed. How Emily had changed. When she first came home from boarding school, she had been a proper little snob. As well as looking down her nose at Dot and Mrs Cooper, she would undoubtedly have been shocked at the mere idea of wearing something second-hand, let alone being grateful for it.

'It would be lovely to have something prettier,' Emily said wistfully.

'We'll have to see what we can do.' Cordelia sat beside her daughter, resisting the urge to place an arm around her. 'Who was there this afternoon?'

Emily rattled off a list of names, hiding Raymond's in plain sight in the middle. Cordelia made a decision. It was time to get this out in the open.

'I'm glad Raymond was there,' she said.

Emily couldn't hide her surprise. 'Are you?'

'When I met him at Darley Court, I liked him . . . and I think you did too.'

Cordelia sensed Emily trembling on the brink. To confide or not to confide? Cordelia sent up a brief prayer that Emily would permit her mother to do for her what Cordelia's mother had utterly failed to do for Cordelia all those years ago.

'Yes . . . yes, I did,' Emily whispered.

'The question is,' said Cordelia, 'now that you've met him again and spent some time with him in the company of others, do you still like him?'

Emily's radiant glow made Cordelia catch her breath.

'Mummy, he's wonderful. He's good-looking with nice manners and he's clever. Do you know why he wanted to be a fire-watcher? It's because he's an amateur astronomer. He spends his fire-watching nights looking at the stars through his telescope.'

Now Cordelia did slide an arm around her daughter's slim shoulders. 'If he wants to look at the stars, he could do worse than gaze into your eyes.'

'*Mummy*,' breathed Emily in delight.

'She's too young,' said Kenneth.

They were in bed. Cordelia had carefully chosen her moment to tell Kenneth about Raymond. They always read for half an hour before lights out, so it was important to speak up before Kenneth could pick up his Graham Greene.

Cordelia's quiet 'Kenneth, can we talk about something?' hadn't exactly arrested his attention, as his soft huff of breath had testified. But when she told him his daughter had met a boy, his gaze swung around and she saw his shock. 'She's too young.' The instant response.

It was precisely what her own parents had said about her. Cordelia ignored the stab of long-suppressed pain. After the way nobody had supported her, she was determined to do everything she could for Emily. Not that she could say so. Kit was her secret.

'It's wartime,' she said lightly. 'Couples meet and there's a sense of needing to make the most of it.'

Kenneth emitted a sound that could only be described as a snort. 'They aren't a couple. They barely know one another.'

'They've met twice now.'

'Did you know about this?' Kenneth asked.

'I thought she was taken with him at Darley Court, so I asked her when she got home this afternoon.'

'You shouldn't have let her go today if you suspected she liked a boy I've never met.'

'That's a little unreasonable.' Cordelia kept her tone light. 'What was I supposed to do? Refuse the invitation on her behalf just in case she'd taken a shine to him?'

'Yes,' was the stubborn reply.

'That shows how much you know about young girls. It would simply have catapulted her straight into his arms. Anyway, the point is that having met briefly at Darley Court, Emily has now spent a reasonable amount of time in his company, *with other people*,' she added, to forestall an explosion, 'and she's found she really does like him.' She paused before saying in a gentle, almost coaxing voice, 'I liked him as well. He's polite and well mannered.'

'How old?' asked Kenneth.

'Young. Honestly, you're not to imagine a man in his twenties on the lookout for a pretty face. He's seventeen, nearly eighteen.'

71

'Coming up to eighteen, eh? So he'll be getting his call-up papers.'

Cordelia sighed softly. 'I imagine so, but I don't think you can use that as a reason to ignore this and hope it'll go away.' She made sure her voice was steady and low-pitched. She wanted to get him on her side, on Emily's side. 'He's a perfectly sweet boy, as far as I can tell, and his parents are pleasant people. Raymond is doing his duty as a fire-watcher, don't forget, and that says something about him. He's good at conversation,' she added. Kenneth would appreciate that.

'At his age? I was tongue-tied until I was twenty.'

'Raymond works in his father's shop and has done in one capacity or another since he was young.'

'He's still young,' said Kenneth.

'You know what I mean. He started off as the messenger boy after school.'

'What sort of shop?'

'His father is a grocer.'

'A grocer!'

'It's a family concern, handed down through several generations.'

'You said that as if you're defending them,' said Kenneth. They're *grocers*. Great Scott, Cordelia – grocers! And our daughter.'

Kenneth shifted his shoulders, practically wriggling in indignation, rumpling the bedding. If they had been in the sitting room, he would have marched across to stand with his back to the fireplace like a Victorian papa.

'Well, that's that,' said Kenneth. 'There's nothing more to it. They're not our sort. And don't say it's wartime and things have changed, because they'll change back again afterwards – and not a moment too soon.'

'What about my friends from the railway? I thought you'd changed your mind about them. I thought you were happy for them to be friends for life.'

'That's different,' said Kenneth. 'This is our daughter. This Raymond boy could end up as our son-in-law.'

'Oh, honestly.' Trying to defuse the situation, Cordelia injected a smile into her voice. 'She's only just met him.'

'Then it's the best time to stop it,' Kenneth declared, 'before anything can start.'

Cordelia knew when to stop arguing. But unless she was very much mistaken, things had already started.

CHAPTER NINE

Colette was home. Home? How weird it felt to be back. Her clothes were still in the hanging cupboard and the chest of drawers, as if Tony had been awaiting her return.

'I couldn't bear to part with anything,' he had told her, almost gulping as he uttered the words, but then his voice hardened. 'It's a good job I didn't.'

That was how he was now. Sentimental and bewildered one moment, granite-faced the next. Colette was frightened. She was still frozen with shock. He had found her and fetched her home and it was her own fault for having kept in touch with Mrs Cooper.

It had started with a simple Christmas card, bearing the message *Love from Betsy*. No address, no details. Colette had firmly intended that card to be the one and only piece of communication, just so that Mrs Cooper would know she was safe and well. But once she was fixed up with her new job and her new billet, it had become unthinkable not to write again, a proper letter this time. The darling lady who had made her freedom possible deserved that at the very least. Colette hadn't included her new address and she hadn't intended ever to send a second letter – or so she had told herself.

But settling into her new life had been hard. An only child born to older parents who had given up hope, she'd had a sheltered upbringing and then, aged eighteen, she had married Tony, who had controlled every aspect of her life from that day onwards. No matter how much she wanted her independence and no matter how desperately she wanted to be free from Tony, being thrust into a new environment with only herself to rely on had been tough . . . and she had again written to Mrs Cooper, the one person in the whole world who knew the truth of her marriage. This time she had, with a fluttering heart, put her address at the top.

When, to Colette's joy, Mrs Cooper replied, she had assured Colette she had memorised the address so there was no need to include it ever again. Moreover, Mrs Cooper had snipped it carefully from the paper and burned it.

Nobody living here knows your handwriting, Betsy dear, so now we can write. I will write every week, but you must write no more than once a month. We don't want your handwriting on the envelope to become a familiar sight.

Mrs Cooper's letters had become a lifeline for Colette in her early weeks living as Betsy Cooper, even though they had made her homesick. No, not homesick. Wilton Close-sick, friend-sick. Her home, the so-called home she had shared with Tony, had ended up being an emotional prison that had ground her spirit into the dust.

Now she was back here again, in the smart little end-of-terrace that Tony was so proud of because it was end-of rather than middle-of. Honestly, you'd think that having a side passage was the be-all and end-all – and that was a thought she would never have entertained before. She would never have dared think critical thoughts of Tony. No, it wasn't so much that she wouldn't have dared. It was because such thoughts wouldn't have occurred to her in the first place. Tony had trained her to believe, to know beyond a doubt, that he was always right, and if she was ever critical, it was of herself, for her own stupidity and inadequacy, never of him.

Tony brought her home on the Wednesday. He wasn't due back at work until the following Monday and he spent

Thursday and Friday with Colette on his arm, parading her around the neighbourhood and knocking on the neighbours' doors to introduce her back into the community – not that he had ever let her play much of a part in the community previously.

'What are you going to tell people?' Colette had asked before they went out the first time.

'That on the night the marshalling yard was bombed, you were knocked out. When you came to, you'd lost your memory and you wandered off.'

Colette lifted her eyebrows. 'All the way to London?'

'Yes.' Tony was unfazed. 'You walked across town to London Road Station and in all the confusion, you ended up on the London train.'

Although his voice was stubborn, there was a pleading glint in his hazel eyes, as if he was begging her to say, 'Yes, that's exactly how it happened. I never meant to leave you.'

'And I've been in London ever since,' said Colette, 'me and my lost memory.'

To her surprise, Tony said, 'No. Too far-fetched. We'll say that in London everything came back to you. You were having nightmares and flashbacks about the bombing and you had a kind of breakdown. You ended up at a sanatorium in the country. When you were well again, you wrote to me, begging me to fetch you.'

'What if I tell people the truth?'

'You can if you like,' Tony said affably, 'but then I'd have to tell them that Mrs Cooper was party to a criminal act of fraud.' He shrugged. 'I don't mind if you don't.'

Colette felt sharp little spikes of alarm inside, but they were followed by a sort of dull resignation. Tony had brought her back and now she was stuck. She could never let him harm Mrs Cooper and that meant she had to concur with whatever story he chose to concoct around her disappearance. She tried to concentrate on being strong for Mrs Cooper's sake, but in the depths of the night she lay awake, biting down on her bottom lip in utter despair.

The one good thing about night-time, the one and only good thing, was that Tony didn't demand his marital rights, but Colette knew it was only a matter of time. It used to be twice a week, Tuesdays and Saturdays, regular as clockwork all through their marriage, apart from when he'd been determined to get her pregnant and at those times it had been practically every night.

Would he want to get her pregnant now? With a baby on the way, she would be tied to him for ever.

To Colette's horror, Tony's father suggested that very thing when Tony took her to visit Father and Bunty on Friday evening.

'A baby, Tony, that's what she needs.'

She? In Colette's head, she clearly heard Dot's voice saying, 'Oh aye, and who's "she"? The cat's mother?'

'Father . . .' Bunty murmured, her cheeks staining pink.

'It needs saying,' Father declared. 'If she's suffered a breakdown, she needs a proper family life to settle into and get her back on track, and that means a baby. Besides, a baby will keep her safely at home. No one expects mothers of babies to do war work.' He nodded, thrusting out his lower lip in a self-satisfied way. 'Yes, a baby. That's what's called for.'

Almost hunched over with embarrassment, Bunty escaped into the kitchen. Colette would have been mortified too, except that she was still so shocked at having been hauled back home.

She followed Bunty to the kitchen. Bunty fussed with the kettle, then opened a cupboard or two for no obvious

77

reason; anything, apparently, so as not to be obliged to meet Colette's eyes. Something inside Colette yearned towards her mother-in-law, this quiet little mouse who was also, so Colette firmly believed, the wife of a man who kept her on the tightest of reins. For Colette, it was seeing her future self in Bunty that had been one of the things that had finally forced her to face up to the truth about her own marriage and made her realise that she needed to escape from it.

Were they going to make the tea in silence?

'How have you been?' Colette asked.

Bunty glanced her way. 'Fine, thank you.'

Fine? Honestly? But Colette didn't challenge her.

Bunty warmed the pot. 'It's – it's nice to have you back, dear. We were so upset when we thought you . . .'

Colette nodded. She had known when she ran away that she would be leaving others to grieve and it had been no use telling herself it was unavoidable. That hadn't stopped guilt thickening in her throat at unexpected moments. Now she would have to face all the people who had grieved for her. When they recovered from the shock of her reappearance, they would be sympathetic about her supposed breakdown and she didn't know how she would bear their kindness.

When the tea tray was ready, she made to pick it up, but Bunty got there first, murmuring, 'No, dear, you mustn't,' as if Colette's breakdown had left her fragile and unreliable.

Back in the parlour, Bunty poured, serving Father first.

He looked at Tony. 'She isn't wearing her wedding ring. Where is it?'

Who's 'she'? The cat's mother?

'It got lost in the sanatorium,' said Tony.

'Lost?' said Father. 'Stolen, I expect.'

Tony smiled at Colette. 'I'm going to buy her a new one tomorrow. I'm sorry, darling,' he added. 'It was going to be a surprise.'

'Put my foot in it, have I?' Father didn't sound at all repentant.

Tony was still smiling at Colette. She wanted to look away, but didn't want to provoke him.

'A symbol of our fresh beginning,' he said.

CHAPTER TEN

Cordelia walked to Wilton Close, enjoying the sunshine. She wore a demure cream dress and linen jacket with a straw hat, a chiffon scarf tied around the crown and hanging down the back; she imagined it floating behind her as she walked. Was the style too young for her? After all, she wouldn't see forty again. Was it silly of her to feel a little older because her daughter was now of an age to be attracted to boys?

She turned the corner off High Lane. Coming towards her from the opposite direction was Alison, wearing a floral dress with cap sleeves and a belted A-line skirt, a pretty style that suited her, but instead of looking cheerful on this fine morning, she looked – well, quite fierce, actually. Then she spotted Cordelia and smiled, a polite, social smile.

Alison had reached the corner of Wilton Close. She hesitated, then stepped forward as if to enter the cul-de-sac, only to stop again and wait for Cordelia.

Cordelia stopped beside her. 'Don't mind me, if you'd prefer to be alone.'

'Oh.' Alison looked startled. 'Sorry.'

'No need. Feeling a bit mis, are you?'

'Do I look miserable?'

Cordelia smiled. 'A little. Should I mind my own business?'

Alison slipped her hand through the crook of Cordelia's elbow. 'Actually, I was remembering this time last year. Paul had left me for Katie and I was distraught.'

'You went through such a difficult time,' said Cordelia. She tried not to sound bracing, but on the other hand, she didn't want to encourage moodiness. 'But it all turned out well in the end, that's the main thing.'

'Yes, it is.'

This time, Alison's smile was genuine and Cordelia experienced a stab of guilt. She hoped she hadn't appeared unsympathetic. She was well aware she often came across as cool, but that didn't mean she was unfeeling. She of all people knew how devastating the effects of a broken heart were.

She squeezed Alison's arm. 'I know you're just about to arrive home, but why not come out again? I'm taking Mrs Grayson to Millington's the jeweller's to see if they can mend her wristwatch.'

Alison glanced at her. 'You mean, come with you and stop moping?'

'Kindly don't put words into my mouth,' Cordelia said with mock severity.

It was the way she sometimes spoke to Emily. That made her think of Dot referring to their young friends as being her daughters for the duration. Were they Cordelia's daughters for the duration as well?

Alison unlocked the door and stood back for Cordelia to go in first. They entered the front room.

'Alison's coming with us,' Cordelia told Mrs Grayson.

'I'm ready.' Mrs Grayson picked up her handbag and went into the hall to take her coat and hat from the hallstand.

After wearing her long hair in a heavy bun since Adam was a lad, the decent cut she'd had last year had taken years off her, but really, that coat she wore – the only word for it was dowdy. The length and caped collar loudly proclaimed the garment's age, but then Mrs

Grayson had had no need of a coat until relatively recently. Likewise that cloche hat. It was desperately old-fashioned, but at the same time too good, through lack of use, to part with.

They set off, Mrs Grayson in the middle. It didn't take long to walk to Millington's. Inside, Mrs Grayson took the wristwatch from her handbag and placed it on the glass counter. Cordelia stood beside her, leaving Alison to wander around, looking at the stock.

Cordelia joined in the conversation about the watch. Behind them, the door opened. Alison cried out. Startled, Cordelia looked at her. Alison's face had drained of colour and she had raised her hands to cover her mouth. What . . .? Cordelia was about to hurry to Alison's side, but Mrs Grayson looked towards the door. She uttered a soft 'Oh!' and crumpled to the floor.

Colette tried to rush to Mrs Grayson's assistance, but Tony's hand clamped around her arm, preventing her. She swung round to look at him – to plead with him.

Tony smiled, but there was frost in his eyes. 'I'm sure her friends will do everything necessary.'

Cordelia had dropped to her knees beside Mrs Grayson, but she was staring at Colette. Then Mrs Grayson stirred and Cordelia bent over her, stroking her hand.

'It's all right, Mrs Grayson. You just fainted. Stay where you are for a moment while you collect yourself.' Cordelia looked at the smartly dressed shop assistant. 'Might we have a glass of water, please?'

Alison walked towards Colette. She walked slowly, with her gaze locked on Colette's face. Colette attempted to step forward to meet her halfway, but again Tony restrained her, though his calm smile would give no suggestion of it to anyone else.

Colette opened her mouth to speak, but what were you supposed to say to one of your dearest friends when you'd just come back from the dead?

Alison reached out a trembling hand as if to touch her, but then her hand stopped moving and something flickered in her brown eyes before her hand dropped away. Was it Colette's lack of response that had stopped her in her tracks? Colette's stomach clenched as a fierce disappointment took hold of her. In her imagination, in her heart, she was hurling herself into Alison's arms, but in reality she was standing stock-still, unable to move unless she wrenched herself free from Tony.

Should she? Or would there be consequences? If there was one thing Colette knew about Tony, it was that there were always consequences. In the old days, if she had deviated from what he expected, there would be sharp-edged remarks to make her feel guilty and small. Consequences. If somebody else annoyed or upset him, he would be unfalteringly polite to them and then take it out on her when he got home. Consequences.

And now the possible consequence was that he might well report Mrs Cooper to the police for her part in the fraud that had enabled Colette to start again as Betsy Cooper. That he was capable of it, Colette had no doubt, even though it would also require him to throw her to the wolves. She might feel desperate enough not to care on her own account, but she cared with all her heart about dear Mrs Cooper.

'Well,' said Tony, 'how very unfortunate.' He smiled at Alison. 'I intended to come to Wilton Close to break the news gently.'

Colette glanced at him. True or false? Would he really have gone to Mrs Cooper's to play the part of the overwhelmed and grateful husband or would he have left her dearest friends to hear it on the grapevine?

Tony turned to her. 'You'd better explain to Alison, then she can spread the word.' His voice was affable, indulgent even, but his fingers dug into her arm.

Colette felt almost light-headed. She didn't want to spout all his lies for him, but she had to go along with it. Heart racing, she uttered the words Tony required.

'I . . . The night of the bombing, I was knocked unconscious. I don't really know what happened when I woke up. I wandered about and . . . and ended up on a train to London.'

'London!' Alison exclaimed.

Tears filled Colette's eyes. 'I wasn't thinking straight. I kept having flashbacks.'

'You poor love,' Alison whispered.

'You had a breakdown, didn't you, darling?' Tony said soothingly. He addressed Alison. 'The poor girl has suffered so much. She needed to be put away in a special hospital to get better.' Raising Colette's hand to his lips, he kissed it. 'But she eventually recovered and wrote to me, begging me to bring her home.'

Alison's eyes were wide. 'I don't know what to say . . . It's a miracle.'

'That's precisely what it is,' Tony agreed. 'I can still hardly believe it myself. It's the same for my parents. I gave them a little time to get used to it before I took Colette round there. Not that it's the sort of thing you can get used to with any speed.'

Colette looked over Alison's shoulder to where Mrs Grayson was now seated on a wooden chair, being fussed over by Cordelia and the shop assistant. Cordelia looked up and met Colette's gaze. Any moment now, she would be required to trot out Tony's lies all over again for Cordelia's benefit.

But Tony had other ideas. He told Alison, 'It's probably better if we leave you to take care of Mrs Grayson. What a shock for her – well, for everyone. I know how that feels, believe me.' He chuckled. 'This is upsetting for Colette too, isn't it, darling? We'll go home now and you can see your friends another time. Excuse us.'

He raised his hat to Alison and made to turn and leave. He had to give Colette a tug, because her feet were rooted to the floor. She almost stumbled as she went with him. Tony opened the door and waved her through, the little brass bell tinkling above their heads.

Tony walked away briskly. Colette had to hurry to match his pace.

'Buying you a new wedding ring was supposed to be romantic and special,' Tony said, 'but those females had to go and spoil it. Typical.'

'You'd best put your hair in a turban if you intend to help,' said Mrs Cooper.

Mabel ran upstairs. She liked wearing her wavy dark brown hair clipped back from her face and hanging loose down her back. Harry loved it that way too, which was a bonus. He said it made her look like a film star. In front of the mirror, she quickly created a ponytail, which she bundled up before deftly tying a headscarf into a turban over it.

Downstairs, Mrs Cooper handed her a wrap-around pinny to protect her clothes. They carried a couple of rugs outside and slung them over the washing line before getting to work with the carpet-beaters. Mabel had intended to tell Mrs Cooper the latest from El Alamein, which she had heard on the Pathé news last night at the pictures, but soon found that carpet-beating was not conducive to chatter.

It was, however, entirely conducive to the venting of feelings and she whacked at the rug with a will as she thought of the likelihood of her Harry being posted goodness only knew where.

Alison appeared by her side. 'Crikey! Watch where you're wielding that thing. Listen. You need to come inside. Something's happened.'

'What?' Mabel asked immediately.

'Mrs Cooper, can you come too, please?' asked Alison.

'I've nearly finished this rug,' said Mrs Cooper.

'Leave it,' said Alison. 'This won't wait.'

'Goodness me,' said Mrs Cooper. 'What is it?'

'Just come inside, both of you.'

Glancing at one another with concern, Mabel and Mrs Cooper followed Alison into the front room, where Mrs Grayson was seated, her face looking drawn, with Cordelia standing protectively beside her.

Cordelia took charge. 'Please sit down. We've got something to tell you and it's going to come as a shock. Please don't look so scared,' she added quickly. 'It's a good thing, not a bad one, but you do need to be sitting down to hear it.'

'Mrs Grayson passed out,' said Alison. 'No, that's not what we want to tell you. What I mean is, she fainted when she realised, so you have to sit down.'

'Whatever it is,' said Mrs Cooper in a thin voice as she took a seat, 'say it quickly.'

'It's Colette,' said Cordelia.

'Colette?' Mabel echoed, feeling utterly stumped.

'She's alive,' Alison blurted out. 'We've just seen her.'

'*What?*' Mrs Cooper pressed splayed fingers to her chest.

'In the jeweller's,' said Alison.

'Let Mrs Masters explain, dear,' said Mrs Grayson.

'Colette's – *alive*?' Mabel stared.

'I know,' said Cordelia. 'It's hard to believe. Apparently, she was knocked unconscious during the air raid that night before Christmas. We don't know many details, but she suffered a breakdown and had to be hospitalised.'

'When she got better, she wrote to Tony to come and fetch her,' Alison finished.

Mrs Cooper's hand moved from her chest to her mouth. She was breathing rapidly. Mabel put an arm around her.

'That's . . .' Mabel shook her head. 'Are you sure? What I mean is – all three of you saw her?'

'Yes, all of us,' said Alison, 'and I spoke to her. Then Tony whisked her away because it was rather upsetting.'

'That sounds like Tony,' said Mabel. Somehow, in her swirling thoughts, Tony's protectiveness was the one thing that made sense.

'But . . .' said Mrs Cooper. 'Poor girl, poor girl.'

Alison sat down on Mrs Cooper's other side and cuddled her. 'We all know how much you liked her, Mrs C. Well, now she's back. It's a colossal shock, I know, but isn't it wonderful?'

Colette sat on the hard wooden pew with tears streaming down her face. She'd tried so hard to be strong and brave, using her loyalty to Mrs Cooper to shore herself up, but while she sat beside Tony in church, a chilly panic had crept up on her. This was happening, it was really happening – it had already happened. Tony had plucked her out of her safe new life and here she was now, on show for all to see, sitting meekly beside her husband in church.

The congregation was paying a lot more attention to her than to the vicar. People kept turning round to look, craning their necks, attempting to catch her eye. She had even been the subject of today's sermon. 'The miracle of hope,' that's what she was, and even more people had turned to gawp at her.

That was when the tears had started. She didn't sob. She didn't gasp or blub. She just caught her breath softly while tears poured down her cheeks. There was no point in wiping them away. There were so many more still to come. It felt as if they might never stop. Then Tony handed her his handkerchief and she mopped her face obediently.

Afterwards, everyone wanted to speak to them. Tony did all the talking. What a well-modulated voice he had. He sounded grateful, humble, overwhelmed . . . though not as overwhelmed as a few days ago. Apparently, he had got used to her return from the dead.

Which was considerably more than she had.

Somehow she stumbled through the day. Tony had taken her to the Town Hall on Friday to start the proceedings to have her death certificate officially made void and had also sorted her out with a new identity card and ration book. Then yesterday, on the way home from Millington's, he had waited outside the butcher's while she went in with instructions to buy something special for Sunday.

'As special as you can, anyway,' he said.

She had emerged from the shop with nothing more than mince, for which she apologised. Sometimes, apologising in advance could divert Tony's annoyance.

But his response was almost flippant. 'It's not as though this weekend is as special as it would have been if I'd got you a new wedding ring.'

Now, at home after church, Colette prepared a cottage pie. It was the oddest feeling, going through the motions, opening cupboards she had never expected to open again and pounding the potatoes with the masher that had been her late mother's.

After the meal, Tony settled down with the newspaper and a cigarette while Colette washed up, spinning out the task as long as she could.

Tony appeared in the doorway. 'What's taking you so long?'

'I've just finished.'

In the parlour, Tony picked up the paper again and disappeared behind it. Colette sat down in what had always been, and had again become, her armchair. What was she supposed to do? She felt edgy, as if she had pins and needles inside. Then she leaned over and dipped her hand down into the needlework bag that evidently had been there ever since she left, and took out her half-finished knitting.

CHAPTER ELEVEN

The new week started with a breakfast-time air raid. Well, it was breakfast time for a lot of folk, including schoolchildren, but if you were a lengthman, like Mabel and her gang, breakfast had long since come and gone. The distant sound of the siren brought goosebumps popping up all over Mabel's arms. Without a word, the four of them picked up their tools and knapsacks and crossed the tracks, looking both ways like children crossing a road. That was what they'd been trained to do and Bernice was a stickler for it. You never crossed a railway track without looking. Just in case.

They needed somewhere to take cover. In one direction was a massive engine shed, where workers would be climbing down the ladders into the inspection pits, or maybe it had a cellar. But engine sheds were targets, which meant there was a chance of being buried alive.

Over in the other direction, an old stone-built railway bridge arched over the tracks, but you couldn't tuck yourself under a bridge, because bridges were targets too. Anything to do with the nation's vital rail network was a target for Jerry. A picture flashed into Mabel's mind of the hammering the marshalling yard had taken last December. She hadn't been there, but she'd imagined it a hundred times, because that was the night Colette had been blown to kingdom come.

Except that she hadn't been.

'This way,' said Bernice.

There was farmland beside the permanent way, with a ditch as the border.

'She loves a good ditch, does our Bernice,' said Bette.

'At least it hasn't been raining,' said Mabel, who had spent more than one soggy hour in a squelchy ditch, taking cover.

They hacked off some leafy branches from nearby bushes and lowered themselves into the ditch, pulling the foliage on top of them. Mabel fiddled with her knapsack, retrieving her wristwatch, which she always tucked away for safe keeping while she worked. It was a good idea to check the time at the beginning of a raid. Otherwise it was difficult to sense how long you'd been taking shelter.

'The siren must have gone off at about five past eight,' she told the others.

It was remarkably short for a raid. Less than twenty minutes later, they were thrusting aside the foliage.

'Back to it,' said Bette.

Standing up, Mabel lifted her tools and her knapsack out of the ditch before climbing out, Louise doing the same beside her. Turning, Mabel offered a hand to pull Bernice up. Laughing, Bernice took it. Mabel gave a heave and staggered backwards as Bernice popped out of the ditch. Before she caught her footing, Mabel banged into Louise, who gave an exclamation.

'Sorry,' chuckled Mabel. Then she registered that Louise's cry hadn't been the laughing exclamation the situation warranted. There had been a sharp edge to it, a sound of pain. Mabel turned to Louise with concern. 'Are you all right? I didn't mean to hurt you.'

'Don't be daft.' Louise's tone was offhand. 'You just bumped into me.'

'Aye, with Bernice's full weight behind her,' said Bette with a grin and Bernice pretended to slap her.

'Less of your cheek, madam,' said Bernice.

They went straight back to work. That was what you did. The all-clear sounded and life carried on.

As the morning wore on and the day grew hotter, Bette took off her cardy and draped it over her knapsack.

'I hate getting up for the early shift,' she said, 'but there's a lot to be said for doing this job in the cool of the early morning.'

After her experience with blood poisoning, Mabel always kept her sleeves rolled down when she was out on the permanent way, but later on, when they stopped to eat their sandwiches and have a breather, she unfastened her cuffs and pushed her sleeves up, leaning her back against a low wall whose bricks were hot from the sun.

Bernice rolled up her sleeves too and Bette drew the front of her blouse away from her body and blew into it to cool her skin.

Only Lou kept her arms fully covered. Mabel remembered her exclamation earlier on – not just of surprise. Surely there had been pain as well? Mabel also recalled an occasion more than a year ago when she had come across Louise with her sleeve rolled up and Lou had pushed it down again the moment she twigged Mabel was there. And Mabel remembered the reason why.

Could Rob Wadden, Louise's violent brother, have come home?

Monday evening was a buffet evening – and thank goodness it was. On any other day, the top of Mabel's agenda would have been her concern for Louise, but today the group needed to be together to pour out their feelings about Colette's return.

Usually, at the end of her working day, Mabel took a bit of time to freshen up in the Ladies before presenting herself to the world, but today a cat's lick was sufficient because she couldn't get to the buffet fast enough. She didn't even queue up for tea. Seeing Persephone and Margaret at a table, she beetled straight over to them.

'No prizes for guessing what you're talking about,' she said, pulling out a chair. She sat down, dumping her knapsack by her feet. 'Oh, sorry, Brizo.' She ducked her head to peer under the table. 'I didn't see you there. Come and say hello.' She fussed Brizo's gingery head, scratching his long, hairy ears. 'There, that's what you like, isn't it?'

'Margaret was just telling me that Colette and Tony didn't go round to Wilton Close yesterday,' said Persephone.

That was what they'd all been hoping for, a Sunday visit. On Saturday, after the emotional bombshell, they had shared out the job of telling their friends. Margaret, Persephone and Dot were all at work, so Mabel and Cordelia had walked to Torbay Road to tell Joan. Fortunately, it was Bob's day off, so Joan had someone to share her shock and give her comfort after Mabel and Cordelia departed.

Later, leaving Mrs Cooper and Mrs Grayson to tell Margaret when she arrived home, Alison had cycled over to Darley Court to see Persephone, while Mabel had cycled to Withington to tell Dot. Cordelia would have liked to be the one to tell Dot, but with Cordelia's domestic responsibilities and their two houses being the furthest apart, it hadn't been feasible.

The one thing they had all said to one another more than once during the course of Saturday was that they couldn't wait to see Colette again, and the same reply they had all made when this was said was, 'They're bound to come over tomorrow.'

But they hadn't.

Now, as the friends arrived in the buffet one by one, all they wanted to talk about was Colette.

'Look, here's Joan,' said Dot. 'Fancy her coming all this way.'

'She must feel the same way we do,' said Persephone. 'We need to be together.'

'Haven't you brought Max?' Margaret asked Joan, budging up to make space.

'I left him with Gran.' Joan leaned down to make a fuss of Brizo, who was ecstatic to see his beloved mistress. 'I had to come. I knew you'd all be here. Did Colette come round yesterday?'

'No,' Mabel told her. 'It was a huge disappointment. We were so sure she would.'

'Perhaps they went to Tony's parents,' Alison suggested.

'Perhaps,' said Cordelia. 'I can understand the need to be with family.'

'But they'd already seen his parents, hadn't they?' said Mabel. 'Isn't that what you said, Alison?'

'Yes,' Alison confirmed. 'When we were in Millington's, he said he'd told them first and given them time to get over the shock, then he took Colette round.'

'Perhaps it's all been a bit too much for her, poor lass,' said Dot.

'Perhaps,' agreed Cordelia. 'It must be an enormous emotional upheaval.'

'Even so,' said Joan, 'I would have expected them to call at Wilton Close, even if they couldn't stay long. Colette visited Mrs Cooper almost every weekend after Lizzie died and they were very dear to one another. You'd think Mrs Cooper would be top of the list for visits.'

'Especially since some of us had seen Colette in the jeweller's on Saturday,' Cordelia added. 'Tony and Colette would know that we'd go straight back to Wilton Close and pave the way, so to speak.'

There was a short silence as they all looked at one another.

'There could be a dozen perfectly good reasons for Colette not to have gone to Wilton Close yesterday,' said Persephone.

'Aye, chick,' said Dot. 'We can all see that – but at the same time, we all know that, putting the in-laws to one side, Mrs Cooper would have been top of Colette's list of the people she wanted to see.'

'Then they must have a very good reason for not coming round,' said Margaret. 'It's no use us speculating. We just have to wait for the visit.'

'Exactly,' said Alison. 'What d'you bet we get home this evening and Mrs Cooper says Colette's been there all afternoon?'

Mabel, Margaret and Alison arrived home having more or less convinced themselves that Colette would have come round to see Mrs Cooper and Mrs Grayson that day.

'Perhaps she'll still be here,' said Mabel, imagining walking in and seeing Colette sitting in one of the armchairs, coming to her feet, tearful and delighted at the sight of her friends.

'Bagsy first hug if she is here,' said Alison.

'She won't be,' said Margaret. 'She'll have had to go home to do Tony's tea.'

They crowded through the front door, jostling one another in their excitement, but the smiles soon dropped off their faces when Mrs Grayson told them that Colette hadn't been round.

'Such a shame,' said Mrs Grayson. 'I'd rather pinned my hopes on it.'

Mrs Cooper frowned anxiously. 'I can't help feeling worried about her.'

Margaret gave Mrs Cooper a hug. 'You're bound to be concerned. You haven't seen her at all. At least Mrs Grayson and Alison saw her in the jeweller's.'

'Not that I saw much,' Mrs Grayson said ruefully. 'I fainted clean away. I feel as if I owe her an apology.'

'There's no call for that,' said Alison. 'I wouldn't be surprised if you weren't the only one who passed out in shock.'

Mabel laughed. 'Can you imagine? "Where's Colette?" "Over there, where all the unconscious bodies are." Poor Colette. It can't be easy to be faced by shock on all sides.'

'I'm sure we'll see her later on,' said Mrs Grayson.

'I do hope so,' said Mrs Cooper.

'It's nice having all you girls getting home at the same time,' said Mrs Grayson. 'Go and sort yourselves out and I'll make the tea. It's marrow cutlets tonight.'

'Perhaps you should have a nap before you go out on first-aid duty, Mabel dear,' said Mrs Cooper. 'You were up very early this morning.'

'If it's a quiet night – and it usually is these days – I'll be able to grab some sleep,' said Mabel.

Later on, she set off for the school in Withington, which was the HQ not just for the local first-aid parties but also for the ARP and Heavy Rescue, as well as the gas, water and electricity chaps. Usually, Mr Wilson, the local first-aid organiser, or Mr Varney, his deputy, gave a quick pep talk at the start of the shift. Tonight, Mr Wilson, the chief ARP warden and the head of Heavy Rescue all stood at the front. Mabel was aware of a certain electricity in the atmosphere. This looked serious.

When everyone had arrived and been signed in, the men gave a brief outline of what had happened at breakfast time.

'A plane flew just above the rooftops in Beswick, near the city centre, and dropped a stick of high explosives,' said the chief ARP man. 'Three streets were hit and three people were killed. We know of seven serious injuries that were taken to Ancoats Hospital, five of them from Palmerston Street, three of them from the same family. Others got off with lesser injuries.'

'Five were trapped in the wreckage,' added the Heavy Rescue man, 'but they were all rescued. At least fifty people had to be evacuated from their homes, thanks to a UXB.'

'It was what we call a pirate attack,' said Mr Wilson. 'We think that Jerry was put off going for his real target by the barrage balloons, so dumped his load this way instead.'

Mabel shivered. Those poor people. It was bad enough when folk were killed or injured as a result of deliberate targeting, but to suffer because Jerry wanted a quick get-away seemed extra cruel.

She left the others talking it over. Her early start was catching up with her and she wanted to snatch some shut-eye, but she was wrenched out of her slumber in the early hours by another air raid.

In fact, it was one heck of a week. Until now, there had been just three raids in Manchester in the whole year, one in January, one in May, during which Max had been born, and the one at the very beginning of July, when two Junkers 88 bombers had passed over Trafford Park daringly early one evening. But as well as the Beswick bombing, this final week of July saw attacks on Middleton Slattocks in the early hours of Tuesday and on Royton and Thornham in one devastating half hour early on Thursday morning, while the last day of the month also began with a raid.

And it wasn't just the air raids that made it a tricky week. Mabel and the others were all worried about Colette, who still hadn't put in an appearance in Wilton Close – though Mrs Cooper did get a visit from the police.

'My heart was in my mouth,' she told the girls that evening. 'I opened the door, saw a constable and thought something had happened to Colette.'

'Why to Colette?' asked Margaret.

'It was just the first thought that popped into my head. Actually, he'd come about a burglary.'

'In Wilton Close?' said Alison.

'No, a house on Edge Lane.'

'What's that got to do with you?' Mabel asked.

'I clean there.'

'Oh, Mrs Cooper,' exclaimed Alison. 'Not another of your ladies. What wretched luck.'

'The policeman wanted to know if I'd seen anyone hanging around recently, but I hadn't,' said Mrs Cooper. 'I couldn't help at all.'

She looked so upset that Mabel seized her hand. 'That's not your fault, Mrs C.'

'I know, dear,' said Mrs Cooper, 'but I feel bad for poor Mrs Ashmore. Apparently, she lost several ornaments. The bobby wanted to know if they were there the last time I cleaned and I know they were.'

'At least that's some information for the police to use,' said Margaret.

'I know what would cheer you up,' Mrs Grayson told Mrs Cooper. 'Seeing Colette.'

'Still no visit?' asked Mabel.

'No,' said Mrs Grayson.

'Well, if she isn't coming to see us,' said Alison, 'we'd better go and see her.' She looked around expectantly.

That was when they realised none of them knew Colette's address.

'I know she lives in Seymour Grove,' said Mabel, 'but I don't know the name of the road. I'm sure one of the others will know it. We're meeting in the buffet on Friday.'

'I'll drop in on Joan,' said Mrs Cooper, 'and see if she knows the address.' She shook her head. 'It's odd to think we don't know where Colette lives.'

'We never needed to know,' Mabel pointed out. 'She always came here.'

'It's not as though any of us is familiar with Seymour Grove,' said Mrs Grayson. 'If we had been, we'd have asked if she lived near the park, or the shops, or wherever. But you only ask that if you know a place yourself.'

Before Mabel went to the buffet on Friday evening, she had something more to worry about. She was already concerned about Louise, but on Friday, when the two of them were working together, Louise stopped for a few moments to stretch her back and roll her shoulders. She stretched her arms too and her blouse came untucked and rode up.

Mabel caught her breath at the sight of an ugly bruise on her midriff.

'Lou,' she began.

Louise quickly pulled down her blouse. 'It's nothing.'

'It doesn't look like nothing.'

'It's just a bruise. I fell, that's all.' Lou's voice was sharp and dismissive. More than that, it contained a warning.

Mabel fell silent. Truth be told, she felt she'd been slapped down. After the help she'd given young Clifford, she'd hoped that Louise might be friendlier, might trust her more, but apparently not. She wanted to do the right thing. She wanted to help, but Louise was determined not to let her.

'It's like last time,' Mabel murmured to Bernice privately later on when the two of them were paired up. 'She was covered in bruises, but she swore blind it was her own fault for being careless, when really it was her brother.'

'Well, he cleared off ages ago, so who's knocking her around now?' Bernice asked. 'Are you saying Rob's come back?'

'Looks like it to me.'

'And what do you propose to do about it?'

'I want to help,' said Mabel.

Bernice sighed. 'We all want to help, love, but you know Lou. She'd never let us. Anyway, what can we do?'

'Report him to the police,' Mabel said at once.

'Trust me, that won't do any good. If all the blokes who slapped their womenfolk around were jailed, the prisons would be full to bursting. At most, Rob would get a ticking off, and what do you think would happen then?'

'He'd take it out on Louise.'

'Aye, he would. He'd blame her for shopping him to the cops.'

Mabel huffed out a breath of pure frustration. 'So we're just supposed to turn a blind eye, are we?'

'Don't take that tone with me,' Bernice rebuked her. 'I don't like it any better than you do, but I've seen more of the world than you have, lass. You had a posh upbringing, with a private school an' everything. I understand you wanting to set Louise's problems to rights, but she wouldn't thank you for wading in. Just do what me and Bette do. Keep an eye on her without making a fuss.'

'She's like a stray dog,' said Mabel. 'You want to be kind, but if you take a step too close, the dog backs away, growling.'

'I know it's hard, love,' said Bernice, 'but there are times when you just can't help.'

CHAPTER TWELVE

Cordelia was as surprised as anybody to find that no one knew Colette's address.

'Isn't that odd,' she remarked, 'when we've known her for such a long time?'

'I don't suppose any of you knew my address when I still lived at home,' Alison pointed out.

'No, that's true,' said Mabel. 'None of us had any reason to know Colette's address because she always came to Wilton Close.'

'Everyone fetches up at Wilton Close sooner or later,' Dot said with a laugh, but then she looked serious. 'All I can think of is to ask Miss Emery.'

Cordelia said quietly, 'Miss Emery might not have kept her address. I don't know what the protocol is when a member of staff . . . passes away.'

That cast a sombre cloud over the group clustered around the table near the fireplace in the crowded buffet. Cordelia thought of the grief they had all gone through after Colette's supposed death and was sure the others were remembering too.

'Well, there's one way to find out,' said Dot.

'There's no harm in asking,' Persephone agreed.

'Miss Emery is away at the moment,' said Mabel.

'On holiday?' asked Persephone.

'Visiting other stations,' said Alison. 'She and the welfare supervisor have a vast area to cover and they're responsible for all of the women. Miss Emery has been away all week, but I gather she'll be back here on Monday.'

'Dot and I will go and see her,' said Cordelia. 'We're both on earlies next week and we've arranged to meet here on Tuesday. That would be a chance to see Miss Emery. I'll nip across to Hunts Bank in a minute and make an appointment.'

'I'll walk over with you,' said Persephone.

They went to the admin building. Cordelia spoke through the hatch to one of the women in the reception office.

The woman looked doubtful. 'Miss Emery will be returning to a full diary.'

'This will only take five minutes, I promise,' said Cordelia.

'Very well, if you're sure.'

Departing with Persephone, Cordelia remarked, 'Miss Emery really ought to have her own secretary. Her position is important enough to warrant it.'

'Tell that to the powers that be,' Persephone answered wryly. 'They don't even think it warrants a proper office.'

Cordelia pictured the three-sided alcove Miss Emery occupied. True, it was the size of a small office, but it was still an alcove without the privacy that a door would afford. Cordelia considered it a highly inappropriate arrangement, not just for Miss Emery but also for all the women who had to go and see her.

'What are you up to this weekend?' she asked Persephone.

'Working, but I'm not starting until two, so I'll have the mornings free. You?'

'A quiet weekend at home – I hope,' Cordelia added, thinking of that week's air raids.

As it turned out, although the weekend was clear of raids, the Masters' household had an upset of a different nature. After a perfect family day on Saturday, complete with a picnic on the meadows, Emily went to the pictures with her friend Lucy.

'If the notice appears on the screen during the film to say there's an air raid,' Kenneth said before Emily set off, 'promise me you'll leave and seek shelter.'

'Oh, Daddy,' Emily wailed. 'Nobody does that. Everyone stays to watch the film.'

'Not my daughter,' Kenneth replied, his voice quiet but firm. 'I mean it, Emily. If you can't assure me of that in a week when we've had four raids and there may be more to come, then I'm afraid you can't go.'

To Cordelia's relief, Emily put her arms around her father's neck and hugged him.

'You old dafty.'

'I just want you to be safe,' said Kenneth.

'I know – and if the notice comes up, I promise I'll leave the cinema.'

When she'd gone, Cordelia and Kenneth exchanged looks.

'She's grown up a lot in the past year,' Kenneth observed.

'And I'm glad she's doing her growing up here with us instead of in the depths of Herefordshire with Auntie Flora,' said Cordelia. 'I missed her so much when she was away.'

'Let's go for a walk,' Kenneth suggested. 'We can call in at the Lloyds and have a drink. It's a beautiful evening.'

It was indeed. After the sultry day, the evening was still warm but the air felt brighter. Walking arm in arm, Cordelia enjoyed looking at the roses, hollyhocks and heliotrope that the neighbours had kept in corners of their gardens. Yes, each and every vegetable plot was essential, but surely the flowers were too in their own way, because it lifted the spirits to see them.

'What are you smiling at?' Kenneth asked her.

Cordelia told him, hoping he wouldn't pour cold water on her idea, but Kenneth was in a mellow mood.

'Flowers as an aid to morale, eh? Well, why not? Talking of morale, have you done anything more about the Christmas dance at Darley Court?'

'I've written to the American base to suggest it. It was a joint letter from myself and Miss Brown, since she'll be the hostess.'

'It's very good of her to offer. I assume all your railway friends will attend.'

Not so long ago, that would have been said in a tone of sarcasm and Cordelia would have found herself on the defensive, but not any longer.

'Yes, though not Mrs Grayson, of course.'

'I've been thinking about that,' said Kenneth. 'Perhaps we could take her there a few times to get used to the journey and the place. We could go by taxi.'

What a generous thought. Cordelia felt a glow of pleasure. 'It's not exactly an essential use of petrol.'

'Isn't it? As I understand it, she wasn't able to join in with the Christmas Kitchens scheme last year because of the travelling. It would be a shame to miss this year's festive event as well. After all, if roses and pansies are good for morale, judicious use of petrol could be too.'

Cordelia was about to respond with words of praise for his thoughtfulness when she noticed their friends the Horsfalls, Lucy's parents, approaching. They were also walking arm in arm. Ernest was a banker and Lucinda had for years sat on the same charity committees as Cordelia.

The two couples met and stopped to chat.

'We're on our way to the Lloyds,' said Ernest.

'So are we,' said Kenneth. 'Shall we go together?'

'It's a pleasant coincidence,' said Cordelia, 'our ending up together on the same evening as Lucy and Emily are out together.'

Lucinda frowned. 'Lucy? She's in Scotland.'

Surprise tingled across Cordelia's skin. Under her hand, the muscles in Kenneth's arm tightened.

'I tell you what, old fellow,' Kenneth said to Ernest with false bonhomie, 'let's save that drink for another occasion.'

The two couples parted, but not before Cordelia had seen their friends' eyes light up with interest. As they walked away, vexation made Kenneth almost march along.

'Where's she gone?' he demanded. 'Why has she lied to us?' He gave a bark of laughter that sounded anything but amused. 'Why am I even asking? We both know the answer to that.'

Cordelia pressed her lips together as dismay washed through her. The silly girl, why hadn't she told the truth? Why hadn't she asked permission? But Cordelia knew only too well the answers to those questions, having herself told numerous lies in order to spend time with Kit. Father would have exploded with wrath had he known.

Please don't let Kenneth explode over this.

'Don't let's be too hard on her,' said Cordelia. 'She's made a silly mistake—'

'Is that how you see it? I'm afraid I view it far more seriously. She's lied to us – blatantly and deliberately.'

'Kenneth . . .' Cordelia began. It wasn't just the lies and the sneaking around that she remembered. It was the damage – the permanent damage. She couldn't bear it if that happened in her own family.

'Kenneth, what? "Kenneth, give her a chance to explain"? "Kenneth, he's a nice lad"? No explanation Emily could provide would even remotely satisfy me, and as for this Raymond boy, he's so nice that he doesn't even collect her from home so he can meet her parents.'

'Well, at least slow down,' said Cordelia. 'I can't keep up.'

Kenneth grumbled under his breath all the way back to Edge Lane, but by the time Emily came home, he was worryingly calm.

'Emily,' he called. 'Come in here, will you?'

The sitting-room door opened and Emily appeared, her blue eyes bright and her skin radiant. Cordelia tried not to look at her daughter's mouth. She remembered all too clearly her own lips swollen with kisses.

'Sit down,' Kenneth said blandly. 'How was the film?'

'It was fun. Bob Hope and Bing Crosby.'

'Anything on the Pathé newsreel that your mother and I should know about?'

'Oh. I . . . don't think so.'

'And how's Lucy?'

'Fine, thank you. She sends her best.'

'Does she indeed? Quite an achievement, considering she's in Scotland. We went for a walk and bumped into Mr and Mrs Horsfall,' Kenneth went on as Emily paled. 'They were most surprised to hear Lucy was at the pictures with you.'

Colour flooded Emily's cheeks. 'Daddy, I can explain—'

'No need. Your mother and I know precisely what happened. You lied to us so you could see that grocer's boy.'

'He's not a grocer's boy,' Emily exclaimed. 'His family has three shops and before the war they employed thirty people. They had a delivery van, not just boys on bicycles.'

'Oh, well, that makes all the difference,' said Kenneth.

'Kenneth,' Cordelia murmured, but he flashed a glance that silenced her.

'A *delivery* van,' said Kenneth. 'The father's next step will no doubt be to enter Parliament.'

Emily jumped up. Her eyes were filled with anguish. *'That's* why I never said anything. I *knew* you wouldn't understand.'

106

She ran from the room, her footsteps clattering up the stairs. A moment later, a door slammed.

'Thank you for your support, Cordelia,' Kenneth said in his iciest tones.

'It isn't a question of support. At least, it is in that I want to support both of you.'

'So you get to sit on the fence while we thrash it out? That's not good enough. You're Emily's mother. You shouldn't let her degrade herself like this.'

'Kenneth! *Degrade*?'

'Yes,' he said forcefully. 'We have a certain station in life to uphold and that doesn't include letting our daughter get taken advantage of by a grocer's boy.'

'If you make a fight out of it, it'll only make her all the more determined.'

'I notice you don't say, "If *we* make a fight out of it." So you've decided to take Emily's side.'

Kenneth went to the sideboard and retrieved the French brandy he had kept in case the country was invaded, so that they could have a swig to fortify themselves in their moment of dire need. Before last Christmas, he had given her a tot for the shock of Colette's supposed death. Now, seeing Kenneth pour himself a finger of alcohol, Cordelia was startled. Did he really view Emily's situation so seriously?

She shook her head. There was nothing to be gained by trying to talk to him just now. She would try her luck with Emily.

Upstairs, she tapped on Emily's door. Emily was lying on the bed. As Cordelia entered, she twisted round and stood up, smearing away her tears. Cordelia's heart melted.

'Darling, I know how upset you are,' she began.

'No, you don't,' Emily retorted. 'You have no idea how I feel.'

Cordelia almost stepped backwards. Was Emily also going to attack her?

'Don't come creeping in here pretending to care,' said Emily. 'You didn't say a word to help me downstairs. You're on *Daddy's* side.'

Cordelia climbed the ladder up to the pair of railway signals high above, passing the platform that gave access to the lower signal and stepping carefully onto the upper platform. Here, she removed the lamp from the signal arrangement, cleaned and replaced it, then returned to the ladder to climb down to the platform blow and repeat the procedure with the other signal. She always took care to do her job properly, but the trouble with working alone in a repetitive manual job was that there was plenty of thinking time. Usually she enjoyed that, but not today. She was still upset by the events of Saturday evening.

On Sunday, the three of them had gone to church, looking every inch the perfect family, but Cordelia's smile had felt stretched thin. On Sunday afternoon, Emily had helped at a Sunday-school event and Kenneth had made a point of walking her there and collecting her at the end.

Frankly, it was a relief to be back at work on Monday. Cordelia crept out of bed for her early start, closing her mind to the thought of Emily and Kenneth getting up and having breakfast with nobody to act as referee. They had to go to work together, but Emily's position as the office junior would ensure she and her father were kept well away from one another for the day.

Tuesday came and at least there was the meeting with Miss Emery to look forward to, Cordelia thought as she walked along the line towards her next set of lights. Sometimes she cleaned lamps on the coaches, wagons and engines in the marshalling yard, but in other weeks she was allocated a section of permanent way along which there would be around a hundred and fifty lamps to be dismantled and cleaned.

At the end of the day, she caught the train back and disappeared into the glorified cupboard that served as the lampwomen's changing room to remove her dungarees and headscarf and put on the clothes that changed her back into the well-dressed lady she was. She checked her face in the tiny mirror before heading into the station to meet Dot.

It was hot and busy on the concourse, tobacco smoke hanging in heavy grey clouds above the heads of the passengers as they queued for tickets, hurried to their platforms or waited with varying degrees of patience, some reading newspapers, others chatting, one elegantly clad woman emitting sharp little sighs and tapping her foot.

Dot was already outside the buffet, dressed in her smart uniform and carrying a handbag and a shopping bag. She smiled as she saw Cordelia. Dot's was such a cheerful smile and Cordelia's spirits lifted. Her friend's warm, commonsensical company was exactly what she needed.

They went first to Hunts Bank, where they found Miss Emery in her ridiculous alcove office. They hesitated at the invisible line where the door would have been and Miss Emery looked up from her desk.

'Mrs Masters and Mrs Green, come in. When I saw in the diary I was to have two visitors, I borrowed a chair. It's out there in the corridor, if one of you wouldn't mind bringing it in.'

Dot picked up the straight-backed wooden chair and lifted it into the office. It was rather a squeeze with three of them in there.

'What can I do for you?' asked Miss Emery.

'We've come for some information, if you'd be so kind,' said Dot. 'We want Colette's – Mrs Naylor's address, please.'

Miss Emery frowned. 'Mrs Naylor? The late Mrs Colette Naylor?'

Cordelia and Dot looked at one another.

'You haven't heard, then?' said Dot.

'This is going to come as a shock,' said Cordelia, 'but Colette is still alive. She was knocked unconscious in the bombing and when she came to, she wandered off. We aren't sure of all the details, but we know she had a mental breakdown. When she recovered, she wrote to her husband and he has brought her home.'

'Are you sure?' Miss Emery's eyes were wide.

'I know, love,' said Dot. 'It's hard to get your head round it at first, but it's true. I haven't seen her myself, but Mrs Masters has.'

'And so has Alison Lambert,' Cordelia added.

'But none of us has seen her since,' Dot went on, 'and we'd like to pop round and see how she's doing. You understand.'

Miss Emery took a moment to collect herself. Then she sat up straight. 'Well, that is good news, though, as you say, it'll take some getting used to. But I'm afraid I can't furnish you with her address.'

'Haven't you kept it?' Dot asked.

'As a matter of fact, it's still on record, but I can't share it with you for reasons of confidentiality.'

Cordelia was disappointed and she could tell from Dot's down-tilted chin that she felt the same. What were they to do now?

'I can, however, go and see her myself,' said Miss Emery, 'though it won't be until Friday.'

'No earlier?' asked Dot.

'I've come back to a full diary. Even fitting it in on Friday will be a squeeze. Then, with Mrs Naylor's permission, I'll gladly pass on her address.'

Dot beamed at her. 'Thanks, Miss Emery. That's a big help.'

As they walked back to the station, Cordelia said, 'It's not the outcome we'd hoped for, but it's a good one all the same.'

'It won't be long before we get to see our lovely Colette again,' said Dot.

Inside the station, they headed for the buffet. Before they could go inside, Dot had to remove her uniform jacket and peaked cap. She pulled a knitted cardy and a felt hat out of her shopping bag so that once inside the buffet she would look like a member of the public, not like a member of staff having a crafty sit-down. While she bagged a table, Cordelia queued up for two teas.

'Any news of the boys?' she asked as she joined Dot.

Dot smiled, pushing her shoulders back. They all had to put on a brave face these days, some more so than others.

'No word from either of them yet,' said Dot, 'but it's early days. North Africa is a long way and I imagine they've been too busy to write, anyroad. How about you?'

There was nobody else in the whole wide world Cordelia could have told. Her long-standing pre-war acquaintances would have seen the situation purely through Kenneth's eyes, but Dot – dear, wonderful Dot – would take both sides into account at the same time as showing understanding to Cordelia.

'And you feel like piggy in the middle,' said Dot when Cordelia had finished.

'Precisely. I understand that Kenneth is the protective father wanting only the best for his precious daughter, but I also understand that Emily is caught up in the excitement of having a boyfriend.'

'And if her father is dead set against it, that might push her even further in. If there's one thing we all know about your Emily, it's that she has a mind of her own.' Dot smiled.

'That was obvious from the way she piked off from the depths of the countryside last year and fetched up back at home.'

'She always had an obstinate streak, even as a little girl,' said Cordelia.

'By, I'm glad I had boys. They're a lot easier,' said Dot. 'If you don't mind me sticking my two penn'orth in, I'd say it's a good thing to have everything out in the open.'

'Do you really think so?' Cordelia asked. 'It doesn't feel that way at present.'

'Oh aye. There'll be ructions, but better that than Emily sneaking about behind your backs. Secrecy doesn't just make things more complicated. It makes feelings more intense an' all.'

That struck a chord. Cordelia pictured her own long-ago situation with Kit. The lies, the creeping out of the house, had made his kisses all the sweeter because there had been an edge of desperation to the relationship, but she couldn't say any of that to Dot, even though, at this moment, the temptation to let it all come tumbling out was strong. She could never breathe a word. Besides, she shouldn't be thinking about herself. She should concentrate on Emily. Cordelia and Kit's love had been over and done with years ago. It was Emily's romance that was happening in the here and now.

Cordelia failed to suppress a feeling of anxiety. She urgently wanted a happy outcome for Emily – but how could that possibly happen?

CHAPTER THIRTEEN

Ever since she had been brought home, Colette had struggled with a state of disbelief. Dread, too. Sometimes she found herself curling forwards, hugging herself, and she had to force herself to sit upright. Her life had an air of unreality about it.

The shock generated by her reappearance had gradually receded. Now she was surrounded by sympathy that she neither wanted nor deserved. The shock had been hard enough to bear, but the sympathy was worse. It meant the story of her breakdown was believed. Knowing that made her feel dull and ill, but in a distant kind of way because she was still wrapped in a cloak of disbelief.

She went to the ironmonger's one morning to see if they had the new head for the garden hoe that Tony wanted. While she waited to be served, she became aware of whispering close by.

'. . . you heard what happened to her, didn't you?'

'Oh aye. Feeble-minded, if you ask me. Where would we be if we all indulged in breakdowns every time a bomb dropped? Under Hitler's thumb, that's where.'

Feeble-minded? Honestly! But in that moment, Colette's previously stunned consciousness snapped into a sharp-edged focus as the powerful sense of disbelief was stripped from her. Time and again in recent days, she had told herself *This is really happening*, but only now did she truly know and accept it, truly comprehend that she was back here for keeps.

Dear heaven, she was back for keeps.

She went home and wept. She sat on the bed, rocking forwards and backwards, grief pouring out of her as if it would never stop.

But it had to stop, because Tony would be home for his dinner and he mustn't find her like this. She had to be strong. She mustn't show weakness. Pulling herself together, she washed her face and patted it dry.

Downstairs, she prepared salad and bread and butter, which she covered with a damp tea towel so it wouldn't dry out. Then she lightly baked some vegetable rissoles that she could warm through when Tony got home.

He was back at work now, but his boss had arranged things so that he was working locally and could come home for his dinner, though Tony couldn't guarantee what time he would arrive, which meant Colette had to prepare the meal early and then prevent it from spoiling if he was late.

While she waited for him, she battled with her fear. Not the old fear of Tony himself, of his sarcasm, of the kindness that wasn't really kindness but a means of making her toe the line. No, her fear now was for herself and her future. How on earth was she to live with Tony again?

She forced the fear to one side by concentrating on Mrs Cooper. That dear lady must be beside herself with worry. She was the only person who knew the truth. Colette longed to see her, but how was she to achieve it? Not only was Tony coming home at unspecified times in the middle of the day, but he had arranged for Bunty to drop in, for the neighbours to knock on the door – the very neighbours whom Colette had never been allowed to befriend in the past.

If she went to Wilton Close, her absence from home would be noted and Tony would find out. Well, maybe she should be open about it. What did she have to lose?

When Tony came home, he kissed her cheek and she let him. The first few times he had kissed her, she had flinched, but she was used to it now.

She waited for him to settle down to his meal. If he approved of the dinner, she would ask. If he didn't, she would bide her time.

'This is good,' said Tony, prodding a rissole with his fork.

'I'm glad you like it. Tony, can I ask you something?'

'Of course. What is it you want to know?'

Wrong-footed, she said, 'It's not that sort of question. I want to ask a favour. I'd like to go to Wilton Close.'

Tony speared a slice of tomato and ate it. 'I'm pleased to hear you asking for permission, as a good wife ought. Of course you . . .'

Elation made her tremble.

'. . . may not go.'

'What?'

'You heard. You can't honestly expect me to let you go there. That woman and all those railway females were a bad influence on you.' Tony's voice was hard, but then he smiled and said kindly, 'I don't want you upsetting yourself.' He held up a hand. 'Let's not spoil our meal, shall we?'

Colette hadn't had much appetite to start with. Now it deserted her entirely, but she made herself finish eating. She had a vague idea that she must keep her strength up.

She put the kettle on while she washed up. Her fingers itched to clatter and crash the plates, but she knew better. She made the tea and took it through. She imagined tipping it over Tony's head, but placed it quietly on the table by his armchair.

The door knocker sounded. Colette went to answer it. Who was checking up on her now?

'Miss Emery!'

The assistant welfare supervisor was as well groomed as always, but her customary composure slipped and she uttered a soft exclamation.

'Gracious me.' She sounded breathless. 'I was told, but even so – seeing you . . .'

Colette was delighted. It cheered her to have a connection, however small, to her old job. 'Please come in.'

'Thank you.' Miss Emery stepped inside.

Colette paused in the parlour doorway. 'Tony, we have a visitor – Miss Emery.'

As Tony rose to his feet, he smiled politely, but his eyes showed he wasn't pleased. He and Miss Emery had locked horns over the job Colette had been given last autumn – and way before that, back on Colette's very first day on the railways, he had decided to accompany her to work so that he could insist upon her being allocated a job he judged to be suitable.

Looking every inch the professional woman, Miss Emery held out her hand to shake Tony's.

'How do you do, Mr Naylor? I don't know the correct thing to say in these extraordinary circumstances, but I'm very happy for you on Mrs Naylor's safe return.'

'Thanks,' said Tony. 'Things couldn't be better.'

'Please sit down,' said Colette. 'I'm so pleased to see you. Would you like a cup of tea?'

'That's kind, but no, thank you. I don't want to take up too much of your time.'

'Take as much time as you like,' said Colette. Please do, she willed. Tony would have to go back to work soon. Please let Miss Emery stay beyond then.

Miss Emery placed her handbag on the floor by her feet. 'I'm here on behalf of LMS to express the company's pleasure at knowing you survived that dreadful raid – though I gather you've been rather ill.'

'Where did you hear that?' asked Tony.

'I'm not here just on the company's behalf, Mrs Naylor. I'm here at the behest of your friends.' Miss Emery glanced at Tony. 'They told me.'

'Friends?' he queried. Then he smiled at Colette. 'You have such good friends. You're very lucky – *we're* very lucky.'

'Mrs Masters and Mrs Green came to see me,' said Miss Emery. 'They'd like to visit you at home.'

'That would be lovely,' breathed Colette, but gratitude was followed by a stab of alarm. She looked at Tony. 'I'd enjoy that so much.'

'Of course you would,' he said indulgently.

'Then may I give them your address?' asked Miss Emery.

'Yes, please,' Colette exclaimed.

'Thank you for your permission. It'll be my pleasure to pass it on. I hope you'll come and see me when you feel ready to return to work.'

'Definitely.' Colette didn't look in Tony's direction.

Miss Emery picked up her bag, a sign she was about to leave. Colette felt a rush of disappointment.

'Must you go?' Another five minutes and Tony would have to leave.

'I'm afraid so. I had to fit in this visit between other appointments.' Miss Emery stood up.

So did Tony. 'You stay there, darling. You know how tired you get. I'll see Miss Emery out.'

Tired? Before Colette could come up with a response, Tony had ushered their visitor from the room. A few moments later, he came back.

'Well,' he said. 'That was unexpected. It's a good thing I was here, wasn't it, darling? Or you might have been tempted to say something foolish.'

But Colette was too happy to care about the little barb. Her friends were going to visit her and nothing else mattered.

CHAPTER FOURTEEN

Mabel sifted through the garments in her half of the wardrobe – well, actually, more than half, but she was always happy to lend her clothes to her friends. She chose a collarless blouse with puff sleeves, which she teamed with a panelled skirt. They would be perfect with her straw hat with a green scarf tied casually around the crown. It might sound daft, but she always dressed nicely when she was going to the telephone box to ring Harry at one of their prearranged times, because she knew he would ask her what she was wearing.

She ran downstairs and looked into the front room to say goodbye.

'I wish the Morgans had had a telephone installed,' she lamented.

Mrs Grayson laughed. 'It's a good job they didn't or you'd never be off the blessed thing.'

'It's nice to see you dressed up for Harry,' said Mrs Cooper.

'Lydia works with a girl who takes her clothes off when she's on the telephone to her boyfriend,' said Alison.

'I hope she doesn't use a public phone box,' Mrs Grayson said with a sniff.

Mabel laughed. 'On that note, I think I'd better go – and I promise to keep my clothes on.'

Chuckling to herself, she walked to the telephone box, pleased to find there was only one person waiting outside. When it was her turn, she shut the door and turned her back on the couple of people who had formed a queue behind her. Popping her coins into the slot, she dialled and waited, pressing button A when the call was answered. She asked for Harry and he quickly came on the line.

She felt the usual thrill of delight at hearing his voice. It wasn't long before he asked what she was wearing and Mabel couldn't help thinking of Lydia's chum. Did she describe herself in her state of déshabillé for her boyfriend?

'Listen, Mabel, can you wangle some time off in August or September?' asked Harry. 'It's high time you met my folks.'

'I'd love to,' Mabel said at once. 'I'm owed leave, so it shouldn't be a problem.'

'Good-oh. Have you got a pencil? Let me give you a couple of dates.'

Mabel couldn't wait to get home and share her excitement.

'You've been invited to meet the parents?' Alison said archly. 'That's a statement of intent, if ever there was one – and no,' she added, 'that isn't the old engagement-ring-mad me talking. That's a plain fact.'

'Please don't read anything into it, any of you,' said Mabel. 'It makes sense for me to meet Harry's parents. He and I have been together coming up for two years.'

'Then it's high time you met his family,' said Mrs Cooper. 'Before the war, no young couple would have dreamed of being together that long without the proper introductions.'

'Has Harry met your folks?' Margaret asked.

'Yes,' said Mabel. 'Ages ago, when I first knew him, before he was my boyfriend.'

'What does his father do?' asked Alison.

'He's a chemist – a pharmacist. He's a bit of a boffin, by the sound of it, a PhD. Dr Knatchbull used to work in a research laboratory, but after Harry finished school, he packed it in to do more training. It wasn't an easy decision because of the reduction in income. In fact, he got a job in the City for a while, thinking it was the right thing to do for his family, but he was never happy. That's what he was doing when I first met Harry, but since then he's become a pharmacist in his local community.'

'I expect the war played a part in his decision,' said Mrs Grayson. 'War makes you focus on what really matters to you.'

The others expressed admiration for a man who had followed his heart.

'As long as the wage is sufficient,' said Mrs Cooper. 'There's no need to look at me like that. It's all very well for a man to make a big change like that, but he has to be able to support his family. I suppose that's why he waited for Harry to leave school.'

'Anyway, that's a gradely start to the week for you, Mabel dear,' said Mrs Grayson. 'We're all very pleased for you. And tomorrow we should be able to organise another visit.'

'To Colette's,' said Mabel. 'Imagine. Two important visits in one go.'

She and Margaret both had the day off tomorrow and it was going to be their job to get Colette's address from Miss Emery. After that, they had decided to go to the afternoon showing at the flicks, which would finish just in time for them to meet up with their friends in the buffet.

Mabel anticipated a happy day, but Miss Emery had an unpleasant surprise in store.

'Yes, Mrs Naylor was glad to give her permission for me to hand over her address, but . . . well, I'm sorry to say Mr Naylor withheld his consent.'

'He did what?' Mabel exclaimed.

'What did Colette – Mrs Naylor – say to that?' Margaret asked.

'She wasn't present. Mr Naylor told me on the doorstep as he saw me out.'

Mabel and Margaret looked at one another.

'But if Mrs Naylor wants to see us . . .' Mabel began.

'My hands are tied,' said Miss Emery. 'Mr Naylor's wishes trump Mrs Naylor's.'

'That's pretty shabby, if you ask me,' said Mabel.

'It's the way of the world, Miss Bradshaw. The husband's views take precedence.'

'But you said yourself that Mrs Naylor was glad to give her permission,' said Margaret.

'Mr Naylor said Mrs Naylor's health isn't yet restored to what it should be and he doesn't want any extremes of emotion for her.'

'Extremes of emotion!' Mabel repeated. Pops would have said 'Balderdash!' to that and she felt like saying it too, but this wasn't Miss Emery's fault.

Miss Emery sighed. 'It's most unfortunate.'

Margaret and Mabel had no choice but to leave. They trailed out of Hunts Bank and, as arranged, went to the pictures. But it didn't matter how good *My Favorite Blonde* was or how much Mabel liked Bob Hope – she just couldn't concentrate. Afterwards, they headed for the station, where they found the others already in the buffet. Not bothering to get tea for themselves, they went straight to the table where Dot, Cordelia, Alison and Persephone looked up eagerly, only for their faces to fall when they saw Mabel's and Margaret's expressions.

'Didn't Miss Emery have a record of Colette's address after all?' asked Persephone.

'Oh, she had it all right,' said Mabel, 'and she's been round there.'

'So why the long faces?' said Dot. 'Wasn't Colette at home?'

'She was,' said Margaret, 'and she gave permission for us to be given her address – gladly, according to Miss Emery.'

'But then Tony saw her out and said "Not likely" on the doorstep,' Mabel added.

In answer to the exclamations of surprise, Margaret said, 'Apparently, he wants to keep her from any extremes of emotion.'

There were more exclamations and this time they held indignation.

'Surely it would be good for her to see us,' said Alison. 'We're her friends.'

'What harm could it do?' said Dot.

'She gave permission in the first place,' said Persephone.

'Evidently Tony's wishes are more important than Colette's,' said Mabel.

'They jolly well shouldn't be,' said Alison.

'He's always been very protective,' said Cordelia, 'and you can't fault him for that, but this does seem a bit much.'

Alison nudged Mabel. 'Here's Miss Emery.'

The assistant welfare supervisor made her way between the tables.

'I hoped I would find you all here,' she said.

'Take a pew,' said Persephone. 'I'll share Margaret's chair.'

Miss Emery sat down. 'I expect I can guess what you're talking about.'

'It's disappointing,' said Cordelia.

'It is,' said Miss Emery.

'What brings you here?' Dot asked when Miss Emery stopped.

Miss Emery hesitated. 'When Mr Naylor said he wanted Mrs Naylor to be spared extremes of emotion, I took the liberty of asking if he was quoting doctor's orders and he told me it's his own way of taking care of her.'

She stopped. Her listeners waited.

'Had Mrs Naylor been under doctor's orders, it would be different.' Miss Emery paused again. 'I wouldn't be sitting here now.'

Mabel sat up straighter, exchanging glances with the others.

When Miss Emery stayed silent, Dot said, 'Aye, well, if she was under the doctor, we wouldn't dream of going against that, would we?' She looked round, gathering nods of consent. 'And she did say she wanted to see us.'

'You do understand, don't you,' said Miss Emery, 'that I can't pass on her address? Not now that Mr Naylor has explicitly denied consent.'

'We can see that,' said Mabel. Where was this heading?

Another pause, then Miss Emery shifted position slightly and said, as if changing the subject, 'I was in Seymour Grove recently. Are you familiar with the Seymour Hotel?'

'We pass it on the bus every day,' said Margaret.

'It's at that junction, isn't it?' said Miss Emery. 'You know the one I mean, where some buses head straight on and others turn the corner. When I was there, I went round the corner.'

'Did you really?' Cordelia said conversationally. 'There's a parade of shops, isn't there?'

'I believe so,' said Miss Emery. 'If you walk along a bit further, there's a pillar box on the corner. I rather think I turned the corner there.'

As they listened, Miss Emery, without once mentioning any street by name, described the route to Colette's road.

'I went as far as an end-of-terrace,' she finished.

'What number?' asked Alison and the others frowned at her.

'I don't remember,' said Miss Emery, 'but there are only so many end-of-terraces in that road.'

'Ta very much, Miss Emery,' said Dot. 'You're an angel.'

'I'm sure I don't know what you mean, Mrs Green,' was the prim reply. Miss Emery stood up. 'Is that the time? If you'll excuse me . . .'

They watched her leave.

'Well!' said Mabel. 'That's a turn-up for the books.'

'Now we can go and see Colette,' said Alison.

'We must be careful never to say where we got her address,' said Cordelia.

'Strictly speaking,' said Persephone, 'we haven't actually got it. But Cordelia is right. We mustn't drop Miss Emery in the soup.'

They talked about the best time to go. Mabel, Margaret, Alison and Persephone would all be free on Saturday evening.

'I'm afraid I won't be able to come,' said Cordelia. 'A party is being held for the fire-watchers.'

'And I've got Jimmy and Jenny that evening,' said Dot.

'Should we postpone it?' asked Margaret.

'Certainly not,' Dot answered at once. 'Me and Cordelia can go another time.' She smiled. 'Spread the visits out.'

'Mrs Cooper will want to see her too,' said Mabel.

'And we can help Mrs Grayson to get there,' said Alison.

'What about Tony?' asked Persephone.

'There's not a lot he can do if we turn up en masse on Saturday,' said Mabel, 'and we'll leave immediately if it seems too much for Colette.'

'We all know what a worrywart he is,' said Alison, 'but he's taken it too far this time. I know he wants to take the best possible care of Colette, but she wants to see us.'

'If seeing us cheers her up,' said Margaret, 'he'll ask for more visits. He only wants what's best for her.'

'Of course he does,' Cordelia agreed. 'He's always wrapped her in cotton wool and now he must feel like doing that more than ever.'

'She's a lucky girl,' said Dot. 'Nobody could wish for a more loving husband.'

CHAPTER FIFTEEN

Cordelia wore dungarees for work and last winter she had taken to wearing smartly tailored trousers for fire-watching. She allowed Emily to wear slacks for fire-watching too, but that was as far as she was prepared to go regarding trouser-wearing for herself and her daughter.

Tonight's fire-watching was to be an exception because of going to the fire-watchers' party beforehand. Mr Sidwell and his wife, who were the hosts, had arranged to hold the party more or less in shifts. The fire-watchers who were due to go on duty that night had been invited to arrive around half past seven, so they could leave in plenty of time; those not on duty had been asked to come later.

'But we'll have a crossover period so both sets can see one another for a short while,' Mr Sidwell had said, 'though how the house will hold everyone, I've no idea.'

So – no trousers tonight. Attending a social gathering meant wearing a dress or a skirt. Fortunately, recent nights had been warm, so Cordelia and Emily shouldn't get cold on the roof of Oswald Road School.

Was Cordelia concentrating so hard on what to wear so as to distract herself from Kenneth's attitude to this evening's party? He had been all set to forbid her and Emily from going until Cordelia had assured him that the Hancocks wouldn't be on duty and hence would attend the later part of the evening.

'But there is going to be an overlap,' Emily had pointed out with a touch of mockery in her voice that she had never before employed when addressing her father. 'It might be better if you lock us in the cellar and throw away the key.'

Later she had apologised for her cheek, but not until Cordelia had been attacked by both her and Kenneth. Honestly! They were the ones at loggerheads, yet she, trying to be the peacemaker, was the one who seemed to come off worst.

Now, Cordelia looked at her reflection, examining her choice of linen skirt with a violet twinset. She looked quite good, all things considered. She went downstairs. Kenneth was in the sitting room. He looked up as she entered.

'How times have changed,' he remarked. 'Imagine such casual clothes being considered appropriate for a formal event.'

'Actually, I thought I looked quite nice.' Cordelia spoke lightly, but she felt a bit miffed.

Kenneth stood up and kissed her cheek. 'Of course you do. You always do. It just seems strange for you to attend an evening party and not wear a long dress and your evening wrap. The war has a lot to answer for.'

'The war is responsible for worse things than that,' said Cordelia. 'Here's Emily.'

They both turned to look at their daughter as she came in, looking trim in a blue blouse patterned with daisies, and a pair of slacks.

'Emily!' Cordelia exclaimed. 'You're meant to be in a skirt.'

'But we're fire-watching afterwards.'

'You'll not set foot outside this front door dressed like that,' said Kenneth. 'I'm not having my daughter looking . . . flighty. Or is that how you want to appear in front of Raymond Hancock?'

'Please, Kenneth,' Cordelia murmured.

Emily looked at her father. 'Is that what you think of me?'

'Of course Daddy doesn't see you in that way,' said Cordelia. She glared at Kenneth. Couldn't he exercise some restraint? 'But, darling, you can't possibly go to an evening do wearing slacks. It wouldn't be respectful to our hosts. Please go and change into a skirt.'

'Yes, please do, Emily,' Kenneth said gruffly. That 'please' was a big concession.

And one Emily ignored. 'Anything rather than let Raymond see me in slacks, is that it? We wouldn't want to inflame his lust.'

'*Emily!*' her parents exclaimed.

'I never thought I'd hear such a word coming from your lips,' said Kenneth, and Cordelia almost laughed.

'Honestly, Daddy, it's not a swear word, you know.'

'Nor is it suitable vocabulary for a young lady,' said Cordelia. 'Come along, Emily. I'll help you get changed.'

She swept the girl from the room and helped her choose a skirt.

'Do you know what would go well with that blouse?' said Cordelia. 'My aquamarine earrings. They're dainty, quite suitable for a girl your age. Would you like to try them?'

Emily's face glowed with delight. 'Yes, please, Mummy.'

The earrings were perfect, as Cordelia had known they would be. It was such a small thing to do to make Emily happy. She wanted Emily's happiness more than anything, and had done ever since she had looked at baby Emily's face for the first time. If only Emily could have met a boy from a background her father considered good enough. But she hadn't and that was that. And Cordelia knew exactly how it felt to care for a chap who wasn't approved of.

What on earth was the answer?

She pushed the thought aside. She didn't want to add to the charged feelings in the house.

The two of them went downstairs.

Kenneth took one look at Emily and said, 'You're wearing earrings.' He gave Cordelia a hard look. 'I thought she wasn't allowed to wear earrings until she's eighteen.'

Cordelia kept her voice calm and polite. 'You know perfectly well she's worn earrings on special occasions. You haven't objected before.'

Kenneth raised his eyebrows. 'This evening counts as a special occasion, does it?'

Cordelia felt like banging his and Emily's heads together, but she maintained her civil tone. 'Yes, it is. We're going to the Sidwells' house to attend a party they have kindly arranged. In my book, that's a special occasion.'

She couldn't get Emily out of the house quickly enough. Her home had always been a place of quiet and courtesy and there had only ever been a sense of strain when Kenneth's mother came to stay. Now, Adelaide's high-handed attitude seemed like very small fry compared to having Kenneth and Emily at loggerheads.

They didn't have to wait long for a bus. Cordelia was aware of Emily's quiver of excitement as she sat beside her and the bus pulled away. She longed to tell her daughter she understood just how she felt, but she must never do any such thing. After years of keeping Kit secret, her old relationship was now constantly bubbling up to the surface. But the current situation wasn't hers – it was Emily's.

It was an excited, chattering group that got ready to go to Colette's. Mabel couldn't wait to get there. She needed to see Colette with her own eyes.

'You mustn't arrive there too early,' said Mrs Cooper. 'You don't want to surprise Colette in the middle of washing up. On the other hand, you oughtn't to be too late either. Tony won't be pleased if you knock after he's put his feet up for the evening.'

Alison laughed. 'They should employ you in the War Office, Mrs C. You have a tactical brain.'

'Get away with you,' said Mrs Cooper. 'I'm just being sensible.'

'Tony might not be there,' Mabel pointed out. 'Isn't he in the Home Guard as well as being a fire-watcher? He's more or less bound to be out.'

Persephone had cycled over from Darley Court. 'I've got a tin of honey biscuits from Mrs Mitchell in my bicycle basket.'

'And I've made carrot scones for you to take,' said Mrs Grayson.

'You must take some tea with you an' all,' said Mrs Cooper.

'It'll be quite a feast,' said Mabel.

'It's a shame Joan can't come,' said Margaret.

'She has a baby to look after,' said Mrs Grayson, 'not to mention a husband. Her place is in the home now.'

How Joan's life had changed, and so quickly too. She had been married for just over a year. Mabel remembered that moment at the very end of Joan and Bob's reception when the happy couple and their smiling guests were all on the platform before Joan and Bob boarded the train, and Joan had tossed her bridal bouquet. No one had been more surprised than Mabel when it had landed in her hands. That was how it had felt – that it had landed there. She hadn't set out to catch it. She had been at weddings where some girls elbowed the competition aside and practically hurled themselves at the bouquet. Mabel hadn't done that. Catching the bouquet had been . . . natural. That was it: natural. Just like the look of understanding between her and Harry had been natural too.

Alison gave her a nudge. 'What are you thinking about?'

'Nothing.'

Alison grinned. 'It didn't look like nothing. It looked very dreamy.'

Mabel retaliated with a nudge that nearly made Alison topple over. It was all part of the high spirits of the occasion.

They had discussed whether to catch the bus to Seymour Grove or go on their bikes and had decided on the latter. They cycled as far as the junction where the hotel was set back from the road and the buses either went straight on or turned the corner. Looking over their shoulders to check for traffic behind them, they held out their arms to indicate they were going right and made the turn. They cycled as far as the pillar box Miss Emery had mentioned, then got off and pushed their bikes so they could make sure they were all in agreement about the route.

'Unless we've gone horribly wrong,' said Mabel, 'this must be Colette's road.'

'Now to find the right end-of-terrace,' Persephone said with a smile.

The first door they tried was opened by a stranger.

'We're sorry to disturb you,' said Margaret. 'We're looking for the Naylors' house.'

'Wrong side of the road, love.' The woman pointed. 'That one down there.'

They thanked her and crossed the road. Mabel knocked and they exchanged bright-eyed smiles as they waited.

The door opened – and there was Colette. Even though she was expecting to see her, Mabel still experienced a sense of shock; then her heart filled with gratitude.

Colette's mouth dropped open and she sucked in an audible gasp. The next moment, they were crowding round her, hugging and laughing and crying.

'You're here. You've come,' Colette wept. 'I've missed you all so much.'

'Of course we've come,' said Alison, dabbing her eyes. 'Nothing would have kept us away.'

'Are you going to let us in?' asked Margaret. 'Or shall we cry on the doorstep all evening?'

That caused laughter and Colette led them into her parlour.

'Tony not here?' asked Alison.

'No, he's out fire-watching.'

'Good,' said Mabel, quickly adding, 'I mean, it's nice it's just us.'

Colette clung to them all again, one by one, before they found places to sit.

'I can't tell you how happy I am to see you all,' she said. 'I've thought of nothing else since Miss Emery came round.'

Alison stood up. 'Come on, Colette. Let's you and me go and put the kettle on. We've brought goodies, even some tea. How's that for planning?'

When they left the room, the others turned to one another.

'She obviously has no idea Tony refused to let Miss Emery pass on their address,' said Margaret.

'Why would he keep it from her?' asked Mabel. 'She's entitled to know.'

Persephone's violet eyes clouded. 'He must have felt he had a good reason. Do you suppose we've made a mistake?'

'How so?' Margaret frowned.

'Colette suffered a breakdown that lasted for weeks – months,' said Persephone. 'What if she's meant to have complete quiet for the time being?'

'Well, we're here now,' Mabel said stoutly, 'and she's pleased to see us. Nothing else matters this evening. Let's have a jolly time together. I can't think of better medicine than that.'

That lifted the mood and they barged into the kitchen to help make the tea and empty the tins onto plates. Returning to the parlour, Mabel looked round at the furniture. Her gaze fell on a low table against the wall, which had a vase on it and a copy of the *Radio Times*.

'May I move these things and put the table on the rug? Then we can sit on cushions and be close to one another.'

'All of us crowded around a table – it'll be like the buffet,' said Alison.

'Oh *yes*,' breathed Colette. 'That would be perfect. I'd love to go to the real buffet.'

Soon they were all settled.

'Please don't ask me about . . . about my time away,' said Colette. 'I'd much rather hear about all of you. I want to catch up with everything I've missed.'

'The most important thing,' said Mabel, 'is that you're now an auntie.' She laughed at Colette's bewilderment. 'We all are. Joan had a baby.'

They told Colette all about Max, about Joan and Bob's move to Chorlton, Margaret's change of surname and Alison's new – 'Not so new now,' said Alison – boyfriend.

'Are you happy?' Colette asked her. 'Is he good to you?'

'Yes and yes,' said Alison.

Colette turned to Mabel. 'What about you?'

Mabel explained about Harry's expected new posting. 'But let's not dwell on that. Cheerful subjects only. That's the rule for this evening.'

'How is Mrs Cooper?' Colette asked.

'She's fine,' said Persephone. 'Magic Mop is doing well. She's taken on a lady to help her out when there's too much for her to manage on her own.'

'And Mrs Grayson is working wonders in the kitchen,' said Margaret. 'She and my sister are penfriends now and Mrs Grayson sends Anna cake and pudding recipes, which the neighbouring ladies get Anna to make for them. They provide the ingredients and give her half a crown for her trouble. Half a crown isn't much for the time it takes her, but it all adds up.'

'Mrs Mitchell over at Darley Court is in charge of a WVS kitchen making chutney, jam and pickles on a grand scale,' said Mabel. 'Mrs Grayson is allowed to do her bit for it in her own kitchen. Mrs Wadden – she's the lady who cleans for Mrs Cooper when needed – has started lending a hand sometimes as her contribution to the war effort.'

Colette closed her eyes for a moment as she released a long, slow breath. 'You can't imagine how much it means to me to hear all this news.'

And she burst into tears.

CHAPTER SIXTEEN

The Sidwells lived in Ordsall. The bus took a long route because of having to avoid craters left by bombs. When Cordelia and Emily arrived, Mr Sidwell greeted them at the door, introducing them to his kindly-looking wife.

'Is that your fire-watching bag?' she asked. 'Let me pop it over here with the others. I'll make sure the flask stays upright.'

It was a pleasant evening of conversation with a quick whist drive against the clock. A young man whose spectacle lenses were as thick as bottle tops took an obvious shine to Emily and Cordelia wanted to tell him he didn't stand a snowball's chance in hell.

She noticed Emily glancing at her wristwatch, and not for the first time. Cordelia leaned over and murmured in her ear.

'Don't keep checking the time, darling. It looks as if you're counting the minutes until we can leave.'

Whereas, of course, Emily was counting the minutes until Raymond arrived. When the second 'shift' of guests began to appear, Emily could barely take her gaze off the door.

When Mrs Hancock walked in, followed by Mr Hancock and Raymond, Emily bounced to her feet before Cordelia could place a gentle hand on her arm. Oh well. If Mr Bottle-Tops hadn't already taken the hint, this would show him exactly where he stood.

Cordelia joined Emily with the Hancocks. Kenneth would expect her to stand guard, but she also wanted to be polite.

If she hung back, it might look stand-offish. Worse, she might appear superior. If there was one thing the war had taught her, it was that people she had previously regarded as her social inferiors were every bit as good as she was.

One good thing she would be able to report to Kenneth was that the Hancocks hadn't arrived until a quarter to nine, and she and Emily needed to leave at nine to be sure of getting back to Oswald Road for a ten o'clock start. As they were saying their goodbyes, Cordelia's heart sank a little when Emily made a point of shaking hands with Mr and Mrs Hancock, which Cordelia knew she was doing purely so as to have an excuse to shake hands with Raymond. Cordelia might be dismayed to see her daughter being quite so obvious, but at the same time she felt a burst of surprise. She would never have dared do that with Kit in front of her own parents.

Remembering to collect the fire-watching bag, she and Emily set off for the bus stop. They were almost there when the air-raid siren started up. The fear Cordelia felt wasn't on her own account but for Emily. All her protective instincts came surging to the fore.

People appeared from nowhere.

'Are you going to the public shelter?' Cordelia asked.

'Aye. This way.'

The shelter was in the park. An ARP warden stood in the park gateway, ushering people in, and there was another warden at the shelter's door.

'Please move right to the back.'

Cordelia took a firm hold of Emily's hand as they found a place to sit. The long benches were hard and there was a stale smell in the air. People were still filing in as the sounds of aircraft engines and ack-ack guns were heard. Then the door shut with a bang. Lamps were lit, as were cigarettes, the smoke lifting into the gloom and hanging there.

An elderly woman opposite Cordelia and Emily got her knitting out. Beside her, a young mother tried to cuddle twins on her lap. Further along, two turbaned women with cigarettes apparently attached to their lower lips talked about 'her round the corner' whose husband had been overseas 'for Gawd knows how long, so where has that bulge in her skirt come from, that's what I'd like to know.'

Cordelia listened in horrified fascination while simultaneously worrying what this was doing to her daughter's innocence.

And then the bombs started to fall.

The moment the siren sounded, they all stood up, knowing from long experience what needed to be done before they could leave the house.

'Have you got your own shelter?' Mabel asked Colette.

'In the back garden.'

Good. That was better than hurrying through the streets to a public shelter. While Colette switched off the gas and electricity supplies and turned off the stopcock, the others went round the house, drawing back the blackout curtains and the ordinary curtains so that a fire that started inside the house would clearly be seen from outside. The buckets of sand and water that stood in the hallway were put outside the front door. Everyone knew the ropes, but it was always a bit odd doing it in a different house. Last of all, they gathered up the goodies. No point in going hungry just because of a raid.

They went outside and Colette opened the Anderson's door. One by one, they stepped down into it.

'It's a cheeky raid, not waiting until dark,' said Alison.

'It makes it easier for our boys to see them off,' said Margaret.

Mabel thought of Harry. Not that he was a pilot with the job of seeing Jerry off. As a bomb aimer, he was part of a Lancaster crew, flying missions over Germany to wreak havoc on the country beneath . . . just as the young Germans flying overhead now were intending to do here.

A whistling sound announced that sticks of high explosives were falling. Moments later came a series of distant crumping sounds. It was always difficult to tell how far away the HEs had fallen. Sometimes an explosion that sounded as if it was in your own back garden turned out to have happened half a mile away.

They carried on chatting, only pausing each time a bomb fell. Mabel glanced surreptitiously at Colette. Did the sounds from outside fill her mind with memories of what had happened before Christmas at the marshalling yard? But Colette gave no sign either of twitchiness or of being lost in thought. That was reassuring.

After half an hour or so, the Andy's door opened and they all looked up. There was Tony, dressed in his Home Guard uniform, with a tin hat on.

'Colette, are you—?'

He stopped at the sight of the faces turned towards him. Another whistling sound made him glance upwards into the sky, then he stepped down into the shelter and turned to pull the door shut behind him before turning round to face them. It was odd: Mabel hadn't felt the small space was crowded when it had just been the girls in there, but now it felt cramped.

'I got permission to come and check on you,' he told Colette. 'This is the first raid since you've been back.' He glanced around at the friends. 'It seems I needn't have worried after all.'

*

The all-clear sounded and everybody in the public shelter got to their feet. The man beside Cordelia puffed out one last jet of cigarette smoke as he rose. As he turned at the same moment, Cordelia received the full benefit of it right in her face. She wafted her hand, but the man didn't notice. Cordelia used one arm to hold the fire-watching bag close to her chest and held on to Emily with her other hand as she shuffled towards the door.

'Mummy, please can we go back to the Sidwells' to make sure they're all right?'

'We have to go straight to Oswald Road. We're on duty.'

'It wouldn't take five minutes to go back,' Emily pointed out, 'and at least one bomb did sound awfully close.'

'They always sound close.'

But when they got outside and Cordelia breathed in the fresh air she'd been longing for ever since the door had closed, shutting them inside the shelter, instead of now breathing in purity, what hung in the air and hit her eyes and the back of her throat was the smell of cordite, brick dust and smoke.

'Come on,' she said to Emily. 'Let's go and see.'

When they reached the Sidwells' road, shock poured through Cordelia at the sight of their house reduced to rubble. Emily took to her heels and flew down the street, Cordelia immediately behind her, her heart thumping with dread.

This house – this house where they had been minutes before the siren sounded – this house she had taken her daughter to – this house – oh my goodness – and all those people—

It seemed as if all the fire-watchers who had been to the party's first shift now came flocking from all directions, white-faced with shock.

Mrs Sidwell appeared from the other side of the rubble, leading several women, including Mrs Hancock. They all stumbled, slack-mouthed and wide-eyed, barely able to stand upright as they beheld the ruins. Willing hands assisted the women to the pavement, where they turned to gape.

'We were in the Anderson,' Mrs Sidwell said in a hollow voice. 'There wasn't room for anyone else, so they all stayed indoors. My husband said he was going to put some under the stairs and others under the dining table. Mr Sobers joked about playing sardines.'

And now Mr Sobers was underneath all that rubble, along with Mr Sidwell and the rest.

Cordelia would have given ten years of her life if it would have spared Emily from the anguish of what followed. The fire-watchers who had left the party early joined in with the rescue effort, alongside neighbours, ARP wardens and a policeman. A WVS van arrived, complete with two huge urns of hot water to make tea, but nobody wanted to stop for a breather. Cordelia thought fleetingly of Oswald Road and her duty, but no duty could be greater than this.

When they carried out the first bodies, Emily sagged as if she might pass out. Cordelia went towards her, but Emily reared up, throwing back her head as if sending a plea to the heavens. When she looked again at the scene before her, her pretty face was grim. She looks like Adelaide, thought Cordelia. Well, if Emily had some of her grandmother's stiff-necked strength, that would serve her well tonight.

'Quiet!'

The call went up and everyone stopped moving. On the rubble, the rescuers crouched down, pressing their ears to bricks, plaster and timber. They looked up, exchanged glances, nodded.

'Can hear something.'

Presently a man was stretchered to one of the waiting ambulances. It felt like awfully bad form to look as he was carried past, but Cordelia couldn't help it. She needed to know. In spite of the thick layer of dust smeared with blood, she recognised him from the training event at Darley Court and felt guilty for not knowing his name.

A few yards away, one of the women from the Anderson shelter uttered a strangled cry and had to be held back from rushing towards the stretcher.

A couple more bodies were brought out, covered by sheets provided by the WVS, and were taken straight to the mortuary van. God, what a job. You heard about plucky ambulance drivers and mobile-canteen drivers. You never heard tales about the dead-wagon drivers. They came and did their job and drove away and everyone tried not to think about them.

Mr Sidwell was dug out – alive, thank God, in spite of a gaping wound that had to be tightly bound to stop the blood pumping out before he could be taken to the ambulance. He was driven away immediately, the ambulance bell clanging, without waiting for another casualty.

The rescuers continued their grim task. Emily had a severe coughing fit and Cordelia broke away to help her sit down and fight for breath.

When she was herself again, Emily said, 'I thought I was choking on tears, but it was the dust.'

Cordelia pressed her lips together to hold in her own emotion at the sight of her daughter's courage. 'No time for tears.'

'I know.' Emily sounded dismissive.

She stood up and returned to the human chain passing chunks of rubble and pieces of jagged-ended timber. They were digging through to the understairs cupboard now, carefully lifting away everything blocking the route, pausing frequently to check that what remained was stable.

At last they got through. From her place in the chain, Cordelia couldn't see exactly what was happening, but it seemed something must be in the way of the cupboard door, something they either couldn't or didn't dare shift. There was an agonising wait while they unscrewed the hinges and lifted the door free.

If Cordelia had expected the people trapped inside to come pouring out, it didn't happen. The rescuer in the doorway peered in and said 'Christ', not loudly, but everyone heard. He must have realised he'd been unprofessional because he immediately started giving orders.

'Stretchers, please. Everybody in the chain, move back. First-aiders and ambulance men only up here.'

Cordelia watched as a prone body was stretchered across the rubble. Towards an ambulance – or towards the dead wagon? A wave of nausea passed through her and she had to bend over for a few moments until it left her and she steadied.

'This one's a young 'un.'

'Raymond!' cried Mrs Hancock. 'It must be. He's the youngest person here.'

A slighter body than the previous one was brought out. Alive? Unconscious? Mrs Hancock tried to move forwards, but the ARP man took her arm.

'Let them do their job, love.'

'Raymond . . .' Emily said, her voice quivering. Her body quivered too.

Cordelia started to go to her, wanting to hold her daughter more than she had ever wanted anything in her life. Then she stopped, almost staggering to a standstill, her mouth dropping open while she watched in astonishment as Mrs Hancock opened her arms and Emily walked straight into them.

CHAPTER SEVENTEEN

Now that she had been back for a while, Colette wasn't as interesting to the congregation. Everyone had become used to her presence. Sometimes she still felt she was reeling around in shock, but she was surrounded by people who thought it perfectly normal for her to be there. Besides, this morning everyone's mind was firmly fixed on last night's raid. Bombs had fallen on Ordsall, apparently, and there had been several deaths. Oh, those poor people, their poor families. Colette tried to pray for them, but her mind kept wandering as she fought to comprehend the suddenness of what had happened. In the moments before their lives were snuffed out, had those people been as happy as she had been?

She closed her eyes and hoped she looked like she was praying, but really she shut them in case they revealed her gratitude and relief at having seen her friends again. As well as feeling guilty and upset at the thought of their grief over her supposed death, she had missed them all the time she had been away in London. She wished she could have apologised to them, but she hadn't been able to because she had to maintain the fiction of her supposed breakdown.

She wished too that she could have asked after Mrs Cooper in a more specific way, but it had been impossible to think of an innocent-sounding question that would have produced the kind of answer she yearned for. Yesterday evening, she had wished that Mrs Cooper had accompanied the girls, but the truth was that it could have led to disaster. If Tony had seen Mrs Cooper's face peering up at him when he opened the Anderson's door, he would have been charm itself at the time, but would he have headed straight for the police station as soon as the all-clear had sounded? Instead of longing to see the dear friend who had helped her to escape, should Colette be willing her to stay away?

Anyway, she didn't want to think about that. She wanted to concentrate on the joy her friends had brought into her house. As they had all talked and laughed together, she had watched each of them, aware of something inside her, something shrivelled and grey, now starting to plump up and become warm and alive.

They had all hugged her before they set off for home and it had been all she could do to restrain herself from clinging to them and sobbing her heart out. She had sat up for ages after their departure, reliving every moment.

Every moment. If only Tony hadn't come back to check on her. She wished he hadn't seen them.

At last, she had taken herself off to bed. She wasn't tired, but Tony would expect her to be in bed when he came off duty, though she would get up as soon as he entered the bedroom, under the guise of making him a cup of tea. Her real intention was to get out of bed and ensure she stayed out of it, because after having left her alone to start with, Tony was now expecting his marital rations. Worse, the old Tuesdays and Saturdays routine had gone out of the window. Now it was any time he felt like it.

And he felt like it a lot because he wanted her to have a baby.

He wasn't the only one. Father and Bunty wanted it and apparently so did the world in general. Mrs Townsend from the local WVS, who had once been kind and welcoming to Colette when she'd been led by Tony to believe that Colette would be joining the ranks, had called round to welcome her home and had delicately suggested that the patter of tiny feet might be just what the doctor ordered. If Mrs Townsend thought that, presumably the whole of the WVS did too. They probably had their knitting needles poised ready.

Movement around her brought Colette back to the present. It was time to stand for the final hymn. Soon everybody was outside in the sunshine.

'Another fine day,' said a woman with a hat similar to one Colette's mother used to wear.

'Not a scorcher of a summer like the one we had immediately before the war,' replied a stooped old lady with a walking stick, 'but a very good summer all the same.'

They both looked at Colette and she made a suitable response. This was her life now. A head bursting with secrets and a tongue that trotted out banal remarks about the weather.

It was a relief to set off for home. Except that it wasn't a relief, not really. She didn't want to go there; didn't want the front door to shut behind her.

No one knows what goes on behind closed doors.

Father and Bunty came round on Sunday afternoon. Father sat in Tony's chair and held forth about what General Montgomery should best do now that he was in command of the Eighth Army, and what Mr Churchill was going to say to Stalin, as if he had chatted over the back fence to Monty and the Prime Minister. Colette thought of the girls at Beeson's. She had loved being a coil girl, but she could never speak of it again for the rest of her life.

If she had the baby everyone wanted her to have, she could never tell him or her about Mummy making coils for the war effort. She could never say that although Daddy had never lifted a finger against her, he had manipulated and controlled her until she didn't know which way was up. She could never tell her child she had run away.

Had Bunty ever tried to run away? It was a startling thought.

And if Colette had a daughter, would she grow up to marry a man who would grind her spirit into the dust, just like her father had ground her mother's? Colette's pulse sped up and her body tensed, the strength and immediacy of her anger taking her by surprise. She wouldn't let her daughter go through what had happened to her.

But how could she prevent it?

'Colette? Look at her, away with the fairies.' Father sounded testy. 'What is it? The lingering effects of the breakdown? You'll have to pull yourself together, Colette. It'll be a bad job if we have to send you back to the sanatorium.'

'Colette's fine – aren't you?' said Tony, not standing up to Father, just appeasing him. 'She was just thinking about what you were saying about the war – weren't you?'

'Yes,' she said obediently. 'I'm sorry, Father.'

Father humphed. 'I should jolly well think so.'

After he and Bunty had left, Tony said, 'You let me down with your daydreaming. It was disrespectful.'

'I'm sorry.'

'Well, we'll say no more about it.'

Tony smiled. There was a note of indulgence in his voice. He held out his hand to her and she had to take it, but sensing he was about to pull her close, she removed her hand, glancing away to hide her expression. Quick, quick. Change the subject. But she couldn't think of anything. Being back with Tony had made her stupid again.

He said, 'I was never more surprised in my life than when I opened the Andy's door last night and saw all those faces looking back at me.'

Heat crept into Colette's cheeks. 'Yes.'

'Did you know they were coming?' Tony asked quietly.

'No. That is, I wanted them to. Miss Emery said she'd give them my address – our address. I thought they'd come at once, but they didn't. I'd almost given up hope.'

'Did they say why it had taken them so long?'

'I didn't ask.'

Tony nodded. 'You have to face it, darling. Maybe you aren't as important to them as you'd like to be. They've had months without you. They've grieved for you – they've let go.'

'No . . .'

Tony reached for her hands, drawing her inexorably to him. 'You poor little love. Don't worry. Don't be frightened. You aren't alone. I will never let go of you. Even when I was heartbroken because I thought you were dead, I never let go.'

Mabel, Margaret and Alison spent part of Sunday afternoon in the garden, sowing spring cabbage and winter lettuce and pruning the shrubs that had finished flowering. As essential as it was to grow food, the garden plants they had allowed themselves to keep mattered too and it was worth taking care of them so as to have the benefit of enjoying their blooms.

'I never realised how much work Tony did out here,' said Margaret.

'He hasn't been round since Colette came home,' said Alison, 'which is fair enough,' she added quickly.

'You know what he's like, how protective he is,' said Mabel. 'He'll be more protective than ever after losing her and then getting her back.'

Margaret laughed. 'His face when he opened the door and saw us all. Mind you, it's not funny really. Not when you think how he didn't want Miss Emery to give us their address.'

'You'd think he'd be glad for Colette to have the company of her best friends,' said Alison.

'Ours is not to reason why,' said Mabel.

As they resumed working, Alison kept glancing over the wall and looking towards the entrance to the cul-de-sac.

'Hey, you,' said Mabel. 'Stop shirking.'

'I'm not. I'm keeping an eye out for Colette and Tony to appear. They used to come here every weekend, regular as clockwork.'

'Colette hasn't been back long,' said Margaret. 'Give them time to settle into a routine.'

They finished work and cleaned the tools before Mabel put them away in the garden shed. There was only room for one person to enter the shed because that was where they stored the bicycles.

Inside the house, they washed their hands – or rather, scrubbed them under the tap. Soap couldn't be used freely these days. Mabel cupped her hands beneath the tap and splashed the back of her neck under her ponytail to cool down.

Mrs Cooper appeared in the scullery doorway. 'Are you finished, girls? Bless you for doing all that. Come and have a cold drink before you do anything else.'

They trooped into the front room and had some of Mrs Grayson's elderflower cordial. 'Though I've had to dilute it so much, it isn't entirely recognisable as elderflower,' said Mrs Grayson, 'but we have to make it last.' She sighed. 'We have to make everything last. You've heard what's happening with the sweets and chocolate ration, haven't you?'

'Isn't it going up later in the month?' Alison asked.

'Aye, up to four ounces per person per week, but only for eight weeks, then it's going down to three ounces.'

'Milk is due to be restricted as well, come the end of the month,' Mrs Cooper added. 'There'll be exceptions, of course, and people who need more will get it.'

The doorbell rang.

'Colette and Tony. What d'you bet?' Alison jumped up and left the room.

Everyone listened as the front door opened. Hearing a man's voice, they looked at one another. Alison returned, leading a policeman, a good-looking fellow in his twenties. Mabel frowned, then remembered.

'Toby!'

'It's Constable Collins when I'm on duty, miss.'

'But you do remember me?' said Mabel.

Toby smiled. 'Yes, you're Mabel – Joan's friend.'

And Toby was Steven's friend. Steven had been the boyfriend of Joan's late and much-missed sister, Letitia. Grief over Letitia had driven Steven and Joan into one another's arms until Joan had seen sense and gone back to her lovely Bob.

'It's good to see you again,' said Mabel.

'You might not think so when you hear why I've come round,' said Toby. He looked at Mrs Cooper and Mrs Grayson. 'Is one of you ladies Mrs Cooper?'

'I'm Mrs Cooper. How can I help you?'

'There's been another burglary, madam.'

'Oh, how very upsetting,' Mrs Cooper exclaimed.

'Quite so,' said Toby. 'I can't help noticing you don't ask whose house has been burgled. It's the Whitfields' house in one of the roads off Edge Lane.'

'Goodness me,' said Mrs Cooper. 'I clean for Mrs Whitfield.'

'Yes, Mrs Cooper,' said Toby. His eyes, which Mabel remembered as being good-humoured, were serious. 'You also clean for Mrs Redmond, Mrs Pearce and Mrs Ashmore. I have to inform you, Mrs Cooper, that you are the only link between all four crimes.'

148

CHAPTER EIGHTEEN

Cordelia's friends listened with widened eyes on Monday evening in the buffet as she described the events of the previous Saturday.

'Good grief,' said Mabel. 'You mean, while we were sheltering in Colette's Andy . . .'

'Eh, love,' said Dot. 'How appalling. To go to a party – and then end up digging out the other guests.'

'Not just guests,' said Persephone. 'Colleagues. Fellow fire-watchers.'

'I have to say I barely knew some of them,' Cordelia admitted.

'It makes no odds,' said Margaret. 'They were all there because of being fire-watchers.'

'I bet you haven't stopped thinking "It could have been me" ever since,' said Dot.

'And Emily,' Cordelia said quietly. 'It could have been Emily.'

Dot matched Cordelia's serious tone. 'Aye, and that's worse, isn't it?'

'What about the casualties?' Persephone asked. 'If you can bear to talk about it.'

'Four died before we could dig them out,' said Cordelia, 'though whether they were killed outright or . . . and two died later in hospital.'

'I'm sorry to hear it,' said Mabel.

'We all are,' said Margaret.

'But the good news is that the rest are going to recover,' said Cordelia. Something impelled her to add, 'There was a young lad there, not much older than Emily. He was knocked out, but he's going to be all right.'

'That must bring it home to you,' said Dot, 'him being near to Emily in age.'

'Yes, it must,' agreed Alison.

A little later, as the group was breaking up, Dot had a quiet word.

'The lad you mentioned, was he the one Emily's taken a shine to?'

Cordelia nodded. For a moment, she felt overwhelmed and had to close her eyes. She felt Dot's hand on her arm.

'I know, love, I know,' said Dot.

But she didn't know. She thought Cordelia's emotions had welled up because of Emily's pain, but in fact Cordelia had in that instant lived the moment when Emily had walked into, not her mother's arms, but another woman's. Of course, what mattered was that Emily had received comfort when she most needed it, but it had come as a body blow to Cordelia that the person offering the comfort hadn't been herself. She couldn't tell Dot. She was ashamed of it, ashamed of herself. Did she really want to be so all-important in her daughter's life? What did that say about her?

She went home. She had been sorely tempted to keep Emily off work today, but Kenneth had refused.

'This is war, Cordelia. One can't take time off just because it's upsetting.'

'You're right,' Cordelia had said. 'Getting on with life and work and daily routines is essential. I've never questioned it on my own account. It's just . . .'

'It's because it's your daughter,' said Kenneth. 'I know how you feel, believe me. I'd do anything to protect her, and I don't just mean saving her from injury. I mean, stopping her from being hurt emotionally. But in wartime, we all have to get on with it and that's a lesson Emily has to learn, if she hasn't already.'

So Emily had gone to work today. If she had found it taxing, there was no sign of it, though her eyes showed how tired she was.

'Was the office a bit much for you today?' Cordelia asked when she sat on Emily's bed to kiss her goodnight.

'No, not at all. It was a breeze – well, a boring breeze, same as ever.'

'You do look bushed, though, darling.'

'I haven't had much sleep. I didn't sleep on Saturday night, and then when we got the good news about Raymond on Sunday, I couldn't sleep that night either, because I was too happy and relieved.'

'I'm more pleased than I can say that he's all right,' said Cordelia. 'Now settle down and get some sleep or you won't be fit to be seen. Night night, darling.'

'Night night, Mummy.'

Emily snuggled down, looking so young that Cordelia's heart ached. Kenneth's words came back to her about wanting to keep Emily safe, not just physically but emotionally. Whatever problems there might be between him and Emily at present, this was nevertheless a happy family with parents devoted to their beautiful, charming daughter.

But they didn't seem so much like a happy family the following evening after work. Kenneth stomped into the house and jabbed his homburg onto the hatstand so vigorously that Cordelia, emerging from the kitchen to say hello, half expected the curved wooden hook to burst through the crown. Emily trailed in behind her father, looking – something made Cordelia expect her to look mutinous, but instead she looked pleased. Pleased?

'What's happened?' Cordelia got the first word in.

'You may well ask,' said Kenneth. 'You won't believe what this young madam did today.'

Cordelia's heart thumped. 'What?'

'She only bunked off work to go and see that boy. I trusted her with an important errand, delivering papers to a client, and she used the opportunity to sneak in a visit to her favourite grocer.'

'Strictly speaking,' said Emily, 'I went there in what would have been my dinner hour, so I wasn't bunking off. And I'm not sorry for it and I won't say I am. I love Raymond and he loves me – so there!'

Mabel and Harry had made their arrangements for the visit to his parents. Although Mabel was excited, worrying about Mrs Cooper took the edge off her pleasure.

'The police can't really suspect her, can they?' asked Alison.

Margaret looked serious. 'They felt certain enough to come round here and – I was going to say "accuse her", but they didn't actually do that, did they?'

'They as good as did,' said Mabel. 'Saying she was the only link – what else could it mean?'

Poor Mrs Cooper had been in what she valiantly tried to pass off as 'a bit of a state' ever since.

'It's just a coincidence,' she kept saying. 'The police will realise that. Pure coincidence.'

But the way she twisted her wedding ring belied her brave words.

'The trouble is, it's such a huge coincidence,' said Joan when she and Mabel took little Max out in the pram on Mabel's day off. 'It looks really bad. There has to be something else to link the burglaries together.'

'If there is, you'd think the police would have found it by now,' Mabel said glumly. 'Listen, there's something else I ought to tell you.'

'About Mrs Cooper?'

'No.' Mabel took a breath. 'About Steven.'

Joan leaned forward and fussed with Max's blanket. Hiding a blush? 'What about him?'

'The constable who came round was Toby Collins.' Mabel waited, but Joan said nothing. 'When he left, I followed him outside and asked after Steven. I thought you'd want to know, especially now that you're living back in Chorlton.'

'Well, he's not somebody I'd want to bump into.'

'You won't have to. Apparently, after – well, he worked his socks off and got promoted to sergeant, which meant going to work in another area.'

'Good,' said Joan. 'I'm pleased – for him as well as for myself. Thanks for telling me.' Her voice sounded a bit clipped and Mabel wasn't surprised when she asked, 'Have they had Mrs Cooper in for questioning? It makes me feel shivery even to ask.'

'They haven't,' said Mabel. 'Not so far, anyway.'

She felt upset at the very idea, so how must poor Mrs Cooper be feeling? When Mabel got home, she put her arms around Mrs Cooper and held her.

Mrs Cooper returned the embrace for a moment, then gently pushed her away. 'Honestly, you girls. I don't think I've ever had so many hugs in my life as I have since Constable Collins came round.'

Mrs Cooper's good-natured courage brought an ache to the back of Mabel's throat, but not even Mrs Cooper could withstand the shock and shame that was to follow.

Mabel came home from work the next day to find Mrs Grayson grim-faced as she bustled about in the kitchen and no sign of Mrs Cooper.

'I sent her to bed,' said Mrs Grayson.

'Is she ill?'

'Not the way you mean. It was her morning for going to Mrs Pearce's and she arrived to be told her services were no longer required.' Mrs Grayson uttered the words in a sharp, sarcastic tone that Mabel had never heard from her before. 'Mr and Mrs Pearce had had a visit from the police to tell them about Mrs Cooper being the only link so far between all these burglaries. So then Mrs Cooper went to see Mrs Redmond, Mrs Ashmore and Mrs Whitfield and they sacked her an' all.'

'They didn't! Oh, poor Mrs Cooper.'

'She cried and cried when she got home and ended up with a pounding headache, not helped by her trying to take her mind off her troubles by cleaning all the skirting boards. She ended up feeling so rotten that she could barely hold her head up, so I packed her off to bed.'

Later, Mrs Cooper came downstairs in her dressing gown, looking wan but determined.

'How are you?' asked Margaret.

'I'm fine, my dears. Well, not really, but I've got to get on with things, haven't I? It was such a shock, that's all. Three of the ladies said it was their husband's decision to get rid of me, and that was bad enough, but then Mrs Whitfield said she couldn't keep me because if she did, she'd have to follow me round and keep watch the whole time.'

The others exclaimed in sympathy, but Mrs Cooper didn't seem to hear.

'This means there'll be less work for Mrs Wadden an' all,' she said. 'I feel bad about that. I know how she relies on it.' She stood up. 'I need to get summat from the sideboard. I'll be back in a mo.'

'Sit down,' Mabel said at once. 'I'll fetch it. What is it?'

'A little notebook in the back of the middle drawer, behind the napkins.'

Mabel went into the dining room and returned with the book. She handed it to Mrs Cooper, who flicked through the pages.

'The question is, do I tear out their pages or just cross out their details?'

'What details?' asked Mabel.

'This has got the details of the ladies I work for – names and addresses, when I go, what needs doing, where the spare key is kept if the lady of the house isn't at home. I keep it private. I mean, Mrs Wadden knows about the notebook, but I don't let her or anyone see inside it; I just tell her what she needs to know.' Mrs Cooper pressed her lips together. 'It wouldn't be right to keep the details of Mrs Redmond and the others now they've sacked me. It might look . . . dishonest.'

'Oh, Mrs Cooper,' said Alison.

Mrs Cooper lifted her chin. 'It's all I can do. I need to look as honest as I can. Do you think – do you think I should tell all my other ladies that I'm under suspicion of theft?'

CHAPTER NINETEEN

Kenneth was practically tearing his hair out at what he saw as Emily's defiance, but Cordelia couldn't help seeing it as courage and it took her breath away. It had all been hole-and-corner and sneaking about when she was with Kit. She had done everything she could to hide matters from her disapproving parents. Yet her own daughter had blatantly declared her love.

As had become the norm, Cordelia tried to smooth things over.

'It's the war,' she told Kenneth. 'Emotions are running high. Many young people are throwing themselves into relationships.'

'If that's intended to make me feel better, you have severely miscalculated.'

To Emily she said, 'I do understand about young love, you know.'

'Excuse me, Mummy, but I don't think you do,' Emily said kindly. 'You were twenty-two when you married Daddy.'

Repeating this to Dot when the two of them met up in the buffet, Cordelia said with a touch of asperity, 'There's nothing quite like being put in your place by your sixteen-year-old daughter.'

'So, young Raymond getting caught in the bombing has made his feelings and Emily's double in size.'

'Yes. Before this, there was a chance it might have fizzled out of its own accord,' said Cordelia. 'Actually, that's not true. I never really expected that to happen.'

'But the protective father was hoping for it,' Dot suggested.

'Banking on it, more like.' Cordelia sighed. 'It should be such a happy time, watching your daughter fall in love. I never imagined it would happen to her so young.'

'Is her age the only obstacle?'

'No,' Cordelia admitted, though she couldn't bring herself to say more.

'I don't suppose the Masters family ever imagined being linked with a family of grocers,' said Dot. 'Don't look like that. It's nowt to feel guilty about. It's the way of the world – or it used to be. I wonder what'll happen after the war. Will we all be expected to go back to our old places in life?'

'Whatever happens,' said Cordelia, 'you and I will stay together.'

That gave her an idea about how next to approach Kenneth.

'You approve of Dot now, don't you?' she asked him.

'Certainly,' he agreed. 'It'd be a pretty poor show if I didn't approve of somebody who played such an important part in rescuing you when you were buried alive. Refusing to leave the rubble in spite of the danger to herself, lying on it and talking to you through a tube, giving you comfort and reassurance – that took real pluck. I admire that. It would have been churlish in the extreme if I had continued objecting to Mrs Green's station in life after that.'

'The Hancocks are similar to the Greens – socially, I mean,' said Cordelia. 'If you can change the habits of a lifetime and think highly of Dot, perhaps you could think of the Hancocks in the same way. They're just as brave. They're a family of fire-watchers.'

'Their courage and sense of duty has nothing to do with it,' Kenneth replied. 'My attitude towards the person who gave my wife such support in a dangerous situation isn't going to sway my attitude towards what is best for my daughter. We've given her everything – music lessons, riding, private schools. She is way above a mere grocer's boy.'

Something prompted Cordelia to say, 'Raymond is an amateur astronomer. On quiet nights, he looks at the stars through his telescope.'

'That's irrelevant.'

'So, it's acceptable for me to be friends with Dot, but Emily will never be allowed to . . .'

To what? To marry Raymond? Cordelia didn't want her daughter marrying beneath her, but – but she knew, she understood, she had lived through it herself – she wanted Emily to find happiness. She wanted Emily and Raymond to be together.

After what had happened to her and Kit, after the way her parents had utterly refused to countenance a relationship between them, Cordelia couldn't inflict that unhappiness and despair on Emily. She couldn't let Emily live the rest of her life mourning a forbidden love.

Mabel was on her way downstairs, humming to herself, enjoying the sensation of being dressed up, excitement fluttering in her belly because shortly she was going to go to the telephone box to ring Harry. Alison, who had preceded her down the stairs, was also dressed up, because she was meeting Joel in town to go dancing.

'See you later,' Alison called, opening the front door. 'Don't wait up.' She pulled the door to behind her, then pushed it open again and leaned into the hall, calling, 'Tony's coming up the path.'

Margaret, Mrs Cooper and Mrs Grayson popped like corks out of the front room.

'Is Colette with him?' asked Mrs Cooper.

As Alison disappeared down the path, Tony paused on the doorstep. 'May I come in?' He chuckled, looking at them all standing there in the darkness. 'What's this, the welcoming committee?'

'Come into the front room,' said Mrs Grayson as Tony closed the front door and pulled the curtain across. 'Isn't Colette with you?'

When Mabel took his coat and hat, Tony made a show of holding his arms out sideways. 'Just me. Nothing up my sleeves.'

In the front room, he waited politely as the others sat. The two ladies had the armchairs as usual, which left the sofa. Margaret sat at one end and Mabel perched beside her on the arm. It felt more comfortable than it would to sit three in a row with Tony.

'How are you, Tony?' asked Mrs Grayson. 'And how is Colette? I'm sorry I fainted when I saw her. I'd like the chance to apologise in person.'

'I'm sure she knows you're sorry,' said Tony.

'She's always such a kind girl,' said Mrs Grayson. 'How is she?'

'That's why I'm here, actually – about her health.'

'Isn't she well?' Mrs Cooper spoke for the first time.

'She seemed fine to us when we saw her at the weekend,' said Margaret.

Tony nodded. 'On the outside, yes, but I'm talking about what's on the inside.' He shook his head. 'She's suffering from nightmares. Flashbacks. That's how her breakdown started.'

Mabel sat up straight. 'She's not heading for another one, is she?'

Tony sighed heavily. 'Let's hope not.' He shook his head again. 'She cries a lot.'

'Poor Colette,' said Margaret.

'I don't quite know how to say this,' Tony went on, 'because it sounds so ungrateful, but when you all piled into our house . . . I know you meant well, but it didn't help. It churned things up for her.'

Shock made Mabel's skin tingle. 'We had no idea.'

Tony gave a sad-sounding laugh. 'I know exactly what you mean. Everybody tells me how well she's doing, but – well, they don't see what I see when her guard's down. I'm sorry to ask this, but I have to.' His voice was soft and serious. 'Will you stay away from Colette? Please. Just for now. It could make all the difference.'

'Well . . . if we must.' Margaret looked round at the others.

'We can write to her,' suggested Mrs Grayson.

'No,' said Tony. 'Thank you, but no. I appreciate all your kindness and I know Colette does too, and she'll appreciate it all the more when she's properly better and can look back on all this. Coming home has been such a strain on her, much more so than she expected – than I expected, if I'm honest. I just thought she was better and everything would go back to normal, but that was wishful thinking. She needs peace and quiet to get used to things.'

'The poor girl,' said Mrs Grayson. 'It's a huge strain on you too, Tony.'

'I'd do anything for Colette,' he said.

'There's going to be a dance on Christmas Eve at Darley Court,' said Margaret. 'We'll all be there. Do you think Colette . . .?'

'Well, it's something to set her sights on, isn't it?' Tony said sadly. 'It's a long way off, but that's probably a good thing. A breakdown isn't something you recover from like getting over a cold. I take it you got our address from Miss Emery. You don't need to answer that. I know she told you – even though I'd specifically asked her not to.'

'If you'd just explained to her about Colette being . . . fragile.'

'I was trying to preserve Colette's dignity.'

'Of course you were,' said Mrs Grayson.

Margaret and Mabel looked at one another and Mabel knew they were thinking the same thing.

'Actually,' said Margaret, 'we did wonder at the time, when we were at your house, I mean, whether there might be more to it than we realised.'

'Let's say no more about it,' said Tony. He sounded brighter, as if he was making an effort. 'I'm so lucky to get her back. She had no identity on her, you know. It wasn't until she finally came to her senses that she was able to tell the doctors who she was.'

'So she could have come home ages ago,' said Margaret, 'if only she'd had her identity card.'

'They're so important,' said Tony, 'for all kinds of reasons. It makes me angry when I read in the newspapers about criminals who use fake identity papers.'

'They normally get a hefty sentence,' said Mabel.

'So do the people who supply the false documents,' said Tony. 'As far as I'm concerned, they should never see the light of day again.'

'Quite right too,' Mrs Grayson declared. 'People who trade in false identities are unpatriotic. They deserve to be hanged.'

Finishing her shift in the marshalling yard on Saturday, Cordelia changed out of her dungarees and headscarf and headed for home, looking every inch the lady. The atmosphere at home was calm, even pleasant, which came as a relief. To her surprise, tears made her eyes prickle and she had to blink them away. It wasn't like her to feel weepy, but honestly, it was a strain coming home and not knowing what fresh battle she might be walking into the middle of.

Kenneth and Emily had apparently had a good day. They had taken Mrs Grayson over to Darley Court so she could start getting used to going there. If Emily had seen through her father's ploy of keeping her by his side for the day, she had let it pass. She was fond of Mrs Grayson and wanted the best for her. Cordelia felt proud. Emily was a good girl at heart.

They were going out to a Red Cross fundraiser that evening. After a simple meal of fritters with salad leaves and radishes from the garden, they had a cup of tea together and listened to the news on the wireless before going upstairs to get ready.

Cordelia put on her plum-coloured velvet evening dress, the straight neckline and high waist of which proclaimed it to be a pre-war garment. After a moment's thought, she drew out a pretty evening shawl, light as gossamer, with the finest of silver threads running through it.

She offered it to Emily, whose cornflower-blue eyes widened with delight.

'Oh, Mummy, *thank* you.'

Cordelia settled it around Emily's shoulders. 'It's perfect on you.'

Her heart swelled as she beheld her lovely daughter, but at the same time a cynical voice inside her asked if it had really come to this. Was she bribing Emily? So what if she was? Emily was a pretty girl and it gave Cordelia great pleasure to see her dressed in beautiful clothes.

'Mummy.' Emily ceased preening in front of the mirror and looked serious.

'Yes, darling?'

'I keep thinking. This time last week . . .'

Cordelia laid a hand on her shoulder. 'I know. It's impossible not to remember. But we've got tickets for tonight and we have to go along. We must smile and join in and show what we're made of. It's all part of being at war.'

'I know, but . . . Raymond might have been killed. He might have *died* – like those others.' Emily turned her agonised gaze on her mother.

'He could have, but he didn't,' Cordelia said gently. 'You just have to be grateful and move on.'

'I understand now what people mean about grasping the good things while you can. Everyone thinks they understand it, but it's not until something like that happens to you that you truly know.'

Cordelia felt as though her heart had cracked open. To hear such words spoken so seriously by a sixteen-year-old. War was a cruel business, not just in the obvious ways of death and destruction, but also because of how it shaped the minds of young people, teaching them lessons that would come as a challenge at any age.

'Are you ready?' Cordelia asked. 'It's nearly time to go.'

They went down together to receive Kenneth's compliments and wait for the taxi. Soon they entered the hall where the dance was being held. They greeted their friends, purchased raffle tickets and settled at a table. Remembering her own advice to Emily, Cordelia was determined to make the most of the evening. The band was excellent and the master of ceremonies was a chirpy young woman.

'A girl as MC.' Kenneth raised his eyebrows. 'That would never have been allowed before the war.'

'You old fogey,' said Cordelia.

She danced a few times, then circulated, chatting with people she knew. The MC announced a ladies' excuse-me. Doing her duty, Cordelia danced with a couple of old boys, getting stuck with the second one as nobody excused her. Kenneth's partners, she noticed, were excused regularly. Well, naturally. Kenneth was a good-looking man. Distinguished. Well-to-do. Highly thought of. No wonder all the ladies were keen to partner him. An unexpected pang tore at Cordelia's heart. With Kit so much in her thoughts at present, she suddenly felt a powerful yearning for all that she had lost, all that she had never had with Kenneth.

Looking at it impartially, she thought what a dratted shame it was that she had never loved him. More than a shame – a rotten waste. Was it – she had never thought of it this way before, but was it selfish of her? Had she withheld herself from Kenneth and from her marriage because of her old loyalty to Kit? Yes, she had. She knew it. But she had never felt guilty about it before.

Kenneth was a good husband. Didn't he deserve a better wife?

CHAPTER TWENTY

It was the last full week of August and only a few days now before Harry took Mabel to meet his people.

'You'll have a lovely time,' said Mrs Cooper.

'I'm sure I will,' said Mabel. 'I can't wait to meet them, but I hate to leave you when you're under this awful cloud of suspicion.'

'It's not as though I'll be here on my own.' Mrs Cooper smiled, though it was a little shaky.

'All the same, I don't like to leave a friend in a bind,' said Mabel. 'I can see how hard this is on you. You're doing your best to keep your chin up and that makes me worry about you all the more.'

'Bless you, chuck, but I don't want you fretting over me.'

Mabel took Mrs Cooper's hands in her own. 'You're such a caring person, Mrs C. You look after all of us so well. Now you need support and I want to help. We all do. Won't you please talk to me?'

Mrs Cooper drew her hands away. 'Oh, my dear child, if you only knew.'

'I can make a good guess,' Mabel said softly. 'You're an honest person. You've never done a thing wrong in your life and here you are, being suspected of theft. I don't mean to rub it in, but I don't want you to feel you have to shoulder the burden alone.'

After a moment, Mrs Cooper blew out a breath. 'I never imagined something so bad could happen to me. There, that's the truth and I feel so guilty about it.'

'Mrs Cooper, why?' Mabel asked, her concern taking a new direction.

'Because I've got no business being upset about this, not after losing my Lizzie. When she died, I thought: that's it, I'll never need to worry about anything else ever again, because the worst possible thing has happened. And now here I am, worried sick, and it feels disloyal to Lizzie to care about it so much.'

'Sweetheart,' breathed Mabel. 'You poor love. You aren't being disloyal to Lizzie.'

'It feels like it. It feels like I'm letting something else be important when nothing, *nothing* compares to the importance of Lizzie not being here any more.' Mrs Cooper jerked her head back and her voice became stronger. 'But I know that's me being daft, because of course this matters. It matters dreadfully. It's changed my life. People look at me in the street, and not in a nice way. I had a postcard in the newsagent's window advertising Magic Mop, and when I went past yesterday, it was gone. It'd been taken down. I went in and asked and the newsagent said that he couldn't have it on display while all these rumours are going around.'

'That's so cruel.'

Mrs Cooper gave a little shrug. 'You can't blame him. He'd had a complaint.'

'From someone who doesn't know you like we do,' Mabel said stoutly.

'And – and I've lost a couple more of my ladies.'

'No!'

'They said it's just until this matter is cleared up, but what they really meant was they think it'll be cleared up when I'm found guilty.'

'Oh, Mrs Cooper, I'm so sorry.'

'I've never had much in my life,' Mrs Cooper said quietly. 'I mean, I had a lovely husband and the best daughter in the world, but I've never had much materially – but what I did have was come by honestly. I've always paid my bills; I've never struggled with debt like some do. I've always held my head up, because – because that's what you do when you're a decent person. You might not have much, but you can hold your head up. And now – the way folk are looking at me . . .'

Mabel enfolded her darling landlady in her arms and gently rocked her as she wept.

Out on the permanent way, it was another long, hot day. No matter how careful Mabel always was about protecting her skin, she had still caught the sun.

'It suits you,' said Louise. 'Me, I just come out in freckles.'

Mabel peered at Lou's face. 'Not that many.'

'You should see my arms.'

Anybody else would have rolled up their sleeves at that point, but not Louise. She looked away and Mabel could guess why. Frustration tugged at her insides. She hated to think of Louise, of anyone, being ill-treated. For it to happen in the home made it worse, surely, because that was the place you were supposed to be safe.

Did Mrs Wadden sport similar bruises? The other day, Mabel had seen Louise's mum in the kitchen in Wilton Close, where she was helping Mrs Grayson with her WVS jam- and chutney-making, and Mabel couldn't help wondering. And what about the younger brothers? Why hadn't Lou told her fellow gang members that Rob had come home?

Mabel knew the answer to that: because they would ask about her bruises. Louise had bent over backwards to keep her brother's violence secret last year, which Mabel and the other two had found deeply upsetting, not to mention frustrating, because they had wanted to help her, even if only by providing moral support.

Now Lou was in the same situation all over again and once more Mabel felt blocked from helping, only this was worse than last time because helping Clifford had made Mabel feel that bit closer to Louise. More than once she'd been tempted to ask Mrs Cooper if she had noticed bruises on Mrs Wadden, but now, with Mrs Cooper's worry over the burglaries, she was glad she hadn't. Mrs Cooper had enough on her plate.

The burglaries.

Something clicked into place in Mabel's mind. The burglaries. Rob Wadden was a thief. That was why he had vanished last year. And he was a brute – hence Louise's bruises before he had disappeared off the face of the earth.

Mabel's heart beat faster as the idea took shape, not least because she was remembering how badly dear Mrs Cooper was being affected by being under suspicion. She was due to meet up with her friends in the buffet after work and she couldn't wait to find out what they thought.

At the end of their working day, Bernice's gang caught the train back to Victoria and went to the Ladies to freshen up. It so happened there were no members of the public in there, so instead of queuing for the so-called 'Out of Order' lavatory, they could use the bent nail Bette kept in her knapsack to unlock the other cubicle doors without having to pay the penny. Well, why not? Male staff didn't have to pay to use their facilities, and they didn't have to share with passengers.

When Mabel emerged from the cubicle, Louise was at the basin, splashing her arms with cold water. She immediately rolled her sleeves down, but not before Mabel had glimpsed the small dark bruises in matching places on each arm. Fingermarks? Mabel's stomach twisted. She met Lou's glance in the mirror. Lou gave her a hard look and dropped her gaze to concentrate on fastening her cuffs. Mabel had to hold in a groan of frustration. If only Louise would accept help.

It made Mabel all the more determined to speak to her friends. Saying goodbye to her workmates, she headed for the buffet. She queued up for her cup of tea, had a friendly word with Mrs Jessop and went to the table where Persephone and Margaret were sitting. Soon everyone was there, clustered around the table.

Their first topic was Colette. Between them, Mabel, Margaret and Alison described Tony's unexpected visit to Wilton Close. Dot, Cordelia and Persephone asked questions that showed their confusion and uncertainty, feelings that were shared by the other three.

'Poor Colette,' said Persephone. 'She seemed so well, all things considered.'

'She must have been putting on her best smile,' said Dot, 'same as we all do these days.'

They all looked at one another and Mabel saw her own worry reflected in the others' eyes.

'And then there's Mrs Cooper,' said Alison. 'You know how the police said she was the only link between all the houses? Well, she lost those jobs.'

There were exclamations of dismay.

'She'll lose more an' all if word gets round,' said Dot.

'Actually,' said Mabel, 'I've come up with another possible link. Bear with me, because this will sound as if I'm talking about something entirely different to start with. You know Louise Wadden, one of the girls I work with? And you remember her brother Rob?'

'Oh aye, we shan't forget him in a hurry,' said Dot.

'You need to explain to Margaret,' said Cordelia, so Mabel briefly described the thieving that they had foiled early last year.

'Only one of the thieves was caught,' she finished. 'The other got away – and that was Rob Wadden.' She looked round the table. 'He's back. I know he is, because Lou is covered in bruises again.'

'What's this got to do with Mrs Cooper?' Alison asked.

'I'm coming to that. Mrs C keeps a notebook with her ladies' details in it: addresses and so forth, including where the spare keys are kept, in case the lady of the house is out when Mrs Cooper goes to clean. Mrs Wadden knows about the notebook, though Mrs Cooper hasn't actually shown it to her. But suppose Mrs Wadden got hold of the notebook and found out where the spare keys are.'

'Are you suggesting that Mrs Wadden . . .?' asked Persephone.

'No,' Mabel said at once, followed by, 'Well, yes, but not because she wants to. I've seen the marks on Louise's arms – and goodness knows where else she's been hit. I think Mrs Wadden is being forced to commit the thefts.'

'By her son,' said Cordelia.

'We already know he's a thief,' said Alison.

'Put like that, it makes sense,' said Margaret.

'What are we going to do?' asked Dot.

'Tell Toby Collins,' said Mabel.

'There's one problem,' said Cordelia. 'We can't tell him without explaining how we know Rob Wadden is a thief.'

'What's wrong with that?' asked Margaret.

'The policeman we dealt with last year, Inspector Stanhope, made it very clear we were never to talk about it to anybody, because of public morale,' said Persephone. 'Hardly anybody knows about the food dumps and that's the way it needs to stay, because they're there in case of invasion. We could tell Toby, but what if, being a lowly constable, he doesn't know about the food dumps and we get him into trouble by telling him?'

'We'd get ourselves into trouble an' all,' said Dot, 'because we'd have disobeyed police orders.'

'Understood,' Mabel said decisively. 'If we can't tell Toby, we'll have to go back to Inspector Stanhope.'

Colette couldn't understand why her friends hadn't been to see her again. For the first couple of days afterwards, she had trembled with sheer gratitude when she looked back on that evening of news and laughter. Why hadn't it been repeated? Yes, her friends all had jobs involving long hours, plus compulsory overtime, plus night-time war work . . . but even so.

She didn't tell Tony she was upset, but he must have realised, because he was sympathetic, though not in a way that made Colette feel better.

'Try to see it from their point of view, darling. You're not a part of their lives now. It must have been downright weird for them to come here and see you.'

Yes, it must have been. Was that why they were now keeping their distance? Colette had always felt guilty for letting her friends believe that she was dead. Were they angry with her? She was sure they wouldn't blame her for her supposed breakdown, but might their shock at her reappearance, on top of the grief they must have gone through, somehow have churned up into a form of anger? She remembered her mother going through a phase of being bitterly angry with her father after his death. Someone had told Colette then that a lot of people felt an irrational anger towards the deceased for leaving them, but Colette had known that Mother's anger had been because her father had left them up a financial gum tree.

It hurt that the dear friends who had meant so much to her weren't flocking around her now. It was hard to believe they weren't . . . and yet she had to believe it because it was happening. A pain formed in the back of Colette's throat, making it difficult for her to swallow. She had missed her friends every single day when she was away and being re-united with some of them had filled her with joy and relief. Surely they must feel the same, and yet – and yet they hadn't come back a second time. The guilt that had tortured Colette for having abandoned the very people she cared about most in the whole world assailed her once more. She had left them to think she was dead; she had left them to grieve. She'd had no option, of course, but she had never ceased to feel wretched about it. The blood in her veins turned sour as guilt washed through her.

Were they waiting for a visit from her? She caught her breath in a mixture of delight and relief. Was this the reason for their absence?

She longed, oh how she longed to go to Wilton Close, but that was the one place above all others she couldn't visit. If Tony were to find out, and he would, there would be appalling consequences for Mrs Cooper. Colette would do anything to protect her dear friend.

No Wilton Close meant no Mrs Cooper, no Mrs Grayson, no Mabel, Margaret or Alison. That left Cordelia, Dot, Joan and Persephone. Colette didn't know the exact addresses of the first three. Persephone lived at Darley Court, but could she get there and back while Tony was out at work? He was still coming home for his dinner. No, she couldn't manage it. Even if she could, she didn't know Persephone's shift pattern.

Victoria Station.

What if she went to Victoria? After Tony set off in the morning, or when he went back to work after dinner, she could give him a few minutes and then run for the bus. Allowing for travelling time each way, how long might she get at Victoria?

But . . . Dot would be on the Southport train. Cordelia and Mabel would be out on the permanent way, Margaret in one of the engine sheds. Alison – well, she could be anywhere. Colette didn't know what her current temporary post was. Only Persephone worked on the station, but she could hardly abandon her post at the ticket barrier to spend time with Colette.

Intense disappointment made Colette's heart feel as if it was shrinking. Then she thought of Miss Emery.

Miss Emery had been kind enough to come and see her to seek permission to pass on the Naylors' address. There was no reason for her to have done this except out of the goodness of her heart.

What if she went to Hunts Bank and asked to see Miss Emery? There was no guarantee the assistant welfare supervisor would be there, but surely it was worth a try. She could thank Miss Emery for her kindness and would it be too much of an imposition to ask if she would pass on a message? Or . . . what if Colette said she was ready to return to work? With Tony's history, Miss Emery wouldn't be at all surprised to hear that he was reluctant. She would realise – wouldn't she? – without any prompting from Colette that an official letter would be required, asking Colette to get a health certificate from the doctor.

Yes! Tony couldn't argue with that. If there was one thing Colette had learned about war work, it was that Tony couldn't stop her doing it.

She drew back her shoulders as a feeling of strength went through her, but she must be cautious. Tony mustn't be allowed to cotton on to the fact that she had visited Miss Emery and had asked to be reinstated.

The next morning, she put her plan into action. She was careful to do everything exactly the same as usual, including behaving towards Tony with the same quiet but restrained courtesy that she had adopted. Civility was important, because she knew better than to antagonise him, though she couldn't bring herself to employ any warmth.

When Tony left for work, Colette saw him off and made herself spend fifteen minutes peeling carrots and potatoes and putting them in saucepans of water before she got ready and set off for the bus stop. On the bus, almost everyone was wearing a black armband. Black armbands had been common earlier in the war when air raids were rife, especially at the time of the Christmas Blitz, but today these were for the Duke of Kent. Colette sensed the shock and distress on all sides, though if she was honest, she felt somewhat distanced from it. Shock and distress? She had felt that way, to some degree or other, ever since Tony had come back into her life. But even so she was truly sorry for the Duke of Kent. She remembered meeting Ivy and Marjorie for the first time and Ivy telling her about the Duchess of Kent's visit to Beeson's, when Marjorie had told Her Grace, 'We all feel we're part of a big national effort to end the war.' Marjorie had said that because of being a war widow and now the Duchess was a war widow too.

Whereas she, Colette, was someone who stood to gain from becoming a war widow . . .

Wicked, wicked, wicked.

Don't think like that.

Alighting from the bus, she walked briskly to Victoria. It was all she could do not to break into a run. She peeled off, heading for Hunts Bank. There was no time to announce herself and seek permission. She went straight upstairs to Miss Emery's office.

She stopped dead – Miss Emery wasn't there. At first Colette thought it was her desperate disappointment that accounted for the twinge of unease. It took her a moment to

174

realise the truth. Miss Emery had always been very tidy. She had to be, having an office that was open to all eyes and much of what she dealt with being confidential. But this was tidiness of a different sort.

The desk had a chair tucked neatly under it, but there was no blotter and there was an empty hole where the ink-well would be; the slender wooden tray for the pencil sharpener and paperknife wasn't there either. Nothing hung from the hatstand. The table was still there, but the typewriter was gone.

Colette was still boggling when a mature gentleman with a bald pate stopped beside her.

'Can I help you?'

'I'm looking for Miss Emery.'

'Ah. You're out of luck. She doesn't work here any more.'

'She's left?' It came out almost as a squeak.

'Not so much left, madam, as got the push.'

CHAPTER TWENTY-ONE

Shock and distress. The nation mourning the death of the Duke of Kent, every single person feeling it as a personal loss. Shock and distress. Miss Emery. *Not so much left, madam, as got the push.*

Miss Emery – sacked. *Miss Emery.*

It was impossible to take in. Just like Tony ringing Mrs Perkins' doorbell had been impossible to believe, and yet it had happened. Colette had become – had been forced to become – an expert at believing the impossible.

Even so – Miss Emery?

Colette trailed home, the journey seeming to take ages. Miss Emery was the embodiment of professional high standards. How could she possibly have lost her job? To have moved on elsewhere, to have been promoted, yes – but to have been sacked?

Colette arrived home. It was important to pull herself together. Tony would be here soon and would expect his dinner on the table. Her shock and distress must be hidden. She busied herself in the kitchen.

The front door opened and Tony called, 'I'm home.'

Colette stayed in the kitchen, her back towards the door, instinctively hiding her expression, but instinct had led her to make a bad mistake.

'What's the matter?' Tony asked from behind her.

She should have gone to meet him at the door, should have hung up his hat for him. What now?

She took a deep breath – a deep, quiet breath. 'Why should anything be the matter?' She forced a smile into her voice as she turned to meet his gaze. 'Dinner's ready. I'm just about to dish up. Go and sit down.'

Would he, wouldn't he? He did.

The meal passed in the ordinary way. They sat on either side of the table and talked, Tony saying more than she did. That was normal. He even complimented her cooking.

'I'm lucky to have such a clever wife to look after me.' Finishing his meal, he put his knife and fork together before asking in a voice that was almost soothing, 'Are you going to tell me what's wrong?'

'It's nothing.'

His voice hardened a fraction, but only a fraction, and he smiled as he said, 'Silly girl. I always know when something's wrong. I can read you like a book.'

Colette felt the same old panic. It was as if the confidence and self-esteem she had gained in London had never existed. Thoughts screeched around inside her head, but not one of them was any use.

'Has one of your friends been to see you?' Tony asked.

'No.' She could answer that at once.

'Are you sure? Because something's upset you. I can imagine a visit from one of them leaving you feeling . . . unsettled.'

'No, honestly, Tony. No one has been here.'

'It's hard for me to believe. If I find out you're lying . . .'

'I swear nobody's been here.' Good heavens, was he about to say her friends weren't allowed to come round? 'It was me. I went out.'

'Where?' Tony's eyes were sharp and angry, but when he spoke his voice was so soft she barely caught the words. 'Have you been to Wilton Close?'

'*No.*' She had to protect Mrs Cooper at all costs. 'I – I went to Victoria.'

Tony jerked his head back in surprise.

'You never said I couldn't,' Colette almost babbled. 'Strictly speaking, it wasn't Victoria. It was Hunts Bank.'

'Hunts Bank,' Tony said, his voice flat. 'Miss Emery.'

'I wanted to . . .' What? What? '. . . to thank her for coming here and for giving our address to my friends. It was such a kind thing to do . . . wasn't it?' She gazed at Tony, trying to read his expression. 'Only – she wasn't there. She – oh, Tony, she's lost her job.'

'Lost it? She was dismissed, you mean?'

'Yes,' she confirmed in a small voice.

To Colette's complete astonishment, Tony laughed. He cocked his head to one side. It made him look . . . smug.

'Well! That was more than I hoped for. What a good day's work that turned out to be.'

'What – what d'you mean?'

'What d'you think I mean? Did you find out why she was sacked?'

Colette shook her head.

'Then allow me to enlighten you. There was a complaint against her.'

'A complaint?' Colette repeated. 'How do you know?'

'Because I wrote it, you idiot. How else? I said she'd broken confidentiality by handing out my address.'

'But I gave permission—'

'And I overruled you.'

'But . . .' Colette's mind was struggling to catch up. As always, Tony was streets ahead.

'As your husband, I withdrew your permission, as I have every right to do. There is no doubt that Miss Emery understood me. Nevertheless, she gave out my address willy-nilly—'

'Not willy-nilly,' Colette tried to object.

178

'—as the appearance here of those females proves.'

'They aren't "those females". They're my friends.'

'Who have totally ignored you ever since, but that's beside the point. Kindly don't change the subject. I reported Miss Emery to her superiors for her breach of confidential information and they evidently took the same view of it that I did.'

Colette shook her head, just the tiniest shake, as anger started to bubble up. Had she ever been angry with Tony before? Or had she been too scared? Certainly, if she had felt anger, she had never dared show it.

'Miss Emery is a good person,' she said, 'and excellent at her job.'

'Except for the small matter of being unreliable with confidential information.'

Colette made fists beneath the table. 'She isn't unreliable. She's decent and hard-working and – and she trusted me with a special job.'

'Oh yes,' Tony scoffed, 'she sent you here, there and everywhere, being a chaperone to the afflicted. You liked that, didn't you? Even though I was against it.'

'I didn't have a choice.'

'How convenient.'

'You shouldn't have reported Miss Emery,' said Colette. Tony's eyebrows climbed up his forehead. 'Shouldn't I?'

'She didn't deserve that,' Colette said stoutly.

'She entirely deserved it.'

Colette lifted her chin. 'Well, I was happy to see my friends and I'm glad she told them – though I wish she hadn't lost her job. That was a vicious thing to do.'

Tony came to his feet. 'Vicious? Who are you calling vicious?' He plonked his knuckles on the table and leaned over. 'I've always done everything I can to protect you and care for you. Ask anyone. I'm the perfect husband

and you're lucky to have me. When I made my wedding vows, I meant every single word. I have done nothing but cherish you. Even after you ran away from home and let me think you were dead, I've taken you back and treated you kindly. A different man, a *vicious* man, would keep you locked inside the house. A *vicious* man would give you a slap to show you who's boss.'

Colette looked him right in the eyes. 'Here we go. I know what comes next. You've never laid a finger on me. Do you have any idea how many times you've told me that? And I was meant to be *grateful* – grateful that my husband didn't hit me, grateful to be married to such a decent man. Well, here's some news for you, Tony. Decent men have no need to point out that they don't hit their wives. For a decent man, it wouldn't even cross his mind. You might have kept your hands to yourself, but you hit me so many times in so many other ways – every time you put me down, every time you made me feel small and stupid and inadequate. You—' Her voice caught as tears welled. She sniffed hard. 'You *controlled* me. You controlled my every move. I could barely think straight because I was so scared. Scared of saying the wrong thing, scared of doing the wrong thing. Scared somebody would be rude to you or make you angry, because you'd take it out on me. Scared of being at home, because I only felt safe at work or—' She stopped herself just in time.

But Tony knew. He stood up straight, his gaze never leaving her face as he walked around the table, stopping at her side. He glared down at her. She made herself keep looking up at him, but her heart was pounding and the breath wanted to burst out of her.

Tony thrust his face close to hers. 'At work or – where? Go on. Say it.'

'Nothing. Nowhere.'

'Nowhere?' Tony asked softly. Then he slammed his fist on the table; Colette jumped and the crockery rattled. 'You were going to say Wilton Close. Oh yes, the best place in the whole wide world, Wilton flaming Close.' He laughed, a sneering sound. He reared up, but when she hoped he would move away, he stayed close beside her, too close, though no longer right in front of her face. 'How dare you prefer that place to the home I provide? How *dare* you? I've given you everything. I've *cherished* you. I'm the one who does everything for you and you're too stupid to see it, let alone appreciate it. This is your *home*, your safe haven. I'm your husband and you're supposed to look up to me and support me. That's what a wife is meant to do, support her husband, not fixate on worthless so-called friends who can't even be bothered to visit her more than once, and not let herself fall under the spell of a grief-raddled old harpy who teaches her to be disloyal to her husband and makes her think she'll be better off elsewhere.'

'Tony – please—'

'*That woman's* life is in ruins since her blasted daughter died and she can't bear other people being happy. That's what made her latch on to you, but you're too dense to see it. *I'm* the one who loves you. *I'm* the one who looks after you. I'm the one who provides you with everything any reasonable wife would be glad of, but are you grateful? Are you proud? Do you thank your lucky stars? Well, do you?'

For a moment, he swung away, then immediately swung back. He glared at her, his breath hot on her face.

'I'm sick of it, do you hear? Ruddy sick. Sick of ruddy Wilton bloody Close.'

Colette gasped as his hand shot out. She flinched from the blow, but he didn't strike her. He grabbed her plate, her knife and fork flying to the floor as he drew back his arm and hurled the plate at the wall.

CHAPTER TWENTY-TWO

Mabel was to meet Harry's parents over the last weekend in August. Were the blooms of the buddleia in next door's garden a richer lilac this year? She laughed at herself. The flowers were exactly the same. She was the one who was different. Her senses were heightened by excitement not just at the prospect of being introduced to Harry's parents, but also because she was to spend so much time with her gorgeous cheeky blighter.

Harry came over from RAF Burtonwood the evening before they were to set off. The strict rules left by the Morgans meant he wasn't allowed to sleep in Wilton Close, so Joan and Bob offered him their sofa.

'I'm afraid Max might disturb you during the night,' Joan said when Harry and Mabel went round.

'And if Max doesn't, there's a dodgy spring that definitely will,' Bob added with a grin.

Having dumped his bag, Harry walked Mabel home, where they indulged in a loving farewell on the doorstep before Mabel slid inside, careful not to compromise the blackout. She leaned against the door after she closed it. Harry's kiss made her feel all weak and tingly. She was the luckiest girl alive.

Upstairs, she got ready for bed. It took a while to drop off to sleep and she was awake early the next morning.

Mrs Grayson gave her an extra slice of toast to keep her going and packed sandwiches and an apple.

'I've popped a beaker in there too,' said Mrs Grayson. 'Alison said lots of station buffets have run out of crockery and it's best to take your own.'

Mabel said, 'Bless you,' and kissed her.

Mrs Grayson blushed and looked pleased. It was a shame she didn't have daughters of her own to take care of. She'd have made a wonderful mum. But as Dot was wont to say, the younger members of their group were her 'daughters for the duration', so at least Mrs Grayson had that.

Harry arrived by taxi and popped inside to say hello and pick up Mabel's bag.

'A taxi,' said Mrs Cooper, impressed.

'Firstly, Mabel's my best girl and she's worth it,' said Harry. 'And secondly, knowing what the trains are like these days, we ought to spend at least part of our journey in comfort.'

Settling in the taxi, holding hands with Harry and waving with her free hand to Mrs Cooper and Mrs Grayson, Mabel was warmed by his consideration. He was undoubtedly right about the train journey that lay ahead.

If your train is late or crowded – DO YOU MIND? a poster had asked early in the war, since which time it had been proved time and again that, with the stakes so high, the Great British public frankly didn't. Passenger trains were usually packed full, sometimes with small children sleeping in the luggage racks overhead. Delays were more or less guaranteed and were often lengthy, trains halting in the middle of nowhere for no obvious reason. Sometimes they would go backwards for an alarming amount of time before eventually heading in the right direction again. Many trains were double the peacetime length and had to stop twice at every station to let passengers disembark or board.

True to form, the train Harry and Mabel boarded at London Road Station was already full, with standing room only. Not that that put off other passengers from squeezing on. With a bit of judicious wriggling, Harry was able to guide Mabel to a spot beside a door.

'Watch out or you'll be swept onto the platform when other passengers get off,' warned a fellow passenger.

Harry grinned at Mabel. 'Don't worry. I'll hang on to you.'

He dumped his bag on the floor against the corridor wall and placed Mabel's on top. He stood against the bags, holding them in position, and slid an arm around Mabel.

'At least we'll have a view as we travel,' he said.

The guard walked past, checking the closed doors were shut properly and slamming those that were still open. As the train started to pull out, a soldier came racing along the platform at full pelt, whereupon several doors towards the rear of the train were instantly thrown wide. Letting go of Mabel, Harry opened their door. Willing hands reached out of the moving train. The soldier grabbed one and was hauled inside. Then came the sound of all the doors banging shut again.

'People wouldn't bother doing that for a bloke in civvies,' commented a man standing too close for comfort. Not that he had any choice in the matter.

Pride swelled inside Mabel. How she loved being the girlfriend of a man in uniform. She indulged in a little day-dream of Harry racing to catch a train and passengers reaching to haul him aboard. Everyone was grateful to ser-vicemen.

Harry murmured, 'That's nice,' and she realised she had snuggled closer. With an embarrassed but loving smile up at him, she drew a couple of inches away, angling herself so as to look out of the window in the top half of the door.

'It's going to be tiring if we have to stand all the way,' said Harry. 'Lean against me if you need to.'

184

'I won't need to. I'm perfectly capable of standing on my own two feet,' said Mabel, 'though that isn't to say,' she added with a saucy smile, 'that I won't choose to.'

'Then let's hope it's my lucky day,' said Harry.

Tony was beside himself with remorse. In the moment before he had hurled the plate at the wall, Colette had felt scared and churned up but determined to fight her corner. But when he had thrown the plate, what she had felt was utter astonishment. Tony had never been violent before. In fact, he had taken pride in not being and had repeatedly reminded her of it. So for him to smash the plate was entirely unexpected.

He couldn't stop apologising. His remorse poured out of him time after time.

'I'm so sorry, Colette. I'm so sorry. You know me. You know I'd never do such a thing, don't you?'

'But you did do it,' Colette said quietly, though out of fairness she had to say, 'I know what you mean, though. It's not something you would do normally.'

'It shows how upset I was.' Tony's hazel eyes were full of pain. His face, which had begun to fill out again and lose its grief-stricken gauntness, was once more hollow-cheeked. 'Not that that's any excuse. It was a shocking thing to do and I'm appalled at myself. I could never have imagined . . . Darling, I'm sorry, I'm sorry.'

He was so distressed that Colette found herself trying to ease his burden. 'I know you are. I know you never meant it to happen. You're not that sort of person.'

'Thank you for saying that – for recognising it.' He scrubbed his face with his hands. 'I'd never do anything to hurt you. I could never strike a woman – any woman, least of all my wife, the girl I adore. Some men give their wives a slap now and then. Old Jenkins at the water board, he does that, has done ever since he got married forty years ago. If Mrs Jenkins answers him back, or if he's had a couple of pints, even when it's just the weak stuff we get nowadays, he gives her a slap to keep her in her place. That's what he calls it. But we've never had that trouble, have we? You know I'd never . . .'

'It's all right, Tony,' said Colette. 'You don't need to keep saying it. Please.'

'You're so kind and understanding.' Tony drew in a deep breath as if savouring the moment. 'What did I ever do to deserve you? My God, Colette, if that plate, if it had clipped you – not that it could have done – but if it had . . . My darling, I would never . . .'

'I know,' said Colette.

It was true. She did know. Tony had injured her in many ways. He had undermined her confidence; he had belittled her; he had made her doubt herself. He had doled out criticism in a loving voice, assuring her it was for her own good. He'd been sharp with her when someone at work had got on his wrong side. She had lived in a state of fear and confusion, never knowing what was coming next, only that whatever it was, she deserved it.

Oh, he had hurt her in more ways than she could count, but she was still in no doubt that throwing the plate had been a terrible aberration, something that should never have happened. Tony was certain of it and Colette had to admit that she was too. Tony had hurt her spirit, her emotional self, but he had never laid a finger on her.

'You know I'd never lay a finger on you,' he said now.

A little chill skittered all through her, just as it used to in the old days when it seemed he was reading her mind.

Tony smiled at her. 'Of course, strictly speaking, I still haven't.'

CHAPTER TWENTY-THREE

It was nearly ten o'clock that evening when Mabel and Harry finally alighted at the station in the Surrey countryside.

'It must have been a pretty station before the war,' said Mabel.

How times had changed. Times were when the platforms of country stations had been dotted with tubs of flowers, with baskets of trailing geraniums hanging from the eaves of the waiting room and the ticket office, each stationmaster along the line vying with all the rest to have the best-looking station of the lot. Now everything looked tired and the only fresh painting that was permitted was for practical or protective purposes, not for decoration.

There wasn't a taxi outside the station. Harry walked across the lane and knocked on the door of a thatched cottage in the middle of a row of identical dwellings. The door was answered by an old lady who greeted Harry warmly and a few minutes later, he and Mabel were perched aboard a rickety cart being driven by the old lady's weather-beaten son.

Mabel had been feeling bone-tired, but now she perked up again, excited about meeting Harry's parents. What would they think of her? Would they like her?

The hedgerow was dotted with greeny-white petals.

'Traveller's joy,' said Mabel. 'That's how I feel.'

As the cart drove into a village about a mile from the station, there was a long house with mullioned windows and masses of leafy stems showing that the front of the building must have been covered by a curtain of wisteria in late spring and early summer. The breath hitched in Mabel's throat in pure delight. What a beautiful house – she would adore staying here – but instead of turning to go through the wide gateway, the cart continued onwards.

'There's something I should perhaps mention,' Harry said quietly.

Mabel felt hideously embarrassed. Had he seen the expectation in her face? She laughed gaily. 'Tell me later. I'm too excited to listen.'

They rounded the village green and duck pond to stop in front of a row of dainty cottages whose front doors opened straight onto the pavement. In the centre of the row stood three shops. Mabel barely spared them a glance, but then her gaze swung back again as she realised that in the window of one stood the tall jars of coloured glass that were the symbol of the chemist.

Before Harry could help her down, the shop door opened and a middle-aged woman with faded dark hair and the same brown eyes as Harry came out. Harry laughed and made a show of moving from side to side as if not knowing which to do first, assist Mabel or greet his mother.

'I think you should help your young lady first,' said Mrs Knatchbull, but Mabel had already climbed down on her own. 'My dear, how splendid to meet you at last. Do come inside. Was the journey frightful? Harry will bring your things.'

Harry saluted. 'Yes, ma'am.'

Mrs Knatchbull led Mabel through the shop and into the back, where there was a kitchen leading to a scullery on one side and a small storeroom and a steep staircase on the other.

Upstairs, Mrs Knatchbull showed Mabel into the sitting room, which overlooked the green and the pond. Dr Knatchbull rose from an armchair. Mabel's first thought was that she'd expected him to be taller. Harry was tall, but his father was of medium height and bald on top, with the aroma of pipe tobacco clinging to his tweed jacket.

'We meet at last,' he said, shaking hands. 'May I call you Mabel? Jolly good.'

Harry's parents were everything that was kind and welcoming and Mabel felt guilty for being taken aback to find that they lived above their shop. But by the next morning, she'd got used to the idea, so at the breakfast table she felt able to say to Dr Knatchbull while he munched his toast, 'It must be good to feel you're helping the community.'

'Well – yes,' he replied, 'though that isn't why I changed career. I simply wanted to apply my skills in this way instead of what I was doing before.'

'Dad used to be involved in research,' said Harry. 'The company he worked for was developing a chemical additive that would make motor oil thicker in a hot engine and thinner in a cool engine, for better lubrication.' In a jokey voice, he added, 'His old colleagues ended up making a pretty penny out of it.'

Later, Harry took Mabel for a walk, during which he said, 'I, er, ought to have mentioned that my parents live above the old man's pharmacy.'

'Lots of shop people do, though I hadn't imagined it for your parents. I don't know why not, perhaps because your father used to be in industry. You must have lived in a house then.'

'Yes, we did.'

Mabel stopped and turned him to her. 'Why did you never say?'

'Because I didn't want to put you off.'

'Oh, Harry.'

'Look at it from my point of view,' said Harry. 'Your father's worth a mint.'

Mabel lifted her chin. 'That doesn't make me a snob. Look what I do for a living, hefting railway sleepers about.'

'That's war work,' said Harry. 'That's a different kettle of fish to my father packing in a lucrative career in favour of . . .'

'In favour of doing what he truly wanted,' said Mabel. 'I admire that. I hope you do too.'

'Of course I want the old man to be happy.'

'Should we head back?' asked Mabel. 'Much as I love the two of us being alone, we are here to be with your parents.'

They spent the rest of the day with Mrs Knatchbull while Dr Knatchbull was in the shop downstairs. During the afternoon, there was a flurry of activity around the village green with women running out of their cottages and knocking on other doors. Mrs Knatchbull jumped up, calling to Mabel to come with her.

'We use the village hall as a canteen for troop convoys,' said Mrs Knatchbull.

Mabel ran to keep up. The hall was alive with busy women and girls of all ages, all seeming to know exactly what to do. Army vehicles pulled up around the green and scores of cups of tea were poured. Mabel joined in with a will, collecting cups, mugs and jam jars the moment they were empty so they could be washed, dried and refilled for someone else. The villagers worked cheerfully and with a sense of pride that seemed to fill the air.

'You've got it down to a fine art,' Mabel said admiringly.

'It's a small thing to do for our boys,' said Mrs Knatchbull.

By the time the convoy had departed and everything was washed up and put away, Dr Knatchbull was shutting his shop. Mabel helped Mrs Knatchbull prepare the evening meal and afterwards the four of them went for a stroll. When they came back, people were emerging from their cottages carrying chairs. Harry and Dr Knatchbull went inside and fetched chairs too.

'We all sit on the green and count the planes out as they go overhead,' Mrs Knatchbull told Mabel. 'We count them back too in the morning.' She paused before she added, 'It can be a terrible thing, counting them back.'

Mabel looked at Harry, then glanced away. She didn't want him to see how much she worried about him flying on his missions. The boys in so many air crews never came home, or else they came home with appalling, life-changing injuries.

But that wasn't what troubled her as she lay in bed that night. It was the memory of Harry saying his father's former colleagues had made a pretty penny.

Did Harry blame his father for leaving his old career and not ending up with a pretty penny of his own? Did it bother Harry that there was a marked contrast between the simple life of the country pharmacist and the relative affluence of the chemist engaged in research that had paid off? Dr Knatchbull had clearly been aware of the financial implications of leaving his research post. That was why he'd taken on that short-lived job in the City instead of going immediately into pharmacy. Had Harry entertained similar worries about the family's financial status as he watched his father's emotional struggles between earning a healthy income and following his true ambition?

Was that what had made Harry determined to marry money?

She went hot and cold at the thought of how she had learned that Harry had originally set his sights on her because she came from money. Her eyes filled with tears, but she pushed the memory away, refusing to let it upset her.

Harry adored her, she knew that, and she adored him, and that was all that mattered.

Mabel sat in the buffet nursing a cup of tea as she waited for Dot to arrive. They were going to see Inspector Stanhope that evening before heading to their respective homes. Before Mabel had gone away for her weekend with Harry, the group had decided that the two of them were the best ones for the job, Mabel because of her knowledge of Louise, Dot because she had been able to give the most detailed information to Inspector Stanhope at the time of the thefts from the food dump.

When Dot appeared, she didn't get a cup of tea but came straight to the table. Mabel quickly finished her drink and they set off through the golden glow of the early September evening.

'I always used to love September when my lads were kids,' said Dot. 'It was the beginning of the school year and I took such pride in sending them off on their first day, all clean and shiny and polished. Mind you, it never lasted.'

'Were they like Jimmy, always getting into scrapes?' Mabel asked.

'Boy will be boys – but there was never a lad like Jimmy. He's more of a handful than his dad and his uncle put together ever were.'

The outside of the police station was protected by a wall of sandbags. They announced themselves to the copper on the front desk, who indicated a wooden bench where they could sit. Dot had made an appointment while Mabel was away, so they didn't have to wait long.

They were shown into Inspector Stanhope's office, where he rose to greet them and waved them into seats before resuming his own behind the desk.

'Do you remember me?' Dot asked.

'I do indeed, Mrs Green. Once met, never forgotten. What can I do for you?'

Mabel began to explain about the burglaries in the Chorlton-cum-Hardy area, but she had barely got started before Inspector Stanhope held up a hand to stop her.

'You've come to the wrong police station. This is a Chorlton matter.'

'On the face of it, yes,' said Dot, 'but we have other information.'

Inspector Stanhope nodded and indicated with a movement of his hand that they could continue. Between them, they told all they knew about the Chorlton incidents.

'We have reason to believe,' said Mabel, 'that the thief is Rob Wadden. Do you remember his name?'

The inspector gave her a keen look. 'Go on.'

'His mother has a little job working for Mrs Cooper,' said Dot.

'The lady who is under suspicion?' Inspector Stanhope clarified.

'Mrs Cooper has a list of where her clients keep their spare keys,' said Mabel. 'We think that Mrs Wadden has used the list to enter the houses secretly and we're certain that it's Rob Wadden who's making her do it.'

Instead of leaping to his feet to shake hands with them for solving the mystery, Inspector Stanhope merely said, 'I have received no word of Rob Wadden having returned to Manchester.'

'But he has,' Mabel exclaimed. 'He definitely has, because he's knocking his sister around. I work with her, so I know.'

'Has she told you this?'

'Well, no. She's very private about it, actually. But she always used to have bruises before Rob disappeared and now she's got them again.'

The inspector rose. 'Thank you for coming to see me, ladies.'

'What are you going to do?' asked Dot.

'My job, Mrs Green,' said Inspector Stanhope. 'Allow me to escort you to the front door.'

CHAPTER TWENTY-FOUR

Cordelia was thoughtful as she and Miss Brown left the US Army base, where the colonel who had been assigned to entertain them had invited them to tea to discuss the proposed Christmas dance and there had been polite jokes about a Yank offering tea to two English ladies. As they'd talked about possible arrangements, Cordelia couldn't help letting her mind wander for a moment. Would Colette be well enough, strong enough, to attend? Surely yes. It was weeks away, plenty of time for Colette to . . . to what, exactly? How did one recover from a breakdown? And it must have been a severe one. It had started before last Christmas and it had been July before Tony had brought her home.

Cordelia and Miss Brown had spoken sympathetically about the soldiers who would spend the festive season so far from home.

'It's good of you to think of going to all this trouble,' said the colonel. 'I know from experience how hard it can be to be away from loved ones at special times.'

Miss Brown asked about his family and he produced snapshots of a pretty woman and three gap-toothed youngsters. Cordelia's heart went out to the whole family. It had been hard enough for her when Emily was away at boarding school, but this family was separated by an ocean and for an unspecified length of time.

'We must do for your boys what we would dearly like to do for our own,' said Cordelia.

'Everyone is being most hospitable to us,' said the colonel. 'Our boys sure love dancing with the local girls.'

As Cordelia and Miss Brown left in a taxi, Miss Brown said, 'You appear preoccupied, Mrs Masters. One might even say, troubled.'

'Not troubled,' said Cordelia, 'but I can't help wondering about this dance. I know that holding it at Darley Court will make it special, but will it be special enough? These boys go out dancing all the time.'

'So I gather,' Miss Brown said drily, 'and my land girls are more than happy to partner them. One of the girls has set her sights on becoming Mrs Hank Wainwright the Third, would you believe? And all of them are mad about jitterbugging.'

'What's that?' asked Cordelia.

'I took the precaution of ascertaining that it happens on the dance floor and not in the bedroom. But I digress. You suggested our Christmas Eve dance might not be enough of a special occasion.'

'I do apologise,' Cordelia said sincerely. 'I don't mean to sound ungrateful when you've been so obliging.'

'Yes, yes, let's take that as read, shall we? Kindly come to the point, Mrs Masters.'

'I'm sure the dance will be a splendid affair, but ideally I'd like to make it even more of an event. Seeing the pictures of the colonel's family made me think of the married servicemen, but what can we do for them?'

'If they're missing their own little ones, maybe we can supply some children.'

Cordelia caught on at once. 'A children's party, with an invitation to our American friends to join us if they care to.'

'Party games with prizes – if we can get hold of suitable prizes.'

'And a visit from Father Christmas,' Cordelia added.

'We could hold the children's party in the afternoon, allowing ample time for clearing up and getting ready for the dance in the evening.'

'Or,' said Cordelia, feeling inspired, 'we could hold an afternoon tea dance in between, for some of the older folk in the local community.'

'Old fogies like me, you mean?'

'There's nobody like you, Miss Brown,' Cordelia retorted. 'You're one of a kind. And the tea dance needn't be just for Darby and Joan. It would be for anyone,' she added with a laugh, 'who doesn't feel up to jitterbugging.'

'Three events in one day,' said Miss Brown. 'What have I let myself in for?'

'I could look for another venue, if you prefer,' said Cordelia, though she knew nowhere else would be as special.

'Certainly not,' said Miss Brown. 'Darley Court will be proud to host your series of events on Christmas Eve.'

'It'll take a lot of organising.' Cordelia nodded crisply as she felt herself preparing to rise to the challenge. This was the type of thing she excelled at, though three events in one go would be a lot of work.

'If anyone can manage it,' said Miss Brown, 'you can.'

One feature of Cordelia's job as a lampwoman was that during the weeks when she walked the line, cleaning every lamp on her allotted stretch of the permanent way, it allowed her plenty of time to mull things over. Each time she climbed a ladder up to a small platform to dismantle and clean a lamp, she was careful to pay due heed, but when she returned to terra firma and set off for her next set of signal lamps, she was free to dwell on her thoughts.

Some lampmen and -women might allow their minds to wander all over the place, but not Cordelia. She had always been able to focus – or was it a by-product of her marriage? Being the perfect wife took concentration. It was also, she had realised a long time ago, an effective distraction from the desperate truth of being married to somebody other than Kit.

But ever since the Red Cross fundraiser, she had started to view her marriage in a different way. What was it like for Kenneth, being married to her? The question made her musings distinctly uncomfortable. Yes, she was a credit to him; yes, she was superb organiser of their social calendar; yes, before the war she had cultivated the most appropriate circle of acquaintances. She had never put a foot wrong.

Shouldn't there be more than that to a marriage, though? Was Kenneth content or did he find the atmosphere of their marriage sterile? To all intents and purposes, it was perfect on the surface, but underneath . . .

Truth be told, she couldn't say what Kenneth thought. Heat made her face tingle as shame washed through her. Had she truly spent all these years not taking her husband's deepest feelings into account? What did that say about her?

For once in a blue moon, Cordelia and Dot had the same day off. They decided to meet up in town to see what fabrics were available in Ingleby's, after which they had a meal in the British Restaurant.

'If you ask me,' said Dot, 'Mr Churchill's ability as a leader isn't just down to his speechifying and his courage. It's to do with his understanding of people an' all. If the old name of Community Feeding Centres had stayed, these restaurants wouldn't be anything like so busy now. They used to sound like charity places before, until Mr Churchill stuck his oar in.'

'Changing their name to British Restaurants was an excellent idea,' Cordelia agreed.

They spent a few minutes choosing what to have, knowing they would get a well-cooked meal of good quality, and all for a maximum price of ninepence.

'Tell me about your plans for the Christmas dance,' said Dot. 'You were a big help to me with the Christmas Kitchens last year and I want to return the compliment.'

'Thank you.' Cordelia smiled. 'I'll hold you to that. I'm going to need help because the original plan has expanded somewhat.'

She explained about the children's party followed by the afternoon tea dance and then the dance in the evening.

'That's a heck of a lot to organise,' said Dot.

'I want it all to be perfect. I thought of the children's party because not all the American servicemen are young and single and I wanted to have an event with a family atmosphere. I hope some of the Americans with children of their own will want to help, and I'm sure they'll find the afternoon tea dance quaint. It's an opportunity to involve more people from the local community, who'll be glad to show friendship towards the Americans since their own sons are away.'

'It's a grand idea,' said Dot. 'Nothing can make up for having your own boys away fighting, but there'll be mums in America who'll be grateful that somebody was kind to their lads far away.'

'It's what I hope to achieve.'

'It'll be a wonderful afternoon and evening. Hard work to pull off, but wonderful.'

'It's going to be more than something for the Americans,' said Cordelia. 'It started out as that, but now I see it as being much more.'

'For the wider community.'

'More than that too. I don't want it to be just another dance. I can organise one of those standing on my head. I want this to be a huge occasion, a special celebration for all of us railway girls. Last Christmas, we were all in a state of grief over Colette. Now we have something to celebrate and I feel as if I want to throw the biggest party in the world.'

'Eh, love, I understand what you mean. Getting Colette back was a miracle. Crikey!' Dot jerked her chin back, a frown forming on her brow as something across the room caught her attention. 'Look over there. Is that . . .? It can't be. Not dressed as a waitress.'

Cordelia turned to look and she too was bewildered.

'Miss Emery!' she exclaimed.

But – dressed as a waitress?

Cordelia and Dot looked at one another in consternation. The poised, professional assistant welfare supervisor, waiting at table? Did she feel their eyes on her? At any rate, she turned round. Even from here, Cordelia could see her face fall, then colour. After a moment, Miss Emery made her way over to them.

'Miss Emery.' Dot spread her hands. 'I don't understand.'

'You evidently haven't heard.' Miss Emery spoke stiffly but with a sheen of tears in her eyes. 'I no longer work for the railways.'

'But you were so good at that job,' said Cordelia. 'Why would you leave?' She didn't ask, 'And why work as a waitress?' but that was the question in her head.

'I should have been more precise in my choice of words,' said Miss Emery. 'I was dismissed.'

'Never!' Dot exclaimed. 'Why?'

'We don't mean to pry,' Cordelia added quickly.

'Yes, we do,' said Dot. 'What on earth happened? Nobody could have done that job better than you.'

'I breached someone's confidentiality.'

'I find that hard to believe,' said Cordelia.

'It's true, I'm afraid,' said Miss Emery. 'Mr Naylor made an official complaint against me for revealing his address.'

'Strictly speaking, you didn't,' said Dot.

'I think that's what's called splitting hairs,' said Miss Emery. 'We all know I did. Mr Naylor was within his rights.'

'I'm so very sorry,' said Cordelia. 'We must bear some of the blame.'

'It was my decision to do what I did,' said Miss Emery, 'no one else's.'

'And now you're here,' said Dot. 'Are you . . . volunteering?'

'No. Fortunately for me, being a larger restaurant, this one has a mixture of volunteers and paid staff. When you've been sacked for breaking the rules of confidentiality, you're very limited as to who will take you on afterwards. Again fortunately for me, what diners choose from the menu isn't regarded as a private matter. Now if you'll excuse me, I must return to my work. I mustn't be seen slacking.'

Unable to come up with any words of comfort, Cordelia and Dot watched her retreat.

CHAPTER TWENTY-FIVE

Usually, meetings in the buffet were arranged through the exchange of messages in the notebook Mrs Jessop kept for them under the counter, but there was no time for that on this occasion. Cordelia and Dot agreed that Dot would speak to Persephone at the ticket barrier and Cordelia would tell one of the Wilton Close girls, who would also pop along to see Joan.

'Joan has to be there,' said Dot. 'Miss Emery has helped her as much as any of us.'

Meeting in the buffet, they bought cups of tea, but only so that they could commandeer a table. Cordelia was sure none of them felt like drinking tea as if this was an ordinary meeting.

When everyone arrived, Cordelia explained what had become of Miss Emery and listened as her young friends expressed their shock.

'How could Tony do such a thing?' asked Margaret.

'Technically, Miss Emery did breach his confidentiality,' said Cordelia.

'But she did it to help us,' said Alison. 'It's our fault as much as hers.'

'The question is,' said Dot, 'what can we do to help her?'

It was Persephone who, after some discussion, hit on the best idea.

'She must have helped a large number of women and girls since the war started. We could have a campaign to get these women to write letters about how she assisted them. If we could get enough letters, it might show the powers that be that even if Miss Emery did make a mistake in this instance, she is nevertheless a valuable member of staff who's made a real difference to others.'

'I don't know how many women LMS employs,' said Margaret, 'but we have only the welfare supervisor herself and Miss Emery to look after the whole lot of us. Miss Emery has worked jolly hard all this time. She deserves recognition for that.'

'I'll certainly write a letter,' said Alison. 'Miss Emery is the person who makes sure I move from post to post in my special training. When I was working in Leeds, the lady who was in charge of me deliberately kept me in menial jobs and it was Miss Emery who sorted her out.'

'And she was the one I went to when I knew I was expecting,' said Joan. 'It was much easier to tell a lady than to have to tell the head porter.' She frowned. 'That doesn't sound like much.'

'If everybody says "It doesn't sound like much", we won't get anywhere,' Cordelia stated firmly. 'Every bit of assistance matters. It isn't just the individual importance of each piece of welfare work. It's the sheer volume.'

'One of the other lady ticket collectors had a problem with one of the men,' said Persephone. 'He was being rather a cad, making suggestive remarks. To start with, she was too embarrassed to do anything, but in the end she went to Miss Emery and it was dealt with. Miss Emery made sure the two of them were always put on different shifts after that.'

'It would have been more to the point if the man had been hauled over the coals,' said Dot.

'Unfortunately, a man would have to do more than simply make suggestive remarks before he was reprimanded,' said Cordelia. 'But that's beside the point. What matters is that Miss Emery dealt with it. Would your colleague write a letter, Persephone?'

'I'm sure she will, especially if she knows we are going to as well. Who else can we ask?'

Margaret spoke up. 'What about the women Miss Emery saw when she went to those other stations? You remember, when we wanted Colette's address, but she'd gone away.'

'Good idea,' said Dot. 'How can we find out who they are?'

'It's easy enough to find out where Miss Emery went,' said Persephone. 'What if we rang each stationmaster and asked to speak to the lady or ladies Miss Emery interviewed? I bet we could drum up some support that way.'

'And I can talk to the staff in Southport,' Dot added. 'There isn't time for me to get off at all the stations in between, but we get ample turnaround time in Southport. I can ask some of the lasses there if Miss Emery has ever helped them – and I can get them to spread the word along the line an' all.'

'That's an excellent idea, Dot,' said Cordelia. 'We must all talk to every lady we've met through our railway work.'

'And ask them to pass it on,' said Alison, 'especially if they work on trains and can get word to other stations.'

'Who should they send their letters to?' asked Joan.

'It can't be to one of us personally in case it all backfires,' said Mabel. 'The last thing we need is for there to be another sacking.'

'Perhaps to my husband's law firm,' suggested Cordelia.

'No,' said Alison. 'That would put people off. Plenty would think they weren't educated enough to write to a firm of solicitors and others would be scared of being dragged into a legal wrangle.'

'I know,' said Margaret and they all looked at her. 'What if the letters were sent here to the buffet, care of Mrs

Jessop – with her permission, of course. She's a good sort. I bet she'd say yes.'

'Everyone would feel comfortable sending a letter here,' said Persephone. 'Clever old you, Margaret.'

'And we mustn't open the letters,' said Joan. 'Nobody must ever be able to say we picked and chose which ones to use. We must show our faith in Miss Emery by trusting that everyone who writes will say good things about her.'

'Aye,' said Dot, 'and to make sure of it, we mustn't badger Mrs Jessop over how many letters have come.'

Mabel looked around the table. 'All right, I'll ask the question. We're all thinking it, so I'll say it: do we tell Colette?'

'Does she even know Miss Emery has lost her job?' asked Margaret. 'We don't want to burden her when she's not well.'

'If she does know,' said Joan, 'she'll be glad that we're trying to help.'

'If she doesn't know,' said Cordelia, 'Tony won't thank us for telling her.'

'Aye,' said Dot. 'We'd best leave well alone.'

'Are we decided on everything we have to do?' asked Cordelia.

'It'll take time for word to get around,' said Alison. 'We need all the support we can get and that won't happen quickly.'

'I'm afraid it won't,' Cordelia agreed. 'We need to set a cut-off date. It's mid-September now, so how about the middle of December?'

'That's three whole months,' Joan cried in dismay.

'Alison's right,' said Mabel. 'It's going to take time. It's all got to be done by word of mouth.'

'I know it sounds like for ever,' said Cordelia, 'but if this is going to have a chance of working, we've got to do it properly and that means giving it the time it needs. We're the ones who got Miss Emery into this fix and it's up to us to get her out of it if we possibly can.'

On Saturday, on her way home from work, Cordelia dropped into Wilton Close to see her friends. As she walked up the front path, the door opened and she smiled, thinking that Mrs Cooper had seen her from the window, but instead Tony appeared.

He gave her a nod. 'Afternoon, Mrs Masters.'

Cordelia's smile had slipped at the sight of him and she quickly pulled it back into place as Tony put on his hat and walked away. Mrs Cooper was inside the doorway. She stepped back to let Cordelia enter.

'What did Tony want?' Cordelia asked, feeling all too well aware of the plan she and the others had made to help Miss Emery if they could.

'He came to say Colette is doing as well as can be expected, but please can we refrain – that was his word: refrain – from visiting her for a while longer, because she's still fragile. He says he'll let us know when she's well enough.'

Cordelia nodded but didn't comment. The way he had complained about Miss Emery had made her see a new side of Tony. On the other hand, he had been within his rights to make the complaint and the decision to sack her had been nothing to do with him.

She had a cup of tea and a chat with Mrs Cooper and Mrs Grayson before heading for home. On the way, she popped into St Clement's Church, as she sometimes did, pausing beside the Book of Notices in which local people wrote the names and ranks of their loved ones who were in danger. It was sobering to think that when the war was over, the Book of Notices would form the basis of the Book of Remembrance. Committing the most recent names to memory, Cordelia slid into a pew to say a prayer for them, adding a general prayer for everyone fighting in the war and a specific one for Dot's two boys.

How much longer would the war last? It had started just over three years ago. Three years! And how low would the call-up age for girls become? Her heart turned over at the thought of Emily receiving her papers.

Leaving church, she turned the corner onto High Lane, where she bumped into Joan and Bob. Joan was pushing the pram while Brizo, on his lead, trotted beside Bob. They chatted and Cordelia admired baby Max while the doting parents lapped up the praise. Cordelia smiled to herself: she remembered it well.

But as they parted and she went on her way, it wasn't the memory of baby Emily that held her mind in a strong grip. It was the picture of Joan and Bob gazing adoringly at Max . . . and then at each other.

It had never been that way for her and Kenneth. Yes, they had both gazed adoringly at darling little Emily, but they'd never looked like that at one other. At least, Cordelia had never once gazed adoringly at Kenneth and she assumed he hadn't at her, though she honestly didn't know. If he had, she'd never noticed. She'd never looked for it, never hoped for it.

Her shoulders dropped for a moment under the weight of sudden disappointment and an unexpected sense of longing went through her. Joan and Bob were so lucky. They shared something she had never had. She hadn't even had it with Kit, because their all too brief relationship had been shrouded in secrecy. Never, not even once, had they felt free to share a loving glance in public.

She tried to shake off her thoughts as she arrived home, but they wouldn't be so easily dismissed and she felt obscurely unsettled as she prepared and served the evening meal. Kenneth and Emily noticed nothing, but they wouldn't, would they? They had their own concerns.

Tonight, they were all to go to another fundraising event, this time an evening of cards.

'Are there spare tickets, do you know, Mummy?' Emily had asked earlier in the week. 'Raymond and his parents might like to come.' She had flicked a defiant glance in her father's direction.

'I think not, Emily,' had been Kenneth's reply. 'It's bridge, not whist.'

'And you think grocers don't play bridge?' Emily had asked. 'I happen to know the Hancocks do. Who do I ask about tickets?'

Later, Cordelia had tried to soothe Kenneth.

'It's better if they come.'

'Indeed? And how do you make that out?'

'So we can keep an eye on Emily and Raymond, of course. Honestly, Kenneth, it's better than the Hancocks not coming and Emily deciding she won't either.'

Now, Cordelia, Kenneth and Emily went into their rooms to get ready.

'Were you thinking of lending Emily a piece of your jewellery?' Kenneth asked, fiddling with his gold cufflinks.

'Yes.' She was pleased he was taking an interest. 'I thought my amethysts.'

'Please don't. They're too old for her.'

'Oh. What about the garnet bracelet?'

'No. I mean, don't lend her anything. She's only sixteen. I don't want her appearing older than she is.'

About to reply, Cordelia thought better of it. Kenneth had submitted to having the Hancocks at the card evening with moderately good grace. Not lending Emily her jewellery was the least she could do in return.

What a pickle. If only Emily could have found herself a nice boy her father could have approved of—

Where had that thought sprung from? She was ashamed of herself. It was precisely what her own parents had wanted for her when she was young.

That brought her thoughts back to her marriage and something squirmed inside her. She might have been the perfect wife all these years, but was perfection any substitute for warmth? Kenneth had always been a generous husband and a devoted father. Didn't he deserve more than cool perfection?

They travelled by taxi to the bridge evening. The organisers had taken the precaution of putting the tables in different rooms, according to the varying standards of play. Cordelia was relieved to find that, within each standard, players drew lots to find partners, so at least Kenneth wouldn't spend the evening fuming because Emily and Raymond had chosen to play together.

Although Cordelia wasn't an expert, she played a confident game. Kenneth was at a different table and while Cordelia was dummy, she watched him play his hand, taking several tricks. The other pair congratulated him and his partner. Kenneth smiled. He was a good-looking man.

Halfway through the evening, there was an interlude for refreshments.

Cordelia went to Kenneth's side. 'Let's step outside for a few minutes.'

Kenneth more or less whisked her through the French windows. 'Are Emily and Raymond out here?'

'No.'

'I thought you meant us to . . .'

'To what?' Cordelia asked.

'You know what I mean. To police them.'

'That isn't necessary. They're inside with Mr and Mrs Hancock. I thought you and I could be out here on our own. Unpoliced,' she added, her heartbeat speeding up. Raising herself on her toes, she placed a light kiss on Kenneth's mouth before dropping back on her heels.

He looked at her, then lowered his face to hers. He started to kiss her, then drew away. Taking her shoulders, he held her from him.

'Kenneth—' she began.

'Don't, Cordelia,' he replied. 'Don't do it if you don't mean it.'

CHAPTER TWENTY-SIX

Knowing that Miss Emery had lost her job was a kind of bereavement for Colette. Yes, she was horrified on Miss Emery's behalf, but her overriding feeling was of being utterly alone in an alien world controlled by Tony. Her friends hadn't been back to see her and now Miss Emery, who might have given her the chance of a new job, had been wrenched away. Colette felt shaky, as if her insides had come unstuck. The fear was worse than when she had previously lived with Tony.

The only good thing was that he was being kind and attentive because of the plate incident – or was it a good thing? Making it up to her, he called it. But Colette knew of old that Tony's kindness wasn't to be trusted. Besides, even if it was genuine, she didn't want it, so she responded coolly.

Sitting in his armchair in the parlour, Tony laughed. 'Are you sulking?'

Sulking? Sulking! He had made her life a misery ever since she was eighteen years old and he had the gall to accuse her of sulking.

'No, I'm not.' She spoke quietly, resting her knitting on her lap. 'I just don't know how to respond.'

'Your husband fusses over you and you don't know how to respond?'

Colette caught her breath. There was a gleam in Tony's eyes that she remembered all too clearly. Pleasant as his voice was, his eyes told another story. Then, as had happened so many times, his face changed and he was all affability. It oozed out of his pores.

'Well then, here's a conundrum for you. I was about to give you something that I know you want very much, but should I, if you don't know how to respond to your husband's kindness?'

He half laughed, as if indulging the little woman in her silly feminine ways. He had always known how to wrong-foot her. In the past, she would have scrambled to do the right thing, smooth things over and bend herself to his will, but not any longer. She had to be careful, always, not to push him too hard. She never forgot the ever-present threat to her dear Mrs Cooper. Nevertheless, she was determined not to cave in like she always used to in the old days. She knew better now. She had to hang on to her pride. She had to be true to herself.

The old Colette would have obediently asked what Tony had got her, but the new Colette wouldn't lower herself. She knew she wouldn't get away with not replying, so she gave a tiny shrug.

'It's up to you to decide,' she said in a neutral voice.

Tony stared at her. Colette swallowed, screwing up her toes inside her slippers. Then Tony got up and walked out of the parlour. Colette knew she ought to feel strong, but weakness washed through her and she trembled.

It was one of Tony's fire-watching nights. Thank goodness. A whole night to herself. Might her friends come round, like they had that other time? Colette couldn't help hoping. Tony believed they'd given up on her, that having grieved for her, they no longer had room for her in their lives. She couldn't bear to think of it. She knew her friends better than that. They were caring and loyal and all thought the world of one another. She had never stopped thinking about them. Even when she had lived so far away, even when she had settled into her new life as Betsy Cooper and had never expected to see her friends again, they had still meant everything to her and thinking of the grief they must be enduring had sometimes made her feel sick with guilt. Was this her punishment now? The others wouldn't have set out to punish her on purpose, she knew. They were too decent and kind for that, but they were now in an emotionally complex situation. After going through the supposed bereavement, was it too much to expect them simply to accept her reappearance? After all the pain they had suffered, followed by the astounding revelation of her still being alive, did they now need time to gather their thoughts and come to terms with everything? Was that why they hadn't come back to see her? There hadn't been so much as a scribbled note enquiring after her health.

Colette struggled to understand it. It was so hard to believe. Yet that disbelief tied in with her life as it now was. Disbelief was the order of the day. It had seemed impossible that Tony should find her – yet he had. Returning to her old home had felt like living in a weird, distressing dream – but it was real. Everything was real. She had been home for two months now. Two months! Some days, she lacked energy and carried a painful lump in her throat. The worst thing of all, the most impossible thing of all – and, as she was now being forced to accept, the most real thing of all – was that this was her life for ever. She struggled against an inner darkness, but could you fight something that would never end?

In the kitchen, she prepared Tony's snap tin. She made a fish paste and cucumber sandwich, cutting it neatly in half, and added a honey biscuit. As she clicked the tin shut, Tony appeared behind her. Instinctively she turned to face him. You should always face the enemy.

'Make another sandwich while you're at it,' Tony said cheerfully.

'I don't need any supper.'

'You'll be glad of it in the early hours, same as I will.'

'What are you talking about?' She didn't want one of those conversations where he tied her in knots. She just wanted him out of the house.

'You're coming with me. This is your surprise present. I know you want to do something outside the home. Why else would you have tried to see Miss Emery? So I've set aside my own wish to keep my wife safe in the house and arranged for you to join the local WVS. You remember how keen they were to have you last year. Well, now's your chance.'

Colette gawped at him. Her eyes popped open, her jaw slackened and she honest-to-goodness gawped.

Tony shuffled his feet like a schoolboy. 'I want you to be happy, Colette. I want to make you happy. I know what an awful you state you got yourself into before you ran away. You felt you had all the cares of the world on your shoulders. I don't want that happening again.' He looked at her almost shyly. 'So I've done this for you. I'm giving you this to make you happy. I'm giving it out of love and consideration, even though it isn't really what I want. It will make you happy, my darling – won't it?'

'Mrs Naylor! You've come back to us. Jolly good. Better late than never.'

As Tony held open the door for her, Colette walked into the school hall, practically into the waiting arms of Mrs Townsend, the WVS lady who had been so welcoming on the previous occasion Colette had been to the evacuated school that had been handed over to Civil Defence for the duration. That other occasion had been thanks to a piece of skulduggery on Tony's part too. Determined to get her to give up her fire-watching job in the marshalling yard, he had accidentally on purpose left his snap tin behind one evening, knowing she would trot along to the school with it and knowing also that everyone would make a fuss of her and do their utmost to persuade her to join the WVS. He had prepared the way very cleverly by explaining to all and sundry what a frightful worry it was for him having her working at the marshalling yard. Colette had felt taken aback when she realised how highly his peers thought of Tony.

'You'll sit between me and Miss Upton, won't you, Mrs Naylor?' said Mrs Townsend. 'But before we sit down, come and look at this. Isn't Mr Naylor an absolute sweetheart? He said he wanted you to have a WVS uniform even if I had to move heaven and earth to procure it. The whole uniform, mind,' she added confidentially. 'Not just the jacket or the hat, which is as much as some can afford. Goodness me, aren't you going to look smart? And if you don't mind my saying, just between ourselves, I'm sure this is exactly what you need to help you get over . . . you know what. You're among friends here, dear. We're all on your side.'

Colette went through the usual experience of not quite believing what was happening. The WVS ladies were kindness itself, which made her feel like an imposter. Their kindness was the last thing she deserved. She hadn't suffered a breakdown. What she had suffered from was a miserable marriage that she had deliberately run away from, leaving her husband, friends, colleagues and neighbours to mourn her.

'Obviously, we have to have ladies on duty overnight,' elderly Miss Upton told Colette, 'but there's plenty to do during the day as well. You might find that easier, less taxing, since you haven't been well.'

It was said to her several times, like the chorus in a song. 'Since you were unwell . . .' 'After what you've been through . . .' Even 'Since your little incident . . .' Her little incident! Nevertheless, Colette was grateful for the kindness. These ladies had no idea of the truth. Living a lie, going along with Tony's story, was a huge strain and Colette felt isolated.

Was this an opportunity to feel less isolated?

She took her WVS uniform home with her and the next day she kept herself busy all morning, so that when Tony asked casually during their midday meal whether she'd tried it on yet, she could blandly reel off a list of the domestic responsibilities that had taken up her attention.

Tony showed no annoyance. 'You're a good little house-wife,' he said.

Later, Colette went upstairs and put on the uniform, gazing at herself curiously in the bedroom mirror. The skirt's waistband needed taking in, but aside from that, everything was fine.

'With your colouring, Colette, you must always dress in pastels,' her mother had told her. 'Strong shades or dull shades will suck out all your natural colour, such as it is.'

But looking at herself in the uniform, Colette didn't feel pale or washed out. The olive green provided a good contrast to her buttermilk-blonde hair and fair complexion.

She imagined herself working for the WVS. She had heard all about it last night. There were regular jobs, such as cooking, jam-making and working in soup kitchens, staffing the clothes exchange and the rest centres and taking the mobile library around, not to mention knitting and making camouflage nets.

'And, of course, there are all the one-off jobs we're asked to do,' said Miss Upton, 'such as providing nursing care in the community if, say, someone has come home from hospital and has to convalesce.'

'There was the time the army asked us to provide rags to clean the AA guns,' Mrs Townsend added. 'It might not sound like much of a task, but collecting on that scale takes organising.'

'And we were called on to provide tea and sandwiches for the police and the Home Guard when they were searching for an escaped POW,' said another lady.

'So you see, we need every pair of hands we can get,' said Mrs Townsend. 'Remember the words of Lady Reading. "The greatest disservice a woman can do at the moment is to consider herself useless." Such an inspiration to us all.'

Colette thought of Lady Reading's words now. Should she take them as her guide? Was it time to accept her new life back with Tony and make the best of it? If she threw herself into war work, would that provide sufficient purpose to make her life worthwhile? Those ladies last night had made it clear they were looking forward to having her as one of their number. Perhaps this was the opportunity to make new friends. Was it time to stop endlessly asking herself 'Is this really happening?' and pull herself together? Was 'Is this really happening?' no more than foolish self-indulgence? It *was* happening and she had better jolly well get on with it.

Was it time for a fresh start?

CHAPTER TWENTY-SEVEN

Colette prepared potato floddies for the evening meal. Everyone was being encouraged to eat more potato and less bread. She grated raw potatoes, seasoned them and then gradually added flour until a soft mixture formed. After frying them gently in dripping, she served them with a simple salad.

After the meal, she washed up while the tea brewed. Joining Tony in the parlour, she sat down.

Tony was seated comfortably in his armchair. He sipped his tea and bestowed an appreciative nod on her. 'What did you think of last night? Did Mrs Townsend lure you in with the promise of plenty of interesting tasks?'

'I tried on the uniform this afternoon,' said Colette.

'You should have left it on for me to see.'

'The skirt waist needs altering.'

'That won't take you long,' said Tony.

Colette looked at him. He really had no idea. 'I shan't be taking it in.'

'That's not like you. Your clothes always fit perfectly – oh!' His eyes shone. 'Do you mean you shan't take it in be-cause – because your waist is increasing? Oh, darling!'

Colette sat up straight, startled. 'No,' she said at once. Then, in a quieter voice, she went on, 'I shan't take it in be-cause I'm not going to wear it.'

Tony made a small, jittery movement with his hand. 'Not wear it? Don't be silly. I spent good money on that kit.' Then his irritation vanished. 'Just because not everyone can afford the full uniform doesn't mean you have to stint yourself. You should be proud your husband thinks so much of you. The other ladies think you're jolly lucky.'

'I know.' Colette put her cup down. 'I'm accustomed to other women seeing me as lucky. It doesn't mean they're right.'

'I beg your pardon?' Sitting forward, Tony put his cup on the table beside his chair without removing his gaze from her.

'I won't alter the skirt because I shan't be wearing it. Nor will I wear the rest of the uniform, because as much as I admire the WVS, I refuse to become a member in these circumstances.'

'What circumstances?'

'The fact is, I don't want to be here. I tried to leave you, but you dragged me back. I know what the rules are, Tony. I know I have to put on a good front and so I'll cook for you and look after the house; I'll be polite to your parents and never breathe a word to anyone about why I really left you. But that's as far as it goes. I won't do anything else. I won't willingly do extra things that suggest all is well and I'm happy.' Her chin jerked in distaste. 'I just won't.'

Tony's jaw hardened. 'So you're declining to do war work because you're a sulky little madam.'

'I'm not sulking. I've never sulked. I've been confused, hurt, upset; I've been all sorts of things back when I was trying to please you and keep the peace, but I've never sulked.'

Tony came to his feet. Any moment now, he would trap her by placing his hands on the arms of her chair. Colette jumped up. They faced one another on the hearthrug. Cold fingers of dread whispered across Colette's flesh. He was too close. He stared down into her eyes. She wanted to look away, but that might make her appear scared. Well, she was scared – but she mustn't look away.

'If I say you sulk,' Tony said softly, 'it's because you sulk.' He caught her wrist and held it tight, bending his face to hers. 'And if I say you're joining the WVS, that's what you'll do. I gave that to you, Colette. I *gave* you what you wanted. Most husbands wouldn't. Most husbands who'd had to bring their errant wives home would tie them to the table leg to make 'em stay put, but not me. I'm trying to do right by you. I'm taking your wishes into account, little as you deserve it. And what do you do? Throw it back in my face, that's what.'

'You can't force me to be grateful. I don't want to be here. I'll be a good housewife and I'll go through the motions in front of everybody else, but I won't join the WVS. I won't put myself alongside all those brave, dedicated, selfless women just so you can kid yourself we're playing happy families – because we're aren't and we never shall be.'

'Did you say "playing"? I'm not playing. I've never been more serious in my life. You're my *wife*, Colette. You're meant to look up to me and do as I say. That's the job of a wife – not that you care. The worst thing that ever happened to you was going to work on the railways. Before that, you were sweet and respectful. But those so-called friends of yours . . .' Tony's mouth twisted and his eyes darkened. 'They've done you no favours with their stupid modern ideas. Well, they've let you down now, haven't they? They've ditched you good and proper – and good riddance to them. You're my wife and you'll do as I tell you.' He squeezed her wrist. 'And if I tell you to join the old biddies in the WVS, that's what you'll do. Understand? I said, *do you understand*?'

Forcing her voice to remain steady, Colette said, 'You can rant at me all you like, Tony, but you can't make me do this. I refuse. Do *you* understand? I refuse.'

The hand grasping her wrist jerked, pulling her off balance. Colette stumbled, but managed to right herself. As she drew herself up again, Tony bent close. She caught a whiff of the thyme she'd put in the potato floddies.

'You'll do as you're told,' he hissed. 'You'll damn well do as you're told.'

'Don't swear at me.' It emerged as a whisper but at least it carried a note of fierceness.

'Are you telling me what to do? Are *you* telling *me*? Is that what you think our lives are going to be like? Stupid little Colette telling me what's what. I don't think so.'

Before Colette knew what was happening, his hand came up and clouted her across the face so hard her neck twanged and black spots appeared before her eyes.

Colette used the spare room that night. In a distant sort of way, she realised it was the first time the bed had been occupied. Apart from Tony's parents, they'd never entertained visitors to a meal, let alone had anyone to stay overnight. Colette didn't even keep the bed made up. She didn't make it now either. She couldn't imagine lying down and sleeping.

She sat on the mattress, feeling stunned, hands in her lap, feet together, just as her mother had taught her. Ladies always sat neatly, according to Mother, and it was true. Colette had watched Cordelia and Persephone.

Something else that was true was that shock could make you feel hot. She had always associated shock with an inner chill, but no, it could make you warm as well. Her blood seemed to have heated up and was swooshing around her body.

Tony had hit her. He had *hit* her. The one thing she had always known would never happen had happened.

She touched her face. It was tender. She ought to leave it alone, but she couldn't help exploring it, investigating the impossible, feeling her skin tighten as it swelled.

221

At last drowsiness overcame her and she curled up on the mattress, not intending to sleep, just needing to rest. The next thing she knew, her eyes flew open and Tony was beside the bed. She lurched upright.

'Come to bed,' said Tony. 'You can't sleep here. Please come to bed. I'm so sorry, darling. You know how dreadful I feel, don't you?'

Oddly enough, yes, she did. He had been so proud of never laying a finger on her.

'Please come to bed,' he whispered.

'I don't want to share a bed with you tonight.'

'I won't expect anything, if that's what you mean,' Tony said gently. 'You poor, sweet darling, you need to recover. We both do. It was a vile thing to happen. Will you forgive me? It'll never happen again. I'm ashamed of myself – there, I've said it. I'm angry too. I never imagined for one moment that I could do such a terrible thing.'

Weariness swept through Colette. 'Not now, Tony, please.'

'Of course, of course. This isn't the moment. I'll make it up to you, I swear. You're the best thing that ever happened to me. You're my darling and my love. I wanted to die after the marshalling yard was bombed.'

'Tony, please.'

'Yes, yes.' There were tears in his voice. 'But you can't sleep in here, darling. Please come to our bed.'

'I want to be alone.'

'Then you shall be.' He jumped at the idea. 'You have our bed, darling, and snuggle down. I'll sleep in here.'

'Are you sure?'

'Of course I am,' Tony said warmly. 'Off you pop. Get some healing sleep.'

After a moment, Colette stood up. She moved around him, careful to avoid contact, and went to the door.

'Oh – darling.'

She turned.

'I can't sleep on a bare mattress. Make up the bed for me, will you?'

After a restless night, Colette got up. There was a dark, tugging sensation in the side of her face when she moved. She was tired, but the feeling dissipated when she looked in the mirror. Her cheek was swollen and there was a narrow mark along the bone where the bruise was coming out. She raised her hand to touch it with her fingertips, but let her hand drop away, the injury untouched.

She got washed and dressed and went downstairs. Was she really going to make the breakfast? Yes, because what else was she to do? The sooner Tony ate his meal and left the house, the better.

'Good morning, darling. Did you get any sleep in the end?'

Tony came into the kitchen. Colette turned to face him.

'My God.' He came towards her, shock and concern all over his face, but she moved away. 'Colette – darling – I'm so sorry.' He covered his face with his hands. 'I don't know what came over me. It'll never happen again, I swear.'

Colette returned to the toast. 'It shouldn't have happened even once.'

Tony groaned. 'Of course not.' He seized her hand and the butter knife clattered to the floor. 'Forgive me. Say you forgive me.'

Withdrawing her hand from his, Colette picked up the knife and washed it.

'You don't want to be late for work.'

Placing his hands gently on her shoulders, Tony smiled at her. 'Not until you say I'm forgiven.'

'Please, not now.'

He removed his hands but was unabashed. 'All right. I understand.' He laughed indulgently. 'You want me to suffer. Well, I deserve to. You have to have your little sulk.'

When they sat down to breakfast, Tony asked, 'Where's your purse?'

Colette looked at him in surprise.

'I need some of the housekeeping,' he said. 'You can't go out looking like that. I'll give the money to the woman next door and ask her to get something from the butcher. Is she registered at Townsend's like we are? I'll collect it from her later. We don't want anybody seeing you in this state, do we?'

When Tony had gone, Colette washed up. Normally she would have done some housework before going shopping, but today she added water to the teapot and had another cup of tea, not caring that it was weak. It was tea. That was what mattered. She pictured her friends crowded round a table in the buffet, enjoying a lively natter. She missed them more than ever.

Presently she washed up her cup and saucer and rinsed the teapot. Then she put on her shoes and her coat and hat. Picking up her handbag, she opened the front door onto a bright, sunny morning.

She went to the newsagent's first.

'I've come to pay the papers.'

When she met Mr Smith's eyes, he dropped his gaze to the counter and shuffled the morning papers as if they needed tidying before he reached under the counter for his record book.

'You don't usually pay midweek. Mr Naylor pays every Saturday.'

'Then I'll leave it for him to do. Good morning.'

She went to the grocer's next. There was a short queue outside. Colette nodded politely to the other women, not reacting when, one and all, they swung their faces in her direction for a second look. She took her place at the end of the line. She didn't deliberately catch anyone's eye, though when it happened, she didn't duck her head in shame, but kept her chin up.

After the grocer's, she went along the road to the fishmonger's. A good housewife bought her fish on the morning of the day she cooked it, but Colette didn't feel like obeying the rules today.

She joined the queue.

'Eh, love,' said an old lady. 'Look at your face. What happened?'

'My husband happened.'

Embarrassed, the old lady turned away.

That reaction more or less summed up Colette's morning. Women who a few weeks ago had competed with one another to be kind to her when she was supposedly recovering from having gone barmy now glanced away from the sight of her bruised face. They didn't know what to say, poor things. Wife-battering wasn't something you talked about. You knew it went on somewhere, but not here, not among your own neighbours. They probably thought she should have claimed to have walked into a door. Either that or she should have stopped at home until she was fit to be seen.

I wonder if any of them ever have to do that.

She went home in plenty of time before Tony was likely to arrive. She didn't feel clever or triumphant. She didn't feel anything. It had happened and she had dealt with it in her own way. No one would say anything, she knew that, but they would know and they would look at Tony through different eyes and that would have to do.

Tony came home bearing the thin slices of ham Mrs Ringwood had bought.

'How are you feeling, darling? Let me look at you.' He cupped her chin; she didn't react. 'It hasn't gone down.' He shook his head. 'You poor darling. I'm so sorry. I swear that was the one and only time. Have you had a nice rest?'

'I'm fine, thank you,' said Colette.

CHAPTER TWENTY-EIGHT

It was the end of September and the sun was lower in the sky in the mornings and evenings. Although the days were still warm and fine, the nights were getting cooler.

Mabel arrived at Victoria Station that morning in plenty of time to catch the six-fifty. Her gang was to meet up next to the bookstall and travel together as usual. Mabel was there first and Bernice and Bette joined her less than five minutes later, but Louise kept them waiting. Then they saw her hurrying and excuse-me-ing her way through the crowd of passengers.

'Everything all right, Lou?' Bernice asked, picking up her knapsack, which she had dumped by her feet.

'Why wouldn't it be?' Louise asked sharply.

'I was only asking,' said Bernice. 'Pardon me for breathing.'

They caught the train to the station just past the section of permanent way they were working on this week. Bernice put Mabel and Bette together.

'Probably so we don't have to put up with Lou's ratty mood,' Bette said sotto voce.

'We'll be changing partners later,' said Mabel.

'You wait. Bernice will get it all out in the open before we swap round.'

When they stopped for their mid-morning break, they trooped onto the scrubby ground at the trackside. Mabel smiled at the sight of a drift of rosebay willowherb. To her, this was the wild flower of the railway and the tall spikes bedecked with rich pink flowers linked her with Grandad.

They wouldn't be around much longer now that October was round the corner; nor would the mayweed's daisy-like blooms, though the pale pink flowers on the knotweed would linger for a while. As for the groundsel, with its flowers resembling teeny-tiny shaving brushes, that would be here for weeks yet.

The four of them sat on the bumpy ground, making themselves as comfortable as they could. Frankly, they were used to roughing it and things had to be pretty bad before anyone complained. Even then, the complaints were usually jokey.

Mabel unscrewed the beaker from the top of her thermos and poured some tea, the others doing likewise.

'Right, Louise,' Bernice said firmly. 'It's time to tell us what's the matter.'

'Why should anything be the matter?'

'Come off it,' said Bernice. 'You've been like a bear with a sore head all morning.'

For a moment, Louise was rigid with obstinacy, but then her shoulders slumped.

'If you must know, we've had the police round.'

'To your house?' asked Bette.

'Aye. It was horrible. They weren't bobbies in uniform, but that was the only good thing. They were detectives in jackets and trilbies, but it was obvious they weren't blokes from round our way, so all the neighbours now know we've had a visit from somebody official, even if they don't know for sure it was the police.'

Mabel's heart beat hard. There was something scary about being the instigator of this event. She had a dozen questions, but didn't dare put any into words.

'What did they want?' Bernice asked.

'Was it because of your bruises?' asked Bette.

Louise gave her a look. 'Don't be daft. The cops don't care about bruises if they happen at home. They wanted to know if Rob was back.'

'Your Rob?' said Bernice. 'I thought you'd seen the last of him. I hope so anyroad, after the way he knocked you around last year.'

Louise's chin jerked up. 'It's nice to know my family has such a good reputation.' Then she seemed to deflate, her eyes shining with tears. 'Actually, we do have a reputation. Round our way, everybody knows Dad was a brute and then he ran off and left us in the lurch. Rob was a hard piece an' all; everyone knows that, though he could be a right charmer when he wanted to get inside a girl's knickers. He got himself a reputation for . . . well . . . if something fell off the back of a lorry, that sort of thing. That's what me and Mum and the boys have to live with. Even though Dad is long gone and Rob took off last year, the neighbours will never forget. It was really hard for our Clifford to get a job when he finished school, because of being a Wadden.'

'I'm sorry to hear it, lass,' said Bernice.

Lou shrugged. 'That's how it is if you're a Wadden. Mabel helped Cliff write a really good letter. That's how he found work in the end. Mum and me are honest and so are the boys, but we're all tainted, all of us. It's so unfair – and now we've had the police round. That doesn't exactly make us look like shining examples of upright and honest behaviour, does it? On top of that, I've got you lot going on at me.'

'Be reasonable, Lou,' said Bette. 'We're your mates. We only want to help.'

'I've told you before. I don't need help.'

'But—' Bernice began.

'Put a sock in it, will you?' Louise broke in.

229

Bernice went from sympathetic to sharp in an instant. 'Oi, you, I won't be spoken to like that. For one, I'm old enough to be your mum, and for another I'm your boss, so kindly keep a civil tongue in your head, young lady.'

Louise's face flushed a dull puce. 'Sorry,' she muttered. 'It just feels like you're all ganging up on me.'

Bernice sighed. 'Oh, Lou, what are we going to do with you, eh? We're not ganging up. We just – I was going to say we just want to help, but you obviously don't see it that way, so we'd best leave it for now, eh, girls?'

Bette nodded, but Mabel felt a frisson of alarm. She had set this train of events in motion, anxious to clear Mrs Cooper's name, but now she felt guilty for hurting Louise. Even so, she couldn't leave things there. She had to know.

'Is Rob home again?' she asked, uncomfortably aware of Bette and Bernice giving her surprised looks.

Lou turned her head and looked her squarely in the eye.

'For your information – no.'

When Mabel reported back to her chums in the buffet, her feelings were conflicted in some ways, but there was one thing of which she felt certain.

'I'm stumped,' she freely admitted. 'I was so sure that Rob was behind the burglaries, but I was wrong. We sent Inspector Stanhope there for nothing.'

'You mustn't feel bad about it,' said Margaret.

'We all agreed with you,' Persephone added.

'You wanted to help Mrs Cooper,' said Cordelia. 'We all did.'

'I don't want to sound as if I'm looking for sympathy,' said Mabel, 'but actually I feel rotten about it. Yes, I wanted to get Mrs Cooper off the hook, but I never thought beyond that. My idea ended up making life unpleasant for the

Waddens. Louise was most awfully upset about her family having a visit from the police.'

'Her poor mam,' said Dot.

'If that was my mum,' said Alison, 'she'd be mortified. Not that it ever would be my mum. We don't have a criminal in the family.'

Dot squeezed Mabel's hand reassuringly. 'It's a shame the Waddens were upset, but it was the only way to find out for sure. We needed to know if Rob was back.'

'Don't forget that Louise was flustered when you asked her about her brother,' said Cordelia. 'Her response seemed to confirm your suspicions. That's why it was necessary to go to the police.'

'I know all that,' said Mabel. 'I just never expected . . .'

'None of us thought of causing the Waddens distress,' said Margaret.

'Not that we would have let it stop us,' said Cordelia. She looked around. 'I'm sorry if it sounds harsh, but it's true. Our first duty in this matter is to Mrs Cooper.'

Mabel nodded. It didn't exactly make her feel better, but she knew Cordelia was right.

'There's still a question that hasn't been answered,' she said.

'Oh aye?' said Dot. 'What's that, then?'

'Who's hurting Louise? Someone is.'

They all looked at one another.

Speaking with reluctance, Persephone suggested, 'A violent boyfriend?'

'She's never mentioned a boyfriend,' said Mabel.

'Surely it can't be that,' said Margaret, 'not after living with a violent father and brother.'

Cordelia sighed. 'Some people can't help following the same patterns of behaviour. If she's grown up with violence . . .'

'No!' Alison exclaimed. 'That's a horrid idea. If she's grown up with it, then she knows to avoid it like the plague.'

'You'd think so,' Dot said sadly, 'but life isn't always that simple. People aren't always that simple.'

Unease rippled through the group. Could it be true? Mabel didn't want it to be – but was she just sticking her head in the sand?

CHAPTER TWENTY-NINE

Never mind what was happening in the wider world. A different kind of war was going on in the Masters' household. Having been forced to accept the impossibility of keeping Emily and Raymond apart, Kenneth had engaged in what could only be described as heavy-handed diplomacy, laying down all sorts of rules for the young couple to follow – though when Cordelia referred to them as the young couple, she was immediately told not to, because it made it sound as if they were engaged.

'Heaven forbid!' Kenneth added, looking aghast at the prospect.

A limit was set on how often Emily and Raymond were allowed to see one another and they could only go out as part of a group, never on their own.

'Not until you're eighteen,' said Kenneth.

Emily baulked at that until Cordelia pointed out that this wasn't a new rule introduced purely to keep her apart from Raymond.

'Daddy has always said you're not allowed to go out with a boy until you're eighteen. You know that.'

'I s'pose so,' Emily was forced to concede.

'Honestly,' Cordelia told Dot afterwards, 'if I ever get tired of my job on the railways, I'm sure I could have a long and fruitful career as a negotiator for the League of Nations.'

'It seems like Emily and Raymond are courting strong,' Dot commented. 'When our Archie was that way with

Pammy, one of the first things me and Reg did was have her mam and dad round to ours, and it was the same when our Harry got together with Sheila.'

Cordelia groaned. 'I hope you aren't suggesting that we invite the Hancocks round for drinks. Kenneth would blow his stack.'

Dot grinned. 'Didn't you say they're good at cards? You could have them round for one of them fancy bridge evenings. There's no need for polite conversation when you're concentrating on playing your hand!'

Cordelia put on a dignified air. 'I'll pretend you didn't say that. Seriously, Dot, I feel as if I'm walking a tightrope most of the time. I'm the one who does all the peacemaking and finds the compromises. You'd think they'd be glad to compromise and each get a little of their own way, but instead of pleasing both of them, I end up pleasing neither. I seem to be in both their bad books all the time.'

Afterwards, she was sorry she'd said so much. It wasn't that she didn't trust and value Dot, but she didn't want to be disloyal to her family. Besides, she definitely wasn't in Kenneth's bad books the whole time, only when they disagreed over Emily's relationship with Raymond. The rest of the time – well, there was something rather exciting about it, actually.

Cordelia was still thinking hard about her marriage, as well as about Kit. Had the time come to leave him behind, along with all her old sorrows and regrets? Not that she could switch off such long-standing feelings just like that – and nor did she want to, if she was honest. Kit was an enormously important part of her life. Without her heartbreak over him, she would never have married Kenneth. She didn't want to forget Kit. Even if she did want to, she knew she'd never be able to. He was part of who she was. He was part of the way her life had unfolded.

But maybe it was time to set him quietly to one side, so that he was still there but she could at last see past him clearly. Or was that easier said than done? It would mean changing the way she had processed all her thoughts and feelings ever since the end of the last war, when she had learned of Kit's death in combat.

It was a daunting idea. To change the way she thought, the way she viewed the world – was it even possible?

Then she pictured Kenneth with the socially perfect but loveless wife. He had always been a generous husband to her and a wonderful father to Emily. He deserved so much more than he had ever received from her.

She must try to do this for him, and also . . . and also she must do it for herself. She experienced a moment of breathlessness as honest surprise bloomed inside her. Do it for herself? Really?

Yes, really. After years of living a half-life in the shadow of her lost love, she yearned for more. It seemed she was learning through observing her young friends. When she thought of the love between Joan and Bob, Harry and Mabel, and Alison and Joel, envy pulled hard inside her belly. Uncomfortable as the knowledge was, she couldn't ignore it. All these years, she had believed her chance of love had perished in the fields of Flanders, but now she pictured Alison, for whom Paul had been the centre of her world. Alison had survived heartbreak and gone on to love another man.

Cordelia didn't fool herself that her love for Kit had been better or stronger than Alison's for Paul. That would be the height of arrogance. What she asked herself now was, if Alison's heart could heal, could her own?

Could her frozen heart ever thaw?

October brought cloudy days and chilly nights. Cordelia thought of Dot's sons and all those other sons fighting for their country, and she thought of young Raymond whose eighteenth birthday would be here before they knew it. Her heart ached for Emily. She knew what it was to love a man who was away fighting, but at least Emily wouldn't have to tie herself in knots finding ways to send and receive letters in secret.

Raymond's mother invited Emily to tea and so Cordelia invited Raymond. Kenneth wasn't overjoyed but didn't object.

'You won't play the stern Victorian papa, will you?' asked Cordelia.

'Demand details of his prospects, you mean, and ask if his intentions are honourable?'

'*Daddy,*' Emily squealed in horror.

'It's come to something when my wife and daughter don't trust me to behave with due decorum in my own house,' Kenneth said grumpily. 'You have nothing to fear. I'll be charm itself.'

And he was – well, maybe 'charm' was pushing it a bit, but he was pleasant and made Raymond welcome, which in turn sent Cordelia's heart fluttering when she saw the emotion shining in Emily's eyes.

'That wasn't too bad, was it?' Cordelia said lightly to Kenneth after Raymond had left and Emily had run upstairs, presumably to hug her pillow and indulge in daydreams.

'It was fine,' said Kenneth. 'He's a perfectly nice boy. Rather interesting, actually, when he started talking about his stargazing. It's just that—'

Cordelia held up her hand. 'Let's leave it at "perfectly nice boy", shall we? Might we talk about Darley Court instead?'

'What's the state of play?'

'I'm going there on my day off.'

'Shall you take Mrs Grayson with you?' Kenneth asked. 'I'll give you the taxi fare.'

'It's very kind of you to do this for her.'

'She deserves it. I know how fond of her both you and Emily are. I tell you what. Why don't I see if I can reorganise things at work and take the day off as well? Then I can come too – as long as I won't be in the way.'

'That's a lovely idea.'

Cordelia's heart gave a little bump of pleasure. Did this mean Kenneth wanted to be with her?

Don't, Cordelia. Don't do it if you don't mean it.

His words came back to her and the pleasure of the moment fizzled out, leaving her utterly still. Was this truly what she wanted? The chance of a fresh start with her husband?

The trip to Darley Court was a success. Mrs Grayson was delighted to see her old friend Mrs Mitchell.

'The two of you had better help us sort out which rooms will be best suited,' said Miss Brown.

Mrs Grayson looked flustered. 'Oh, I couldn't impose.'

'Well, I could.' Mrs Mitchell tucked her hand through the crook of her friend's elbow, adding with mock severity, 'I'm the housekeeper and what I say goes when it comes to allocating rooms.'

'We'll need the ballroom for the two dances,' said Cordelia. 'We must decorate it as best we can. Lots of bunting and little Union flags. It's a pity we haven't got any little American flags.'

'If we can get together sufficient paper,' said Kenneth, 'we can get the local children to draw some and colour them in.'

'Good idea,' said Miss Brown. 'It would be a worthwhile job for the Guides or the Scouts.'

'There should be flags from all of the Empire,' said Mrs Grayson.

'And all the Allies,' added Cordelia.

'There'll be clearing up to do after the tea dance,' said Mrs Mitchell. 'I'll see to it we have enough help.'

Miss Brown nodded. 'And tell the land girls there won't be any Americans if the clearing up isn't done. They'll have the ballroom sparkling like a new pin in thirty minutes flat.'

'The music is sorted out,' said Cordelia. 'I asked the band that did the War Weapons Week dance last year. The band-leader is an excellent master of ceremonies.'

'So now we just need somewhere for the kiddies' party,' said Mrs Grayson.

'Come this way,' said Mrs Mitchell. 'I thought the board-room,' she added to Miss Brown.

'You have a boardroom?' said Kenneth.

'We began calling it that shortly after the war started,' Miss Brown told him. 'It's a meeting room, really. It used to be a grand old drawing room called the saloon, if you please. Ridiculous name. I never liked it. It sounds like the Wild West. When I offered Darley Court to the powers that be as a centre for meetings and training for Civil Defence, we cleared out all the good furniture, put in the biggest table we could lay our hands on and called it the board-room. The various groups that use Darley Court equipped it with noticeboards and so forth.'

They entered a long room, currently dominated by a table of considerable size that bore testament to the lavish dinner parties that must once have been held in Darley Court, though never, Cordelia was willing to bet, in Miss Brown's time. It was impossible to imagine that lady bothering with such things.

'What do you think?' asked Mrs Mitchell.

Cordelia smiled. 'Masses of space for musical chairs and oranges and lemons.'

They made more plans, then the taxi arrived to convey Cordelia, Kenneth and Mrs Grayson back to Wilton Close.

As the vehicle pulled up outside the house, Kenneth said, 'Don't get out, ladies. Is Mrs Cooper at home?'

'I expect so,' said Mrs Grayson. 'She's not out cleaning this morning and if she's been shopping, she should be back by this time.'

'Good. I'll see if she'd like to come out for lunch with us. Keep the meter running, please, driver.'

Cordelia felt a ripple of pleasure. She hadn't known Kenneth had this in mind. After a minute or two, he escorted Mrs Cooper from the house and she settled in the back seat. Kenneth gave the driver directions and they set off for a little place in West Didsbury that Cordelia remembered well.

'We used to come here regularly before the war,' she told their guests, 'but I haven't been for ages.'

As they were shown to a table and presented with menus, she warmed towards Kenneth. How good of him to give Mrs Cooper and Mrs Grayson this treat. It was clear they were thrilled, all the more so because it had come as a surprise.

During the meal, Kenneth asked Mrs Cooper about the burglaries and Mrs Cooper looked upset.

Cordelia leaned towards her. 'We needn't discuss it if it distresses you.' She frowned at her husband.

'No, indeed,' he agreed. 'I really just raised the subject so I could give you one of these.' He reached into the inside pocket of his jacket and removed a business card from his wallet. 'If the need arises, show the police this card and say you wish your solicitor to be present.'

'Do you think it might come to that?' Cordelia asked.

239

'Just a precaution.'

Cordelia steered the conversation onto smoother ground and they all enjoyed their meal. Afterwards Kenneth paid the bill and asked for a taxi. He and Cordelia returned the ladies to Wilton Close. Cordelia climbed out of the vehicle to say goodbye to her friends, watching as Kenneth escorted them to the front door.

She slid back inside the taxi. Before he joined her, Kenneth poked his head through the front window to address the driver.

'Torbay Road, please. You'd like to call on Joan, wouldn't you?' he asked as he got in. 'I haven't seen the baby yet. I ought to meet him before he starts school.'

Cordelia caught her breath in delight. What a day of surprises this was turning out to be.

Joan was pleased to see them.

'Goodness.' Kenneth addressed Cordelia as he looked at baby Max. 'Doesn't this take you back?'

They chatted for a while, Kenneth fondling Brizo's ears as the dog leaned heavily against his legs.

'He's having a day off from his charity work at the station,' said Joan.

'Would you like us to take him for a walk?' Kenneth offered.

'That's awfully kind,' said Joan. 'He'd love it.'

'We've both got the day off,' Kenneth explained, 'so it's good to have something different to do.'

'He's got a ball,' said Joan, 'but be careful where you throw it, because he doesn't always bring it back.'

They headed for Chorlton Park with the dog trotting eagerly between them.

'It was good of you to treat Mrs Grayson and Mrs Cooper,' said Cordelia, 'though I wish you hadn't brought up the burglaries.'

'I wanted to give Mrs Cooper my card.'

'That was good of you as well.'

'It's worth remembering that if Mrs Cooper's reputation is called into question, then so is ours. You're the one who recommended her to Mr Morgan as his housekeeper.'

'Is that why you gave her your card?' Cordelia asked.

'It's certainly a factor, but the main reason is that she's a decent soul and I don't like to think of her in trouble.'

'Mrs Grayson enjoyed her trip to Darley Court. She looked quite sparkly-eyed.'

'It's good for her to get out and about and to have something different to interest her. It can't have been easy for her to be trapped inside her house all those years.'

How Kenneth's attitude had changed towards the Wilton Close ladies. Cordelia was proud of the way he had not just climbed down but had turned his former disapproval into a warm interest and generosity.

'Are you pleased with how the visit went?' Kenneth asked.

'Things are shaping up,' said Cordelia, 'though there's still a lot to do.'

'I had an idea while we were there.'

'You should have said. What was it?'

'I could dress up as Father Christmas – for the children's party, I hasten to add.'

'Really? You'd do that?'

'Your surprise isn't exactly flattering, you know.'

'It would be wonderful if you would. I wonder where we could get hold of a costume.'

They arrived at Chorlton Park and went in. Most of it was now given over to allotments, but there was still space for playing and dog walking. Kenneth let Brizo off his lead and threw the ball. Joan was right. Brizo knew what he was supposed to do, but didn't always do it, and Kenneth and

Cordelia had to fetch it for him several times. In the end, they discovered that the most effective way to play was to stand some yards apart and throw the ball between them, which Brizo found madly exciting and he chased to and fro after it with a will.

Cordelia laughed at the dog. This was fun.

Fun? When was the last time she'd had fun? And with Kenneth, of all people.

CHAPTER THIRTY

Colette missed her friends more with each day that passed. It was October and they hadn't been round since the night of the raid in August. Two whole months. She had hoped so much that their absence had come about because they needed time to adjust to her return from the dead – but two months! Could Tony be right? Having mourned her, had they moved on and left her behind? Surely not. She refused to believe it. Tony was wrong. He didn't know them like she did.

And yet, if Tony was wrong – where were they? Could they be waiting for her to return the visit? But if so, they wouldn't have waited this long. They would have been concerned when she didn't appear and would have come back to Seymour Grove long since. She knew that – and yet they hadn't come.

It was puzzling and unsettling and she felt horribly alone, which in turn made her feel scared. She had to make herself go to the shops, because supposing she went out and one of her friends had the day off and popped round to see her, but she wasn't there. She couldn't bear to think of missing seeing a friend . . . somebody she trusted.

She didn't trust Tony. She couldn't trust anyone locally. No matter what they thought of her bruised face, they all knew about her 'breakdown', and while they treated her with a mixture of kindness and curiosity, she sensed they were on the lookout for some sign of nerves or instability. Had Tony asked them to keep an eye on her?

She also had to run the gauntlet of the pitying disapproval of the WVS ladies when she saw them out and about. Tony presumably had made her sound weak and feeble, possibly even feeble-minded, when he made her excuses for not joining their ranks. No doubt he had also portrayed himself as the anxious, doting husband and everybody – WVS, Home Guard, fire-watchers, simply everybody – would feel sorry for him while admiring his devotion to his delicate wife.

Sometimes Colette wondered if she would go mad. Life had been hard in the old days before she had faced up to the truth of her marriage. She had crept about and kow-towed, which had been difficult and upsetting, but that had been the person she was in those days. She hadn't had to pretend. It was only when she'd opened her eyes to the way Tony treated her and kept her under control that the pretending had started. She'd had to keep her thoughts and feelings closely hidden so that Tony wouldn't guess what was going on in her head while she planned her escape.

Living that way had been an awful strain, but nothing compared to the strain she lived under now. Back then, Tony had believed things were the same as always, but now there were no secrets between the two of them. The only secret was between Colette and the outside world. She had to keep up appearances according to Tony's requirements or else place Mrs Cooper in danger.

And now – now she had another worry. Her monthly was late. Was it because of the worry – or had Tony and Father got their wish? Was there a baby on the way?

Colette placed the cutlery on the wooden draining board beside the plates and took the used washing-up water out-side to tip it on the vegetable garden. Carrying the bowl back into the scullery, she put in into the sink. *Clink*. A tiny sound reached her ears and she moved the bowl aside. There in the bottom of the big Belfast sink was her wedding ring. It had slipped off and she hadn't noticed.

How appropriate. It wasn't as though she was truly married. The law said she was and the church said she was, but the Betsy part of her knew different. As Betsy, she had known freedom; she had known choice. Above all else, Betsy had lived without fear.

Colette clung to the remaining shreds of Betsy. If Tony ever wore her down to the point where there was no Betsy left, she would become another Bunty.

Bunty Naylor, Father's downtrodden mouse of a wife, who barely raised her head in his presence and hardly spoke other than to agree or apologise.

Looking back, Colette knew that in the old days, she'd been part of the way down the road to becoming a second Bunty. Was that how all the Naylor wives ended up? Tony had learned it from his father. Had Father learned it from Tony's grandfather?

It could have ended up happening to Colette if she hadn't woken up to the truth of her situation.

Betsy or Bunty.

She must hang on to Betsy at all costs.

Colette placed the wedding ring on the window ledge while she dried her hands. She didn't want to put it on again, but she had to. She had to do everything Tony required. It was only after she'd put her foot down about joining the WVS that she'd realised, after his initial anger, it actually suited Tony this way. Not joining kept her stranded at home with no company. Had she joined, she would have had to play along with Tony's story about her. Either outcome would have worked well for Tony.

She slid the ring onto her finger. The strain she was living under had made her lose weight. She hadn't known fingers could lose weight, but hers must have because the ring that had been a perfect fit back in July was now loose. She moved it from the base of her finger to the tip and back again several times.

Ought she to ask Tony to take it back to Millington's to be made smaller? But that would be like saying she wanted to wear it, and she didn't. Oh, she didn't.

The days grew shorter. In the queues outside the shops, women remarked on the darker evenings and the earlier blackouts. Although there were still some days of brilliant sunshine, the whole world felt dark to Colette. Was this how she was to spend the rest of her life? What sort of man employed blackmail to keep his wife tethered to him? Was Tony content with the way things were?

She found herself looking at other women in queues or at church. What were their lives like? Was she the only one living a lie? Or were there heaps of lies going on all around her? And nobody knew about other people's lies, because everyone kept their secrets and pretended that their lives were normal and just as they should be.

She tried to pull herself free from this train of thought, which, however intriguing, was deeply unhelpful, to say the least, because it dragged her down into an inner darkness of fear and despair. What if she ended up having a real breakdown? Nobody would be surprised. To them, it would simply be a relapse. Weren't there special doctors who talked to you when you were sick in the head? But if she talked about being unhappy with Tony, when everyone knew he was the perfect husband, the doctors would think her utterly doolally.

Maybe that was the answer, she thought wryly. Get herself packed off to Prestwich. She shuddered. Some things shouldn't be joked about. Prestwich was where the lunatic asylum was. You sometimes heard that a person had been 'sent to Prestwich'. Sometimes it was an old person with senile decay. Whoever it was, you knew you were never going to see them again.

Colette wasn't entirely sure how she got through the days. In spite of the strain she was under, she felt bored silly a lot of the time. She missed her job dreadfully. She had given up work, of course, when she married Tony, but had worked full-time again since early in 1940 and now she wondered how she was to fill her days, with just a husband and a house to look after.

Was there going to be a baby to take care of too? That would certainly fill her time. Would it also fill her heart and make her life worthwhile? Or would protecting her child from Tony's ways make the strain unbearable?

If she had a son, would he learn from watching his father that women were to be kept in their place?

She desperately didn't want to be pregnant – and what did that say about her? What kind of woman didn't long for a baby?

She woke up each morning in a state of dread lest nausea overwhelmed her. If she suffered from morning sickness, her condition would be impossible to keep from Tony. He would be cock-a-hoop.

Or maybe she wasn't pregnant. Maybe it was stress interfering with her body's workings. She wished she knew one way or the other.

She tried to shake off her thoughts as she got the dinner ready. When Tony came home, she removed her apron before taking her place at the table. She waited a moment, her knife and fork hovering above her plate, while she checked whether Tony approved of the meal. He gave a nod of appreciation and Colette was relieved, but then she felt annoyed. Waiting for approval was a Bunty sort of thing to

247

do. But Colette had done it every day before she'd run away and now she had slid back into the habit. When the atmosphere in the house depended entirely upon whether one person was pleased or displeased, you couldn't help holding your breath to see which way things would go.

Tony laid down his knife and fork.

'Where's your wedding ring?'

Colette stared at her ring finger. Her heart thudded. Her finger was bare. She had put the ring on after it fell off in the sink. Since then, it had come off again. When? She hadn't heard it fall. It could be anywhere. It might not even be in the house. It could be lying in the sawdust on the floor of the butcher's shop.

She opened her mouth to say so, but Tony spoke first.

'You've taken it off.'

'No, I haven't. I lost it.'

'How convenient. A show of defiance, more like.'

'No, honestly, Tony—'

'*No, honestly, Tony.*' He put on a high-pitched, whiny voice, mocking her. But it wasn't just mocking. It was threatening too. 'No, honestly, Tony, *what*?'

She couldn't swallow as fear coursed through her, the same way it had always done. This was the point where she was meant to grovel. Well, she wasn't going to. Resolution pushed her old fears aside.

Betsy or Bunty.

Betsy every time.

'You're right. I did take it off.'

'You did what?'

'You heard.'

Placing his hands on the edge of the table, Tony shoved his chair back and came to his feet. He marched round the table and towered over her. Colette gazed up at him, refusing to back down.

Tony's lip curled and his nostrils flared. Colette knew she was the only one who ever saw this expression on his face. To everyone else, he was always affable. He was nice-looking when he was in a good temper. She was the only one who knew what he looked like angry.

'Well, you can jolly well put it on again,' Tony said softly.

Betsy or Bunty.

'No, I can't. I dropped it down the drain. When I say "dropped", I mean on purpose, not by accident.'

Tony drew back his fist. Colette's instinct was to flinch, but a moment later she drew herself up straight. She wouldn't cower.

One blow. She could cope with one blow. This time to-morrow, she would be parading it around the shops.

But Tony didn't stop at one.

CHAPTER THIRTY-ONE

Colette opened her eyes. No – just one eye. The other eyelid flickered, or tried to. She ached all over. Did that make it sound as if she ached only on the outside? She ached on the inside as well. There was a dark pain down one side of her ribcage. Why single out that one in particular? Maybe because it was a specific sharp pain and the rest were dull aches that throbbed.

'Colette? Colette, darling, can you hear me?'

Tony. Tony sounding quiet and loving and full of concern.

Colette's one good eye saw a white . . . sheet? For a moment it was like looking at a sheet hanging on a washing line. Then she realised it was a curtain on a rail that went . . . that went around the bed where she was lying. Her gaze followed it all the way round until her line of vision was interrupted by Tony, looking dreadful. Was this how he had looked when he'd first believed her to be dead?

His face, always narrow, was haggard, his eye sockets hollowed out. His hair, usually neat, was messy, as if he had raked his fingers through it. He was seated beside her, leaning forwards.

'Colette? Darling?'

His voice cracked. Colette focused her single eye on him. His eyes pleaded with her and she looked away. Why were they letting him sit beside her? Shouldn't he be in a cell at the police station?

Tony's chair scraped lightly on the floor as he stood up, the white curtain whispering as he went through it. Colette breathed in and out. She had a cracking headache.

The curtain parted again, a *whisk* this time instead of a whisper, and a nurse appeared.

'Your husband says you've woken up. How are you feeling, Mrs Naylor?'

She picked up Colette's wrist and took her pulse. Colette wanted to ask, 'What's he doing here?' but it seemed rude to interrupt the nurse while she was counting. The nurse returned Colette's hand to the bed and smiled down at her. It was a restrained, professional sort of smile.

'I'll fetch Sister.'

The moment she was gone, Tony dropped into the chair and leaned forwards, his gaze full of pain and urgency.

'Darling, I'm so sorry. I never meant – I never intended . . .' He shook his head, eyebrows gathering. 'Can you ever forgive me? Look at you. Look what I've done.' He swallowed hard. 'This is appalling. I'm so dreadfully ashamed. I'd never have believed it of myself. Please, please say you'll let me make it up to you. I swear I'll spend the rest of my life making it up to you and I'll never, ever raise a hand to you again.'

'That'll do for now, Mr Naylor.' A middle-aged nurse wearing a different cap swept into the cubicle. 'Save the rest of your apologies for later. Goodness knows, Mrs Naylor deserves them. Wait outside for now, please.'

'Outside the curtain?' Tony asked, hopeful and humble.

'Outside the ward, please. Mrs Naylor needs attention. Doctor will want to examine her and we can't have you here for that, can we?'

Tony stood and leaned over Colette. 'I'll be just outside, darling, and I'll come back in as soon as Sister allows me.'

He bent closer and Colette turned her head away before he could kiss her. Tony cleared his throat and shifted awkwardly.

'I suppose I deserved that. Poor darling.' Tony addressed the sister. 'Take care of her, won't you?'

The curtain swished again as he left and Colette listened to his footsteps fading away. She fixed her gaze on Sister. Now that Tony was gone, Sister would help her. Sister would—

'Poor chap,' said Sister. 'He deserves to suffer, of course, but I know remorse when I see it. Your husband, Mrs Naylor, spent most of yesterday in my office in floods of tears. Not very manly, I know, but, well, impressive in its own way. I think we can safely say there's a husband who's learned his lesson.'

After the doctor examined her, he told Colette, 'Rest now. Nurse will tidy your bedclothes while I go and speak to your husband.'

'He's the one who did this to me,' Colette objected.

'I apologise, Doctor,' said Sister. She raised her eyebrows at Colette. 'You shouldn't answer back when Doctor speaks to you. It's most inappropriate.'

'That's all right, Sister,' said the doctor. 'Circumstances, and all that. Mrs Naylor, I am aware of how you came by your injuries. Rest assured, I've already had words with Mr Naylor. We can't have behaviour of this sort. One expects a certain amount of it from the lower orders, but it's not acceptable in your husband's rank in life. Carrying on like the great unwashed won't be tolerated, and I jolly well told him so.'

Colette stared from her good eye in disbelief. Carrying on like the great unwashed – was that how wife-battering was viewed?

'Not to worry, Mrs Naylor,' the doctor went on kindly. 'I know for a fact that Mr Naylor has seen the error of his ways. He won't hit you again. I've never seen a man more full of remorse. It was rather pleasing, actually,' he added, apparently taking the credit for Tony's anguish. 'You need have no fears for the future.'

Colette wanted to throttle him. The doctor could see for himself what Tony had done, yet Tony's extravagant sorrow seemed to make it all right.

'I'll inform Mr Naylor of the extent of your injuries,' said the doctor.

'Tell me,' said Colette. 'Please,' she added when Sister gave her a look.

'Your job is to rest and get better, Mrs Naylor,' said the doctor and the nurse held the curtain aside for him to pass through on his lordly way.

Sister remained behind for long enough to order the nurse to draw back the curtains, then she too disappeared. As the curtains swooshed aside, Colette realised she was in a ward full of women who all looked at her with great interest. Colette felt a jolt of surprise. Those curtains had made her feel separate and private. Now she knew that every word had been overheard by all these strangers, who must have been dying for the curtains to be drawn back so they could see for themselves the extent of the damage that had been inflicted by the now remorseful husband whose station in life meant he should have known better.

Colette pressed herself into the mattress, her skin crawling with humiliation. This was different to choosing to walk around the shops in Seymour Grove. That had made her feel strong and resourceful. She didn't feel strong now. She felt vulnerable and ill. Shocked as well. Shocked to the core that Sister and the doctor both seemed to have accepted Tony's shamefaced assurances that he would never assault her again.

Tony appeared and sat beside the bed.

'I've been given five minutes. Sister says that after this I have to keep to visiting times, the same as everyone else. It's good news, darling.' Tony tried to take her hand, but Colette slipped it under the covers. 'You're going to be fine. As bad as it looks, the damage is superficial – well, aside from your ribs.' His cheeks burned. 'You . . . you bruised your ribs.'

'No,' said Colette, her voice low and insistent. '*I* didn't bruise them. *You* did.'

'I know, I know. There's no need to rub it in.' Tony shifted uncomfortably, glancing around the ward beneath lowered eyelids. 'We don't want to tell everyone our business.'

'I want you to leave,' said Colette. 'Now, please.'

'Darling, I know I hurt you and I bitterly regret it. I was a brute, but that wasn't the real me. You know that. You know I'd never hit you.'

'You did hit me.'

'But I didn't mean to. I told you. That wasn't the real me.'

'I'm tired,' said Colette.

'Of course you are, poor little love.' Tony looked round as the nurse appeared at the foot of Colette's bed. 'Come to shoo me away, have you?' He stood up, smiling down at Colette. 'Get your beauty sleep, my darling. Everything's going to be all right, I promise.'

Fury boiled up inside Colette to the point where she couldn't distinguish between the pain and the anger. How dare Tony say everything was going to be all right?

But her anger drained away when she remembered Sister's attitude and what the doctor had said. They had accepted Tony's apologies. Well, she hadn't and she never would.

Presently, the nurse returned and pulled the curtains around the bed once more, but Colette wasn't fooled this time. It wasn't real privacy, just an illusion.

'There's a policeman to see you, Mrs Naylor, if you feel up to it.'

Colette's whole body weakened in pure relief. A policeman! Now she would make herself heard. She struggled to sit up, but the pain in her ribs prevented it.

A policeman appeared at her bedside. He kept his head bent over his notebook as if he didn't want to look at her injured face.

'Can you confirm your name and address, please? Mrs Anthony Naylor?'

'Colette Naylor.'

'Wife of Mr Anthony Naylor?'

'Yes.'

On her wedding day, her mother had said with tearful pride, 'Mrs Anthony Naylor. You'll never have to worry about anything ever again.'

'Can you describe what happened, in your own words?'

'My husband lost his temper.' Her voice was thin and calm, but her heart thumped. 'He attacked me. I thought he would hit me once, but he . . . carried on. He didn't stop. When I fell to the floor, he kicked me. He bruised my ribs.'

'I have a list of your injuries. There's no need for you to go into detail.'

'It's not the first time,' said Colette.

'Makes a habit of it, does he?'

'Well – no. This was the second time.'

'Was it this bad the first time?'

'No. Nothing like as bad.'

The policeman nodded. 'Good. That fits in with what Mr Naylor told me.'

'You've already spoken to him? Before you came to me?' Alarm bells rang in Colette's head.

'To his credit, he insisted on speaking to me the moment I appeared. Very cut up, he is. It's obvious he's appalled by his own actions. And the doctor has assured me you'll make a full recovery.'

'You mean . . . that's all there is to it?' Colette's ribs tightened and she couldn't breathe. She felt light-headed. 'Aren't you . . . aren't the police going to do anything?'

'We prefer not to interfere between man and wife. Domestic disputes aren't for the police to oversee. Our job is to catch criminals, not to sort out marital problems.'

Colette's eyes filled with tears. Her good eye went blurry. Her swollen eye, with tears trapped inside it, felt as if it might burst.

The policeman coughed. 'There now, Mrs Naylor. It's a bad business, but your husband couldn't be more ashamed of himself. He swears he'll never lay a finger on you again.'

Tony wouldn't let Colette have visitors. It beggared belief. He was the one whose brutality had put her in hospital, yet he, as her husband, could decree who was and was not allowed through the ward doors to see her. Not that many people knew where she was.

'The neighbours know, of course,' said Tony. 'They saw the ambulance. I – I thought it best to say you fell down-stairs. Better that way.'

'Better for you,' said Colette.

'Better for both of us, darling,' Tony said tenderly. 'What happened was deeply regrettable and it's not the kind of thing you want people knowing about. They might get the wrong idea.'

'The wrong idea?' Colette said softly.

A dull flush invaded Tony's cheeks, but he said stoutly, 'Yes – the wrong idea. It's never going to happen again, so it would be damaging for others to know.'

'Have you told your parents?'

'They'd like to come and see you, obviously, but I told them it would be better to wait until you're home again.'

'And the bruises have faded,' Colette added.

'Be reasonable, darling.'

Colette said nothing. She had asked the nurses not to let Tony in at visiting time, but nobody had listened to her, so she was forced to lie there while he wove his falsehoods.

Tony talked about her going home, but of one thing Colette was certain. She would never live with him again. No matter what it took, she wasn't going to the end-of-terrace in Seymour Grove.

'Do my friends know where I am?' she asked. If she hadn't been so desperate to see them, she might not have spoken to Tony at all.

'Of course they do. I told you. I went to Wilton Close specially. They're all very sorry and concerned.'

'About me falling downstairs.'

Tony sighed and put on a puppy-dog expression. 'Now then, darling, please don't be difficult.'

Colette glanced away. She knew he was lying and she couldn't afford for him to read it in her face. He hadn't been anywhere near Wilton Close. If he had, her friends would have queued up outside the ward at visiting time twice a day every day.

She knew now that he had somehow kept them from her all along. She couldn't imagine how he'd managed it, but there was no doubt in her mind. It showed how clever he was. Her friends had strong characters; they were capable and independent – far stronger and more independent than

257

she'd ever been. Yet Tony had prevented them from seeing her. He wasn't just clever. He was ruthless.

How could she get a message to them? She couldn't trust Sister or the nurses because Tony had charmed them and they believed in his contrition. He made a point of speaking to them every visiting time, to check on her progress and thank them for looking after her.

Then the hospital's lady almoner came to see her, sitting beside Colette's bed with a clipboard. Colette noted the sharp glance the lady almoner gave her face before she smoothed her expression.

'I believe you'll soon be ready to leave us, Mrs Naylor. Part of my role is to ensure you'll receive the correct care when you go home. Mr Naylor tells me he has received offers of help from the neighbours and that your mother-in-law will come round every day. Your father-in-law says she can move in with you, if necessary.' The lady almoner smiled. 'I wish I had more patients like you.'

Colette's heartbeat raced, the sound filling her ears. She couldn't go home, she couldn't, but nor could she walk out of hospital wearing her nightclothes, which at present looked like the only other possibility.

The lady almoner made to stand up.

'Would you do something for me?' Colette asked quickly.

The lady almoner settled down again. 'If I can.' She looked sympathetic, but something in her eyes said that she had other patients to get to.

'Please could you contact somebody for me?'

'That's for your husband to do, Mrs Naylor.'

'He – he won't.' Making sure she sounded polite and quiet and, God help her, sympathetic towards Tony, Colette went on, 'He's so protective of me, you see, and he's been so good about sorting out the help for when I go home, but what I really want is to see my friend, only my husband won't want me to see her, because . . .' and here she lowered her voice '. . . because he's ashamed of . . .' She waved a hand, indicating her face. 'Could you please drop her a line to say where I am? I'd be very grateful.'

'Well . . .'

'She is the Honourable Persephone Trehearn-Hobbs and she lives at Darley Court.' Seeing that the lady almoner looked impressed, Colette added, 'Her father is something big in the War Office. I know she'd be glad to hear from you.'

'Very well,' said the lady almoner.

'Today – please,' Colette pressed.

'It depends if there's time. I shan't provide any details, naturally. I'll just say you're here.'

Colette had to bite her lip so as not to beam her head off. If anybody could dash aside Tony's rules and persuade the nurses to let her in, that person was Persephone. Oh, please let her come here soon.

CHAPTER THIRTY-TWO

Mabel listened in horror, feeling chilled right to the centre of her being. She had thought that Colette's return from the dead was the biggest surprise of her life, but this was even harder to take in.

Persephone, her lovely violet eyes troubled in a way Mabel had never witnessed before, sat on the sofa, angled towards Mrs Cooper, holding her hand.

'Colette said I should ask you. She said you'd confirm everything.'

Mrs Cooper's thin shoulders sagged in despair. 'It's true. It's all true. I helped her to escape. She was desperate. To say she was under Tony's thumb doesn't give any idea of how bad it was. He controlled her every waking moment.'

'Why did she never say anything?' asked Mabel. 'How could she have been so unhappy and none of us noticed? How is that possible?'

'It's possible, believe me,' said Mrs Grayson. 'Situations develop slowly. Then one day you wake up and realise you're trapped in the middle of something bad and it's too late to do anything about it.'

Mabel nodded slowly. Mrs Grayson's personal trouble had its roots in the loss of her baby and the lack of support from Mr Grayson and his parents. What had started as grief and loneliness had escalated into fear of leaving the house. Mabel felt a stab of shame. When she'd first met Mrs Grayson, she had thought her bonkers. Had she – had all of them – made a comparable mistake with Colette?

'We just thought Tony was overprotective,' she said wonderingly. 'I always thought how lucky Colette was to have such a loving husband.'

'We all thought that,' said Persephone.

'Me an' all,' said Mrs Cooper, 'until I found out different.' A shudder passed through her. Her face was sickly pale. 'I've been so worried ever since she came back. I've not known what to think. I knew she'd never have chosen to come back. All that nonsense about her writing to Tony and asking him to fetch her made my blood boil because I knew it was all lies, but there was nowt I could do. I was so frightened and worried for her. All I wanted was to catch the first bus to Seymour Grove and give her a hug, but it was safer to wait for her to come here.'

'Only she never did,' said Mabel.

'It was agony listening to the rest of you talking about Tony being overprotective when I knew what he was really like. Then, after you girls went round to see Colette, Tony popped in here. Do you remember? He went on about Colette needing peace and quiet – and then he somehow twisted the conversation so that it was about fraud and false identities and I knew that was a warning to me to keep my mouth shut or he'd report me to the police. What I did was against the law, you see. I gave my Lizzie's identity papers to another person and that's a crime.'

Mrs Grayson pressed her fingers to her mouth. Her hand was shaking as she removed it, letting it fall into her lap. 'Oh my goodness,' she whispered. 'That evening when Tony came here, I said . . . I said that fraudsters deserved to be hanged. Oh, my dear Mrs Cooper, I had no idea.'

'I know you didn't,' said Mrs Cooper.

'What must you have thought?' said Mrs Grayson.

'If you must know, I thought what a rogue Tony was,' said Mrs Cooper. 'Colette used to tell me how clever he was and how manipulative, and there I was on the receiving end of it. I went weak all over and I had to hold my breath to stop it bursting out of my body.' She closed her eyes for a moment and shook her head.

'Everything is out in the open now,' Persephone said comfortingly, 'and that's what matters. Normally, we'd all get together and talk about it, but there isn't time for that. Colette will be discharged soon and she's desperate not to be sent home. She needs somewhere to go.'

'She can come here – can't she?' Mabel said at once.

'No,' said Persephone. 'This is the one place she specifically said she couldn't come to. She said it would make things difficult for Mrs Cooper.'

'Tony would report her to the police,' said Mrs Grayson. 'Even if he didn't, she can't be involved in the break-up of a marriage. The Morgans wouldn't like it – and our girls' parents would have something to say too.'

Mabel thought about it. 'Mumsy and Pops would be shocked. Ending a marriage is a serious matter, but surely you have to take the reasons into account before you pass judgement.'

'Unfortunately,' said Mrs Grayson, 'there are far too many people who aren't interested in the reasons, but it doesn't stop them passing judgement. That was my experience. I was the innocent party when my husband left me, but there were those who held me to blame.'

'But it wasn't your fault,' said Mabel.

'I descended into a terrible depression. You wouldn't have to go far to find folk who'd say it was no wonder Benjy looked elsewhere. Anyroad, we're meant to be talking about Colette.'

'I'll ask Miss Brown if she can come to Darley Court,' said Persephone. 'I'm sure she'll say yes. Colette needs a breathing space and it's probably the safest place. If anywhere else took her in, Tony might come banging on the door, but it would take some gumption to march up to Darley Court.'

Mrs Cooper pressed her hand to her chest. 'My heart is going nineteen to the dozen.'

'Of course it is,' Persephone said solicitously. 'Everyone knows how much you love Colette.'

'We all love her,' said Mabel, 'and we want to do our best for her. I'm still struggling to take it in. I always thought she was happy.'

'We all believed they were the perfect couple,' said Mrs Grayson. 'It just goes to show. You never know what really goes on in someone else's marriage.'

'It wasn't easy for me to get into the ward to see Colette,' said Persephone. 'The nurse said she's not allowed visitors.'

Mrs Cooper's breath caught in a gasp. 'Are her injuries very bad?'

'It's not that,' Persephone quickly reassured her. 'Apparently, Tony said the staff shouldn't allow anyone in.'

'And what did the staff say to that?' Mabel asked indignantly.

'He said he wanted her to have complete rest, so she'd get better sooner. If anything, the nurses were touched that he cared so much. They certainly didn't think it necessary to ask a doctor to overrule him.'

'How did you get past them?' asked Mrs Grayson.

'I didn't, to start with. I found the lady almoner and she kindly came with me to the ward – after I'd dropped a few names. It was lucky for me Tony wasn't there. Colette is due to be discharged the day after tomorrow, so tomorrow we need to take her to Darley Court.' Persephone looked at Mabel. 'What hours are you working?'

'It's Mabel's day off,' said Mrs Grayson.

'And Alison's,' said Mrs Cooper.

'Jolly good,' said Persephone. 'The two of you will have to fetch her during afternoon visiting. I wouldn't be able to do it until the evening and that would be trickier because Colette says Tony is always there for the whole evening session, but in the afternoons it depends on his work. With luck, he won't appear tomorrow afternoon – but even if he does, even if he has every doctor in the hospital to back him up, you have to save Colette.'

Mabel and Alison loitered at the top of the staircase, their gazes shifting between the stairs and the people, all but one of whom were women, grouped outside the ward doors.

'We need more visitors,' said Alison.

'There's still time for more to come,' said Mabel. She was jumpy with nerves. Everything was riding on this.

The plan was as straightforward as they could make it. They had a taxi waiting outside and they'd tipped the driver lavishly to make sure he stayed put. Alison had a coat draped over her arm and she carried a bag containing clothes and a headscarf. When the doors opened, she was to walk into the ward along with everyone else, leaving Mabel outside to keep watch at the top of the public staircase.

Inside the ward, Alison was to drop something as she passed Colette's bed so that she could give quick instructions to her. Then she would keep walking and disappear into the lavatory at the far end of the ward that the patients who weren't bed-bound were permitted to use. There, Colette would join her to get dressed. Wearing the coat and headscarf, keeping her head down, Colette was to walk out of the ward.

There had been a long discussion last night as to whether Alison should hang back and create a diversion by bumping into something and making a fuss to draw attention her way while Colette left, but in the end it had been decided that the two of them leaving quickly and quietly together would be best.

Their plan depended on two things – a good number of visitors and Tony's absence.

As two o'clock drew closer, more visitors came up the stairs, some heading towards Colette's ward, others going in the opposite direction. Just before the clock struck the hour, Alison nodded to Mabel, who whispered 'Good luck,' and Alison went to insert herself into the waiting group of visitors.

Then the doors opened and everyone went in, the doors shutting behind them. Below her on the stairs, Mabel heard footsteps. Her heart beat hard as she went down a short way, but the newcomer was a man with his mackintosh flapping open. He ran past Mabel, who returned to the top of the stairs, where she could also see the ward doors. If Alison emerged and Mabel wasn't there, that meant Tony had arrived and Alison would shunt Colette through a side door and leave the building via the fire exit.

More footsteps – a doctor appeared on the half landing, then a couple of porters in brown overall coats. How long did it take to throw on a few clothes? Footsteps – someone running up the stairs. Mabel looked over the bannister rail and felt a chill of alarm. Tony was heading for the half landing.

She ran down and got there first.

'Tony! Fancy seeing you here. Is there a problem with the hospital's water supply?'

Was she overdoing it?

'Remember,' Persephone had said yesterday evening. 'Tony thinks we don't know Colette's in hospital. He'll be more scared by seeing you than you'll be of seeing him.'

'No,' said Tony. 'I'm here visiting.'

'Not your mum or dad, I hope,' said Mabel. 'Sorry. I don't mean to be nosy. How's Colette? We've all kept our distance, but we think about her all the time. Is she recovering?'

'Yes – thanks for asking. She's doing well, but I'd like to keep things quiet for her for a while yet. It's important after the kind of problems she's had.'

'Please tell her I asked after her.'

'I will.'

Liar, thought Mabel. 'And how are you coping? It can't be easy for you. You've gone from the joy of getting her back to dealing with these worries.'

'That's beside the point. I'd do anything for Colette.'

'I know you would.' Mabel hated herself for flattering him. 'We've always said what an attentive husband you are.'

'What brings you here?' Tony asked.

'My friend works here—' She started to elaborate, but Tony broke in.

'Sorry, but I need to get on.'

'And I'm keeping you talking. You won't forget to tell Colette I said hello?'

But she was speaking to Tony's back. Praying that she had provided Alison and Colette with sufficient time, Mabel ran downstairs to the front entrance. Outside, she found her friends. There was a yellowing bruise on one side of Colette's face.

'The taxi's gone,' said Alison. 'He swore he'd wait.'

'Here comes another,' said Mabel, waving it down. When it pulled in, she recognised the driver.

'A bobby said I couldn't wait here,' he said, 'so I've been driving round the block. Hop in, ladies.'

Alison ran round to get in the other side while Mabel hovered behind Colette as she edged into the middle of the seat. Just as Mabel was about to follow, a hand grabbed her arm and yanked her backwards.

'Colette! What are you doing? Get out of there.'

Tony reached in and tried to pull Colette, who cried out. Mabel caught hold of Tony's arm and tried to haul him away.

'Here! What's going on?' demanded the driver.

'That's my wife in there,' said Tony, 'and you're about to take part in a kidnapping.'

'It isn't kidnap,' said Colette. 'It's what I want.'

'Darling – please,' said Tony. 'We can talk about this. I've always taken care of you. Don't spoil things now. You know how much I love you.'

Summoning all her strength, Mabel launched herself at Tony, taking him by surprise as she delivered an enormous shove that sent him staggering sideways. Before he could right himself, Mabel slammed the door shut. She just about caught Alison's yell of 'Drive!' and Colette's 'Please' before the taxi pulled away.

She turned to face Tony. He stared at the disappearing vehicle, then glared at her.

'You can't take a wife away from her husband. Colette's rightful place is with me.'

'Not any longer,' Mabel retorted.

'You think you're so clever.'

'No, actually I think you're the clever one,' said Mabel. 'You had all of us fooled.'

Tony took a step towards her, an ugly look in his eyes.

Mabel stood tall. 'Go on, Tony. Do to me what you did to Colette. I dare you.'

CHAPTER THIRTY-THREE

Normally, when Cordelia and Dot got together on their own in the buffet, they were never stuck for what to say, but today they sat and looked at one another. There was bleakness in Dot's eyes and Cordelia recognised the shock and above all the sadness she herself was feeling.

'I don't know where to begin,' said Dot. 'To think Tony had us all fooled for such a long time.'

'His protectiveness seemed so plausible,' said Cordelia, 'and Colette never gave any indication.'

'Folk don't, though, do they?' said Dot. 'They show you what they want you to see.'

Cordelia's chin dropped for a moment. That remark had hit close to home. Dot had unknowingly described Cordelia's whole adult life.

'It's all about appearances,' Dot went on, 'and not washing your dirty linen in public.' She shook her head. 'If you'd asked me, I'd have said Colette had the cleanest linen of anyone.'

'We all thought so,' said Cordelia. 'We all thought Tony the perfect husband. Too protective, of course, but we took that as a sign of how he worshipped her.'

'I wonder what will happen next. Leaving your husband is one heck of a thing to do.'

'It shows how bad things must have been,' said Cordelia. 'Colette's a serious girl and she's a thinker. She's not the sort to do something unless she really means it. Look how much planning went into her running away and starting a new life. It wasn't exactly spur of the moment.'

'That's another thing,' said Dot. 'Mrs Cooper knew ever since the summer of last year and she never breathed a word. She must have been worried sick.'

'Evidently it was on the evening of the War Weapons Week dance that she found out,' said Cordelia. 'That was, as you say, one heck of an evening. It was when Paul met that new girl and ended up leaving Alison, and now it turns out it was also when Mrs Cooper glimpsed the real Tony.'

Dot lifted her shoulders and shook them in a theatrical shudder. 'It doesn't bear thinking about. That poor girl – and we all thought she was so happy. I feel like I've said them words a hundred times in the past day or two.'

'I think we all have. It's hard to believe.'

'You never know what goes on in other folks' marriages,' said Dot. 'That's the truth of it. It's made me look at my own, I don't mind telling you. It's not the ideal marriage in many ways. I learned early on that life with Reg wouldn't be all hearts and flowers, but I always treat him with the respect he deserves as the head of the household.'

'Does he show you similar respect?'

'Since you mention it, no, but that's no reason for me not to.'

Cordelia nodded. That fitted in with what she knew of Reg. From odd things Dot had said, Cordelia had formed the impression that Reg Green was a pretty graceless and unsupportive husband.

'But the point is,' said Dot, 'that he's always been a good provider and no one in the family has any reason to be scared of him. There's a lot to be said for that.'

Frankly, not being scared of her husband was something that Cordelia had always taken so completely for granted that she had never even thought of it before, but she thought of it now and wondered how many wives lived in fear of their husband's temper. How many wives looked on the war as a time of respite from having to live under the same roof as an abusive man? It turned her cold to think of it. She pictured the elegant, well-dressed ladies who had been her acquaintances ever since she got married. Did any of them have reason to be afraid? The trouble was, it was impossible to tell.

Cordelia had been brought up to keep her hands to herself, but now she placed her palm gently over Dot's hand as she said quietly, 'I appreciate the confidence you showed in me by speaking openly about your marriage. I'd like to show similar confidence in you by admitting that recently I have been looking for ways to become a better wife.'

Dot looked surprised. 'A better wife? You? You're kidding.'

'I'm not. This isn't an easy thing to admit, and you're the only one I can say it to, but . . . I know I look like the perfect wife. I always have. I've dressed the part, organised the social events, made friends with the right people. But . . . well . . .' She seemed to run out of words.

'Eh, love,' said Dot.

'I'm sorry. I'm not making much sense.'

'It's all this talk of secrets and keeping up appearances. It's made us all look inwards. It's made us look at the women around us with new eyes an' all. If it's made you think about yourself, that's only natural.'

'You're a wise woman, Dot Green.'

'I've been called worse things,' Dot answered with a smile. 'You might not have explained yourself clearly to me about what you mean, but do you understand in your own head what you're on about?'

It was Cordelia's turn to smile. 'More or less.'

'That's all that matters.'

Afterwards Cordelia thought of Dot treating Reg with the respect he was entitled to as head of the family. Dot never said it in so many words, and Cordelia wouldn't have dreamed of asking, but did Dot treat Reg with respect even though she didn't necessarily feel respect for him? If so, was it a form of behaviour that held their marriage and their family together?

Cordelia didn't love Kenneth, but what would happen if she treated him as if she did? Would it enrich her life? Would it lead to real closeness . . . to more fun?

Could she build a new relationship out of that?

Tomorrow, Saturday, would be the last day of October. Mabel still felt churned up over what had happened to Colette. She only had to picture rescuing her from hospital and standing up to Tony in the street for her pulse to pick up speed.

That Friday evening, the friends met in the buffet to make arrangements to go to Darley Court on Saturday afternoon to visit Colette. Not everyone could go. Margaret would be working, as would Persephone.

'We could sort out a different arrangement,' said Mabel.

Margaret shook her head. 'You know how hard it is for all of us to manage something at the same time. I'll go on Sunday.'

'I live there, so don't worry about including me,' Persephone added.

'Joan is taking Max to meet Colette on Saturday morning,' said Dot.

'Mrs Grayson will be at home cooking all day,' said Mabel. 'There's a sickness bug among some of the WVS ladies, which means production has fallen behind and Mrs Grayson has taken on extra work, so she can't come with us, but Mrs Cooper will.'

'It'll be quite a reunion, her and Colette seeing one another again,' said Alison.

'It's best if I go to Darley Court at a different time,' said Cordelia.

The others looked at her and voices asked, 'Why?'

Cordelia looked from Mabel to Margaret and Alison. 'You may have noticed that I haven't been to Wilton Close to perform my monthly check.'

'I hadn't noticed,' said Alison, 'but what of it?'

'I've written to the Morgans to apologise and say I'm too busy. If I stay away, I can pretend not to be aware that Mrs Cooper is under suspicion.'

'But she's innocent,' said Margaret.

'Of course she is,' said Cordelia. 'But I have an obligation to the Morgans. Strictly speaking, I ought to tell them – and then Mr Morgan would probably ask me to look for another housekeeper, which is the last thing any of us wants.'

'What about being innocent until proven guilty?' Alison demanded.

'Come on, lass,' said Dot. 'Think about it. Would you want a suspected thief living under your mam and dad's roof?'

'It's for the best if I don't see Mrs Cooper at present,' said Cordelia.

'Does she know?' asked Mabel.

'No, and there's no reason to inform her. It would only make her feel worse.'

Alison blew out a breath. 'I don't know about Mrs Cooper feeling worse, but this has certainly made me feel worse.'

'Don't turn it into a drama, chick,' Dot advised. 'We don't want Mrs Cooper to realise.' She smiled around the table. 'Are we all set for tomorrow, then?'

Mabel counted off on her fingers. 'There's going to be you, me, Alison and Mrs Cooper. Shall we meet you there, Dot?'

'Nay, love. I'll come over to Wilton Close and we'll go together.' Dot started gathering her things. 'I'll love you and leave you. I want to get home and listen to the news on the wireless and find out what that German Afrika Korps is up to.'

She spoke lightly, but no one was fooled. Dot was worried sick about her boys.

'From the recent reports,' said Margaret, 'it sounds as if General Montgomery knows what to do.'

'Aye, chick, let's hope so.'

The meeting broke up on an unsettled note. As they were leaving the buffet, Mabel glanced across at Mrs Jessop. Oh, how she would love to ask if letters in support of Miss Emery were arriving, but they had all agreed that they mustn't do that.

When Mabel got home, she gave Mrs Cooper a hug.

'None of us can stop thinking about Colette, but that doesn't mean we've forgotten your troubles.'

'I know, chuck.'

Mrs Cooper smiled but her eyes looked strained. It was easy to see how deep her anxiety ran. Mabel had noticed her occasionally fiddling with her watch strap or closing her eyes as if making herself remain calm. Even her quiet assertions of innocence sounded shaky and worried rather than defiant.

'I'll feel better tomorrow,' she said, 'after I've seen Colette.'

CHAPTER THIRTY-FOUR

On Saturday afternoon, Mrs Wadden arrived to help Mrs Grayson in the kitchen. Mabel had never observed it before, but was there a resemblance between Mrs Wadden and Mrs Cooper? Not that they looked like sisters or anything like that. It wasn't that kind of resemblance. But they were both skinny women with work-worn hands.

Then something else struck Mabel and she felt an unpleasant jolt in the pit of her stomach. It wasn't their thinness that made them similar. It was the worried look in their eyes; it was the way their heads drooped when they thought you weren't looking. And there was something that made it worse too. Mabel didn't know about Mrs Wadden, but she knew for a fact that Mrs Cooper hadn't been this way before. It was the burden of being under suspicion that was weighing her down.

The doorbell rang again and it was Dot.

'Is that the time already?' Mabel asked, surprised.

'Nay, chick. I've come early. I reckon me and thee owe Mrs Wadden an apology for getting the police sent round to her house.'

'She doesn't know it was us.'

'Maybe she deserves to know. She's probably been worried sick it was one of the neighbours.'

'I know from what Louise said that they were shamed by it.'

'There you are, then,' said Dot. 'You never know. She might end up telling us who's hitting Louise.'

Mabel nodded. 'I feel wretched for not realising Colette needed help. I want to help Louise if I can.'

They entered the kitchen, which was filled with the sweet tang of blackberries and chopped apples. Mabel introduced Dot and Mrs Wadden to one another.

'What are you making?' Dot peered into a pan. 'Is that rhubarb?'

'It makes the blackberry jam go further,' said Mrs Grayson, 'and we'll use beetroot to bulk up the crab-apple jelly. Nobody will be any the wiser.' She sighed. 'Do you remember the days when jam had sugar in it? Now you can use sugar or fruit, but not both.'

'If anyone can make sugarless jam taste like the real thing, it's you,' said Mabel.

'How are you keeping, Mrs Wadden?' Dot asked.

'I'm fine, thanks.'

'Are you sure, love? You look a bit peaky.'

Mrs Wadden shrugged. 'You know how it is. Money worries, and three growing lads.'

'Aye, they'd eat you out of house and home if they had half a chance. I remember it well.'

'Mind out, love,' said Mrs Grayson.

She lifted a heavy pan and Dot stepped aside to make way. In so doing, she accidentally knocked Mrs Wadden's arm. Mrs Wadden caught her breath in a sharp gasp.

'No harm done.' She rubbed her arm.

'Sure?' asked Dot.

Mrs Wadden dropped her hand to her side. 'You just gave me a fright.'

Dot's eyes narrowed. 'Anyroad, we'd best get out of your way, ladies, before I do more damage. I don't know my own strength.'

As Dot turned to reach for the doorknob, Mabel said, 'But I thought we were—'

'Oh aye,' Dot said cheerfully.

Turning back, she gave Mrs Wadden a sharp tap on her arm in the place she'd been rubbing. Mrs Wadden gave an exclamation, which she tried to bite back, but it was too late.

'Eh, love, I'm sorry,' said Dot. 'Have I touched you where it hurts?'

'It's nowt,' said Mrs Wadden.

'Then you won't mind rolling your sleeves up and showing us,' said Dot.

'You can't make me.'

'We just want the truth,' said Dot. 'There's summat going on in your house and I want to know what it is. Your Louise is being hit regular and I'll bet next week's housekeeping that you are an' all. We know your Rob hasn't come home, so what's going on?'

'Nowt. Mind your own business.'

'But it is my business,' Dot told her, 'and it's the business of everyone under this roof. I reckon that what's going on in your house is tied up with what's happening to Mrs Cooper's customers.'

Mrs Wadden snorted. 'Don't be soft.'

'Soft, am I?' said Dot. 'Well, let's see. Me and Mabel and one or two others – and I don't mean Mrs Grayson or Mrs Cooper, mind – we thought it were you that was stealing from Mrs Cooper's ladies, choosing ones whose houses you'd never been to yourself and finding out about their spare keys from Mrs Cooper's notebook.'

'I don't know anything about any notebook,' said Mrs Wadden.

'That's not true,' said Mabel. 'Mrs Cooper said you knew about it.'

'We thought your Rob had fetched up at home,' said Dot. 'We thought he were battering Louise and forcing you to steal for him. We were so sure, we went to the police.'

Mrs Wadden's mouth dropped open. 'It was you. You shopped us.'

'Aye, we did. We felt we had good reason. I were all set to apologise to you for it, but now I'm not so sure, not now you've refused to roll your sleeves up.'

'I don't have to prove owt to you.'

'Listen, love,' said Dot. 'Mrs Cooper is a dear friend of mine and I know she's as honest as the day is long. She doesn't deserve what's happening to her. All this suspicion, and losing her customers.' She shook her head. 'Nay, she doesn't deserve it.'

Mrs Wadden looked scared and mutinous.

Mrs Grayson stepped in. 'What I know of you, Mrs Wadden, is that you're devoted to your Louise and the boys. You're worried sick about not being able to provide adequately for them. That tells me a lot, Mrs Wadden. It tells me you're a good mother. You work in that shop and you clean for Mrs Cooper and you're helping me in the kitchen as your war work. You're a good person at heart. I have no doubt of that . . . whatever else might be happening in your life.'

Mrs Wadden chewed her lip. 'You're all ganging up on me, that's what you're doing.'

'That's what Louise said,' Mabel recalled. 'Bernice, Bette and I wanted to help, but she accused us of ganging up. I thought she might have a violent boyfriend, but if you're being hit as well . . .' She frowned, trying to make sense of it.

'It's Mr Wadden, isn't it?' said Dot. She looked at Mabel. 'Didn't you say Rob learned his violent ways off his dad?' To Mrs Wadden, she said, 'Has Mr Wadden come back? Did Rob learn his thieving off his dad an' all?'

The fight went out of Mrs Wadden and she sank onto a chair. Even though Mabel took this to be a sign of admitting the truth, she still couldn't quite accept it.

'If the police had found any sign of Mr Wadden living in your house,' she said, 'surely they'd have followed it up.'

'He isn't living at home,' Mrs Wadden said in a dull voice. 'He's stopping with a mate. I were never more surprised in my life than when he turned up after all this time. Louise was beside herself. She said he couldn't move back in because he'd lead the boys into bad ways. He gave her a good slapping for that. Poor lass. She's always done her best for the youngsters. Anyroad, he realised he could do better for himself by not moving back in. If he came home, he'd have to tip up money for the family, but if he stayed away . . . Lou has no idea. You have to believe that. She'd be appalled if she knew.'

'If she knew what?' Mrs Grayson asked gently.

'If she knew her mam is thieving to pay her dad to stop away,' Dot suggested.

'No!' cried Mrs Wadden. 'I never stole owt. I just . . . I gave him the information about the spare keys to houses I'd never been to. He made me do it,' she added desperately. 'He comes round and – and belts our Louise. She thinks it's because she didn't want him moving back in. As if he'd let that stop him! Really he hits her to make me carry on doing what he wants. He makes me do it. He *makes* me. That's why I wanted to come here to help in the kitchen – because it gets me out of the house, somewhere that he can't follow me. And I'm sorry about Mrs Cooper's troubles, honest to God I am. She's a generous lady and she's been good to me. But he makes me. You don't know what it's like. He *makes* me.'

In the end, only Mabel and Alison went to Darley Court. Dot and Mrs Cooper had both gone to the police station with Mrs Wadden. Mrs Wadden had wept and trembled and begged for time, but Dot had been adamant.

'Time for what, love? Time to get cold feet?'

'I could . . . I could tell him you've worked it out. Then he could do his disappearing act. That would sort it out. Me and Lou would be safe.'

'But Mrs Cooper would still be under suspicion,' said Dot. 'The only way to clear her name is to tell the police and let them do the necessary.'

'Should I come with you to the police station?' Mabel asked Dot.

'You get over to Darley Court and see Colette. She needs her friends. I'll see this through.'

Mabel felt torn. It didn't seem right to walk away from such an upset. Mrs Cooper was shaken to the core at the revelation that her trusted employee had betrayed her and Mrs Wadden was well on the way to full-blown hysteria. But if anyone could cope with all that, Dot could, and she was right about Colette needing her friends.

Mabel and Alison talked it over as they made their way to Darley Court.

'Should we keep it from Colette?' asked Alison. 'We don't want to upset her. On the other hand, it might be good to give her something else to think about.'

'Let's tell her,' said Mabel. 'She'll want to know, because it concerns Mrs Cooper.' She heaved a troubled breath.

'What's the matter?' asked Alison.

'I should be jubilant that we've proved Mrs Cooper's innocence – and I am. But I wish it had been anybody else but the Waddens.'

'I didn't know you were that friendly with Louise.'

'I don't think she lets anyone get truly close to her, but I helped her younger brother earlier this year. In fact, it was Louise who asked me to. It meant she trusted me.'

'It isn't your fault that Mr and Mrs Wadden did what they did,' Alison pointed out.

'I know, but I can't help feeling uncomfortable.'

Together, they entered through Darley Court's wide gateway, passing the gatekeeper's lodge, where the land girls lived, and went up the long drive to the mansion with its many windows criss-crossed with anti-blast tape. As they approached, the front door opened and Colette came out to meet them.

'I've been watching for you.' She glanced past them. 'Are the others coming later?'

'We'll explain all that,' said Alison. 'Let's get inside. It's parky out here.'

'There are various meetings and training sessions going on,' said Colette. 'There's a small sitting room Miss Brown says we can use.'

She led the way into a room Mabel remembered from when she had briefly lived here early in the war. The velvet curtains and pelmet were of deep red with cream fringing and the marble fireplace had blue hearth tiles. Beaded cushions lay on the chairs and the sofa.

'How are you?' Alison asked as they settled themselves.

'A lot better, thank you,' said Colette. 'My ribs are still sore, but nothing like as bad.'

'That's how you are physically,' said Mabel. 'How are you in yourself?'

Colette thought for a moment. 'Stunned. So much has happened.'

'The main thing,' said Alison, 'is that you're not on your own any longer.' She hesitated before she said, 'I used to be so jealous of you and Tony. Back when all I wanted was to get engaged to Paul, I couldn't believe your luck. You seemed to have everything I longed for.'

'It's hard to believe we couldn't see what was in front of us,' said Mabel.

'There's no reason why you should have seen anything,' said Colette. 'Neither Tony nor I ever gave anybody cause to wonder.'

'You should have told us,' said Alison.

Colette's blue eyes filled. Mabel knew what Dot would say.

'Don't make this Colette's fault. She was caught in a terrible situation and she coped with it as best she could.'

Alison flushed. 'I know. I'm sorry. Anyway, I'm not one to talk. When Paul dumped me, I turned away from all my friends, so I'm the last person to criticise others for keeping something to themselves.'

'Have you got plans?' Mabel asked Colette.

'I'm building up the courage to go home – no, I don't mean I'm moving back in. I need to pack my things and de-register at the butcher's and so on. That's something I've learned: you can't leave your husband without the butcher and the fishmonger being the first to know.'

'So you're going to stay here,' said Mabel. 'That's good.'

'I can't hide away for ever,' said Colette. 'Everyone already believes I suffered a breakdown. That's what Tony said – and so did I. This is going to look like I've had a relapse and I won't have a hope of a normal life if everybody believes that. The truth has to come out once and for all – and the only way to do that is to make an official complaint to the police and have Tony arrested.'

CHAPTER THIRTY-FIVE

Early in November, there was a warning on the evening news not to switch off the wireless and go to bed. Cordelia and Kenneth glanced at one another. With Emily in between them, they sat up and waited until the midnight news came on, read by Bruce Belfrage, who was well known for continuing to read the nine o'clock news one night in 1940 in spite of a bomb landing on Broadcasting House. Tonight he had an important announcement concerning the war in Egypt.

'The Germans are in full retreat.'

They all hugged one another and Cordelia surprised herself by weeping in relief. The country had waited so long for good news of the war, and this was the best possible news for her dear friend Dot – as long as her two boys had survived.

'It's thanks to General Montgomery,' said Kenneth. 'Good man, good show.'

Cordelia and Emily had been selling poppies recently and now it felt more important than ever. Some people bought several poppies and it wasn't just that they were buying for other family members. You often saw people wearing three or four at once. One for each son overseas? Or because after three years of war, their hearts were full?

'You only have to look into the faces of the older people who buy them to see how heart-rending it is for them,' said Emily. 'They spent years thinking their poppies would only ever be for the Great War, but here it is happening all over again.'

'I know, darling,' said Cordelia. 'Women who lost their husbands first time round are now losing their sons.'

Cordelia felt proud of Emily's sensitivity. What would happen when Raymond was called up? Poor Emily would suffer agonies of worry, along with all the other sweethearts left behind. Cordelia couldn't bear to think of her daughter suffering, but it was inevitable. At least Emily and Raymond's love was out in the open – not like hers and Kit's. Secrecy had made everything so much more painful.

Remembering Kit didn't hurt as much as it used to. Was it because she had thought of him so much recently and become used to it? Or maybe it was because she had linked Emily's romance with Kit, and Emily was of greater importance to her.

Or . . . was it because she appreciated Kenneth more now? Was that why memories of Kit were less painful?

Was she fooling herself? As if appreciation could compete with all-consuming passion!

But it had to if Cordelia were to have any hope of achieving the kind of relationship she envied so deeply in her young friends. The sense of desolation she had lived with since Kit's death had taken on a new form, becoming an ache of longing for a truly loving marriage.

Thoughts of Colette were never far away either. Colette had lived a secret life of fear and nobody had guessed. Cordelia knew all about living a secret life. Colette's had been entirely different from hers, but the simple fact that the two of them had hidden the truth for such a long time shook Cordelia to her core.

Colette's secret was now out in the open. Was it time to reveal her own secret too?

*

The moment Mabel and Margaret arrived home from work, Mrs Grayson emerged from the front room. 'He's been arrested,' she announced with a satisfied air.

'Who – Tony?' Margaret asked, taking the words from Mabel's mouth.

'No. Mr Wadden. That nice young Constable Collins came round to tell us.'

'That's good news,' said Mabel. 'Where's Mrs C?'

With a wide smile, Mrs Grayson stood aside to wave the two girls into the front room. Mabel went straight to Mrs Cooper and hugged her.

'I'm sorry you had to be put through such a nasty experience, but it's over now.'

'Your reputation will be restored,' Margaret added, 'and so will Magic Mop's.'

'I can't tell you what a relief it is,' said Mrs Cooper, looking tearful.

'You must visit Mrs Pearce and the others and let them know your name has been cleared,' Mabel said encouragingly.

'I will, of course,' said Mrs Cooper, 'but it won't be that simple. I'll have to tell them the truth. It's partly my fault.'

'Yours?' said Margaret. 'How?'

'Because I employed Mrs Wadden.'

'But she deceived you,' said Margaret. 'No one can blame you for that.'

'There's blame,' said Mrs Cooper, 'and there's responsibility. I'm not to blame for the dishonest actions of another person, but Magic Mop belongs to me and that means everything to do with Magic Mop is my responsibility. This has damaged Magic Mop's good name and . . . I hate to say it when I know she's hard up and it was her husband making her do it, but I can't keep Mrs Wadden, not after this.'

'You don't trust her any more,' Margaret said quietly.

'It isn't a question of whether I trust her, chuck,' said Mrs Cooper. 'If she carries on with Magic Mop after what she did, then nobody will ever trust *me* again.'

The inside of the bus smelled of damp coats and tobacco. Mabel rubbed gloved fingertips over the steamed-up window. Not that there was much to see other than early-morning darkness blurred by rain. It looked set to be one of those days that never got light properly. Mabel glanced around at her fellow passengers. Across the aisle was a pretty girl in a belted mackintosh and a jaunty rain hat. She was going to spend the day in an office, keeping dry, lucky thing.

Rain was the worst weather for working on the permanent way, as far as Mabel was concerned. Being wet made you cold, no matter how physical your job was, and you had to take extra care handling the tools.

When the bus arrived in town, Mabel jumped off, angling her jump at the last moment to avoid landing in a puddle, and half ran to Victoria Station. She found a spot by the bookstall, their agreed meeting place. As well as her knapsack, she had a bulky cloth shopping bag.

'What's in there?' Bette asked, appearing beside her.

'Old sacks. The gardener at Darley Court sent them. Mrs Grayson cut them up the front and made armholes.'

'A sort of jerkin.'

'Not glamorous, and rather scratchy, but an extra layer of warmth and they're moderately waterproof. There's one for each of us. I've got mine on under my coat.'

Bette looked down at herself. She always wore her coat tightly belted to show off her hourglass figure. 'I'll lose my trim waist if I put it on under my coat – and I'll look like a sack of potatoes if I wear it on top.' She started unbuttoning. 'Here, hold my coat while I put it on.' She laughed and pulled a face. 'You were right when you called it scratchy.'

Someone cannoned into Mabel from behind and she staggered. She turned, expecting to receive an apology, only to find Louise glaring at her. Louise gave her another shove, but Mabel saw it coming and steadied herself.

'Louise! What d'you think you're playing at?' Bette demanded, shocked.

'What *I'm* playing at? How about what *she's* playing at?' Louise's usually pale complexion was stained with anger. 'Ask *her*.' Squaring up to Mabel, she delivered a sharp jab to the shoulder.

'That's enough of that, thank you,' said Bette. 'This is how you behave, is it, pushing and shoving? You, who know what it is to be knocked about. You're the last person that should raise your hand to another.'

Louise's reply was to jerk her chin and look sullen, but only for a moment. She fixed her gaze on Mabel. 'It's all your fault. You had to go and tell the police, didn't you?'

Something inside Mabel trembled beneath the harshness of Louise's scrutiny, but she lifted her chin. 'Yes, as a matter of fact, I did. Was I supposed to let Mrs Cooper take the blame for those burglaries when I knew your family was involved somehow?'

'It's so easy for you, isn't it, with your father's money and your top-quality clothes? Even the so-called rough clothes you come to work in cost more than ordinary folks' Sunday best.'

'What has your father being a thief got to do with my father having money?'

'You don't know what it's like to be poor,' Louise shot back, 'to scrimp and save and never have enough. Only we can't save, because you have to have summat left over

286

before you can do that and owt we have left over is snaffled by my dad.'

'That still doesn't make it right for him—'

'I know that! I'm not stupid!'

'No, lass,' said Bette. 'You're just upset. What's gone on?'

Mabel turned to her, keeping a wary eye on Louise. She hated saying it, but she had no choice. 'You know Lou's mum works for my landlady's little cleaning business? Well, Mrs Wadden gave Mr Wadden information so he could burgle the customers' houses.'

Louise let out a howl of rage. 'Oh, that's right! Blame my mum. He *made* her do it – he *made* her. But you don't care about any of that, do you? Shall I tell you what's happened now?'

'I know your father was arrested,' said Mabel.

'Oh aye, he was carted away, and good riddance to bad rubbish. But d'you know what else happened because of you? My mum lost her job in the corner shop, that's what. They didn't want her after she'd aided and abetted a thief, did they? So now she's lost both her jobs. Our Clifford has held on to his by the skin of his teeth, but he's been told he'll never be allowed anywhere near the office or the money. So that's what's happened to us Waddens. Satisfied, are you? I'll tell you summat, Mabel Bradshaw. I don't care what Bernice says: I shan't be working with you in future and if she says otherwise, she can go and boil her head.'

When Mabel and the others climbed aboard the train, Louise made a point of entering a different carriage in an obvious snub that made Mabel feel even worse than she did already. How was the gang to get through the day with Louise determined to be at loggerheads? Mabel thought of helping Clifford and how this in turn had helped the whole Wadden family, but now Lou couldn't stand the sight of her.

But Bernice seemed to take the situation in her stride. 'Lou can be a right stroppy little so-and-so when she wants. Admittedly, this is taking it to extremes, but I s'pose it's an extreme situation. She'll come round.'

'Do you think so?' asked Mabel.

'She'll have to,' Bernice said drily. 'I'm not having her picking and choosing who she works with. Don't you go feeling bad about what's happened. You did the right thing. If the Waddens are suffering now, it's because Lou's dad is a bad 'un.'

It didn't matter how true that was. Mabel couldn't help feeling rather a rotter. She'd focused all her efforts on helping Mrs Cooper and it had never occurred to her to think events through as far as what might become of the Waddens. Not that that would have held her back from helping Dot get the truth out of Mrs Wadden, but not having considered the consequences made her feel she hadn't handled matters as well as she might have.

Louise's comparisons of their backgrounds, one deprived, the other privileged, had been unsettling too. Mabel chewed her lip. Was that how she appeared to Louise? The young Lady Bountiful clearing up the mess left by the undeserving poor?

An uncomfortable day followed and the rain didn't help. Bernice accepted a sack jerkin, but Louise made a scornful sound and turned away, as if Mabel was trying to buy her off.

'It's a filthy day,' said Bernice, 'so what I suggest, girls, is that we don't bother with a morning break. We'll work straight through and award ourselves a longer dinner hour. If we walk back to that shed we found yesterday, we might have a sporting chance of drying out. Bette and Mabel, you can be together for the morning and I'll have Miss Sunshine with me.'

Without a stop for tea to punctuate the morning, it felt endless, but the prospect of being stuck in a hut with Louise didn't make the prolonged dinner hour something to look forward to. Or would Louise insist on sheltering under a tree with rain dripping down her neck, just to make a point?

'More fool her, if she does,' said Bette. 'She's got no business making you her whipping boy.'

When they hurried into the abandoned shed and gave their coats a shake, Bernice came in last and shut the door.

'Right. That's not opening again until we've got this sorted out, and I know I said I wanted a long dinner hour, but I don't want it to be *that* long, so think on, young Lou. We've all got homes to go to.'

There was a charged silence, then Louise said in a low voice, 'You lot might have, but us Waddens might not for much longer.'

The shed, bare and dirty, suddenly warmed with a swell of sympathy.

'Let's get settled, then Lou can tell us everything,' said Bernice.

They sat on the floor, leaning against the wall, legs stretched out in front of them, flasks by their sides.

'Go on, then, Lou,' said Bette. 'We're all ears.'

Louise heaved a sigh. 'It might be nowt. It might just be her next door stirring up trouble, which would be just like her. Yesterday she took great pleasure in telling Mum that our days in the street are numbered, because the landlord will chuck us out once Dad is found guilty.'

'He wouldn't take it out on your mum and the kids . . . would he?' said Bernice.

Louise shrugged. 'Dunno. We'll see.' She flicked a glance in Mabel's direction. 'If you're waiting for me to have another go at you and say this is down to you an' all, I'm not going to. I've calmed down.'

'Me and Lou had a long talk this morning,' said Bernice. 'She was het up before and who can blame her?'

Was Bernice feeding her a cue? Mabel said sincerely, 'I'm sorry about your family's problems, Lou. It must be hard.'

'You don't know what it's like,' said Louise and Mabel felt a shiver at hearing Mrs Wadden's words repeated. 'I shouldn't have yelled at you this morning, but . . . I spent all night hating you because if you'd just kept your nose out . . . But you had to do summat, I know that, and it's not your fault. It's my dad's fault. He's . . .' Louise shut her eyes tight for a moment. 'He's a rotten dad and a rotten husband and I've spent my whole life wishing he was different, but he's not. He is the way he is and he'll never change. He had my mum frightened stiff of what he'd do to me if she didn't help him with his thieving. I'm so angry with myself for not knowing that summat was going on.' She laughed bitterly. 'I was pleased with myself because I thought I'd made him stay away. I thought, without him there, the boys would have a chance to grow up decent.'

'You weren't to know,' said Bernice. 'Your mum thought she was protecting you by keeping it secret.'

'But I should have known, because I know what he's like. If I'd been like Mabel and stuck my nose in and asked questions and made Mum tell me the truth, I might have found out, and Mum might still have her jobs. How are we supposed to manage now? The thought of it makes my heart beat so fast, it feels like it's about to explode.'

'I wish I could tell you everything will work out,' said Bernice, 'but we all know it's not that simple. You and your mum have got hard times ahead.'

Lou shrugged. 'Shall I tell you what the stupidest thing is? All I wanted was for my dad to love me. Even though I grew up being slapped around, even after he cleared off and left us, I used to daydream about him coming home and saying he couldn't live without his kids and he'd never hit us again. I – I was still daydreaming about that up to a year or so ago. There: I told you it was stupid.'

'There's nowt stupid about wanting your father to love you,' said Bette.

'It depends on who your father is, doesn't it?' said Louise. 'I shan't make that mistake again.'

CHAPTER THIRTY-SIX

Cordelia took the brass poker from the stand on the hearth and stirred up the fire to coax more heat from it. It really needed a few more lumps of coal, but that would be a dreadful extravagance. Before the war, she wouldn't have thought twice about heaping the coal on, but now everybody had to eke out what fuel they had.

Replacing the poker, she straightened, standing in front of the flames. Her father's voice popped into her head, informing her that it was selfish to hog the fire, but she stayed put, her gaze landing on the clock on the mantelpiece. She didn't like it, had never liked it, yet it had always held a fascination for her. It was a brass skeleton clock, its workings on display inside the glass dome. It stood on four bun feet on a wooden base, to which a small silver plaque had been fastened.

> *Presented by his colleagues*
> *to Mr Kenneth Masters*
> *on the occasion of his marriage.*
> *24th January 1920*

From the first moment she had set eyes on it, part of her had resented the fact that Kenneth's colleagues had failed to put her name on the wedding present, but it was the thoughtlessness she didn't like rather than the absence of her name. That, frankly, had always struck her as appropriate. It wasn't as if theirs was a great love match. Emotionally speaking, she had been distanced from her wedding and her marriage, so why acknowledge her? She didn't deserve it.

Now, though, her missing name touched her in a new way, because she no longer wanted to be absent from her marriage. Even though she was confused over what she might or might not be capable of feeling for Kenneth, she definitely wanted a closer, more fulfilling relationship. After all the years of emptiness, her heart yearned for more.

Behind her, the door opened and she looked round as Kenneth entered. He sat down with his book.

'Should I put a little more coal on the fire?' Cordelia suggested. 'Honestly, I feel like Bob Cratchit sometimes.'

'Well, I'm certainly not Mr Scrooge, refusing to use the coal. A quarter of a scuttle a day is what we allow ourselves and we've done what we can to get the best out of it.'

They had indeed. Cordelia glanced around the room. Once, the furniture had been arranged to look stylish and smart, but now the suite was clustered around the hearthrug and Cordelia and Emily had used old towels to make draught excluders. Elegance might have gone out of the window, but now that she'd got used to it, Cordelia thought the room rather cosy this way – or it would be if Kenneth and Emily were on better terms.

Kenneth politely set his book aside. 'Would you prefer to talk?'

'Feel free to read,' Cordelia replied with equal civility. 'I'll get on with my crochet while Emily isn't here.'

She picked up her knitting bag and took out the piece she was making. It was a necklace of small daisy-type flowers for Emily for Christmas. It was very fiddly to make, but now it was growing in length, it looked lovely. But Cordelia hadn't been at work for more than a few minutes before she set it aside and said, 'Would you mind if we talked?'

'Let me just finish this chapter. I'm nearly there.'

Doubts assailed Cordelia as she waited, but she was determined not to back down.

Kenneth popped his bookmark into position and closed the book, putting it on the table next to his chair. They still referred to it as his drinks table even though alcohol was impossible to find these days unless you used the black market.

'You look serious,' said Kenneth. 'Is this something I should be worried about? Please don't say Emily wants to get engaged.'

That startled her. 'No, it's nothing of that sort.'

'What, then?'

Cordelia felt thrown. How was she supposed to go from her daughter's love life to her own from before she met her husband? But this needed saying, so she had to.

'There's something I want to tell you and it isn't easy to talk about, but I think we've become . . . friendlier recently . . .'

'Friendlier.' Kenneth's voice gave nothing away.

'Yes, and I – I like it. I'd like us to feel closer and I think that means being honest with you about something that happened a long time ago.'

'I see.' Still that neutral voice.

'It will help you understand why I've never sought real closeness between us before.'

'Are you referring to Kit, by any chance?'

Cordelia's eyes popped open. 'You – you know about Kit? You know about us – him?'

'Your father told me. He called it your shabby little secret.'

Impossible! Cordelia tried to gather her thoughts.

'But it wasn't a "little" secret, was it?' said Kenneth. 'I realised that early on. It hasn't been easy living with a wife who's in love with a ghost.'

'You never said anything,' Cordelia whispered.

'Would it have done any good? It would very likely have bound you to Kit even more. I took my lead from you, Cordelia. You set the tone for our marriage. You've always been an exemplary wife. I couldn't have asked for a more gracious hostess, a more skilful organiser or a more acceptable addition to my social circle. I certainly couldn't have wished for a better mother for my daughter.'

All these years, that was precisely what Cordelia had set out to be, the perfect wife, but hearing her attributes listed by Kenneth brought her no satisfaction. She realised as if for the first time what a cool and unfeeling person she must seem.

But she wasn't unfeeling, she knew she wasn't. Once, she had worshipped Kit and for the past sixteen years, she had loved Emily with all her heart. Unfeeling was the last thing she was.

'I'm sorry,' said Kenneth. 'I appear to have taken the wind out of your sails. Perhaps you'd care to explain how your telling me about Kit would bring us closer emotionally.'

'I thought – I hoped you'd understand why I've . . .'

'Kept your distance.'

'Yes, all this time.'

'It so happens I already know that,' said Kenneth. 'What did you intend the outcome to be?'

Cordelia found herself stumbling over her words in a way that was most unlike her. 'Well, as I say, I'd like us to be closer.'

'Have you developed new feelings for me?'

'Not exactly, but I hope that I can.'

'I don't think it's the sort of thing one has a choice about.'

'Possibly not, but . . .'

'If you've finally got over Kit, then I'm pleased for you, but if recovering from your lost passion means you're now in the market for a new fling, that isn't really what a husband wants to hear.'

'Kenneth! That's unfair.'

'Is it?' Kenneth held up a hand. 'Let's leave it there for now, shall we? But there is one thing that I'd like to say now that the Kit affair is out in the open. It has grieved me, Cordelia, yes, and angered me at times, having to watch you push Emily into Raymond's arms. It's been hard sharing you with Kit all these years, but being obliged to stand by while you have attempted to give yourself and Kit a happy ending through Emily and Raymond, that has been the hardest thing of all.'

A letter arrived for Mabel just as she, Margaret and Alison, for once all on the same shift, were setting off for work.

'Read it now, if you like,' Margaret said once they were settled on the bus. 'We won't disturb you.'

'No, it's from Harry and she wants to read it all on her own,' Alison teased.

Later, Bernice said, 'I don't know why you didn't leave it behind at home.'

Mabel smiled, but didn't say anything. Would she sound soppy if she said she just liked having it about her person?

The letter burned a hole in her pocket all day. Finally, travelling home on her own, she read it on the bus, unable to wait a moment longer. Harry wanted her to telephone him. For once, she didn't go home to get dressed up but went straight to the telephone box in her work clobber and put the call through to his base. Harry wanted to make arrangements to come over to Manchester to see her, but was reluctant to say why, though Mabel could guess.

'You've got your posting, haven't you?'

'Let's leave it until I see you,' said Harry. 'Some things are better said in person. Before I go, tell me what you're wearing.' There was a smile in his voice.

'You cheeky thing. You know perfectly well what I'm wearing.' Mabel laughed. She had already told him she was telephoning on the way home from work and here she was in her old brown coat, slacks and a brick-red jumper that Mrs Grayson had knitted out of a man's pullover she had found on the market and unravelled. With her green crocheted scarf looped around her neck and a headscarf of a clashing green keeping her hair out of the way, she must look a sight.

'Sounds glamorous to me,' joked Harry.

The call had ended on a happier note than it deserved, Mabel thought as she headed for Wilton Close. She felt torn. She wanted to tell the others why she thought Harry was coming over, so they could sympathise and help her not to feel so glum, but suppose she was mistaken? Then she'd look a proper clot. It was best to wait for Harry.

But when she saw him, she felt so wound up that she couldn't wait for him to say the words.

'You've got your posting, haven't you?' she asked. 'You're being sent away.'

Harry reached for her hand. 'We knew it was going to happen.'

Mabel had been dreading this for ages, but she put on her best smile. She didn't want to make this difficult for Harry. If she was going to have a bit of a weep, she'd save it for later.

'Where?' she asked.

'The new Bomber Command. The camp was built last year.'

'Where?' Mabel asked again. This time her voice was little more than a thread.

'Near High Wycombe,' said Harry and when she frowned and shook her head, he added, 'It's not a million miles from where Joan went that time to look for her family. Wing Commander Alan Oakeshott is in charge.'

Was she meant to have heard of Wing Commander Oakeshott? 'It sounds just right for you.'

'It is – apart from being so far from you, of course.' Harry kissed her and rested his forehead against hers. 'I'll miss you.'

'We're no different to any other couple,' said Mabel. 'Everyone has to make sacrifices.'

'There's my brave girl,' Harry murmured.

Mabel would much rather be his nearby girl, but she mustn't say that.

'It's a real feather in your cap, going to Bomber Command,' she said. 'We can write all the time and you'll soon sort out the telephone arrangements. I'm so proud of you, Harry Knatchbull. I tell you what. I've just found out that I've got a few days off over Christmas. Can you see if you can get leave then as well? Then you can come to Annerby with me and spend Christmas with Mumsy and Pops. They'd love to have you.' Mabel smiled, though she felt trembly inside. 'It'll give us something to look forward to.'

On Sunday the 15th, as the church bells rang out to celebrate victory at El Alamein, Colette walked on her own through the grounds of Darley Court, thinking about the North African campaign and Dot's two sons – or was she using this subject to distract her from the anxiety that kept her awake at night as Tony's appearance in the magistrates' court drew closer?

The certainty she had felt when she'd resolved to report him to the police and insist upon pressing charges hadn't gone away. She knew that for her own sake, it was the right thing to do, the only course to take. But her resolve was accompanied by other feelings, principally shock and shame that her marriage should have come to this. All her mother had wanted was to see her safely married to a suitable man, by which she meant one with a steady job and a sensible head where money was concerned. Tony had certainly fulfilled those criteria.

For Colette, the most important thing had been that she loved him – and she had, oh she had, He was good-looking and kind and he made a fuss of her, but not so much of a fuss that she felt unworthy. His parents had welcomed her too and she had believed she was such a lucky girl.

On top of all that, Tony had a job for life with the water board. After the financial despair that had followed Colette's father's death, that was something to be profoundly grateful for. Colette had been careful not to make too much of it when she talked to her mother, in case Mother thought it was Colette's primary reason for getting married. Imagine if she told the neighbours!

How strange. Six years ago, she hadn't wanted anyone to think she was marrying Tony for any reason other than love. It had mattered what people thought. It had mattered how they were perceived as a couple. Now she had thrown him over to the extent of wanting him to go to prison. She wanted it for her own protection; she wanted it so that there would always be a record of what he had done – and didn't that make her sound vindictive and hard-faced? She wanted neither of those things. She only wanted to be safe.

But dragging her husband to court was a matter for profound shame. She would always be pointed out from now on as the girl who'd married a wife-beater. She'd got married with high hopes, filled with happiness and . . . and trust. She hadn't known then how important trust was. She hadn't given it a thought, taking it utterly for granted. She'd been heartbroken when her mother died, but now she was grateful that Mother wasn't here to see this. She would have been devastated.

'I'll never be able to hold my head up again,' she said inside Colette's mind.

Colette wanted to feel strong and determined, maybe even defiant, but it wasn't that simple. Bad things had happened to her, and bad things were . . . were greater than the sum of their parts. Wasn't that the expression? It was more than a controlling husband who had turned to violence. Bad things . . . made you ashamed.

CHAPTER THIRTY-SEVEN

Colette walked into the magistrates' court building with Cordelia and Alison on one side and Mrs Cooper firmly linked on the other. Everyone else was at work. She drew extra strength from having Mrs Cooper by her side. Dearest Mrs Cooper, who had given her so much help last year, not just by making it possible for her to escape, but also by simply being aware of her situation, which had meant that Colette wasn't alone. She would have crumbled to dust without that support.

'Where would you like to sit?' Cordelia asked quietly as they walked into the courtroom, where the rows of public benches were at the back.

After a moment, Colette said, 'In the middle.'

A large part of her wanted to sit at the front, but that might look like gloating. The middle seemed safest. They took seats and waited.

'Who are those men over there?' Colette whispered as another set of seats across the room started to fill up.

'Reporters,' said Cordelia.

That gave Colette a chilly feeling. She lifted her chin, trying not to feel humiliated. Then she felt annoyed. Ghouls, trading on other people's misfortunes. She remembered a court case from last year that had involved a married couple. Everyone at work had followed the story with great interest. Were her old colleagues now going to drool over her own case?

But it wasn't her case. She tried to derive strength from that. It was Tony's case and he was going to plead guilty. All he had to do was admit to having beaten the living daylights out of her, and that would be that. Open and shut. No story here. No juicy details.

More people walked in. A couple of clerks sat at desks. Father and Bunty appeared. They stopped when they saw Colette. Then Father led Bunty to seats further back. Colette felt glad and uncomfortable at the same time. She didn't want to see them, but she didn't like them being able to see her.

A gentleman in a crisp suit strode in, carrying a briefcase. He went to a table in front of all the seats, placed his briefcase on it and began taking out papers. As if he sensed he was under scrutiny, he looked round, straight at Colette. Did he know who she was? She looked away.

Then a side door opened and Tony walked in and was shown into the dock. Colette's breath caught in her throat and Mrs Cooper held her hand. Colette made herself look at her husband. He looked smart in his pinstriped suit and a dark tie, his hair slicked into place. The gentleman who had opened the briefcase went to stand beside the dock and spoke to him; Tony leaned towards him. It must be his solicitor. They both looked at Colette and she felt colour flame in her cheeks. Were they also looking at her companions? Colette couldn't be sure. Then the solicitor resumed his place.

Cordelia leaned closer. 'It won't be long now.'

A door opened at the rear of the chamber and everyone stood as the magistrate walked in. He was round-faced and bald with big blue eyes. His seat was on a dais that raised him higher than everyone else. When everybody had settled back into their seats, the magistrate glanced at his notes and nodded to a clerk, who stood up to announce the case, ending with '. . . the case to be heard by Mr Unsworth.'

Tony was then asked to stand up to confirm his name and address before the charges were read out and the reporters scribbled madly.

Tony's solicitor rose to his feet. 'If I may, Mr Unsworth?'

Mr Unsworth indicated with a slight move of his chubby fingers that he might.

'Jeremy Wagstaff, acting on behalf of Mr Naylor. Mr Naylor pleads guilty to the charges laid against him and wishes the court to know he is deeply remorseful, but he also wishes the court to be aware of certain mitigating circumstances.'

Alarm streamed through Colette and she sat up straighter. What was going on?

Mr Unsworth gave Mr Wagstaff a stern look that perhaps wouldn't have been expected from his round, bland face. 'I was given to understand this was a straightforward matter, Mr Wagstaff. Are you telling me there's more to it?'

'Indeed I am, sir. Mr Naylor was undoubtedly in the wrong to beat his wife as he did, but it could be said he was pushed beyond endurance.'

The clerk whose desk was in front of the magistrate's bench stood up and Mr Unsworth leaned forward and listened to him, then nodded and the clerk resumed his place. Mr Unsworth addressed Mr Wagstaff.

'I'm prepared to listen to what you have to say, but if it turns out this is a matter for the Crown Court, I will not be pleased to have had my time wasted.'

'Of course, sir,' Mr Wagstaff agreed. 'Mr Anthony Naylor is a man of heretofore good conduct. I have testimonials written by his employer, the captain of his Home Guard brigade and the local organiser of his fire-watching unit.'

He handed some papers to a clerk, who passed them to the magistrate. Mr Wagstaff waited while Mr Unsworth read them.

'That shows the calibre of the man,' said Mr Wagstaff, 'a man who, in his determination to serve his country, has taken on not one but two significant commitments to assist the war effort. But the court needs to know what manner of husband he is. May Mr Naylor be permitted to speak for himself?'

Tony stood up as Mr Wagstaff turned to him.

'Mr Naylor, could you tell the court about your wife?'

'She's the most wonderful girl in the world,' said Tony, his voice ringing with warmth. 'It was the best day of my life when she married me.' He looked straight at Colette. 'Darling, if you can find it in your heart—'

'That's enough,' said Mr Unsworth.

'I apologise,' said Mr Wagstaff, but he didn't sound in the slightest bit sorry. 'Mr Naylor, this has been a year of huge emotional upheaval for you, is that not so? Could you explain why, please.'

'Colette – that's my wife's name – Colette was believed to have been killed last December.'

'And for how long did you believe her to be dead?'

'Until the summer.'

'I see you frowning, Mr Unsworth,' said Mr Wagstaff. 'It is indeed a bizarre story. Please elaborate, My Naylor.'

'She was thought to have died in an air raid, blown to smithereens,' said Tony, 'but the truth was that she ran away because she couldn't cope. Don't ask me to explain, because I don't understand it myself.'

'She ran away?' Mr Wagstaff repeated. 'What, she left you a note and bought a train ticket with the housekeeping?'

'No, she . . . she faked her own death.'

'All on her own?'

'No, she had help from . . . from a friend.' Tony hesitated, as if it was too much for him. 'A friend of us both, or so I thought. A lady called Mrs Cooper, whom Colette was attentive to after her young daughter was killed early in the war. We were both attentive. I worked in her garden and did odd jobs around the house.'

'I see,' said Mr Wagstaff. 'So before all this, you would have said you had every reason to trust this Mrs Cooper?'

'Yes, sir,' Tony said sorrowfully.

'And is Mrs Cooper here today?'

'She's sitting beside my wife.'

Everyone looked at Colette and Mrs Cooper, who surreptitiously squeezed one another's hands. The reporters had a good look, then bent their heads over their notebooks.

Mr Unsworth removed his gaze from Mrs Cooper and addressed Mr Wagstaff. 'Do you wish to question Mrs Cooper?'

'No, I think not, thank you, sir. I wouldn't wish to embarrass her by raising the matter of how she has recently been under suspicion of stealing from the ladies she cleans for.'

Colette gasped, a sound that was echoed by Cordelia and Alison. Mrs Cooper didn't utter a sound. Colette was appalled. Her dear friend had been annihilated in a single stroke.

'Let us leave Mrs Cooper out of this and concentrate on Mrs Naylor,' said Mr Wagstaff. 'Mr Naylor, how did you explain her happy return from the dead?'

'We told everyone she'd suffered a breakdown. I did everything I could to protect her reputation.'

'Did Mrs Naylor settle back into her old life?'

'I helped her all I could. I tried to get her to join the local branch of the WVS and they were all set to welcome her, but she just . . . wasn't ready.'

'Poor lady,' said Mr Wagstaff. 'She is clearly a very sensitive creature. It has been a lot for you to cope with, Mr Naylor, on top of your essential work with the water board and the two important jobs you do for the war effort. Now, let us come to the nub of the matter. On the day in question, why did things get out of hand?'

Tony pressed his lips together, looking extremely uncomfortable.

'Come, sir,' said Mr Wagstaff. 'This has to be brought into the open.'

Tony lifted his chin, looking brave. 'Colette told me that she'd . . . she'd dropped her wedding ring down the drain. On purpose.'

'And that was when you lost your temper.'

Now Tony hung his head. 'Yes, sir.'

'A little louder, if you please. You have to address yourself to the bench.'

Tony looked at Mr Unsworth. 'That was when I lost my temper, sir.'

Mr Unsworth frowned. 'Your wife dropped her wedding ring down the drain, you say?'

'Yes, sir.'

'Deliberately,' Mr Wagstaff added for good measure. 'Did she in fact do this, Mr Naylor?'

'Well . . . she said she'd done it. She was definite about it, but then I found the ring later when she was in hospital.'

'Where had she hidden it?'

'In one of the drawers in the sideboard.'

Colette couldn't help making a small movement. 'I didn't hide it,' she whispered to her companions. 'I lost it.'

'In other words—' Mr Wagstaff began.

'I trust you aren't about to put words into your client's mouth,' said Mr Unsworth.

'Naturally not, sir. Allow me to rephrase.' Mr Wagstaff turned back to Tony. 'Mrs Naylor hid her wedding ring and then informed you that she had disposed of it.'

'Yes, sir.'

'Down the drain.'

'When I found it, all I wanted was to put it back on her finger.'

Colette crumpled inwardly. Why was Tony being allowed to rewrite history this way?

'Mr Naylor,' said Mr Wagstaff, 'was this the first time you had hit your wife?'

Tony's shoulders slumped. 'No. I hit her once before – but only once, I swear, in all the time we've been married.'

'And what did Mrs Naylor subsequently do on that occasion?'

Tony dipped his chin. It made him look deeply embarrassed. 'She . . . I was told she walked around the local area and went in the shops so everybody could see her.'

'Indeed? Not exactly the action of a modest lady, if I may say so.'

Immodest! Colette's posture stiffened. It had been a way of standing up for herself. Was that wrong? And why were these men allowed to talk about her in this way? It wasn't fair.

'What did you do,' Mr Wagstaff asked Tony, 'when you learned your wife had flaunted her injured face around the neighbourhood?'

'Nothing, sir. I was so dreadfully ashamed of what I'd done. All I wanted was to preserve my marriage and get things back to how they used to be.'

Mr Unsworth had been scribbling notes. Now he put down his fountain pen and eyed Mr Wagstaff. 'What has this to do with the subject of this hearing, which is the attack that hospitalised Mrs Naylor?'

'It perhaps sheds light on Mrs Naylor's character, sir. Any other lady would have hidden her injuries, but Mrs Naylor chose to show them off. She then went through the fiction of disposing of her wedding ring . . . perhaps knowing what the result might be . . .?'

With a great gasp, Colette shot to her feet. Cordelia dragged her back down, hissing, 'Sit down. It won't do any good.'

'What's going on?' demanded Mr Unsworth, looking across. 'I will not tolerate misbehaviour in my courtroom. Please continue, Mr Wagstaff.'

'Thank you, sir. Then we come to the time Mrs Naylor spent in hospital. Should I list her injuries?'

Mr Unsworth sifted through the papers in front of him. 'No need. I have the information in front of me.'

'When she was in hospital, Mrs Naylor was interviewed by a police officer. She could have made an official complaint against her husband at that stage, but did she? No, which suggests she was close to forgiving him. Alas, I fear that subsequently poor Mrs Naylor has been badly advised.'

'By whom?' enquired the magistrate.

'She has certain friends whom she met through her former work with the railways. Two of them removed Mrs Naylor from the ward. No attempt was made to have her properly discharged. It was a ridiculous act perpetrated by a pair of foolish girls with no knowledge or understanding of the married state. Could it be that her so-called friends prevailed upon Mrs Naylor to press charges against her husband? Just a thought.' As if the idea had just this moment occurred to him, Mr Wagstaff looked across at the public benches before turning to address Mr Unsworth. 'In fairness to Mrs Naylor, I feel it behoves me to invite one of her companions to speak up for her.'

'Are you sure?' asked Mr Unsworth.

'It's only right to give the court the full picture, sir, in case anyone should imagine I am over-egging Mr Naylor's pudding, as it were. If I might ask Mrs Masters to come forward.'

Colette had never seen Cordelia look flustered before. Cordelia quickly controlled it and resumed her customary cool manner. She was asked to confirm her name and address, then she looked at Mr Wagstaff. Colette felt confident. Mr Wagstaff might think himself very clever, but he had met his match in Cordelia.

'Mrs Masters, when did you first meet Mrs Naylor?'

'On the day we both started working on the railway. That was in February '40.'

'Did you subsequently come to know Mr Naylor?'

'Yes. The Naylors were regular visitors at the home of a mutual friend.'

'That would be Mrs Cooper?'

'Yes,' Cordelia confirmed.

'And in all the time before Mrs Naylor's disappearance and presumed death, did you and your friends ever discuss – I'm not suggesting for one moment that there was gossip – but did you share your opinions of the Naylors' marriage?'

'We did,' said Cordelia. 'We were all in agreement that Mr Naylor was attentive to the point of overprotectiveness.'

'Did Mrs Naylor ever express discontent at this?'

'Never,' Cordelia admitted.

'Did you or your friends ever feel concern on her behalf at that time?'

'No, never. In fact, we thought her lucky to have such a loving husband.'

'Thank you, Mrs Masters. You may return to your seat.'

'But—'

'Thank you, Mrs Masters,' Mr Wagstaff repeated in a firm voice.

The usher stepped forward and Cordelia was obliged to return to the public benches. As she approached, she gazed at Colette, looking shocked.

Mr Wagstaff nodded his head, appearing to be lost in thought. 'Ah, yes. "We thought her lucky to have such a loving husband." There it is, from the lips of one of Mrs Naylor's own friends. It fits exactly with comments made to my clerk by others known to the couple – neighbours, shop-keepers, the WVS ladies who were so keen to welcome Mrs Naylor into their ranks, the brave men of the Home Guard, the local fire-watching unit. Everyone speaks of the adoring husband and the fortunate young wife; the wife who under-went some sort of mental crisis that led her to run away, leaving her husband, friends and neighbours to grieve her loss. Mr Naylor has spoken of the fictitious breakdown he claimed she'd suffered from in order to explain her dis-appearance in the least damaging way, but maybe it wasn't as fictitious as all that. A sensitive young wife, a rather spoilt young wife, if I may say so, was overwhelmed by the rigours of wartime and simply couldn't cope a moment longer.'

He paused and looked around. Colette thought he would look at her and she braced herself, but he didn't. He carried on speaking, oozing sympathy not just for Tony but for her too.

'When Mrs Naylor came home, my, oh, my, what a lot Mr Naylor had to deal with. He did all he could to preserve his wife's good name and keep their marriage intact. He came home from work in the middle of every day at great per-sonal inconvenience to make sure she was all right; he asked the neighbours to keep an eye on her. In what can only be described as her reduced mental state, Mrs Naylor rewarded him with provocation of the most destructive sort. If it wasn't reduced capacity, it was sheer bloody-mindedness, but it has to be one or the other.'

In the course of this speech, Mr Wagstaff's voice had gone from syrupy to hard. Throughout Colette's body, her muscles tightened against the fear that was creeping over her.

'This is a woman who knowingly and deliberately pretended to have disposed of her wedding ring – the very ring that is the most sacred of all objects to every decent wife – and not merely disposed of it, but dropped it down the drain. What greater insult or injury could she possibly have inflicted on the husband whom we all know to have been so loving and anxious to care for her? A man whose single fault as a husband – if such a thing can be said to be a fault – is to be overprotective. Mr Unsworth, sir, my client is beside himself with remorse for the injuries he inflicted upon his dear wife, but I hope and pray you can appreciate that there is far more to this case than the bald charge laid against him.'

CHAPTER THIRTY-EIGHT

'This has lasted far longer than expected,' Mr Unsworth announced tetchily. 'I need to consider this matter and take advice. This hearing is adjourned for twenty minutes. After that I have a long list of cases to get on with.'

He marched from the chamber, barely allowing time for everyone to rise politely. Colette dropped back onto her chair, exhausted. How had this happened?

'Colette?'

She looked up. Father and Bunty were standing there. Distress rolled in her stomach.

'These are Tony's parents,' she told her friends.

Cordelia spoke up. 'I'm sorry. Colette can't talk to you just now. This has been most upsetting for her.'

'For her?' Father demanded. 'What about for our son? And you,' he barked at Mrs Cooper. 'Was that fellow correct? Did you really—'

'Excuse us,' said Cordelia.

With her friends forming a protective group around her, Colette found herself being hurried towards the door.

'Is there somewhere private we can go, please?' Alison asked the usher, and after glancing at Colette, he showed them to a small room with a table in the middle and chairs around it.

'That was a good idea, Alison,' said Mrs Cooper.

'It was worth a try,' said Alison. 'It's the sort of thing Persephone would have asked for – and got.'

Colette sank onto a chair, dumped her elbows on the table and rested her head in her hands. The sensation of disbelief that she had battled with after Tony had dragged her home had returned with full force.

Lifting her head, she dropped her hands to the table. 'It felt as if I was on trial, not Tony.'

'He had a very clever solicitor,' said Cordelia.

'I should have had a solicitor to speak up for me.'

'You shouldn't have needed one,' said Cordelia. 'With Tony pleading guilty – and there's no doubt whatsoever that he's guilty – he should simply have entered his plea and received his sentence.'

'Now the magistrate wants to think it over,' said Alison, 'so maybe Tony will get a different sentence.'

'Don't say that,' said Mrs Cooper.

'Why not?' asked Colette. 'It's true. Tony is going to get off leniently.' An idea popped into her head. 'Could we send a message to Mr Unsworth, asking him to see me?'

'I'm sure he wouldn't agree to that,' said Cordelia, 'but even if he did, I don't think it would help.'

'Why not?' asked Alison. 'Colette deserves to be heard.'

'She does,' Cordelia agreed, 'but in all honesty, Colette, could you in the twenty minutes available get Mr Unsworth to understand your marriage?'

'No,' Colette said quietly. 'I could give him a dozen examples of Tony's unkindness and all he'd think is that Tony isn't quite the all-round good egg that he's been painted. He wouldn't see how it ground me down and wedged me entirely under Tony's control. It would just make me sound pathetic and spiteful. Let's be honest. I know how much my friends care about me and trust me, but it would have been a lot harder for you to believe the truth about Tony if I hadn't had Mrs Cooper to back me up and describe how things were and tell you how worried she was about me.'

She looked at her friends. Cordelia and Alison's silence told her this was true.

'It's a hard thing to understand,' said Alison. 'In fact, I don't understand it, not in the sense of being able to say, "This is what was going on Tony's head." But I do believe you, Colette,' she added earnestly. 'Every single word.'

'Mr Unsworth thinks I'm a crackpot who pushed Tony to the brink,' said Colette.

'If only Tony had pleaded not guilty,' said Mrs Cooper. 'Then the hospital staff and the police would have been called as witnesses.'

'It wouldn't have done any good,' said Colette. 'They were all on his side. He was so full of remorse that they all wanted me to forgive him.' A slow sigh seemed to drag up echoes of soreness in her ribs. 'We'd better face it.' She clutched Mrs Cooper's hand. 'Tony is going to get off lightly.'

The twenty minutes sped past. Cordelia made sure they were all back in their seats in the public benches before the time was up. Colette wasn't at all sure she wanted to be there. What was the point? But she had come this far and she ought to see it through to the end. She pulled her mid-blue wool coat further round her for comfort.

'All rise.'

The door at the back of the chamber opened and Mr Unsworth came in and took his place. Colette resumed her seat, wishing she could carry on descending and slither through the floor. She didn't look at Tony and she didn't look at the reporters.

'This is a most unsavoury case,' said Mr Unsworth. 'There is no doubt at all that Mr Naylor caused his wife's injuries and that these injuries were significant enough to keep her in hospital for a number of days, though not, apparently, for as many days as they should have. I have consulted with some fellow magistrates as to the best way to deal with this matter and I am ready to give my verdict.'

Tony stood up. Colette couldn't help glancing at him. His face was expressionless.

'Mr Naylor, the injuries you inflicted on Mrs Naylor were of a nature that had you injured a stranger in that way would have seen this case referred directly to the Crown Court, where you would automatically have faced a longer prison sentence. I have heard the mitigating circumstances and I sympathise with what you have been through. Nevertheless, the court takes a serious view of your behaviour. The degree to which you injured your wife went well beyond simple chastisement. We can't have men treating their wives in this way.'

Mr Unsworth paused, as if allowing the gentlemen of the press to catch up.

'Nor can I overlook the fact that we are a nation at war. Mr Naylor, you have shown yourself to be a man of patriotism and honour. Therefore, I am going to offer you a choice. You can go to prison, which will give you a record for the rest of your life – or you can join the army without a stain on your character.'

CHAPTER THIRTY-NINE

The latter half of November brought first heavy rain, the pavements vanishing beneath puddles and fallen leaves, and then fog. Kenneth had never liked Cordelia's job as a lampwoman, to start with because he felt it to be beneath an educated lady of her rank, and during spells like this because he was plain worried about her safety.

'All the lampmen and -women take extra care in the fog,' said Cordelia and then thought what a pointless thing it was to say, because every single person, regardless of where they were or what they were doing, had to do that.

It was eerie walking the line and her working days lasted two or more hours longer because of having to take such care. Walking through dense grey murk was no laughing matter. Kenneth produced a walking stick and Cordelia got used to waving it to and fro across the ground in front of her. More than once, it saved her from coming a cropper.

Wearing additional layers beneath her warm green herringbone overcoat and with her red-patterned silk scarf keeping her neck and chin covered, Cordelia shifted her knapsack to a more comfortable position on her back and set off for the next set of signals.

The most important thing when the world surrounding you was opaque was to make sure you went in the right direction. She did this by removing her knapsack before she climbed the ladder up to the signals and placing it a yard away in the direction she needed to head next, so that when she climbed down again after cleaning the lamps, she could feel about for it with her walking stick. Plenty of lamp workers told stories of descending a ladder and setting off back the way they had come. It was an easy thing to do when you were in the middle of a pea-souper.

The other thing Cordelia did was stay close to the permanent way so that the swish of her walking stick repeatedly touched the sticking-out ends of the railway sleepers as she walked. That was especially important today as she could hear a stream close by and she didn't want to stumble head first into that.

Walking through the fog was scary, no matter how sensible you were. She remained alert for the sound of an approaching train. It was impossible to tell which track it was on, the one beside her or one further away, so she had to assume every time that it was going to pass right next to her. Rather than walk away from the track and possibly lose her bearings, she would lie down on the ground until the train had gone by.

Cordelia smiled to herself. Kenneth had hoped the thick fog would keep Emily and Raymond apart. Honestly! As if a bit of bad weather would thwart the course of true love.

The youngsters had arranged to take today off work with some friends. It had been organised ages ago and, to Kenneth's disappointment, the fog hadn't made them put it off. Even at breakfast this morning, he had tried to persuade Emily out of it, but she wouldn't budge.

Cordelia's hope that, as he got to know Raymond, Kenneth's attitude would soften hadn't come to anything. Kenneth liked Raymond well enough and didn't mind saying so, but his feeling about the social gap between the two families hadn't altered in the slightest and he didn't mind saying that either.

By the end of her day at work, Cordelia was chilled and exhausted. Non-stop concentration was taxing. She travelled home on the bus, wiggling her toes in an effort to warm them, glad to think of the stew she had prepared last night, which Emily should be gently warming through at this very moment. Cordelia's mouth watered. She had put in extra potatoes. Before the war, she had liked to serve a hearty stew with chunks of crusty bread fresh from the baker's oven, but these days, the national loaf, no matter how healthy, wasn't a patch on pre-war bread for texture or flavour.

But when she opened the front door, there was no savoury tang in the air to greet her and she couldn't even switch the lights on, because Emily hadn't done the blackout. Cordelia caught her breath. Emily! Had something happened? An accident?

It was galling, and she had possibly never hated the war as much as she did at that moment, but before she could do anything else, she had to do the blackout. Still in her coat, she rushed around downstairs, drawing both sets of curtains across each window, then she switched on the lamp in the sitting room before going upstairs.

She heard crying and with her heart in her mouth, she hurried into Emily's room and found Emily a sodden little heap on the bed. Cordelia gathered her child in her arms and held her, kissing her hair.

'Darling, darling, what is it? What's happened?'

Emily twitched and a puffy face appeared close to Cordelia's.

'It's Raymond. Oh, Mummy, he doesn't want to see me again. He's called it off.'

Emily was inconsolable. That first night, Kenneth moved into the spare room and Emily slept with Cordelia. Not that she actually slept. She cried and talked and cried more. Cordelia was shocked by how deeply she herself felt hurt.

All along through Emily's romance, she had looked back and compared present circumstances to past unhappiness and she had thought a lot about her own long-ago heart-break. But now she found that her daughter's pain hurt her as a mother far more than her own distress had hurt her when she was young.

'Why?' Cordelia asked. 'I thought the two of you were so happy.'

Emily gulped. 'So did I – and Raymond too. He *was* happy, I know he was, but . . .'

Emily's anguish filled the house and her parents were worried about her. Cordelia had the additional worry of hoping Kenneth wouldn't say anything that showed he was glad the relationship was over. At the moment, he was as shocked by the news as she was.

'It's all because of that bomb that flattened the Sidwells' house on the night of the fire-watchers' party,' Cordelia confided in Dot in the buffet a few days later. 'Before that, Emily and Raymond were obviously attracted to one another, but what happened that night – the fear, the strain, the sheer emotional upheaval – was what truly threw them together. Bound them together, I should say.'

'It's understandable,' said Dot. 'Emotions run high in wartime. You've only got to look at the number of weddings to see that.'

'As far as Emily is concerned, from that night onwards, her love for Raymond became the real thing, not a schoolgirl infatuation but a lasting love. She thought they were going to spend their lives together.'

'But Raymond doesn't feel the same?'

'That's just it.' Cordelia breathed out a short sigh. 'He did, to start with. The bombing had the same effect on his feelings that it had on Emily's. He was very much in love with her until . . .'

'Until he went off the boil,' Dot finished. 'Sorry, love. I don't mean to sound flippant.'

'Don't apologise,' said Cordelia. 'That's exactly how it happened. I don't doubt that his love for Emily was genuine at the time. It just wasn't of the permanent variety. As far as he's concerned, they had a wonderful few months together, but now his feelings have subsided and it's over.'

'Poor Emily,' said Dot. 'Poor child.'

'That's exactly the right word. "Child", I mean. Ever since she came marching home unexpectedly last year, I've watched her grow up, including falling in love, but now it's as though she's gone back to being my child again, my little girl, and all I want to do is cuddle her and kiss it better, which of course is impossible. I'd no idea being a parent could hurt so much. I'm sorry, Dot. I shouldn't be saying this to you, of all people. You know all about the anguish parents can go through.'

'Just because I have my fears about my boys doesn't mean I haven't got time to share your worries about Emily. That's what friends do for one another.' Dot laughed. 'If everyone kept their worries to themselves, the world would be a much quieter place, but I don't think it'd be any better for it.'

'You've still not had word from them?' Cordelia asked.

'No, we haven't, but we haven't had a telegram either and that makes us luckier than a lot of mams and dads.'

Gathering their things, they left the buffet to go home, pausing for a minute or two in front of the station's Great War memorial. The noise and bustle vanished as Cordelia concentrated on thoughts of the fallen men not just from the last war but from this one also. She closed her eyes and said a prayer for Dot's sons.

Shortly, she was waiting at the bus stop. A gas-bag bus came along, its nose-to-tail roof rack containing a long bag of 'town gas', whatever that was, which powered the vehicle. Travelling home in it, Cordelia wondered how Emily had coped during the day. It seemed cruel to send her to work when she was so desperate, but at the same time Cordelia knew it was the best thing for her, providing her with something else to focus on.

'Huh,' Emily had said when Cordelia had gently pointed this out. 'If I had an interesting job, maybe, but it's grotesquely boring being the office junior.'

Always a slender girl, Emily had grown thin since Raymond had ditched her. The effect was to make her look older and Cordelia felt she was glimpsing her baby girl as she would be in her twenties. She shivered. The last thing she wanted was to wish Emily's life away.

The one good thing, as Cordelia saw it, was that Emily was prepared to talk about what had happened. In fact, she could barely shut up about it. Given how she personally had been forced to live out her own heartbreak in silence, Cordelia was grateful for it and was happy to have the same conversation over and over as many times as Emily needed.

Most of all, Cordelia was grateful for Kenneth's support and sensitivity. Yes, his sensitivity.

Emily had been wary of him at first and had burst out with, 'I suppose you're glad now.'

'Glad? To see my daughter unhappy? Emily, I just wish I could take the pain away from you and suffer it myself.'

'But you always said—'

'Never mind what was said before. That was then. I know that all you want is for Raymond to come back and say he made a mistake, but since that doesn't look like happening, would a hug from your old dad do any good?'

'Oh, Daddy.'

Emily practically ran into his arms and clung to him while he stroked her hair, looking at Cordelia over the top of her head. Even though Cordelia was filled with sorrow for her daughter, there was a new warmth inside her too. Kenneth's tenderness towards Emily touched her deeply. Then she felt guilty. What had she expected Kenneth to do? Rub Emily's nose in it? Crow in triumph?

Of course not. He loved Emily every bit as much as she did. In that moment, something inside Cordelia reached out to her husband, a mixture of gratitude, respect, trust and affection . . . Maybe something more than affection? She caught her breath.

After all these weeks of watching Emily's romance, of mourning her own lost love and trying to reach towards a new happiness for herself, was this the moment when it happened? Had poor Emily's heartbreak given Cordelia the final push into a new beginning for her own heart?

CHAPTER FORTY

December brought hard frosts and the scrubby land beside the permanent way that last week had been a sad display of spiky twigs now twinkled beneath brilliant winter sunshine. Mabel set to work with a will. The victory in North Africa had given everyone new hope. Christmas was on its way and she couldn't wait for Harry to join her at home in Annerby. What could be better?

She had stopped feeling guilty about Louise's family too, but the next morning Louise arrived at Victoria first thing with huge circles under her eyes.

'You look rough,' said Bernice. 'Didn't you sleep?'

Lou shook her head. Her face was pale and drawn. 'We're being chucked out. The landlord won't have us any more.'

The other three exclaimed in sympathy.

'With the time that's passed since your dad was arrested,' said Bette, 'I assumed things must be all right regarding your landlord.'

'Dad went to court yesterday,' said Louise. 'Fair's fair. At least the landlord waited for him to be found guilty.'

'You never said his case was coming up,' said Bernice.

Louise shrugged. 'It's not the sort of thing you shout about.'

Mabel felt wretched for Louise's family and a flash of her old guilt returned. Mr Wadden was a thief and a bully, a violent husband and a violent father, and none of that was Mabel's fault. But she had wanted to find out the truth behind Louise's bruises, and she'd also been determined to clear Mrs Cooper's name. In pursuing those aims, she had uncovered the truth about Mr Wadden's activities and the knock-on effect was that Louise, her mum and her younger brothers were now going to lose their home. It was all very well for Mabel to know it wasn't her fault, but she still felt bad about it. It was horrible to think that doing what was right for Mrs Cooper had turned out so badly for the Waddens.

That evening in Wilton Close, Mrs Cooper assured Mabel, 'It's not your fault, chuck. You did nowt wrong.'

'I know I didn't,' said Mabel, 'but it's made me feel rotten all over again.'

'Aye, love. Me an' all.'

Mabel looked at her landlady in surprise. 'You? What have you got to feel rotten about?'

'Sacking Mrs Wadden, of course. I know it had to be done and I know Magic Mop wouldn't exist now if I'd kept her on, but that doesn't mean I have to feel good about it. If you ask me, she deserved another chance, but my ladies wouldn't have stood for it.'

'I wish I could make things right for the Waddens,' said Mabel.

'It shows what a good heart you have,' said Mrs Cooper.

Mabel huffed a little sigh. It was no use having a good heart if you didn't put it to work. She was determined to help Louise's folks – but how?

She gave it some thought, half listening to Mrs Grayson reading out something about the Beveridge Report from the newspaper. Sir William Beveridge wanted to introduce a scheme of social insurance covering things like family allowance, sickness and unemployment benefits and pensions. Something clicked into place in Mabel's mind. The Beveridge Report had made her think of Pops. He had always had a social conscience. Now she knew exactly what to do.

She put on her outdoor things and poured her telephone change inside her glove before presenting herself just inside the front-room door to say goodbye.

'I'm going to the phone box.'

'It's not a Harry evening, is it?' asked Mrs Cooper.

'No. I need to have a word with my dad.'

Taking her torch with her, she set off through the pitch-dark streets. For once, the telephone box was empty. Good. It was a chilly night for queuing up.

Soon she was speaking to Mumsy.

'Mabel, how lovely to hear your voice. I take it this call means you've heard from Harry.'

'Harry? No.' Mabel was taken aback, but she didn't have sufficient change to allow herself to be distracted. 'Mumsy, I need to speak to Pops. It's important. Is he there?'

Her father came on the line.

'Mabs, is everything all right?'

'With me, yes, but very much not so for a girl I work with. She and her family need help.' Mabel outlined what had happened to the Waddens.

'And you're telling me this because . . .?'

'Because they deserve a fresh start. Can you possibly provide jobs for them? And could Mumsy sort out a billet?'

'That's a tall order,' said Pops, but Mabel could tell he was thinking about it. 'Mother, grown-up daughter, three young boys.'

'The oldest boy is of working age. An apprenticeship would be a marvellous opportunity for him.'

'I'll write in a day or two, Mabs, and let you know,' said Pops. 'Mind, if they do come here, they're not to leave a forwarding address with anyone. I'm not having the no-good father turning up unannounced in the future.'

'Understood. Thanks, Pops.

'I haven't done anything yet.'

'You're a love,' said Mabel. 'Before I go, Mumsy asked me if I'd heard from Harry.'

'You mean you haven't? We had a letter from him, giving his apologies but he can't come for Christmas after all. Duty calls and all that. It's a rotten shame, but you shan't let it get you down, shall you, Mabs? We'll make sure you have a splendid time. Chin up, old girl. Worse things happen at sea.'

Her friends assured her that there was no need for her to see Tony again before he joined up. Indeed they were keen for her not to, but Colette knew she must do it.

'Are you sure?' Persephone pressed her. 'There's really no need.'

'Actually,' said Miss Brown, 'there's every need – isn't there?' She removed her spectacles and treated Colette to a penetrating look. 'Sometimes one just has to face up to things.'

Colette nodded. Miss Brown was right. Colette couldn't help feeling surprised. What could an elderly lady from a privileged background know of such things? Yet Colette had sensed complete understanding in Miss Brown's uncompromising gaze.

'I really felt she knew,' Colette confided in Persephone afterwards.

'I should think she does. I'm not suggesting that anything has happened to her that is comparable to what has happened to you, but, well, she hasn't always had it easy. She wasn't born to all this, you know. She inherited after all the male heirs died off, taking the title with them. A spinster in her thirties seemed a pretty hopeless case for taking on Darley Court and the estate and there was a lot of feeling against her at the start.'

'Poor Miss Brown,' said Colette. 'She seems perfectly capable to me.'

'And, of course, she is eminently capable,' said Persephone. 'Everyone knows that now, but at the time she had to prove it and it's not the sort of thing you can prove overnight.'

Colette nodded. 'That's what she meant about facing up to things.'

Now Colette was ready, or as ready as she would ever be, to face up to things – to face Tony. Her friends wanted him to come to Wilton Close or Darley Court or, failing that, for the meeting to take place on neutral territory, but Colette knew she had to go home for this. Home? Could Seymour Grove be home again? Perhaps, once Tony was gone.

Gone. For the duration, however long that might be.

When she arrived in Seymour Grove, she alighted from the bus and walked through the familiar streets, seeing a couple of women she had known ever since her early married days. She braced herself for conversation, only to catch her breath in shock when they crossed the road. They pretended not to have seen her, but Colette knew they had. She hadn't wanted to speak to them, but this was worse.

Then an old lady who lived round the corner from her and Tony came up to her and said, 'It's nice to see you again, love,' and Colette could have wept with gratitude.

When she got home, she hesitated on the step. Should she use her key? What was the protocol for a runaway wife?

While she was dithering, the door opened and there was Tony. She hadn't seen him since that day in the magistrates' court. His mouth was a tight line that reduced his narrow lips to a slash, but she could see in his eyes how vulnerable he was. For a moment, she felt guilty. No. No guilt. This wasn't her fault.

'Hello, Tony.'

He stood aside to let her in. She walked into the parlour. Everything was clean and neat. Had Bunty been looking after Tony in her absence?

Tony entered the room behind her.

Colette waited a moment, then asked, 'May I sit down?'

'For pity's sake, Colette, this is your home.'

Colette unfastened her blue coat and sat down. Her knitting bag was beside her chair, just as it had been when Tony had brought her back from London. Had he told Bunty to leave it be?

'Aren't you going to take your coat off?' Tony asked.

'I'm not stopping long.'

'Is that all I get? Is that all *we* get? Aren't we worth more than that?'

'Please sit down, Tony. I don't want you looming over me.'

'I'm not – oh, very well, if it makes you feel better.' Tony sat on the edge of the seat, leaning forward, every line of his body speaking of urgency and strain. Then he smiled. 'Well, here we are. It's so good to see you again. I've been worried about you.'

'There was no need.'

'It came as a shock when you took your ration cards. It made me realise you meant it. You've made your point, Colette. I should never have done what I did and I'll regret it until the day I die. I can't bear to think of how I hurt you. You didn't have to take me to court to make me sorry. I was already sorry. You know I was.'

'Let's not go over all that,' said Colette. 'I don't think we'll see eye to eye.'

'You're right,' he said with schoolboyish eagerness. 'Let's not dwell on the bad things. Let's remember the good times. There are far more of those.'

He rattled off a string of memories: a picnic in the park, a day trip to Southport, a visit to the theatre, helping at the church fête, planting daffodil bulbs in the back garden, going to his works dance. He was right. They were happy memories . . . on the surface. But any happiness Colette had experienced had been derived from not being made to feel belittled or anxious. Her happiness hadn't been happiness at all. It had been a desperate gratitude that Tony was being kind.

'You'll move back in, won't you?' said Tony. 'I'll enjoy picturing you in our house while I'm away. Don't worry about the rent. I've made arrangements about my wages. It will make everything more bearable if I know you're here.'

'Tony,' Colette began, then stopped.

'What?' His voice was warm. 'Tell me.'

'You make it sound as if everything is going back to how it was.'

'It can't do that.' Tony laughed. 'Not with me joining up. I've been thinking. I've done nothing but think. This will be good for us. I've decided to make the best of it. Time apart from one another will heal the wounds and make us ready to be together again. It'll be something for us both to look forward to.'

Colette stared. Did he really believe that? She stood up.

'I'm sorry, Tony. I thought that us seeing one another would – actually, I'm not sure what I thought. I should go.'

Tony rose to his feet, reaching out a hand towards her. 'Don't leave. I don't want you to go.'

'I'm sorry.' Colette fastened her coat. 'You want things to go back to how they used to be and they can't.'

'No – no – you're right. Things won't be the same. They'll be better, I swear it.'

'I have to go.'

'All I want is for us to have another chance. We deserve that, don't we?'

'Goodbye, Tony.'

'You really don't have to leave Darley Court,' said Persephone, sitting on the bed in the guest room Colette had been given when she came here. It was next to Persephone's room and the two girls shared a bathroom. Truth be told, as much as Colette loved the bedroom with its elegant furniture and padded window seat, she loved the bathroom more. The deep, claw-footed bath was like something out of a Hollywood film.

'I feel welcome here,' said Colette, 'and I'm grateful for everything, but I ought to go back, at least until I decide what to do. It isn't good for a house to stand empty, especially in winter.'

'If you're sure,' said Persephone, sounding not at all sure herself.

Colette wasn't sure either, not in her heart, but her head told her it was the right thing to do. After the way the magistrate had come down on Tony's side even though he was guilty, Colette had felt a strong need to restore her personal reputation in the community she had been a part of for so long. That meant going back and holding her head up. She hadn't done anything wrong and that was the best way to show it. It was also important to do it for the sake of any of the local women whose husbands knocked them about in secret or abused them verbally. Colette was sure these women existed; she couldn't be the only one, even if she had thought she was at the time. She wanted the others to see her going about her daily life in a confident way. If they felt cowed inside their own homes, if they had bruises to hide, she wanted to give them hope.

She packed her things and after thanking Miss Brown and Mrs Mitchell for their hospitality, she set off, declining offers to accompany her home. She didn't especially want to go on her own, but she felt it was right.

It wasn't easy to leave Darley Court and she ended up setting off later than she'd intended. She had somewhere else to go to as well and she'd meant to drop off her things at the house before going out again, but now she decided to go straight to town. She went to Victoria and put her things in Left Luggage, then went across to Hunts Bank and asked to see Mr Mortimer. He was the gentleman who had given a talk to all the new recruits on Colette's first day. Persephone had told Colette about the plan to invite letters in appreciation of Miss Emery and she was hugely proud of her friends for finding a way to help the assistant welfare supervisor. It was exactly the sort of thing they would do. By now, Mrs Jessop would have taken all the letters to Hunts Bank and Mr Mortimer would have received them. Colette wanted to make sure her voice was heard as well.

'I don't have an appointment,' Colette told the middle-aged secretary, 'but please tell Mr Mortimer that it's Mrs Naylor to talk about Miss Emery.'

Two minutes later, she was sitting in Mr Mortimer's office. He looked as immaculate as she remembered, with his smartly pressed suit, his bow tie and the watch chain hanging in a loop from the little pocket in his waistcoat. His hair was slicked back, his moustache neatly trimmed. He picked up a wire in-tray from a shelf beside his desk. It was full of letters.

'You wanted to talk about Miss Emery. I've heard an awful lot about her recently.'

'Are those letters in support of her?' Colette was pleased, but, if you could feel both ways at the same time, she was disappointed too. After all these weeks and the effort that had gone into spreading the word, she would have hoped for more letters. 'Is that all of them?'

'No,' said Mr Mortimer. 'These are just the ones I've opened so far.' He indicated a sack over in the corner. 'The rest are in there.'

Colette almost laughed in delight.

'Did you organise this?' asked Mr Mortimer.

'No,' Colette said truthfully. She hesitated, not knowing whether Mr Mortimer was going to hand out glory or blame. She needed to be able to report back to her friends. 'What makes you think it was organised? Surely it can't have come as a surprise to you that Miss Emery is so highly thought of?'

Mr Mortimer sighed and replaced the tray.

'I'm here to add my voice to all those others,' said Colette. 'It was my husband who caused Miss Emery to be fired.'

'He complained that she had broken confidentiality and she admitted it.'

'I want to make it clear that she didn't breach my confidentiality. I gave permission for my address to be given to my friends.'

'Nevertheless, your husband—'

'He withdrew my permission without telling me, so as to keep my friends from me. He has just been up before the magistrate for having beaten me. He pleaded guilty. There was never any doubt as to his guilt.'

Mr Mortimer coughed and didn't meet her eyes. 'I, er, read about it in the *Evening News*.'

Heat crept across Colette's face. 'I don't propose to embarrass either of us by discussing the ins and outs of my marriage, Mr Mortimer. I would simply ask you to bear in mind, while you read all those glowing testimonials to the quality of Miss Emery's work, that I gave her my permission willingly, and the person who withdrew my permission is also the brute who put me in hospital.'

Colette put her key in the lock. A moment later she was inside her house. Her house. Tony was gone and she had it to herself. Would she stay? Take in a lodger? Would she hand back the key to the landlord? She wasn't sure what her position was. Was she under an obligation to keep the house for Tony's sake?

She didn't want to be plagued by thoughts like that just now. She didn't want to spoil the pleasure and, yes, the pride she felt at having spoken up for Miss Emery. The old Colette would have been scared of doing such a thing.

She put down her luggage and took off her hat and blue coat and unwound her cream wool scarf, pulling off her gloves. The house was chilly. She went into the parlour and set about laying the fire. Then she made herself a cup of tea and sat on the hearthrug. She would drink this and then go to the shops and re-register. It would feel odd, cooking for one. She had never done that before. People said it was easy not to bother when it was just for yourself. She mustn't fall into that trap.

'Hello, Colette.'

Her heart bumped and she spilled her tea.

'Careful,' said Tony, walking into the room.

She stared up at him. 'I thought you'd left.'

Tony smiled. 'Did I give you the wrong leaving date? So sorry. My mistake.' Then his voice hardened. 'You didn't think I'd leave without a proper goodbye, did you?'

The inside of Colette's head swirled. For a few seconds, black spots appeared in front of her eyes. She couldn't speak.

'That's what I like to see,' said Tony, 'some proper respect.'

Everyone thought he'd gone. There was nobody to help her.

'What do you want?' she whispered.

'I'm not going to slap you around, so you can take that look off your face for a start. I just want to say goodbye, that's all. I gave you every opportunity to do it the nice way by reconciling and starting again, and you wouldn't. So now we're going to do it this way, with me reminding you that you are my wife and that will never change. There will be a lot of divorces when this war is over, what with all these spur-of-the-moment weddings and the number of babies that are going to be difficult to explain when the husbands come home. But I'll tell you now, just in case your friends have put any silly ideas in your head: there will never be a divorce for you and me. We shall be together for ever.'

Tony bent down and kissed her hard on the mouth.

'Goodbye, darling.'

CHAPTER FORTY-ONE

Hearing that the Waddens were going to move away and start a new life in Annerby gladdened Mabel and made her proud of Pops for making it happen. All her life she had been aware of being nouveau riche and not quite good enough, but by crikey, no amount of breeding could have made Pops a better man. He and Miss Emery's old boss, the welfare supervisor for women and girls, had between them enabled Louise to quit her railway job, no easy matter when you were engaged in war work, but Louise and Mrs Wadden would now have war jobs in Pops's factory, where young Clifford was to be tried out to see if he was worthy of an apprenticeship.

Bernice and Bette were upset that Louise was leaving, and Louise was too, but they all knew this was for the best.

'Thanks, Mabel,' said Lou. She sounded almost shy.

'Don't thank me,' Mabel said warmly. 'Thank my dad when you meet him.'

'It's such a good thing for the boys,' enthused Louise. 'They'll have the chance to grow up and get jobs in a place where no one has heard of Dad or Rob. It'll make all the difference.'

'We'll miss you, Lou,' said Bette. 'You may be scrawny, but you know how to wield a crowbar.'

The Waddens' good news went some way to making up for Mabel's disappointment that Harry couldn't get away for Christmas. Determined to be sensible about it, she coped by throwing herself into the preparations for the

Christmas festivities at Darley Court. She helped carry the boxes of decorations and garlands, oohing and aahing along with her friends and Miss Brown's land girls at the beauty and quality of the strings of coloured beads, blown-glass baubles, tartan streamers, delicate paper lanterns, red velvet stockings tipped with fur, and an exquisite wooden nativity set.

'And we have more bunting than you can shake a stick at,' said Miss Brown.

Putting up the decorations was a pleasure for everyone. They sang as they worked, the most popular song being 'White Christmas' from the film *Holiday Inn*, which was lifting everyone's spirits at the moment. Persephone master-minded the decorating operation in her usual pleasant way, but with an eye for detail and an understanding of the best order in which to do things that made the others joke that you could tell she was a general's daughter.

'We want all the guests, young and older, to feel they're walking into something magical,' said Persephone. 'The decorations must start in the front hall – in fact, on the day itself, we must decorate around the outside of the front door as well.'

'Leave the door to us,' said one of the land girls. 'We'll cut masses of holly and intertwine it with as many ribbons as we can lay hands on.'

'The guests must have decorations all around them,' said Persephone, 'including up above as they enter the building, all the way to the boardroom, where the children's party will be held, and the ballroom. We also need plenty of decs for those rooms, so we must be careful how we apportion everything. And I think we should have a Union flag and a Stars and Stripes hanging side by side from the hall ceiling.'

'That would be perfect,' said Mabel.

'Very appropriate,' Alison agreed. 'A good reminder.'

'And don't forget we've got the paper flags the children made,' said Cordelia. 'I've got them in boxes at home. We'll bring them with us next time, won't we, Emily?'

Emily nodded. Mabel was pleased to see her here. Cordelia had discreetly told the rest of them about the boyfriend who had changed his mind.

'No, that's not fair,' she'd said. 'He didn't change his mind as such. The friendship was what he wanted for some time, but then he grew out of it.'

'And Emily hasn't,' Margaret said sympathetically.

'No, she hasn't,' said Cordelia. 'Raymond will be called up soon, which at least gets him off the scene.' She looked round at the others. 'You'll all keep an eye on Emily, won't you? But don't say anything.'

They had all promised. Emily was more or less a little sister to them and they were very fond of her. Now, although she was helping with the decorating, it was clear she wasn't her usual self.

'But top marks to her for coming along,' Alison whispered to Mabel. 'I hope this takes her mind off it for a bit.'

Mabel hoped so too. It certainly put her own disappointment over Harry into perspective and she made a point of behaving in a jolly way even though she didn't altogether feel like it.

Cordelia and Dot sat in the buffet, just the two of them, comparing notes about Christmas.

'There's not a turkey to be had, of course,' said Dot.

'Of course,' Cordelia agreed, a wry note in her voice. 'It's only to be expected with the government controlling the price. I believe farmers can make hardly any profit from turkeys. What will your mock turkey be this year?'

'We aren't having anything mock this year,' said Dot. 'My sister Minnie keeps chickens and she's promised me one. Mind you, it's not exactly in the first flush of youth, so it'll need to be boiled slowly before it's roasted. It'll want smothering in fat an' all. But however it turns out, it'll be better than the year me and the lady up the road swapped rabbits.' She smiled. 'Better for my nerves, anyroad. I spent the whole meal dreading the children asking awkward questions.'

'What have you got them for Christmas? They're growing up now.'

'Aye, thirteen last birthday,' said Dot. 'They'll be finishing school next summer. The time goes so quick. Gone are the days of toys.'

'Not that toys are easy to come by these days,' said Cordelia.

'I've knitted a cardy for our Jenny and a pullover for Jimmy, and I got Jimmy a model kit of a Hawker Hurricane. You'll never guess what I found in the shops for Jenny. Velvet slippers. Eight and sixpence, plus three coupons.'

'She'll love them,' said Cordelia.

'Aye, she will. She likes pretty things, does our Jenny, and after bringing up two boys, it's a big treat for me to have a girl to buy for. How's your Emily doing?'

'Soldiering on. What choice does she have? I hear her crying herself to sleep and it makes me want to crown that boy, but it isn't his fault. I know that.'

Dot started to answer, then a figure appeared beside their table and they both looked up.

'Miss Emery,' said Dot.

'I'm pleased to see you both,' said Miss Emery, 'though I was hoping more of you would be here.'

'Just us today,' said Dot.

'Will you join us?' asked Cordelia.

Miss Emery sat down. 'Thank you. I want you and your friends to be the first to know.' She smiled, and for the first time it wasn't a small, professional smile but the real thing. 'I've been given my job back.'

'Well, that is good news,' Dot said warmly.

'I'm sure I have you and your friends to thank for it. I should make it clear that Mr Mortimer has no idea about that. As far as the powers that be are concerned, dozens of women wrote letters of support quite spontaneously when they heard I'd left, but I imagine that certain people had something to do with it.' Miss Emery raised her eyebrows at them.

'I can't think what you mean.' Dot smothered a smile.

'No, I don't suppose you can,' Miss Emery replied. 'But if anybody did help matters along in my favour, I'd like them to know how deeply grateful I am.' She had to pause for a moment, her eyes suspiciously bright. 'It's the best Christmas present I could possibly have had.'

Even though Cordelia was completely accustomed to the blackout, there was something odd about going from a conversation about Christmas straight into total darkness outside. There ought to be lights everywhere, welcoming the festive season and making everyone feel jolly.

She travelled home on the bus. She was looking forward to this evening because she and Kenneth and others from church were going carol-singing, but would Emily want to come with them? That had been the plan, but since then Emily's world had fallen to pieces. Even if she came, her heart wouldn't be in it.

Cordelia felt torn. She was half dreading the event for Emily's sake, but looking forward to it for her own, which made her feel guilty, as if she wasn't putting her daughter first, which was what she'd done for the past sixteen years. It was Emily who had made her life worthwhile and given it true meaning. Realising that things had changed for her was sobering, but at the same time made Cordelia feel she was on the brink of something special. She couldn't help smiling to herself. The world might not be filled with twinkling lights, but she felt as if she was twinkling in her heart. How silly – and yet how wonderful.

At home, she gently heated up the Scotch broth she'd prepared yesterday, while she cooked some liver. She loathed liver and wouldn't have touched it with a bargepole before the war, but it was very good for you and Emily needed building up. Like many middle-class housewives, Cordelia had adopted the British Restaurant style of catering, namely either a starter and a main course or a main course followed by a pudding, but never all three together. It wasn't patriotic.

'Shall you come carol-singing with Mummy and me?' Kenneth asked Emily.

'Do come, darling,' Cordelia encouraged her. 'It'll do you good and you have such a pretty voice.'

She and Kenneth looked at one another, sharing their concern for their daughter. But there was more than that in the look. There was something that gave Cordelia a little lurching sensation in the pit of her stomach and she went all tingly in a way she hadn't since she was a girl.

'I'll come,' said Emily. 'I suppose I ought to see Lucy and get it over with.'

'Get what over with?' asked Kenneth.

'Didn't I mention it?' Emily asked in a breezy voice that fooled no one. 'Charlie's coming home for Christmas and they're going to get engaged.'

Cordelia felt as though a door had slammed shut in her chest. Oh, poor Emily.

Emily looked at her plate and put down her knife and fork. 'May I leave the table? I'm not hungry.'

'Eat a little more,' said Kenneth, 'and we'll decide on a plan of action for tonight. You must spend a bit of time with

Lucy, Emily. She's your friend and she deserves that consideration. Then I'll whisk you away to help with the song sheets and Mummy can practise saying, "Oh, what a shame. We have other arrangements for that evening," in case Lucy's mother mentions an engagement party. And when we get home, we'll open the chocolate I bought for Christmas and gorge ourselves. Will that make it all a bit more bearable?'

'Daddy, you're lovely,' said Emily.

'Yes, you are,' said Cordelia, and meant it.

'Well, I don't know,' said Kenneth. 'A man mentions chocolate and suddenly all the ladies in the room are his greatest admirers.'

And Emily laughed. She actually laughed. Whatever else happened this festive season, Cordelia felt nothing could be better than that.

CHAPTER FORTY-TWO

Christmas Eve

The children's party was a huge success. All the friends were there to help, apart from Mabel, who had gone home to Annerby yesterday. At Miss Brown's suggestion, some ancient curtains had been borne down from the attics and the WVS had cut them up and sewn them into velvet and chintz sashes for all the children.

'Some children will have party clothes and others won't,' said Miss Brown. 'This way, everyone gets something special to wear and afterwards it can all go to salvage.'

One set of red velvet curtains had been used to make a Father Christmas suit for Kenneth. The coat was to be stuffed with cushions and one of the WVS ladies had produced a curly white wig that had belonged to her late mother and which she had allowed Cordelia to chop up and turn into a beard. Last year, Kenneth would never have offered to dress up in this way. He had been far too much of a stuffed shirt. It brought home to Cordelia that she wasn't the only one who had changed in recent months.

She couldn't have been more delighted with how the party went. From the moment she saw the first children walk into Darley Court's grand entrance hall, where their eyes popped open at the sight of the holly-bedecked bannisters, mantelpiece and hearth, and the two huge flags hanging proudly, symbolising the friendship of two great

nations, she was sure the afternoon was going to be everything she had hoped for.

She had asked if a piano could be moved into the board-
room for the party.

'But I never expected a baby grand,' she whispered to
Persephone.

Persephone grinned. 'This is Darley Court, you know.
Only the best for our guests.'

Persephone and Alison took turns to belt out popular
tunes on the piano: 'Run, Rabbit, Run' for musical chairs,
'It's a Hap-Hap-Happy Day' for pass the parcel and 'We're
Gonna Hang Out the Washing on the Siegfried Line' for
railway stations, as well as the traditional tunes for oranges
and lemons and who stole the watch and chain?

The Americans, bless their generous hearts, had provided heaps of chocolate bars, so many, in fact, that not
only could every single game have first, second and third
prizes, but there were going to be enough left over for every
child to have one to take home.

While hunt the thimble was in progress, to the accom-
paniment of 'Bless 'Em All', Cordelia and her team of
helpers started putting out the plates of sandwiches and
fairy cakes on a long table in the next room. The food might
not be very Christmassy, but the room was decorated and
one of the land girls was going to play carols while the children tucked in.

Once all the sandwiches and little cakes had been demol-
ished, there was a loud knock on the door.

'Who's that?' asked the children, looking round.

'Is it Father Christmas?' asked one tot.

'No, honey, it's the US Army,' announced a handsome
young American soldier, walking in, followed by more soldiers, much to the delight of the children – and also,
Cordelia noticed, to the delight of the women helping.

Although it was a lovely surprise, Cordelia's heart sank. Yes, the arrival of the soldiers was exciting and wonderful, but was Kenneth in his guise as Father Christmas going to be upstaged? That would be such a shame.

Then Persephone appeared and called for silence.

'In a moment, I'm going to ask all the children to stand up and tuck their chairs under, so we can all walk outside in a nice line, because we've got a special visitor.'

Cordelia frowned. This wasn't part of her plan.

Everybody trooped outside and there, coming up the drive, was an American jeep in the back of which was a big chair and sitting on it was—

'Father Christmas!' shouted the children, jumping up and down in excitement. 'It's Father Christmas.'

A little girl tugged at Cordelia's hand. 'Is he the American Father Christmas? Is he different to our Father Christmas?'

But Cordelia was too choked with tears of pride and happiness to answer.

'Success follows success,' Miss Brown remarked to Cordelia as they watched couples waltz around the floor during the afternoon tea dance.

'People keep congratulating me as if I'm responsible for everything,' said Cordelia, 'but I couldn't have organised it without a lot of help. It was a team effort.'

'With you at the helm, Mrs Masters. Ah, Mr Masters,' Miss Brown added as Kenneth came over, now dressed in his suit and tie. 'Is your wife always this bashful about accepting compliments?'

Kenneth smiled. He was growing more distinguished as the years went by and while Cordelia had been proud to be on his arm, she had always thought he looked rather austere. These days, however, he was smiling more and she had realised what kind eyes he had. How could she never have noticed before?

'I'm always happy to receive compliments on Cordelia's behalf,' he told Miss Brown, 'because I know what an excellent organiser she is.'

Cordelia looked around the ballroom. The band members were playing more quietly than they would this evening, as befitted the genteel air of an afternoon tea dance. Plenty of couples were on the floor and it was good to see the different ages mixed up. The Americans were gallantly dancing with elderly ladies as well as with the girls. Where was Emily?

Cordelia found her in the kitchen, helping to prepare the tea, which was to be served on pretty china and cake stands and brought to the tables surrounding the dance floor. Mrs Mitchell was in charge of the kitchen, assisted by her band of helpers, including Mrs Grayson, Mrs Cooper and Colette.

'Wouldn't you like to dance?' Cordelia asked Colette.

Colette shook her head. 'I'm happy here, thank you.'

'Have you seen Emily?'

'She's through there, polishing the cutlery.'

Cordelia went to help her daughter.

'Don't you feel like dancing, darling?'

Emily shook her head and Cordelia's heart reached out to her. Like Colette, but in a completely different way, Emily had been hurt by a man. It was understandable that she wanted to hide herself away, but at the same time Cordelia wanted so much for her.

'It won't always be this way, you know,' said Cordelia.

'What won't?'

'I know how badly hurt you are,' said Cordelia and Emily flicked a glance at her that said she couldn't possibly understand, but Cordelia persevered. 'But you will recover and

345

you will feel better. It takes time. The most important thing is, please don't close yourself off.'

'If you're saying what I think you're saying, Mummy, please stop.' A sharp note entered Emily's voice. 'I'm not interested in finding another boyfriend.'

'Not now, obviously, but—'

'Never,' Emily stated flatly. 'The way I feel, I can assure you it will be never.'

'Darling, please listen. I can't bear to see you unhappy and my heart aches for you. Please don't close your heart, no matter how desperate you feel. The truth is, my darling, you will never find true happiness unless you are willing to reopen your heart.'

CHAPTER FORTY-THREE

There was a fireplace in Mabel's bedroom in Kirkland House, but in these days of wartime shortages the upstairs fires weren't being used. Mabel looked at the evening dresses in her wardrobe. Mumsy had asked her to wear something special, but honestly, she felt more like pulling on a woolly and two pairs of socks. Did she possess an evening gown that she could wear a vest underneath?

'It's Christmas Eve and I'm holding a sherry party,' Mumsy had said.

'You've got sherry?' Mabel had asked, impressed. 'I thought nobody had any alcohol left these days.'

Mumsy lifted her chin. 'I got your father to buy six cases when war was declared.'

Mabel laughed. 'No wonder lots of guests are coming. They're probably all gasping for a drop of the hard stuff.'

'Don't be vulgar, Mabel.'

Now, as Mabel stood in front of her open wardrobe, there was a knock on her door and Mumsy came in. She wore a black velvet gown adorned with beads.

'Aren't you dressed yet, Mabel? Our guests will start arriving soon.' Mumsy came to stand in front of the wardrobe. 'Wear this one.'

She reached in and took out a silk-taffeta gown with a sweetheart neckline and tiny sleeves. The fitted bodice, with its slightly dropped waist, was a soft green, while the flared skirt was a toning darker green.

'It's rather flimsy,' Mabel said doubtfully.

'It's warmer downstairs,' said Mumsy. 'Besides, you'll be too happy and excited to notice the temperature.'

It was true that Mabel was looking forward to seeing old friends again, but even so, Mumsy's claim seemed to be stretching a point.

'Wear it to please me,' said Mumsy. 'You'll look beautiful in it. I'll help you put it on.'

The gown was indeed lovely and seeing her reflection made Mabel feel special. Nevertheless, she reached for a diaphanous wrap and draped it around her shoulders.

'It's either this or I wear my dressing gown over the top,' she told Mumsy in a pretend stern voice.

Together, they went down to the drawing room, where there were logs on the fire. The Bradshaws were by no means reliant on the measly coal allowance for heating, but Pops had insisted on there being no fires upstairs so that nobody could ever accuse them of enjoying unpatriotic comforts.

Guests arrived and the room started to fill. Mabel was pleased to see Mr and Mrs Wilmore, the parents of her late friend Althea, whom she had grown up with and whose loss had changed the course of her life.

To Mabel's great joy, Mumsy had invited half a dozen of the old folk Mabel used to visit when she lived here, including dear Mrs Kennedy, who had always been her particular favourite. Dear Mrs Kennedy had always been a little bird of a woman with swollen knuckles in once busy though now pretty well useless hands, but now she looked even more frail and Pops guided her straight to an armchair that had been drawn close to the fire so she could keep warm.

Mabel kissed Mumsy. 'Thank you. It's a lovely surprise.' She smiled wickedly. 'Though I'm not sure what the book of etiquette would have to say about mixing the classes in a social event.'

'We both know precisely what it would say,' answered Mumsy, 'and under normal circumstances it wouldn't be correct, of course, but this is a special occasion. I want you to be happy, Mabel, and that trumps etiquette.'

About to make a joke out of it, Mabel changed her mind when she saw the serious look in Mumsy's eyes. She knew how much her parents loved her.

The local doctor and his wife arrived. Pops circulated, pouring sherry into the best crystal, which twinkled in the firelight.

'I think the last guest has arrived,' said Mumsy. 'Mabel, would you mind?'

She gave Mabel a push towards the door. Mabel opened it – and stopped dead. There stood Harry. He came forward and reached to close the door behind her, so that they were alone in the hall.

'Harry!' Mabel could hardly believe her eyes. 'You're here? You came after all.' She thought she might burst into tears.

Taking her hand, Harry led her into the library, where a cheerful fire welcomed them. He took her to the hearthrug and stood facing her.

'I was always going to come,' he said, the firelight casting a glow over his handsome features. 'I wrote to your parents and we arranged this surprise.'

'It's certainly that.' Her heart was still racing.

'A good one, I hope.'

'None better.'

'Good. That's what I hoped you'd say. You mean everything to me and I hope I mean just as much to you.'

Mabel moved closer. Harry bent his face to hers and she happily accepted his kiss, warmth and desire and utter rightness pouring through her, filling her veins with joy.

When the kiss ended and Harry lifted his head, he kept his eyes closed for a moment. Then he opened them and looked deep into her eyes. She thought he was about to speak, but instead – her heart thudded – he sank down onto one knee. He took one of her hands and gazed up at her. Mabel trembled with anticipation as he produced a small box from his pocket and opened it to reveal a ruby that flashed in the firelight.

'Mabel Bradshaw, you are the most wonderful girl in the world and I don't deserve you, but that doesn't stop me adoring you and longing to spend the rest of my life with you. Will you marry me?'

'Yes,' Mabel said almost before he had finished asking. 'Oh, yes.'

She held out her hand and Harry slipped the ruby onto her finger. She hardly had time to gaze at it before he was on his feet, claiming a kiss.

'Mrs Harry Knatchbull,' he whispered and Mabel shivered in delight. 'Do you like the ring?'

'I love it. I've always loved rubies.'

'That's what your mother said.'

'Did she?' Mabel laughed. 'We'd better go and tell people, hadn't we? Though I don't suppose it's going to come as a surprise.'

'You don't mind that, do you?'

'Not at all, though you're a brute to put me through the misery of thinking you wouldn't be here.'

'I thought about proposing in Manchester so we could celebrate with your friends,' said Harry, 'but this way seemed more appropriate.'

'It's perfect.' Mabel spoke from her heart.

Leaving the library, they crossed the hall to the drawing room. As they entered, everyone was already looking their way, sherry glasses at the ready.

Mabel laughed. 'Yes, you can drink a toast.'

While all their guests chorused 'Mabel and Harry,' Mumsy rushed across the room, followed by Pops. Mumsy kissed Mabel while Pops pumped Harry's hand.

'Congratulations, darling,' said Mumsy. 'I'm so happy for you.'

'It was very naughty of you to arrange all this behind my back,' said Mabel, 'though I should have guessed when you dug out the sherry.'

'Let me see the ring.'

Mabel held out her hand, slightly splaying her fingers. 'Oh.' Her arm was bare. 'My wrap must have slipped off when we were in the library. I didn't notice.'

'Didn't you? And are you warm enough?'

'Yes, thanks,' said Mabel, laughing again.

'Told you,' said Mumsy.

CHAPTER FORTY-FOUR

The evening dance at Darley Court was in full swing, the ballroom crowded with dancers. As well as plenty of local people, another contingent of Americans had arrived.

'That'll keep the land girls happy,' Miss Brown said drily.

'And not just the land girls,' Cordelia added.

Miss Brown went off to circulate and Cordelia spotted Dot, who had a broad smile on her face. Cordelia went over to her.

'You look happy.'

'That doesn't begin to express it.' Dot's hazel eyes positively glowed. 'Our Pammy had a letter from Archie today. He's fine and so is our Harry.'

'Oh, Dot, that's marvellous news. I'm so pleased for you.'

'Thanks, love. Happening today of all days, it feels like all my Christmases have come at once. It's like a miracle.'

'A Christmas miracle,' said Cordelia.

'That's the best kind.'

'I know how worried you've been,' said Cordelia.

'Do you? That's more than I did. I've been trying to hold it inside for so long. I couldn't let myself see how bad I really felt.'

Cordelia nodded. 'But now that it's over, it's come flooding out. You must be exhausted.'

Dot grinned. 'I've no time to be tired tonight. I'm going to dance every dance.'

'I feel a bit that way myself,' said Cordelia.

'Oh aye?' Dot eyed her shrewdly. 'I know you, Cordelia Masters, and I know that when it's an event you've organised yourself, you spend the whole time flitting about making sure everything is as it should be. So if you're in the mood for tripping the light fantastic, there must be another reason. I haven't forgotten you saying how you wanted to be a better wife. I take it things have worked out for the best.'

'Very much so,' Cordelia admitted and laughed.

'Then stop flitting about being in charge and go and dance with your husband.'

'Is that an order, Mrs Green?'

'Dashed right, it is, Mrs Masters.'

They parted. Cordelia stood at the edge of the dance floor for a minute, enjoying the spectacle. All the ladies had made an effort to dress up, even those who didn't possess formal evening attire. Cordelia was wearing a full-length evening gown that rippled as she moved.

Kenneth appeared by her side. 'Would you like to dance?'

Cordelia said, 'Actually, no,' and saw the disappointment in his face.

'Busy organising, are you?'

'What I should have said is, I'd love to dance with you, but first I'd like us to talk.'

They left the ballroom and sat in an alcove beneath an arch of tiny silver stars.

'Is everything all right?' Kenneth asked. 'Is it Emily?'

'She's fine – well, she isn't, but she's coping.'

'The poor girl, she's really going through it.'

'Kenneth, I know that a good deal of our conversation has always been devoted to Emily, but I'd like to talk about . . . us. Some time ago, I kissed you and then you seemed to be going to kiss me, but instead you said, "Don't do it if you don't mean it." Well, I do mean it. I know that now.'

353

'Cordelia—'

'Please let me say this. I want to say everything and then you can decide if it's what you want. You know about Kit. My love for him came from his good looks, his artistic temperament and his sense of fun.' Cordelia paused for a moment as she remembered how Kit's eyes used to sparkle. 'The feeling I have for you is very different to that all-consuming madness. I've always admired you and respected you, but the deeper feeling I have for you now has grown out of seeing your sensitivity towards Emily. That seemed to reach right inside my heart. We're both devoted to her and what I feel for you now has grown from that shared devotion. It's . . . a love that has been sixteen years in the making.'

'Love?'

'Yes.' Cordelia kept her gaze on his face.

'Say it. Say the words I have dreamed of hearing ever since I met you.'

'Ever since . . .?'

'Oh yes. I have loved you for so long, Cordelia.'

She reached for his hand. 'I always knew I had a good husband. I always knew my daughter had the best possible father. I spent years trying to believe that that was enough, that it was as much as I could hope for, but I was wrong and it was seeing my young friends so happy in their relationships that made me realise I wanted, needed more. I've looked at you through new eyes in recent months and I've seen myself through new eyes too. My heart has woken up, Kenneth. I love you. You are the one my heart wants.'

Kenneth leaned over and kissed her tenderly, making her heart flutter. Dot wasn't the only one to have a Christmas miracle. Kenneth stood up and held out his hand to her.

'Would you like to dance?' he asked. 'It will be our wedding dance.'

CHAPTER FORTY-FIVE

'Are you sure you don't want to go and dance?' Mrs O'Brien, one of the helpers, asked Colette. 'A young thing like you shouldn't be working non-stop in here. You should be on the dance floor, having a good time.' She glanced down at Colette's hand and Colette was too late to hide it in the folds of her apron. 'You won't find a husband in the kitchen.' Mrs O'Brien laughed.

'Colette!'

'In here, chuck, if you've got a minute.'

The two voices called through the open doorway from the big scullery, where Mrs Grayson and Mrs Cooper were working side by side at one of the sinks.

'Excuse me,' Colette murmured to Mrs O'Brien and darted away.

'We thought you needed rescuing,' said Mrs Grayson.

'I did, a bit. More than a bit. She meant well.'

'If nowt else,' said Mrs Cooper, 'it shows that not everyone knows the story of you and Tony, so take heart from that.'

It had been a long afternoon and evening, but thoroughly worthwhile. It had taken ages to clear up after the children's party – not that anybody minded. As well as the washing-up, there were the floors to sweep and the furniture to be dusted. Cordelia was adamant that the rooms must be returned to Miss Brown in the condition in which they'd been received, which meant that every fingermark had to be removed. All the furniture had to be put back too, though Miss Brown had said the baby grand could stay there for now.

Then there had been the afternoon tea to prepare for the tea dance, after which all that beautiful china had to be lovingly washed and dried. The band members were all offered a snack before they started again, and the ballroom had to be cleaned and made ready for the evening.

'We're on the final stretch now,' said Mrs Grayson. 'There'll just be the clearing up to do when the dance finishes. The American boys have offered to put away all the tables and chairs.'

'I hope everyone has had a good time,' said Mrs Cooper.

'I'm sure they have,' said Colette, 'especially the children.'

'What about you, love?' asked Mrs Cooper.

Colette breathed out a deep, gratifying sigh. 'It's been a good day. It's taken me out of myself. I'm looking forward to spending Christmas Day with the two of you.'

'And we can't wait to have you. There will be no Mabel or Alison, but Margaret will be there and we've invited her father.'

'Much better than last year, when they were estranged,' said Mrs Cooper. 'And we've got the Waddens coming an' all.'

'That's kind of you,' said Colette.

'I wouldn't want me and Mrs Wadden to part without being on good terms. She did a bad thing, but she was forced into it and I want her to know I don't hold it against her.'

'It's going to be a lovely day,' said Colette. Then she put her arms around Mrs Grayson. 'I want to say how sorry I am for the grief and upset you went through last Christmas because of me.'

'It wasn't your fault,' said Mrs Grayson. 'You did what needed doing. I understand that. We all do. But last Christmas was hard. This year, though, is going to be wonderful.'

'I'm looking forward to the church bells being allowed to ring,' said Mrs Cooper. 'There's hope in the air this Christmas, with the way the war's going.'

They all looked round as Mrs Mitchell appeared in the doorway.

'Look at you three,' said the housekeeper, 'all huddled in here like the naughty children at the back of the classroom.'

'We're just about finished,' said Mrs Cooper.

'Until the next lot,' said Mrs Grayson.

'The kettle's boiling,' said Mrs Mitchell. 'Come and take the weight off your feet.'

As Mrs Grayson went off with her friend, Mrs Cooper looked at Colette.

'You go, chuck. I'm just going to step outside for a few minutes.'

'I'll come with you.'

They fetched their coats and went outside. It was chilly and overcast. The sound of the band carried faintly through the night air – a foxtrot.

Mrs Cooper said, 'I stood outside last Christmas Eve, thinking about you.'

Colette said nothing, but slipped her arm through her friend's and stood close.

'We had a little memorial service for you,' said Mrs Cooper. 'Not at church, not a proper service. Just a special few minutes between ourselves in Wilton Close. All your friends were there. We talked about you and what we valued about you.' She shook her head. 'I don't know how I got through it. The others were so hurt and upset, but I knew you were all right. I'd received that Christmas card from you, so I knew for certain you'd got away. I hadn't been completely sure before that, because the marshalling yard took such a hammering and I'd been asking myself, what if you really had been killed? After everything we'd

357

planned, what if you really had been killed? Then your card came and I knew you were safe.'

'And you had to sit and listen while everyone talked about me and said their goodbyes,' Colette said quietly, picturing it. 'I'm so sorry you had to go through that.'

Mrs Cooper squeezed Colette's arm with her own arm at the same time as lifting her other hand to touch Colette's cheek.

'Eh, love, don't say that. All I wanted was for you to be safe. When Tony brought you back from London in the summer, I were terrified. I knew you'd never have come willingly. All that claptrap about a breakdown! But I never dared breathe a word to anyone, because I was scared for you – aye, and for myself an' all. I don't mind admitting it. Tony came round – it were the evening he warned us all off visiting you – and somehow or other, he got us all talking about identity papers and fraud and prison sentences, and I knew he meant it as a warning to me. I knew that he knew what I'd done for you to help you get away from him.'

'You had that fear hanging over you at the same time as you were under suspicion for the burglaries.' Colette put her arms around this dear, brave lady to whom she owed so much. 'It's over now. It's all over.'

Mrs Cooper pushed her away slightly, keeping hold of her hands. 'I'd do it all again. Don't imagine I regret it, because I don't.' She gave Colette a watery smile. 'You're my Betsy, you are.'

'Betsy Cooper.' Colette smiled. 'I loved being Betsy. You gave me much more than you know when you let me have Lizzie's papers. I didn't just get a new name. You gave me my freedom. Betsy had a good life. *I* had a good life as Betsy. I had a job and new friends, and I was thankful for the things I *no longer* had: the fear of saying the wrong thing or doing the wrong thing, the fear that someone at work would annoy Tony and he'd take it out on me. I used to be scared the whole time, but you took that away. I'll be grateful to you until the day I die.'

'Oh, chuck.'

They moved, standing side by side again, arm in arm. It felt right for them to stand close like this. Indoors, the sweet strains of a slow waltz finished and there was the faint sound of clapping before the band struck up a lively quick-step.

'Things didn't turn out the way we meant them to,' said Colette. 'Betsy was meant to stay away for good. Coming back was hard. Living with Tony again was hard. But things worked out in the end.'

'Only because he beat you so badly that you ended up in hospital.'

'No, things worked out because I stood up for myself and insisted on pressing charges against him. He had no option but to plead guilty, though it was horrible when his solicitor tried to make out it was my fault.'

'At least he's gone now,' said Mrs Cooper.

'I've been promised he won't be given leave after his basic training,' said Colette. 'He'll be shipped straight out. The further away the better, as far as I'm concerned.'

'He might get killed,' said Mrs Cooper. 'God forgive me for saying it, but he might get killed.'

'He might. He might not. But he's gone now and I hope "now" lasts a very long time. Not that I want the war to go on and on, but you know what I mean.'

'Aye, chuck. You're a brave lass.'

'I don't think I am.'

'Your friends think you are.'

'Can I tell you something? It's not the sort of thing people talk about, but I feel as if I want someone to know and you . . . you're the right person.' Colette hesitated. 'My mother would have died of embarrassment if I'd said it to her.'

'There are lots of things folk don't talk about, as you know all too well,' said Mrs Cooper. 'If you've got summat to tell me, I'll listen and I'll do my best not to expire from shock.'

That made Colette smile as well as giving her the little push she needed. 'Tony was desperate for us to have a baby and I . . . I thought he might have got his wish, but . . .' And here came the bit where Mother would have died. 'I don't know whether it was an early miscarriage or a very heavy monthly, but . . . there's no baby.'

'That's probably for the best,' Mrs Cooper said gently.

'A baby would have tied me to Tony for ever,' said Colette, 'and that would have been unbearable.'

'Aye, it would.'

'So why did I sob my heart out?' asked Colette, finally getting to what she really wanted to say.

'Because life's complicated. Because you married a bad 'un, but you've got what it takes to be a good mother. Or maybe because you were plain exhausted after everything you've gone through. The main thing is to be positive. Like you say, if you had a baby, you'd be stuck with Tony for keeps.'

'I know and that would be intolerable.'

'But you still cried,' Mrs Cooper said gently. 'That's because you're a good person. You can wonder about the child that never was at the same time as being glad to be free of your rotten scoundrel of a husband. Some folk might not think you can, but you and I know better, don't we, eh? Don't you fret about what others might think, love. You know who your friends are and we all love you and want nothing but the best for you. Shall I tell you what I think? I know you never wanted to come back here. It were never meant to happen and you've gone through all sorts of pain since Tony brought you back. But he's gone now and you're still here. I know you made a good life for yourself as Betsy, but you're Colette again now – Colette without Tony wielding his power over you. You're my miracle, that's what you are.'

Colette's throat felt thick with emotion, but she managed to say, 'I'll tell you what the real miracle is. I've got choices now. I've never had choices before, except briefly when I was Betsy. It's extraordinary. I feel all light and excited inside. Choices – me! I'm going to see Miss Emery after Christmas and ask for a job.'

'Good for you,' said Mrs Cooper. 'Maybe you'll get your old job back. You liked that and you were good at it. What about the house? Will you stop on?'

'For the time being, while I find my feet. I certainly won't be living there when Tony comes home.' Colette shivered. 'It all comes back to him, doesn't it? I feel as if I want to shake him off for good and stop thinking about him.'

'That'll come,' Mrs Cooper said soothingly, 'like it did when you were Betsy.'

Colette smiled. 'I learned a lot by being Betsy and you're the one who gave me that chance.'

From inside the building came the faint but immediately recognisable sound of 'We'll Meet Again', not just the music but everyone singing along.

'That's the last song you want to hear,' said Mrs Cooper. 'You don't want to meet Tony again.'

'No, I don't,' Colette agreed, 'but this song isn't about him. It's about decent people being separated from their loved ones. It's about all the good things we're fighting for. It's about Vera Lynn making all the boys overseas feel a little bit closer to home. It's about how much I missed you and all my friends when I was away in London and thought I would never be able to come back.' Colette linked her arm through Mrs Cooper's. 'Now let's go indoors and sing with everyone else to celebrate all of that.'

Welcome to

Penny Street

where your favourite authors and stories live.

Meet casts of characters you'll never forget,
create memories you'll treasure forever,
and discover places that will stay with
you long after the last page.

Turn the page to step into the home of

MAISIE THOMAS

and discover more about

The Railway Girls...

Dear Readers,

There are two wonderful things about writing a book for publication. I bet you can guess what the first one is. Yes, that's right – the sheer pleasure of writing the story. And the other one? It's the fact that it's everybody else's job to make my book as good as it can possibly be! It takes a lot of hard-working people to produce a book. In this letter, I'd like to introduce the team of talented colleagues who are responsible for getting this book into your hands.

If you read my step-by-step guide to planning a Railway Girls book (which can be found a few pages on from here), you'll learn more about how my editor, Katie Loughnane, and I work together. It is my job to create the story and plan the book, which is done in consultation with Katie. Katie also chooses the titles and briefs the Design team on the covers for my books, which happens very early on in the process. Ask any traditionally published author and they'll tell you that it's normal (and a little alarming) to look on Amazon and see a book available for pre-order that they've nowhere near finished writing yet!

The cover designer for the Railway Girls series is Emma Grey Gelder. When a new viewpoint character appears in a story, Emma works with a photographer to cast a model to be that character, then organises the photo shoots, making sure the girls are in outfits appropriate for the 1940s, whether they're dressed for work or in their own clothes. Out of the many pictures that are taken, Emma selects the best one of the three models together. After that, it's time to think about the cover as a whole and choose the background image and any seasonal touches, such as snow for the Christmas titles.

After I've finished the manuscript, I send it to Katie, whose job is to edit it – which means making suggestions that will bring out the best in it. For example, in *Miracle* Katie thought of ways to make Mabel's crime-solving plot more of an emotional journey.

When I have revised the story and Katie is happy with what I've done, she passes the manuscript over to Rose Waddilove, my managing editor. Rose is the person who oversees the copy-editing and proofreading process.

The copy-editor for the series is Caroline Johnson. The role of the copy-editor is to check everything in the story, whether it's a wartime date or the colour of someone's eyes, and to make sure there are no continuity errors. I personally keep lots of notes about the characters and the plots so I don't make mistakes, but my notes are nothing compared to Caroline's. I don't mind telling you that I made a mistake in *Miracle*, but fortunately Caroline picked it up immediately and saved the day.

My proofreader is Rachel Cross, who has been with the series from the beginning. Rachel's job is to do the final check to make sure that no mistakes have slipped through. You will have seen how many people have worked on the book by the point where Rachel receives it and you'd think that, between us, we'd have found every single error. Yet a handful always survive and Rachel has the task of finding them.

When it comes to marketing, the series is looked after by the wonderfully creative Hope Butler, who devises campaigns that are specific to each individual book. She is also responsible for the content across the Penny Street channels. As many of you will already know, Penny Street is a lively online community for readers who love enthralling and heartfelt historical fiction. Hope is the person who created the dramatic and beautiful promotional video of a train crossing a viaduct as part of the publicity campaign for *Hope for the Railway Girls*.

Marie-Louise Patton is my publicist for the series, providing copies of each book to her media contacts and to magazines and newspapers as well as to book-bloggers. She is the one who ensures there is a buzz of anticipation for each new title ahead of publication.

The person responsible for creating the finished book you are holding in your hands (or reading on your e-reader) is Tara Hodgson. As my production controller, she liaises with the type-setter and the printer to ensure everything runs smoothly and that the paperbacks have a high-quality finish. She also makes sure that the books are delivered to retailers promptly so that they receive their stock ahead of publication.

The Sales team is made up of Claire Simmonds, Jade Unwin, Mat Watterson, Olivia Allen and Evie Kettlewell. Right from the start, they've been the ones who have worked to get the Railway Girls titles on bookshelves in the various supermarkets and on the high street, as well as with online retailers.

So, as you can see, a published book isn't just the work of the author. There is a whole squad of people who contribute to the process and I can't begin to tell you how grateful I am to every-one who brings out the best in my books and makes sure that the reading experience for all of you is as good as it can possibly be.

I should also mention that I received a lot of help with this letter. Katie wrote a document for me called *The Lifecycle of a Book* to make sure that I got everything in the right order. She and Rose also ensured I had everyone's names so that no one was missed out. Therefore, it feels right to end this letter with …

Much love,

Maisie, Katie and Rose xx

A STEP-BY-STEP GUIDE TO PLANNING A RAILWAY GIRLS BOOK

1. Firstly, I think of who my three viewpoint characters will be, and what their plot lines could look like, and discuss them with Katie, my editor. I value her input because she understands what will make the most satisfying book for you, the readers.

2. To ensure the timeline of the book is accurate, I make a list of which day of the week was the first day of each month in the timeframe of the book. I also note what day of the week Valentine's Day, Christmas Day, etc. took place, as well as the dates of Easter Sunday and the bank holidays.

3. I list the important wartime events, with dates. For example, in *A Christmas Miracle for the Railway Girls*, events in North Africa are very important. I had to research exactly when the news of victory was broadcast on the wireless, which is why Cordelia, Kenneth and Emily stay up late to listen to the news. I was also lucky enough to find out who the newsreader was.

4. I list, with dates, things that happened on the home front. Changes to the rationing rules is an obvious example and, in this book, Cordelia, Dot, Mrs Cooper and Mrs Grayson mention the start of the new rationing year and the fact that sweets and chocolate will be rationed.

5. I think ahead: do I need to sow the seeds of something that's going to happen in a future book? For example, in *Hope for the Railway Girls*, Mrs Wadden started working for Mrs Cooper, which didn't seem significant in *Hope*, but performed a key part in *Miracle*. And something that happened at the end of *Hope* – or rather, something that *didn't* happen – has paved the way for a plot development in a future book. One thing I can promise you is that everything in my books happens for a reason … even if the reason won't become apparent until a couple of books down the line.

6. Using a separate sheet of A4 for every scene, I write down the main points of each scene for each viewpoint character, including how each scene will end. For me, it's essential to know from the outset how each scene finishes.

7. I cross-check to see if the three central characters have a similar number of scenes – it doesn't need to be exact, but it helps if they have approximately the same. Having said that, in *A Christmas Miracle for the Railway Girls*, Colette has a chunk of scenes in the middle of the book, because that was what was needed. It isn't an exact science!

8. I check each set of plot-strands against historical dates. My books are woven around real events and the individual plots reflect this.

9. Now, the scenes for the three characters have to be merged together into a single sequence.

10. Next, I put the scenes into a month-by-month timeline, starting at the end of the book. Why start at the end? Because this is what everything is building up to. You might expect a timeline to start at the beginning, but I find it easier to start at the end and work backwards.

11. Although it's important to balance the book fairly evenly in terms of the three character viewpoints, it's more important to create an overall plot that makes sense in terms of the time that is passing. (For example, I read a book a few years ago in which there were four key characters, one of whom was pregnant, so her condition dictated the amount of time the story had to last. But this stretched another character's plot to snapping point, because his plot would have been far more believable if it had been wrapped up in a matter of a few weeks.)

12. Finally, I go through the individual scenes to add references to details of life on the home front and also real events. Many of these references are date-sensitive, but obviously there are others that aren't. These details can only be added to a scene if they fit there naturally. Yes, books take a lot of research, but it must never look like research – it must be woven seamlessly into the narrative. It's always exciting to reach this stage in the process because this is when the plotlines and all the detailed elements from the time period merge together and bring the book to life.

So there are the 12 steps that go into the planning. After that, it's time to start writing the book!

BIBLIOGRAPHY

These are the books that helped me write *A Christmas Miracle for the Railway Girls*. I am grateful to all the authors.

Asa Briggs, *Go To It! Working for Victory on the Home Front 1939–1945* (Mitchell Beazley, 2000), which enabled me to create the factory where Betsy works.

Mike Brown, *Christmas on the Home Front* (Sutton Publishing, 2004).

Mike Brown, *Put That Light Out! Britain's Civil Defence Services at War 1939–1945* (Sutton Publishing, 1999); and John Christopher (editor), *Air Raids: What You Must Know, What You Must Do! The Wartime Guide to Surviving the Blitz* (Amberley Publishing, 2014), both of which contributed to the training session at Darley Court.

Glynis Cooper, *Manchester at War 1939–1945* (Pen & Sword Military, 2018), in which, amongst other things, I found the gas-powered bus.

Frank E Huggett, *Goodnight Sweetheart: Songs and Memories of the Second World War* (WH Allen, 1979), which provided the music for the Christmas celebrations.

Norman Longmate, *How We Lived Then: a History of Everyday Life During the Second World War* (Pimlico, 2002), which helped with Mabel and Harry's travels and life in the village in which Dr and Mrs Knatchbull live.

Susan Major, *Female Railway Workers in World War II* (Pen & Sword Transport, 2018), which helped provide details about Cordelia and Mabel's work on the permanent way.

Raynes Minns, *Bombers and Mash: the Domestic Front 1939–45* (Virago, 1999), which helped with the cooking.

Peter J C Smith, *Luftwaffe Over Manchester: The Blitz Years 1940–1944* (Neil Richardson, 2003). This is the book I always turn to for information about air raids.

Donald Thomas, *An Underworld at War: Spivs, Deserters, Racketeers and Civilians in the Second World War* (John Murray, 2003).

Megan Westley, *Living on the Home Front* (Amberley Publishing, 2013).

* * * *

Not all the books I consult are war-related.

Pam Forey, *Wild Flowers of Great Britain and Europe* (Dragon's World, 1993) helped me make sure the wildflowers beside the permanent way appeared in the correct season. It also helped me identify a wildflower I have always associated with the railways, thanks to holiday journeys in childhood. My mum told me they were lupins, but they aren't – they're rosebay willowherb.

Lance Hattat, *The Gardening Year* (Parragon, 1997) helped with the work in Mrs Cooper's garden.

And also John Peacock's utterly gorgeous *20th Century Fashion: the Complete Sourcebook* (Thames & Hudson, 1999 edition) and his *The Complete Fashion Sourcebook* (Thames & Hudson, 2005), books which I delve into not just for research but also for pleasure.

Turn the page for an exclusive
extract from my new novel

Courage
of the
Railway Girls

COMING APRIL 2023
Available to pre-order now

CHAPTER ONE

Saturday 2nd January, 1943

Standing in front of the dressing-table mirror in her pretty bedroom, Emily drew a deep breath and tried to make her shoulders relax, but it wasn't easy. She felt so miserable and tense these days that her shoulders were practically up at the same level as her ears. Just a few short weeks ago, she had been the happiest she had ever been in her whole life, and now...

Now, *right now*, this afternoon, she was going to hold her chin up and put on a brave face for the sake of her friends. Yes, *her* friends, she reminded herself, not just Mummy's friends; they were hers as well and you didn't let your friends down. The thought gave her a feeling of determination and she looked squarely at her reflection. Lord, but she'd changed. She had lost weight and her forget-me-not blue jumper and navy A-line skirt were looser than they ought to be. Her face was thinner too and her dark hair had lost the shine she used to be so proud of. She looked a fright – but what did it matter? It didn't. She didn't care. Gone were the days when she had loved looking at herself, when she had gloried in gazing at her reflection. Being in love had made her cheeks glow and her blue eyes sparkle – yes, they really had sparkled. She wouldn't have believed it if she hadn't seen it for herself, because it sounded like the sort of daft but rather appealing description you found in books.

Well, there was no point standing here gawping at herself. 'That won't butter any parsnips,' she murmured. It was something she'd heard Mrs Green say. She loved Mrs Green. She'd loathed her to start with, but that had been back when she'd still been a silly little snob who didn't know any better.

Emily lifted a hand to straighten the Peter Pan collar of her white blouse before turning away to sit on the bed and remove the slippers she'd been given for Christmas so she could put on her shoes. She'd had to carry on wearing her old school shoes for some time after she'd come home from boarding school until Mummy had taken her to the market to look for a suitable second-hand pair. Mummy had said it was more sensible to do this than to splurge precious clothes coupons on new shoes. Emily had longed for a pair of stylish sling-backs, but she'd been more than happy with a pair that had almond-shaped toes and, oh bliss, heels. They were proper grown-up shoes, not silly schoolgirlish flatties. Grown-up shoes for a grown-up young woman. That was what she'd thought at the time; she remembered thinking it. But now she knew that being an adult wasn't all it was cracked up to be.

She went downstairs into the sitting room, where Daddy was reading the newspaper while he waited. Thanks to the fuel shortages, the furniture hugged the fireplace, though Mummy might restore the old arrangement in the summer.

Daddy lowered the paper as she walked in. 'You look pretty, darling.'

Emily smiled. Daddy was always good for a compliment. But she felt a stab of sadness too. She didn't feel pretty; she felt washed-out and wretched and the thought of never seeing Raymond again filled her with despair.

But she was *not* going to dwell on that today. This afternoon, they were going to Mrs Cooper's house in Wilton Close to celebrate Mabel's engagement.

As if he could read her thoughts, Daddy stood up and came over to her, looking down into her face. 'You'll be all right this afternoon, won't you?'

'I managed at Lucy's engagement party, didn't I?' Emily answered. 'I'm an old hand at it now.'

Her old chum Lucy had got engaged at Christmas – the same time as Mabel, as it later turned out – and Lucy's parents had thrown a party for the happy couple in between Christmas and New Year. It was supposed to be an impromptu party, but it was obvious it had been planned down to the last detail. Beforehand, Mummy and Daddy had thought there might well be a party and they had wanted to spare Emily from having to attend.

'Mummy can practise saying, "Oh, what a shame. We have other arrangements for that evening," in case Lucy's mother mentions an engagement party,' Daddy had said.

But when the invitation came, much to her own surprise, Emily had second thoughts.

'Mummy, could you please say that we have other arrangements that evening, but that we'll drop in for a while on our way?'

'Are you sure, darling?' Mummy had looked concerned.

'No,' Emily said bluntly, 'but I think we ought to.'

'Good girl,' said Mummy.

Her parents always liked it when she did the decent thing. They'd brought her up to be polite and it turned out that the need to do so applied even when you were heartbroken.

After that, Mummy had come home from work with the news that Mabel had returned from her Christmas visit to Annerby sporting a ruby engagement ring that she was flashing left, right and centre, 'along with the happiest smile you can imagine,' according to Mummy. And this afternoon there was to be a get-together at Mrs Cooper's, where Mabel lived, for her friends to celebrate the wonderful news with one of the railway friends' tea parties that they all loved so much.

Emily felt better about going to this party than she had about attending Lucy's. Was that because she and Lucy had been friends for simply yonks, ever since they were little girls, and these today were new friends? But that made it sound as if her new friends weren't as important and that most certainly wasn't the case. She'd only known them since the summer of '41 and, truth be told, she hadn't been at all keen in the early days. These days, shame could still make her face tingle when she recalled how she'd looked down on Mrs Green and Mrs Cooper for being working class. Back then, she'd felt ashamed of her mother for wanting to be friends with people of that sort. She hadn't liked Mabel, Alison and the rest either, fearing that they were simply out for what help they could get from Mummy, maybe free legal advice from Daddy. Why else would girls in their twenties pal up with someone of Mummy's age?

How wrong she had been, how completely wrong. Emily had learned to value people according to their characters and their actions instead of making harsh and unsubstantiated judgements based purely on age or class. She'd been rather a twerp, actually, and dearly hoped her railway friends had forgotten her old snobby ways. She still experienced the occasional twinge of doubt in case they only accepted her because she was her mother's daughter, but with her sensible hat on, she knew this wasn't the case.

Emily looked round as Mummy walked into the room. She didn't miss the glance that passed between her parents when Mummy saw Daddy standing close to her. They'd been very protective ever since Raymond dumped her, which was perfectly sweet of them, of course, and she adored them for it, but it could feel a bit, well, smothering sometimes. There were moments when she just wanted to say, 'It doesn't matter how kind you are or how much you watch over me. You can't change the way I feel,' but she never did.

Mummy looked swish but not over-dressed in dove-grey with her trademark pearl earrings. Mummy always looked nice. Elegant. You'd never imagine she spent her working days out on the railway tracks, dismantling, cleaning and reassembling the lamps belonging to signals and to engines, coaches and wagons. In her snobby days, Emily had been obscurely ashamed of her mother's job. Essential war work it might be, but it wasn't exactly suitable for a respectable, educated, cultured lady from the upper middle class. Daddy had thought so too, but they had both come round since then.

'All set?' Mummy asked, smiling.

'We'd better do the blackout before we go,' said Daddy. 'It'll be dark when we get home.'

'I'll do it,' said Emily and ran around the house, pulling first the ordinary curtains and then the blackout curtains, twitching them at the edges to ensure they covered the entire windows plus a bit more. Sometimes it was hard to remember what life had been like before the blackout. Just think: small children who had never known any different would think this was normal.

In the hall, her parents were togged up in their outdoor things, complete with warm scarves and leather gloves. Mummy had a rather gorgeous wine-coloured coat with a top-stitched collar and a grey felt hat with an upswept brim. Emily had been obliged to wear her school gabardine for quite some time after she had come home, until dear Mrs Cooper, who helped with the WVS's clothes exchange, had tipped Mummy the wink about a nut-brown coat in good condition and Mummy had quickly exchanged Emily's gabardine for the brown coat as a surprise. It had been an especially kind thing to do because, even though Emily was the one to benefit, it had been her mother who had done the exchange and that meant she couldn't visit the clothes exchange again for a whole month.

Emily's new-to-her coat was flattering, with a tie-belt made of a length of fabric that had to be fastened in a knot, and a slight flare below the waist. And Mummy's pale pink hat with magenta trim looked especially good with the coat – to the point where Mummy hadn't exactly given the hat to Emily, but she raised no objection when Emily wore it so much.

Not that it mattered these days. Emily had cared most awfully what she looked like when she was seeing Raymond, but now – so what?

Shrugging on her coat and winding her scarf around her neck and tucking it in, Emily was soon ready to go.

'Have you got everything?' Daddy asked.

They were taking with them a plate of sardine sandwiches and a coconut pudding, as well as a contribution to the afternoon's quantity of tea leaves.

'You can't have a tea party without plenty of tea,' said Mummy. 'And we're taking a quarter of our Christmas cake. Dot's bringing a quarter of hers too.'

'So we don't all scoff Mrs Grayson's,' said Emily.

'I expect hers will be the best,' said Mummy, 'even though we've all had to make eggless cakes this year.'

They walked to Wilton Close, which took about twenty minutes.

The afternoon was chilly and damp. Daddy would probably cut along to the telephone box and ring for a taxi to bring them home later when it was dark and cold. That was the sort of thing he did.

When they arrived, Mrs Cooper opened the front door as they were still walking up the path and they hurried inside. Daddy took their coats and Mummy vanished into the kitchen to hand over her dishes to Mrs Grayson. Then they went into the front room to a flurry of greetings and cries of 'Happy new year!' Those who were sitting down jumped up to hug Mummy and Emily, and Emily could *almost* – almost – feel she was a true part of what was happening. Everyone knew of her unhappiness and wanted to make her welcome and she appreciated that, she really did, even though it could be rather off-putting knowing that everybody knew the private business of her heart. But all the same, the very unhappiness that the others wanted to alleviate was precisely what made her feel distanced from what was going on.

But she could play her part. If there was one thing she'd learned about herself recently, it was that she could act the part of Emily Masters to perfection. So she smiled and offered best wishes for the new year and cooed over Joan's baby and tickled his chin and generally behaved as if there was nowhere she'd rather be. And then she joined her mother, who was with Mabel, admiring her ring.

'May I see?' asked Emily. 'It's gorgeous.'

Mabel immediately took it off. 'Do you want to have a go? Try it. Everyone else has.'

Emily blinked. Not so long ago, she had daydreamed about her own engagement ring. She had thought that would be the first ring to go on her finger. Next thing she knew, Mabel's arms were round her and Mabel was whispering in her ear.

'Sorry, kid. Me and my big mouth. I wasn't thinking. I'm just so excited.'

Part of Emily wanted to dissolve into floods of tears, but she was made of sterner stuff than that, or at least she wished she was. Pretending she was strong was the best she could do. With a small wriggle, she freed herself from Mabel's embrace before others could realise.

'That's all right. I'd love to try it on.'

She pushed the gold band with its deep-red ruby onto her ring finger. There. It turned out that ring fingers weren't so special after all. You could put any ring at all on them. She took it off and handed it back, making sure she was smiling.

'It's beautiful. Congratulations.'

'Thanks. I'm very lucky.' Mabel replaced her ring and looked at it. The rich red stone was perfect for her colouring. She had such glorious dark-brown hair, which she wore scooped away from her face and hanging in natural waves down her back. Mabel removed her gaze from her ring, laughing at herself.

Joan appeared, slipping an arm around Mabel. 'Before Christmas, she'd have been gazing adoringly at Max. Now all she cares about is her ring.'

'I don't blame her,' said Emily and slipped away, duty done.

She spent some time in the kitchen, helping Mrs Grayson, then she volunteered to take Joan's dog Brizo for a quick walk before they had tea. She loved Brizo, with his soulful eyes, his soft floppy ears and gingery, golden-brown shaggy coat. She made the suggestion quietly so no one would offer to accompany her, but even so, Colette joined her. Emily was fascinated by Colette, but then presumably everybody was. Colette was a quiet individual, softly spoken and gentle in her manner. She seemed like a completely ordinary person, yet she had had to put up with being treated appallingly badly by her husband; and nobody had had the slightest inkling of what was going on until Tony had beaten her black and blue and put her in hospital. Instead of being sent to prison, he had been allowed to join the army, which seemed grossly unfair, but at least it meant he was a long way away – but for how long? Everyone was saying that the tide was turning.

'I hope you don't mind me tagging along,' said Colette, pushing a strand of buttermilk-fair hair behind her ear.

'Of course not.'

'I'm glad to have a chance to have a word, actually,' Colette added, and Emily's heart beat harder for a second or two. 'I just wanted to say that I know what it's like when people are watching – kind people, I mean, people who care and who want to make things better, only they can't, because nobody can. Whatever has hurt you, you have to live with it and find your own way out the other end.'

'That's exactly it,' Emily exclaimed. 'Everybody back in the house knows about Raymond and me, and I know they all care deeply, but they can't make it better.'

'It's the same for me,' said Colette. 'I love my friends and I appreciate everything they've done to help me, but when push comes to shove, I still have to live with my feelings. Nobody can take them away.'

'No, they can't.'

'If ever you want to talk to somebody who – and I mean this in the kindest possible way – won't try to help you feel better, but will just let you feel what you feel, then I'm here.'

'Thanks,' said Emily, feeling that a little piece of her burden had lifted. It was flattering too to be paid attention to in this way by someone older than herself and to be talked to as an equal. The other girls were in their twenties, but she was only sixteen, with her seventeenth birthday coming up in March.

They walked Brizo as far as the police station on Beech Road and back again. When they returned to Wilton Close, there was chatter going on in the kitchen, which suggested it was nearly time for tea. Emily slipped into the front room. Fussing Brizo, she took him into a corner and sat on the floor with him. Soon the room was full and Emily wasn't the only one sitting on the carpet. Plates were passed around and tea was poured while everyone chatted. Emily smiled and laughed occasionally as if she was joining in, but she wasn't really. She felt distanced from what was going on, as if her deep sorrow and heartache lifted her out of the occasion.

She looked round at everyone. Mummy was sitting on the sofa between Mrs Green and Mrs Cooper. It was Mummy who had got Mrs Cooper the job of taking care of this house while the owners, Mr and Mrs Morgan, were away in North Wales for the duration. Mrs Cooper didn't just take care of the house, she took great care of the residents as well, helped by Mrs Grayson, who was a wonderful cook and turned out tasty, nutritious meals in spite of all the shortages and rationing. With them lived Mabel, Margaret and Alison, all of whom worked on the railways.

Joan used to work on the railways as a station porter at Victoria Station, and then briefly in Lost Property, before she had Max. Now she was a housewife. Her husband Bob was here too. Emily liked him. He was what she imagined a big brother would be like, kind and good-natured with a lively sense of humour. He wasn't film-star handsome like Mabel's fiancé Harry, but he was the sort of person you felt comfortable with and that counted for a lot. Harry wasn't here this afternoon because he'd had to go back to Bomber Command straight after Christmas.

Next to Joan, dandling Max on her knee, was Persephone, who was the most beautiful girl Emily had ever seen, with her honey-blonde hair and her violet eyes, but as Mrs Cooper said, she was lovely on the inside as well. Educated in a boarding school herself, Emily recognised in Persephone the confidence that came from living away from home, but in Persephone's case it was more than private education. It was the confidence that had been bred into her through generations of titled ancestors stretching back to when Adam was a lad.

Daddy was talking to Mr Green and Bob while Mrs Green sat with Mummy and Mrs Cooper. Mrs Green was Mummy's great friend even though they were poles apart socially.

She caught Mrs Green's eye without meaning to and quickly buried her face in Brizo's thick coat before Mrs Green could speak to her. She was quite all right tucked away here in her corner. All she wanted was to be left alone. It wasn't difficult, because Mabel was the centre of attention.

'Where's the wedding going to be?' asked Alison.

'At home in Annerby,' said Mabel. 'Mumsy can't wait.'

Alison pulled a face, but then she smiled. 'I suppose it was too much to hope that you could get married here.'

'Of course she can't,' exclaimed Mrs Cooper. 'She has to get married from her parents' house.'

'It's going to be a June wedding,' said Mabel, 'and I hope some of you will be able to come, though I know it'll be tricky to get time off.'

'You must tell us as soon as the date is confirmed,' said Mummy.

'It's so exciting,' said Margaret.

'There's something else I ought to tell you,' said Mabel. 'I expect you've already worked it out for yourselves, but I ought to say it anyway.' She pressed her lips together, looking emotional. 'When Harry and I tie the knot, obviously I'll go to live down south. Harry has applied for married quarters.'

'Of course you have to live with Harry,' said Mrs Grayson.

'No, you don't,' Joan teased, though her eyes were suspiciously bright. 'You could get wed and come back to us.'

'I think Harry would have something to say about that,' said Alison and the others laughed, so Emily joined in, though she didn't really feel she was part of the conversation. Not because she was being left out, but because … oh, just because.

'We'll all miss you, love,' said Mrs Green and there were murmurs of agreement.

Mabel wiped away a tear. 'But we'll keep in touch, won't we?'

'Of course!' everyone cried reassuringly, dashing away a few of their own tears.

'If there's one thing I can guarantee about this lot,' Alison declared, looking round, 'it's that they're superb at keeping in touch. I was snowed under with letters last year when I was packed off to Leeds.'

After everyone had finished eating, Margaret and Joan went to boil the kettle again so that more tea could be squeezed out of the pot.

'Don't start drinking yet,' said Mrs Green, standing up when all the cups had been refreshed. 'We need to have a toast. It's a shame Harry can't be here, but we all want to wish the very best to our lovely Mabel – a wonderful future and a long and happy marriage.'

'Mabel,' everyone said, raising their teacups, and 'Congratulations,' and 'Harry's a lucky man.'

Emily joined in, but it was like she wasn't really there. She was an observer rather than a participant. Lucy and Charlie. Mabel and Harry. Things were meant to happen in threes, weren't they? She wasn't sure she could bear it if Alison and Joel got engaged too.

Except that she would bear it. It wasn't as though she had a choice. She didn't have a choice about anything these days. The one choice she had made, to be with Raymond for ever, had been ripped away from her.

She watched all the smiling faces around her and saw Mabel's happiness. Was it always going to be this way for her from now on? Was she always going to feel she was on the outside looking in?

SIGN UP TO OUR NEW SAGA NEWSLETTER

Penny Street

The home of heart-warming reads

Welcome to **Penny Street**, your number **one stop for emotional and heartfelt historical reads**. Meet casts of characters you'll never forget, memories you'll treasure as your own, and places that will stay with you long after the last page.

Join our online **community** bringing you the latest book deals, competitions and new saga series releases.

You can also find extra content, talk to your favourite authors and share your discoveries with other saga fans on Facebook.

Join today by visiting
www.penguin.co.uk/pennystreet

Follow us on Facebook
www.facebook.com/welcometopennystreet/